ALSO BY MEG M. ROBINSON

<u>Chloe Chadwick Series</u>
Finding Salus
Waking Salus
Remembering Salus
Saving Salus

Megaverse Series
<u>Immortal Love Series</u>
Seeking Eternity
A Fury's Heart
The Last Lemurian
Grim Favors

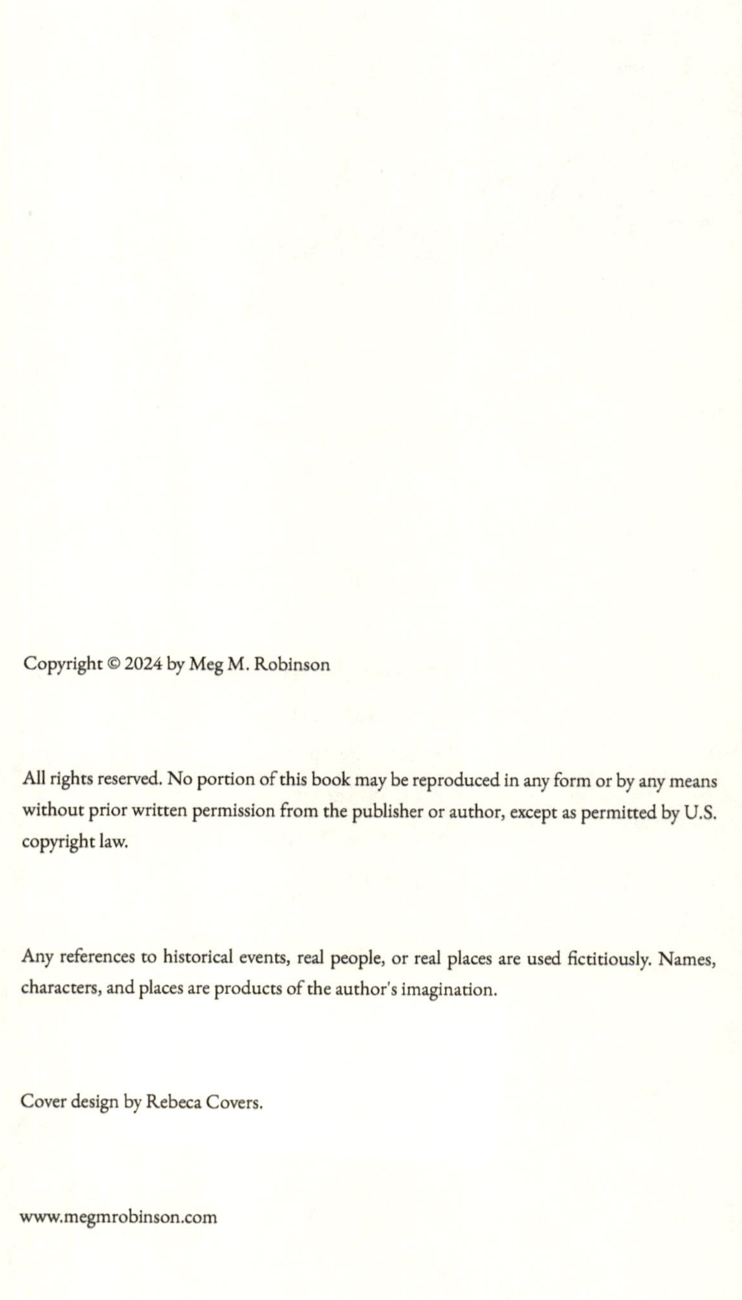

DANCE WITH DEATH

MEG M. ROBINSON

ARCANE CROW PUBLISHING

DEDICATION

This is for everyone who's dealt with anxiety, and those who help them get through it.

CHAPTER 1

Mira was not going to stay dead. Blanche wouldn't allow it. She never should have died, and Blanche blamed herself for the untimely death, which meant she was going to fix it. She had to. Now she just needed to figure out how the hell she was going to pull it off.

Currently, she stood with her toes at the edge of a pit humans had yet to find, deep within an inhospitable, unexplored cave in Bulgaria. Back at her family home in Vermont, her sister Mira rested in Blanche's bed. Or her body did, anyway. It had been two weeks since Mira's death, but her body hadn't yet deteriorated thanks to a spell Blanche had cast. A spell that also kept anyone from removing Mira's body from that bed. It was a necessary precaution.

In the few days she had been at home after Mira's death, she'd tried everything she could think of to do the impossible. Except there was no spell she'd found to resurrect the dead, even for necromancers like herself. Historically, only the gods had been able to grant life, and they were stingy about who they gave it to. Most often such gifts came with loopholes, so more often than not, the person who was supposed to be returned to life never actually left the underworld. Still, Blanche had tried. She'd spent hours praying to every death and underworld deity she knew of, and thanks to her sister's research and her own upbringing, she knew of quite a few. They had, much to her displeasure, ignored her. Except for one, and he'd given her a magical jolt that had left her paralyzed for half an hour as a warning. A warning she'd ignored.

She'd even tried to summon a reaper, but none of her modified spells had done any good. Not that she was surprised. Most people thought reapers were little more than myth. Her family knew otherwise, considering ninety-five percent of her family was made up of necromancers and banshees. All creatures of death. There was little about death or death magic they didn't know. Still, while they knew reapers existed, the species was elusive.

The only other thing she'd thought of that she could attempt at home was reanimating Mira's body, and that was something she'd never do. She'd never subject her sister to an existence as a revenant. To be forever mindless, with no pleasure, no joy, nothing but a hunger that could never be sated. It would be torture, and she wasn't willing to do that to her baby sister. No, she would settle for nothing less than true resurrection. Which was why she had taken a plane to Bulgaria.

The Arcane knew of quite a few places humans didn't, or that they'd forgotten. One such place was this pit, but even among the magical community, it was considered more legend than truth. Some said it was nothing more than an extremely deep hole. Others that it was a bottomless pit, and that anyone who entered it would fall until they starved to death. But the story that had brought her here was a rumor that had been around far longer than she had.

Legends said it was a doorway to the underworld. All it took was a literal leap of faith. But whether the rumor was true or not, if she jumped, she'd still end up in the underworld one way or another. The only question was...which one, and would she be alive or dead when she reached it? But for Mira, she'd take the risk. And that risk was why she hadn't told her parents or brother where she was going, or even that she was leaving. If she was wrong...they'd have lost two people in under a month. There was a chance that would happen, so she'd hidden a letter with Mira's body. She didn't want them to have to wonder what had happened to her. Not knowing could be worse than any alternative. But if she was right, she could be *in* the underworld, alive, and ask whichever god ruled it to help her.

It was harder to turn someone down when they were in front of you than when they were in a completely different realm. Or she hoped.

The cavern around her was dark, with only the ball of fire floating above her palm providing light. Staring down into the pit, she felt her heart hammer with fear. This might be her best chance, and she was determined, but that didn't eliminate the possibility that this could go all wrong. Beyond that, she was in this forbidding place all alone.

The pit was a vaguely oval shape, about twenty feet across at the narrowest point, with a small outcropping at one of the narrow ends. That was where she stood now. The bottom—if there was one—was impossible to see.

Now, she was willing to risk her life for Mira, but she wanted to do it with as good a chance of success as possible. Previous members of the Arcane who had visited had done their best to measure this pit, but no matter what method they'd used, none could ever say they'd found the end of it. A few claimed it went straight through to the other side of the world, but Blanche had checked into that. A hole directly through the Earth came up in the ocean west of Australia. It was possible they'd meant it less literally, but she had no way of knowing.

The years muddled truths, even with the Arcane being longer lived than humans.

But there wasn't any way she going to find out if she didn't jump, and standing here worrying about it would get her no closer to answers.

Blanche closed her eyes and drew in a deep, slow breath. Closing her fist, she extinguished the fireball. Before she could talk herself out of it, she acted. She didn't simply lean a foot over the hole and let herself fall. It was too passive, and would run too much risk of her body banging against the jagged sides of the pit. Instead, she threw her arms out to the side and leapt out into the so-called pit to hell.

She tumbled end over end for a moment before she ended up horizontal, her arms spread out to her sides. Her eyes remained closed against the wind that slapped against her face and tore at her clothes. Heart pounding in her chest, she clenched her fists as she waited for something to happen. She was half expecting to hit bottom, but could honestly admit she had no idea what would become of her. She could only hope and pray to the gods of the underworld to protect her.

First seconds, then minutes ticked by, with nothing new occurring. There wasn't even a change in the air around her. Tentatively, she cracked an eye open, but saw nothing but darkness. Unsurprising, really, but it was a let down.

Blanche brought a hand up, shielding her eyes to try to prevent them from watering. It was only partly successful, but she wanted to be able to see what was coming. Then again, not having that warning that she was about to hit the bottom might be a good thing. But as soon as that thought occurred to her, the walls around her began to glow. It was faint, and if her eyes hadn't adjusted to the dark long ago she might not have even noticed it. The glow was a pale blue, and actually kind of...pretty. Odd, even to her, but pretty.

With nothing else to do, she studied the walls. That was her only excuse as to why it took her so long to realize they were brightening. It happened so gradually that she would have only noticed if she hadn't been staring. The farther down she got, the brighter it got, until she was shielding her eyes not just from the rush of air, but the intense light coming from the rock. Another few minutes and she had to close her eyes and cover them, the glow was so intense.

Then, just when she was about to check on the light again, her body slammed into something hard and flat. It knocked the breath out of her and she curled onto her side and into the fetal position, gasping as she tried to fill her lungs. The difficulty she had in breathing had her already high pulse quickening, but it evened out when she was finally able to take her first deep breath.

It took her several minutes to be able to breathe normally, and only then did she allow her eyes to open. The intense light was gone, replaced by a gentle flickering. When her eyes adjusted to the dimness, she saw there were multiple torches leading the way down a narrow stone staircase.

Everything hurt as she pushed herself up to a sitting position. It didn't matter, though. She was alive. She'd reached the bottom and had lived. Now she had to figure out exactly where she was and find the deity that ruled this underworld. Assuming she'd actually ended up in the underworld.

Giving her body more time to recover, she looked around. It didn't take long. Other than the staircase which spiraled down around the edge of the room, there was nothing. It was simply an oval-shaped cavern with no ceiling. The floor was rough and uneven, made of matte black rock, which explained the various cuts and scrapes over her body and the now torn clothing.

Though she wanted to stay put longer, to let the stings ease, she forced herself up to her feet. She'd get nothing if she stayed on the floor licking her wounds. Her first step resulted in her leg trying to buckle, and she hissed as pain shot from her knee. She took a slow breath, then tried walking again, keeping as much weight off her bad leg as she could.

The stairs were hell on her knee, so she leaned against the wall as much as she could. Still, it was slow going, and the fact that the stairs seemed to go on forever didn't help anything. After a solid five minutes, she lowered herself to one of the steps, taking a break. She hated the necessity of it, but the landing had been rough on her. It had proved that this pit was magical in some way, though. If it wasn't, the fall would have flat out killed her. There was no way in hell she hadn't reached terminal velocity. Though she hadn't timed it, she estimated she'd fallen for close to ten minutes.

Rising, she continued on her downward journey. Her body insisted she take a break twice more. Eventually she started counting stairs just to give her mind something to do and reached 1,022 before she reached the bottom. Though she wanted to sit down again, she forced herself to walk down the even more narrow passageway. And once again, it seemed to take forever before she reached something new. A closed door made out of the same stone as the passage.

This whole experience was alien and frightening, but she walked up to the door, only to discover there was no knob, no handle, no visible way of opening it. Baffled, she spent a few minutes examining it. The hinges were made of bronze and there were carvings over every inch of the door, but the language wasn't one she knew. It resembled cuneiform, but there was something off about it. That suggested this was some sort of Mesopotamian afterlife, but she wasn't taking anything for granted.

Finding nothing useful, she tried to dig her nails into the almost invisible seam opposite the hinges, but wasn't able to pry it open. She did break a nail at the quick, but barely felt it, the rest of her body ached so much. With that failing, she placed a hand on the door and shoved, though the door should open toward her. Shockingly, it worked, but not because of anything she'd done.

The door swung open toward her, forcing her to step back quickly. Standing in its place was a man. If he wasn't seven feet tall, she'd be shocked, and he had the broadest shoulders and chest of any man she'd met before. His black hair was short, but his thick beard easily reached his chest. Bronzed skin was on display as he wore nothing but a wrap-style skirt that hit his knees. Well, the skirt and a belt with a sword hanging from it. A very sharp-looking sword.

His brown eyes narrowed when he caught sight of her. He said something rapidly, but the language was completely foreign to her.

Interrupting his angry words, she shook her head. "I don't understand."

Exasperation joined the anger, but his next words were in heavily accented English. "You're not dead. What are you doing here?"

Blanche quickly flipped through her knowledge of Mesopotamian gods, relieved her unusual education was paying off. If this was a Mesopotamian afterlife as she suspected, then she was looking for Ereshkigal or Nergal. It didn't matter whether this was the Sumerian,

Babylonian, or Assyrian underworld; those religions had shared those gods. And though she tended toward snark over respect, she'd brush up on her use of the latter if it meant bringing Mira back.

Inclining her head, she told him, "I have come to humbly petition the lord or lady for a favor."

"What favor?"

"I'm seeking a way to bring my sister back to life," she answered, head still bowed.

He snorted, which was such an unexpected sound that her head jerked up to meet his eyes. The anger was gone, but the annoyance that had replaced it wasn't much better. "You're not Sumerian. Why would my lord or lady even listen to someone who isn't even a worshiper of theirs?"

"I am a necromancer, as is my sister," she said, refusing to refer to Mira in the past tense. "Because of that, we revere most deities of the dead and the underworld, and have often prayed to them."

"And when was the last time you prayed to either Nergal or Ereshkigal?" he challenged.

"Just a day ago," she admitted truthfully.

"No doubt a plea to resurrect your sister."

She couldn't argue with that, so only nodded.

He shook his head and waved a hand dismissively at her. "They do not have time to waste with such things. You and your sister are mortal. It is the way of mortals to die. Once dead, you are meant to stay dead. We do not undo that which fate has decreed should happen. Begone."

"Please," she begged. Ego had no place at the moment. If she had to humble herself to resurrect Mira, she would without hesitation. "I have tried everything I can think of. She didn't deserve to die. I will do anything to make things right."

"I believe you," he said, showing the first trace of compassion, but it was gone just as quickly as it appeared. "But the fact remains that we have never before brought a mortal back to life, and there is no reason for that stance to change. The most I can do is wish you luck with another god."

She didn't have a chance to protest further, because with another wave of his hand, he sent her back to the edge of the pit. Despair filled her belly and she dropped to her knees, nearly falling into the pit once more. She didn't scream, but only because her throat had tightened. She didn't cry because she no longer had tears to spare. She could only stare into the abyss before her and silently rage that she had failed.

Time passed, but she neither knew nor cared how long she sat there. Eventually, her stomach growled, reminding her that she hadn't eaten since before leaving home. Only then, and grudgingly, did she pull herself to her feet and summon a weak fireball for light. She made it out of the cave and back to the plane that would take her home, no longer feeling all her many injuries. They were still there, still sapping her strength, but her mind had tried to just turn off. Who knew grief was an anesthetic?

When she arrived home, her family spoke to her, apparently concerned, but their words were just a buzzing in her ears. Her parents hugged her, not realizing they were squeezing on bruises and scrapes. Her brother yelled at her, apparently annoyed when she could only stare blankly at him.

Eventually, she was able to retreat to her bedroom. Kneeling beside the bed, she touched Mira's cool hand and whispered a promise.

"I'll figure something out. I swear it. I won't give up until you're back with us."

It had been two days since Blanche had returned from Bulgaria and nothing had changed. Her injuries were starting to heal, but she hardly noticed. Her clothes had been changed, but only because the rips kept distracting her. She'd continued researching and beseeching death deities, but it had been as fruitless as her trip. Though she was losing hope, she wasn't giving up.

She kept her attention focused on the book in her lap, very careful not to look at her sister's body. Every time she did, she was inundated with guilt, and guilt wasn't conducive to problem solving. She turned the page, struggling to find something, some tiny clue which would tell her how to find someone who could help. Who *would* help. It was likely a hopeless task, but she refused to give up. She owed it to Mira.

A sharp knock made her glance toward the door with a sigh. Ever since she'd returned, her family had been trying to talk her out of this. Her parents, her brother, even the ghost of her grandfather had begged, argued, and demanded she release the spell on Mira and allow them to put her to rest. Her mom had even tried to take the stasis spell down by force, but to everyone's shock, had been unable to. Marguerite had always been stronger than her daughters, so the fact that she couldn't undo this one spell was surprising.

She didn't respond to the knock, just turned her attention back to the book, but her brother wasn't going to be put off.

"Come on, Blanche. Let me in. You can't hide in there forever," he called. When she remained silent, she heard a thunk that she suspected might be his head dropping to the door. "Look, I know it hurts. Mira's dead, and we all feel it. We all miss her. But you know as well as anyone else that we need to put her to rest. You know what can happen when someone doesn't receive that which they're owed."

She did. It wasn't how revenants were created, or even ghosts—vengeful or otherwise. Nor was it even likely that she or the rest of her living family would personally suffer for the lack of proper rituals. It would be Mira who would deal with the consequences. Like the dead in the old Greek stories, stuck on the wrong side of the Styx, with no coin for Charon. It was almost as bad an existence as that of a revenant.

"Blanche, you can't keep doing this to yourself," Aidan said, voice quieter now. "But I get the feeling that doesn't matter to you." There was a sound that made her think he'd slapped the door and his voice strengthened, hardened. "But it damn well should matter that Mom and Dad are suffering. Not just because she's dead, but because you're selfishly trying to absolve yourself of guilt and keeping the rest of us from mourning."

That struck a nerve, and she drew her knees up to her chest even as she heard his footsteps leading away from her door. Her breathing quickened, as did the beat of her heart, in what she knew could very well be the precursor to an anxiety attack.

Was he right? Was she just being selfish? In her mind, she was trying to help all of them, but even she had to admit it was beginning to feel like a fool's errand. Could she keep putting her family through this in the off chance that she might find a way of bringing Mira back? She probably had a better chance of winning the lottery while simultaneously being struck by lightning.

Her gaze was drawn to the serene look on her sister's face, and her chest tightened painfully. How could she let Mira go? But how could she hurt her family? There was no way to win. No way to make this right.

Hot tears rolled down her cheeks as she fought to draw breath. What was she going to do? Who did she let down? Who did she hurt?

There was only one option left to her. If it didn't work, she would have no choice but to take down the stasis spell protecting Mira and allow her family to inter her in the family catacombs. It was risky and had no better chance of success than anything else, but she had to try.

In a voice too quiet to even be called a whisper, she spoke the words that Death himself had told her just a few weeks back. Words meant to summon the original and most powerful deity of the afterlife.

The many shadows in the room drew together as she watched, forming the silhouette of a man. That silhouette quickly turned into a man wearing black leather pants and a form-fitting black tee-shirt that stretched across his muscular chest and exposed the black and silver swirl tattoos on his arms. His black hair was short on the sides, but stylishly shaggy on top. His skin was tanned and there was dark scruff on his jaw, but it was his pale silvery-blue eyes that commanded her attention. They were fixed on her and they were pissed.

"What the fuck do you want?" he demanded, his voice deep, smooth, but with an edge that further betrayed his current mood. "I thought I told you never to summon me again."

He was gorgeous, but he would normally terrify her. This was Death, the single being more powerful than the gods, who was said to be the only person incapable of being killed. His power filled the room, a cold chill that could smother even her. He could snap his fingers and send her to Tartarus or Hel, but right now all she could feel was grief and growing panic.

"My sister," she told him, her voice wobbling as she pointed to Mira. "Please, bring her back. She died helping get your scythe, so can't you just do this one thing?" He didn't say anything, just folded his arms across his chest and stared. "Please, Death," she begged. "I'll do anything, but I can't stand knowing that she died because I brought her into that whole situation. Bring her back?" Her voice cracked on the last word and she pushed the book off her lap before she slid off the bed. She'd kneel, she'd prostrate herself. She'd literally do anything as long as he agreed.

"No."

The single blunt word had her labored breathing stopping for several seconds, and she shook her head. "Please reconsider. It's just one person. You don't need another soul. She—"

He disappeared before she could continue to plead her case, the room warming in his absence.

For several heartbeats—rapid ones—she simply stared at where he'd been, unable to process her failure. Then, when it sank in, she threw her head back and let everything she was feeling—the grief, the frustration, the rage—out in a scream that burned her throat. Her power burst out of her, as uncontrolled as her emotions. Within moments, ghosts slid through the walls and into the room, swarming her, all hoping to be the one to possess her and taste life again.

For the first time in her life, she wasn't entirely sure she cared if they succeeded.

CHAPTER 2

The necromancer wouldn't shut up. Death sat on his throne, one knee draped over the arm as he rubbed at his temple. For four days she had been calling him. Not just using the summoning he'd taught her, but the one she'd used the first time he'd met her and her friends. The annoying as hell summoning that always felt like a spike driving into his temple.

He really should have killed the god who had figured that spell out before he could write it down. As it was, he had thought he'd destroyed all copies of it. Apparently he'd missed one, but that was a mistake he was going to rectify. Just as soon as she shut the hell up.

Groaning, he closed his eyes and let his head thump against the back of his throne. "I swear, I haven't had a headache in more than ten thousand years. I'd forgotten how much I fucking hate them."

A man chuckled and Death cracked open an eye to see which of the twins had dared to laugh at his suffering. They stood nearby, with Abaddon leaning against one of the columns. Both of them had the dusky skin of the Sumerians, black hair, and bright blue eyes ringed with black, and their features were identical, but the brothers were almost as different as life and death. Abaddon's hair was short, while his beard and mustache were thick. They were kept short as well, but full. He was tattooed, with matching bands around both wrists, but otherwise he dressed in what Death thought of as 'rich casual'. Tailored jeans and a white button-down shirt. Abaddon had always been a little uptight.

Grim, on the other hand, was more casual—and the one who had chuckled. His hair was longer and pulled into a bun, while his beard and mustache were kept short and neat. The tee-shirt and faded jeans he wore were his standard uniform when he wasn't working, and the shirt revealed the full sleeves of tattoos the man wore proudly.

"You find this amusing?" Death asked, voice low and dangerous.

Grim shrugged. "Little bit. I don't know why you don't just respond to her. It would make her stop calling you."

"I don't know why you haven't just killed her," Abaddon said bluntly. "That would end the incessant calling, too."

"Yeah, but for all we know, she could end up here when she died, and then she'd have even more access to him," Grim retorted.

Death sighed and reminded himself that he liked the twins. They were the oldest reapers and some of his oldest—and almost only—friends. "You know I don't kill people just for annoying me." He paused and grimaced as Blanche called for him again. "Usually," he corrected, as he was now reconsidering Abaddon's suggestion.

"Then what are you going to do?" Grim asked as he pulled a heavy silver coin out of his pocket and began running his thumb along one side, as though feeling the image that had long-since flattened due to centuries of the same motion.

"Hell if I know," Death said, running a hand through his hair. He couldn't ignore the necromancer, that much he knew. He'd have to decide something, because allowing her to constantly summon him without penalty would send the wrong message. Most weren't aware he truly existed, but those who did needed to fear him, respect him. He was Death. Powerful, terrifying, and the only truly immortal being in existence. He wasn't here to fulfill the whims of all the mortals who were sad over losing someone.

In the end, they all ended up here in Cindatha, the realm of souls.

"If you don't want to kill her, why not just give her what she's asking for? Bring her sister back and she'll stop bugging you," Grim advised.

Abaddon shook his head and echoed Death's thoughts. "That would just lead to her telling people and then everyone would start begging for people to be brought back to life."

"So make that part of the deal," Grim countered. "Bring the sister back, but she can never summon you again or tell anyone what happened."

"Didn't Death say her friends witnessed the sister dying, though? When she shows up alive and well, they'd know something had happened."

Death tuned out the bickering brothers. They'd go on like that for hours if he let them, and they were two of the extremely few people who dared to relax around him—and even they had a healthy respect for him. Still, Grim had a point. He even had a good idea. A deal...It had worked out well for him last time, even if it had gone poorly for the sister.

His lips curved as a thought occurred to him. He could offer a deal...one that she'd never agree to. And since she couldn't agree to it, she'd have to stop calling for him. Which meant he wouldn't have to bother killing the mortal, and he could finally get rid of his first headache in millennia.

He rose, cutting Abaddon off mid-sentence. "I'll be back," he told them, disappearing even as Grim smirked and Abaddon started to ask him a question.

Blanche sat on the floor, her head resting against the soft mattress Mira's body still rested upon. She hadn't bathed since Death had refused her and she'd had to fight off ghosts, so her long black hair hung limply around her face. A face that was paler than usual, so the dark smudges beneath her blue-gray eyes were darker, seemed deeper. Since she also hadn't eaten in those four days, she was aware she'd lost a few pounds as well. Her shirt and cargo pants now bagged on her.

Maybe Aidan and her parents were right. She should just give up and perform the rituals to ensure Mira's soul would be laid to rest properly in the afterlife. A soul that Blanche had captured the moment Mira had died. A soul that was currently housed in the locket that rested against Blanche's chest.

It had been all she could think of to do, especially when Suni's healing had failed to save Mira. If Mira's soul had gone to the underworld, there would have been almost no chance of bringing her sister back.

Blanche drew the locket from beneath her shirt and traced a finger over the softened edges of the ivory crow on the blackened silver. Inside, it held strands of hair from her parents and both her siblings. A way of connecting to them, no matter how far apart they might be.

The metal was icy now, despite having been against her warm skin, a result of the soul held within it. Her finger trembled as she pressed the tip of her thumbnail against the latch. All she had to do was open it, and she'd free Mira's soul, allow her to pass on.

But then Mira would truly be gone.

Before she could force herself to go through with it, the room darkened and chilled as a familiar power flooded it. Startled, her hand jerked, and the locket fell back to her chest as she stared up at the expressionless face of Death.

"I didn't call you," she said dumbly, uncertain if she should be pleased he was here, or fearful of what he intended.

"For once," he said dryly. "Dare I ask why you stopped after doing it over and over again for the last few days?" She didn't have the chance to even begin to answer when he cut a hand through the air and shook his head. "Don't care. I've decided to make you a deal."

Scrambling to her feet, Blanche clung to the bedpost for support. The lack of food had left her legs weak, but she refused to deal with Death while her ass was on the floor. "What's the deal?" she asked, ignoring the warm hope trying to form in her belly.

Death smiled, but it was as icy as his silvery-blue eyes and made her heart sink. Whatever deal he had, she was going to like it even less than she had his last deal, she knew it. "I will grant you the ability to bring your sister back to life. It will be as though she'd never died at all. She'd be whole, with her mind, body, and powers intact."

That was exactly what she wanted, but there had to be a catch. There was always a catch. "And in return...?" she prompted.

His smile widened, showing that Death, of all people, had dimples. A fact which didn't reassure her at the moment. "In return, you will agree to come to the realm of souls with me, to forever reside in Cindatha, never returning to this plane or any other. And to be clear, there will be no way for your to communicate with your sister from there. You will leave your phone here."

In that moment, everything within her froze in shock. Her breath held, and she would later swear her heart even skipped several beats. Leave? Spend eternity in the underworld? An underworld she'd never even heard of? For all she knew, it was worse than Tartarus or Hell. And to never see her family again? Not even in death? That was exactly what she was trying to prevent.

Turning, she glanced at the phone on her nightstand, then looked at Mira's body. Her heart started beating again, and she exhaled. The decision wasn't actually a difficult one. She owed Mira for getting her killed. This was simply setting things right.

Straightening her shoulders and lifting her chin, Blanche turned back to Death. She wasn't sure what he saw on her face, but his smile slipped slightly. "I accept."

The smile faded entirely, his face returning to the emptiness it had shown when he first appeared. "Are you certain? This will be the last time you will ever see your family. No one would fault you if you needed some time to consider."

She firmly shook her head. "No, I don't. I accept your bargain. Bring Mira back to life, and I'll do what you ask." Her brow furrowed. "But why did you say you would give me the ability to bring her back? Why not just do it yourself?"

"Are you really questioning me when I've just agreed to give you what you want?" he asked, though she thought he said the words through gritted teeth.

"No," she quickly said.

With one sharp nod, he strode toward her, firmly gripped her chin, and tilted her face up. She found herself staring up at him, but it only lasted an instant before his mouth was on hers. It wasn't gentle, it wasn't tender. It was a rough kiss, but she only had long enough to register that he was kissing her before pain shot through her. It jolted through her lips and went clear down to her toes, feeling like she imagined being struck by a bolt of lightning might feel, if lightning froze instead of burned.

Blanche tried to scream against his mouth but she felt paralyzed. The whole thing had the single virtue of being over quickly, though it certainly didn't feel like it at the time.

He released her and stepped back. "You have five minutes."

She slumped back against the bedpost, once again needing its help to remain on her feet. Her whole body tingled, and not in the good kind of way. It took her one of those five minutes just to relearn how to breathe and speak. "I...I don't know how to bring her back."

"I gave you the power. Use it like you use any other power." He arched a brow and glanced pointedly at her locket. "You might want to start with letting that out. Souls tend to dislike being contained."

Though she doubted it was as easy as he made it sound, she shifted over and sat beside Mira. Undoing the clasp on the locket's chain, she took several calming breaths, trying to forestall the panic that the entire situation was creating.

"Three minutes," Death told her, tone bored.

"Would you shut up for a second?" she snapped before she could think better of it.

"Careful," he told her in a warning tone. "My patience for your actions is at its end. I can call the deal off now."

She couldn't allow that. Before he could follow through on his threat, she dropped the spell around Mira's body and placed the locket against Mira's chest, over her silent heart. Her other hand rested against Mira's cold cheek. Not letting herself think of everything that could go wrong, she hit the latch with her nail, opening it.

Blanche could feel Mira's soul sliding free of its confinement, and closed her eyes, digging for the new power that rested deep within her. Biting her lip hard enough to draw blood, she pushed that power into Mira and prayed with everything she had that this would work.

It had to work.

The fleeing soul hesitated and hovered over Mira's body. Still pushing with the magic Death had forced into her, she waited, flattening the hand on Mira's chest, desperate to feel the heart beneath start beating again.

When it finally did, she let out a sob as her eyes flew open. Mira's eyes shifted beneath her lids, but Blanche continued to wait. Until she saw Mira look at her, heard Mira speak, she wouldn't believe she'd done it. She couldn't afford to.

Then Mira let out a little moan and her eyes fluttered open. They were fogged by confusion, but there was life in them.

"Mira," Blanche whispered, dropping the locket and gathering her sister into a fierce hug.

"Blanche? What's going on?" Mira asked as she weakly returned the embrace.

"Two minutes," Death intoned behind them.

"Who…" Mira tried to pull away, to see who had spoken, but Blanche refused to release her.

"You died," she whispered in her sister's ear. "In the catacombs in Abydos. Revenants got you."

Mira stiffened and shoved Blanche back, her gaze going straight to Death. "What did you do?" she asked, but the question clearly wasn't for the intimidating man only feet away.

"What I had to," Blanche answered, without a trace of remorse. "But you need to listen, because I don't have much time."

"No, you—"

Blanche covered Mira's mouth with her hand and kept talking. "I have to go, and I won't be allowed to come back, but I'll be okay. This was my decision. I want you to remember that. I want you to tell Mom, Dad, and Aidan that. This was my choice, and I'm content with it."

Mira shoved Blanche's arm away, her expression showing that she couldn't decide if she was angry or sad. "You're leaving? Now?" Her gaze snapped to Death. "You. This is your doing!" she accused, trying to push past Blanche to climb off the bed.

"No!" Blanche grabbed Mira's arm, terrified that if Mira attacked Death, that he'd just kill her and Blanche would still be forced to go with him. And she very much doubted that he'd give her time to bring Mira back a second time. For all she knew, it had been a one time only thing, and she'd never be able to do it again. "This was *my* choice. Not his. I begged for this. I begged to bring you back."

"It's time. Say your goodbyes," Death ordered.

"I love you, Mira. You and the rest. Let them know that, okay?" Blanche begged, doing her best to prevent her tears from falling. Mira was alive. Everything else she could deal with. Even an eternity in an unknown underworld.

"I love you, too, Blanche. I just wish you hadn't done this," Mira whispered.

The shadows again coalesced in the room, but this time they engulfed Blanche as well as Death. The world turned an odd shade of blue-black before she felt a tug in the center of her body. Then she was gone, pulled to the realm that would become her home, with the man who would become her captor.

Mira watched Blanche and Death disappear and tried to make sense of what had just happened. The last thing she remembered was being in the catacombs, trying to keep revenants away from Evane as Suni did her best to save him. There had been pain, then a timeless sort of blackness. She wasn't sure if she'd been there for minutes or years.

Then she'd felt a pull that had drawn her back to the light. No, to her body, if Blanche had told her the truth, and she'd never before doubted Blanche. She wasn't going to start now, but she did need more answers than she'd gotten in the few minutes before Death had stolen her sister.

Pushing out of the bed, she was surprised to find she felt good. No weakness, no dizziness. Instead, she felt like she'd just woken from the best nap ever.

She left Blanche's bedroom and went downstairs in search of whoever might be home. She'd just reached the bottom step when she saw her dad just coming inside. His gaze landed on her and his eyes widened. His legs buckled and he blindly reached out for the doorframe. He didn't manage to grab it before he dropped to his knees and all color drained from his face. Throwing his head back, he let out a wail that made her flinch and cover her ears.

"Dad!" she yelled, trying to be heard over the banshee shriek, but it was a useless attempt. Very little was more piercing than the voice of a banshee. Hurrying forward, she knelt in front of him and risked uncovering one of her already aching ears to grab his arm. "Dad!" she tried again.

The sound ceased as abruptly as it had begun, and let her hear the sound of footsteps quickly approaching.

"Mirabelle," he whispered in a hoarse voice. "Are you a ghost?"

"No," she assured him, tightening her hold on his arm. He might not be a necromancer, but he lived with three. *Had* lived with three. He knew ghosts could only rarely touch the living, and certainly not until they'd been dead for a while. Then again, she had no idea how long it had been since Abydos.

He lifted an unsteady hand and touched her cheek. Reassured that she was real, he pulled her into a tight hug. She wrapped her arms around him, saying nothing when he squeezed too hard and her ribs began to ache.

"Holy shit. She did it."

Her brother's voice made her glance over, and he looked just as stunned as their dad did.

"Elliot? What is it? Did something happen to Blanche?" her mom was calling as she rushed toward the foyer.

"Mom! It's Mira! Blanche did it! She fucking did it!" Aidan yelled.

"What?" her mom shrieked, doing a passable imitation of a banshee herself.

It took only seconds before Mira found herself surrounded by family, with both Aidan and her mom speaking over each other as they touched her so they, too, could prove that she was real.

She had most definitely been dead.

It took quite some time before they calmed down enough for her to do more than promise that she felt okay. Now she just had to get some answers...and tell them that they'd gotten one daughter back, only to lose another.

CHAPTER 3

Blanche and Death appeared in a long hallway. The stone that made up the floors, ceiling, and walls was a dark gray with veins of silver, deep blue, and dark red spearing chaotically through it. Both sides of the hallway had doors, each one identical, with torches in the space between the doors. It reminded Blanche of a medieval castle, but without the rugs and wall hangings that normally softened structures made of stone. The lack of any of those homey touches actually seemed to suit Death, though.

Something about Death's method of teleportation left her feeling woozy, and she reached a hand out, bracing it against the wall. To her surprise, it wasn't cold, but as warm as flesh, which was kind of creepy. She jerked her hand away, staring at the spot she'd touched, and she heard Death sigh.

"This is...Cindatha?" she asked when she turned back to him. "An underworld?"

"The Underworld, yes," he confirmed. "Or the realm of souls. Whatever you wish to call it."

Her brow furrowed as something occurred to her. "Are there ghosts around?" she asked as she looked up and down the hallway, searching for signs of them even as she used her magic to check for their presence.

One dark brow lifted. "Why?"

She hesitated, not really wanting to give him something to use against her, but reasoned that, as master of death, he'd likely be able to sense it in any case. "I'm a receptacle. I'd like to know if I'm going to need to be constantly fending off attempts by the local ghosts to possess me." Attempts that would eventually succeed. Sometimes she hated being so easy to possess. Most times, actually.

"It's a little late to be worrying about that, isn't it?" he asked with no trace of emotion. "You're never leaving here."

Did he have to be so blunt about that? So cold and unfeeling? Unfortunately, he wasn't wrong. She'd agreed to this and had to deal with the consequences. All the consequences. "And what is it you want me to do now that I'm here?"

His eerie pale blue eyes seemed to bore into her as he stared, unblinking, for a long moment. "Stay out of my way," he finally answered before he disappeared.

Her jaw clenched as she stared at the spot he'd just inhabited. Her first instinct was to yell at him to come back, to tell her there was more for her here than just hiding from ghosts, but she bit her already sore lip. Screaming at the man who could subject her to so much worse than this wasn't a good idea.

But being alone gave her no distraction from her thoughts. Thoughts which were back in her family's home. With her parents, her brother...and the sister she'd brought back from the grave. How were they handling Mira being back? Hell, how was Mira? Blanche had never dealt with it herself, but she had to imagine it would be jarring. It was jarring enough having been the one to do it.

Lifting her hands, she stared at them as though her power was centered in them, though she knew that wasn't how it worked, at least not for her. But her touch had brought life back to Mira. Except she still wasn't sure why Death had given her the power to resurrect rather than just doing it himself. He was obviously powerful enough, so why had he opted to give her this power that no one but the gods had ever before possessed? Not even all gods could do what she'd done just a few minutes before.

Dropping her hands, she looked around and sighed. Not that it was going to be a useful skill here. And that was if it hadn't been a one time thing.

But for now, she had a more immediate issue. She was stuck in some unknown underworld by herself, and had no idea where to go or what to do. Her body was suffering from neglect—especially since she hadn't truly taken care of the injuries she'd sustained in the pit—and her hand was throbbing from all the times she'd cut it to try summoning Death. All of those things combined had her searching desperately for some place private, because she felt a panic attack stirring in her chest.

The door next to her was locked, though she sharply jiggled the handle. Turning to the door on the other side of the hallway, she made a sound unfortunately close to a sob when the handle turned. She rushed inside, relieved to see it was not only a bedroom, it was also unoccupied.

Closing the door behind her, she leaned back against it then sank down to the floor. Her eyes closed as she drew in slow, steady breaths, in through her nose and out through her mouth, trying to calm herself before the panic grew out of control.

Simple breathing exercises weren't helping, so she tried to distract herself. Forcing her eyes open, she looked around the room, making herself detail everything she could. The first thing she noticed was the bed. It was large, with four posts like hers back on Earth, though without the canopy her bed had. The bedding was wine colored, and there were several fluffy pillows piled around the headboard. A steamer-style trunk rested at the foot of the bed, and she gave herself a moment to imagine what could be inside it. Blankets, probably, though it could be clothing for whoever called this room their own. No, that was probably in the wardrobe that sat on the wall across from the bed.

Now that she noticed the wardrobe, she saw there was a second door beside it. Feeling marginally calmer, she braced a hand on the floor and pushed to her feet to investigate. Huh. An attached bathroom, with what looked like modern plumbing. That was more than a little surprising, but it was also just out of place enough to help pull her mind away from the panic attack.

With the anxiety receding, she found herself annoyed with the way Death had just bailed on her. Okay, so he had probably not expected her to take the deal and hadn't planned for what to do with her, but it was still a dick move. Which meant she was now going to push the last of her panic attack away by snooping. After she cleaned up.

To her relief, there were soap and towels in the bathroom, so she cleaned the blood from her hand, then splashed water on her face. There wasn't anything she could do about the rest of her, not until she showered, which sadly, wasn't going to be now.

Done, she slipped out of the room, shut the door, and moved down the hallway, but every other door she tried was locked. Dismayed, she came to the only other things in the hallway—a wide staircase in the center that curved down in a large U, and a straight staircase opposite it that led up.

Her steps were wary as she went down the stairs, finding herself in a large, circular room. Like the upper floor, it was basically empty but for three more hallways; one directly across from the stairs, one to the left, and one to the right. Stepping out onto the smooth floor, she slowly turned and saw there were two doors as well, set on either side of the staircase and back a good eight feet.

Blanche could feel her anxiety starting to rise again. Since Death had disappeared, she hadn't seen a single other person—living or dead. While she was by no means questioning her decision to give her life for Mira's, she truly hoped that she wasn't in for an eternity of solitude. Even the occasional ghost might be good, though she'd prefer beings who couldn't possess her if she had a choice.

Forcing herself to think of other things, she strode down the middle hallway, her steps quick, purposeful. This hallway was also full of doors, but they were smaller than the ones upstairs had been, and each had a small, barred window set about eye level. Her unease deepened as she peeked in the window of the first door. Inside was a small, empty room with nothing but a pallet and bucket.

Cells. Why in the hell would Death have cells? She'd expect it in Tartarus or any of the other hell realms, but this wasn't an underworld she'd ever heard in conjunction with any afterlife. Were there even any souls here? He'd called it a realm of souls, but so far it was as bare as the rooms. Where were the souls? What religion led its believers here upon death? It was a mystery, and she didn't like it. How could her family not have ever heard of an underworld connected to Death himself?

She shook her head and moved on, hoping she'd find the answer some place in this castle.

It was no surprise when every other door led to a cell, at least until she got to the end of the hallway. There she saw a set of huge double doors, clearly different from the rest. They had to be twenty feet tall and made out of the same stone as the rest of the castle. They were carved, not with images of death as she expected, but a scene which resembled a lush rainforest. About six feet from the ground was a thick wooden bar, meant, she was sure, to keep the doors closed, but she saw nothing supporting it.

Curious, she tried to shift the bar, but wasn't able to budge it. Trying again, she used her magic as well as her arms, but still the bar didn't rise an inch. But that presented another question. She was in the underworld, but had her powers. Did that mean she was still alive? Or had Death killed her when he'd brought her here? That could be why she could never leave.

Unwilling to risk another panic attack by considering her own death, she made her way back to the circular room. Debating for only a moment, she turned right and headed down that hallway. Unlike the others, there was only a single door here, set at the far end of the hall. And this one gave her a low feeling of...not quite dread, but it was the closest word she could think of to describe it. There wasn't any fear like she'd normally expect with dread, but it was definitely not a positive feeling. Somehow she was both drawn to it and repelled by it, the conflicting emotions causing her belly to churn.

Moving closer, she rested her hand against the polished wood. There was something inside, something important, and her pulse quickened as she slid her fingers down to the old-fashioned handle.

No knob here, but a handle older than she'd ever seen, and she was more than two hundred years old. It wasn't just the style of it, though that looked ancient, but the metal itself looked old.

Drawing the door open, it creaked ominously, but that didn't stop her from stepping inside. The room was perhaps only ten feet squared, and almost as empty as everything else she'd come across. There was a torch on both the left and right walls, illuminating the pedestal in the middle of the room. It wasn't a separate piece, but part of whatever stone made up the floor. And resting on top of that pedestal was a sarcophagus. It was unlike any she'd seen before, and she'd seen hundreds of sarcophagi and coffins, from dozens of cultures. This one was made of ceramic rather than stone or wood, but she recognized none of the carvings on it. They certainly weren't Egyptian, or any other language she knew.

Normally tombs, graves, and other aspects of death didn't bother her. She was a necromancer in a family of necromancers. Her family's home had catacombs beneath it, filled with the remains of their loved ones. She'd grown up seeing ghosts and learning about funerary rites. Death was normal. It was natural. And, except for Mira's death, it was as commonplace to her as working nine to five was for humans. But something about this one sarcophagus, this one death, made her skin crawl and her blood chill. It wasn't a sensation she was used to, and she found she disliked it immensely.

In any other situation, she'd investigate. She'd examine the carvings, see if she could shift the lid to peek inside, and use her magic to thoroughly check it out. Not today. She'd already dealt with way too much that day. She wasn't going to mess with what looked like an ancient sarcophagus in Death's fucking house. There was no telling what it could do to her.

Leaving, she closed the door quietly behind her. Feeling drained, she took a minute to simply lean against the wall beside the door and breathe. There was no reason she could think of why just being in the room should have affected her, and certainly not after such a short time. But she'd also never truly been in any realm but the realm of the living—except for that short trip to Kur. For all she knew, this was normal for all living beings in the underworld. She could wake every day feeling tired and powerless. She seriously hoped not, but if so, she'd deal with it. She'd figure out how to deal with everything here.

With that falsely optimistic thought, she put distance between herself and the sarcophagus, returning to the circular room that seemed a great deal safer than it the first time she'd seen it.

At least that room didn't hold a corpse.

CHAPTER 4

Blanche didn't stop to consider her options this time, but continued straight across the room, taking the last unexplored hallway, ignoring the doors by the stairs for now. Since the first had contained cells, and the second a tomb, she was almost afraid to consider what she might find down this one. But with nothing else to do, she opted to continue exploring.

The first door she came to was open, but it was completely empty. No furniture, no rugs, nothing. Just a large room that echoed when she stepped inside. Odd, but whatever. It was Death's castle. He could leave rooms empty if he wanted to. The next room was the exact same, right down to the size. As were the three after that. Now Blanche was confused. One empty room she could see, but five? What was the point of having a bunch of useless rooms?

After leaving the last bare room, she continued down the hallway but her steps paused after a few feet. She heard music but hadn't yet seen anything that could play music. It sounded like a violin, and though she couldn't name the song, it was something equal parts eerie and beautiful.

Her steps carried her toward the closed door that was at the end of that side of the hallway. The music was definitely coming from this room, and she wondered who was playing it. Death? One of the souls that might live here? Or maybe it was a recording, because whatever it was, it was played wonderfully. She couldn't decide whether to smile or weep.

Trying the knob, she found it locked and pressed her hand against the wood, leaning into it. Closing her eyes, she forgot about the shit show her life had been the last few weeks and let herself get lost in the poignant melody.

That song blended seamlessly into the next, then a third, but when that one was done, the violinist went silent. Blanche wanted to bang on the door, to call to them to continue, but without knowing who was on the other side, she wasn't sure how wise that would be, and she'd already made enough bonehead moves for one day.

Sighing at the silence that was even more deafening now that she'd heard the music, she pushed away from the door. She hoped they'd come back, but for now, she had a few more doors left to try. At least one of them was bound to have *something* in them. Or so she hoped, because otherwise her life was about to get extremely boring.

When she opened the door across from her, she made a low sound of pleasure and relief when she saw it was a library. And not a simple home library, either. There were multiple stories, all filled with books upon books. She'd never seen so many in one place, even at the library near her house. Which meant the odds were good there was something here she'd enjoy reading.

She took a step into the room, fully intending to investigate, when a loud, low-pitched snarling made her freeze. Slowly, without moving her head, she scanned the room, and it didn't take long until she found the source of the sound.

Stalking her was an honest-to-gods saber-tooth tiger. Despite the name, it was tawny in color, more like a lion, though it lacked a mane. It was huge, and those long canines looked way longer than they had on fossils she'd seen in museums. Its paws looked like they could cover her entire head without even trying. But the worst part was the cold, feral look in its amber eyes.

"Fuck me," she whispered, doing everything she could to avoid turning and running. That, she knew, would just inspire it to chase her. Nor could she do nothing and wait for it to reach her and eat her. So she did the only thing she could think of. She called for help.

"Death! Get your ass here before your overgrown house cat makes a meal out of me!"

The tiger didn't seem to be bothered by her screaming, but neither did Death seem to notice. Or maybe he noticed and just didn't care. Either way, it meant she was on her own.

"Nice kitty kitty," she murmured as she took a slow step back. The movement caused another snarl, and she stopped. The huge cat, however, did not. It kept coming, and Blanche had a feeling she was about to know what those eight-inch fangs felt like. Desperate to do something, she shoved a hand toward the tiger, pushing with her magic, trying to force it back, but it didn't do more than make it pause for a second.

"Death!" she yelled once more as the predator shifted in a way she'd seen in pet cats. It was preparing to pounce. Drawing in a breath, she lifted both hands, ready to blast it with fire. It was the only chance she had.

Just before she was going to release the magic, a tall figure stepped between her and the tiger.

"Sa!" he said sharply.

Blanche had to lean around the man to see the tiger. It had sat and cocked its head, but the moment her face was in view, its eyes shot to her and it stared. Hungrily, or at least that's what she thought it looked like.

"Dude. She's not lunch."

"Really not," she agreed, straightening.

The man stepped to one side and turned so he could keep both her and the cat in view. "Sorry," he told her. "Guess no one told him there was company."

"Not sure I'd call myself company," she told him dryly. "And I didn't know I'd be here a couple hours ago."

The man shrugged. "Still. He isn't used to seeing strangers here. Not like there are a whole lot of visitors."

"Gee, I can't understand why," she said, making no effort to mask her sarcasm.

He grinned. "Fair enough. I'm Grim."

Her eyes narrowed. "Grim? So am I going to run into nothing but people with death-related names here? Pick up a baby name book or something. Variety's never a bad thing."

Rather than being offended, he laughed. "Can you think of a better name for Death than Death? And my name's just as fitting, I promise. Besides, the big guy's name is Sa. Not death-related," he said, pointing his thumb toward the tiger.

That's what he said, but Sa probably meant death or something in some obscure language. "Uh huh. Well, I'm Blanche."

"I know," he said, smirking. "Want a tour?"

"What, there's something more than a bunch of empty rooms, cells and tomb?" she snarked.

The smirk froze. "Tomb?"

Blanche folded her arms over her chest, keeping an eye on the tiger as she wasn't quite sure he was as tame as Grim made him sound. "Yeah, tomb. You know, room with a dead body in it?"

Grim nodded slowly. "Yes...there's more than cells and tombs. Like the library," he said, jerking his head back to the room behind the tiger.

She looked away from the feline to the books beyond. It really was impressive, and her fingers itched to get her hands on some of those books. "Please tell me those aren't off limits." Not that it would stop her if they were, but it would help to know if she needed to be sneaky about it. Then again, if Sa was the guard, she might never get close to a single book.

He shook his head. "Not at all. But you should know that Death gets pretty pissed if anyone messes up the books. So don't dog ear them or write in them or anything and you'll be fine."

"Noted." As much as she wanted to dive in right now, she was curious about what else was here. "So...that tour?"

"Right." Grim waved a hand at the cat. "Come on, Sa."

The cat grumbled but stretched, gave a huge yawn, then padded out of the library. He didn't stop, but started back down the hallway. Hopefully to find something to eat that was not her.

Grim shut the door behind Sa, then opened the door at the end of the hallway. "You like movies?" he asked, blocking the doorway with his body.

"Doesn't everyone?"

"Surprisingly, no," he said before he opened the door.

At first she thought she was looking at another wall of bookshelves, but after a moment she realized it was what looked like thousands of movie cases. "Holy shit." She pushed past him into the room and saw that it was a long rectangle. Both long walls were completely full of movies, shelves stretching from floor to ceiling. Between them was the most comfortable looking couch she'd ever seen, with two recliners set behind it and on a riser. They faced a blank white wall, and when she looked at the other end, she saw a projector and table with the electronics to play all the movies.

While she absolutely preferred books to movies, she had to admit to wanting to spend some time in this room, too. She knew some people who had money, but she'd never been in an actual home theater.

"I'm kind of confused," she admitted.

"About what?"

"There are a shitload of empty rooms, but then this huge library and theater? Doesn't make sense."

"Oh, that. Yeah, Death isn't big on interior decorating, but we kind of harassed him until he gave us something to kill the time. You can only read a book so many times, you know? Though I've caught him in here more than once, so if you hear him bitch about the theater, just know he's full of shit. Now come on. You can play with the movies later," Grim told her, taking her elbow and drawing her out of the room. He headed to the last door in that hallway and gestured her inside. As surprised as she'd been to see modern plumbing upstairs, the sight of a small but fully equipped kitchen seemed even more out of place. It had a table, but it only looked big enough for four people. Death clearly wasn't one for big parties. Not that she was surprised.

"Hungry?" Grim asked.

Her stomach, of course, chose that time to growl since she hadn't eaten in a few days, but she couldn't help but think of a Greek story she'd heard when she was just three or four. "Ah...I don't think that's such a good idea."

He arched a brow as he walked to a fridge and grabbed out a beer. "Why not?"

"Seriously? Persephone ate a few pomegranate seeds and got stuck in Hades for half of every year. I can't even imagine what a full meal would have done."

He chuckled. "Okay, first off, aren't you stuck here anyway? So what would it matter if that story was true? If you're not leaving, then you're not leaving."

He had a point, but she didn't want to tell him that. "What's the second thing?"

"That story's pure bullshit." She gave him a skeptical look, and he nodded. "Seriously. It's what Demeter put out there to try to save face. She was pissed and insulted that her daughter would choose to leave her and live with Hades." He rolled his eyes and shook his head. "I promise. Seph loves her husband and is perfectly happy where she is."

"And you would know...how?"

"Partly because I've met pretty much all the death and underworld deities out there. And Hades is pretty good friends with Death." That actually didn't surprise her—much—but his next comment did. "That's actually why Cerberus guards the gates to Hades."

"I'm not following."

"You know how a lot of people like one-upping each other? Well, Hades got jealous of Sa, and when he heard about a three-headed dog being born..."

She stared at him. "Are you fucking kidding me?"

"Nope. But since you know it's safe for you to eat, are you hungry?"

Her stomach demanded she say yes, but honestly, her nerves had her wondering how wise putting anything in it would be. Still, maybe something light would stay down, and since she did seem to be alive, she'd need to eat sometime. Although, was there really going to be a difference between life and death since the rest of her eternity was apparently going to be spent here?

"Yeah," she decided. "But nothing too heavy?"

"Easy enough." She expected him to show her where she could find fixings for sandwiches or something, but he set about cooking something with pasta. She sat at the table and expressed her surprise.

Grim smirked. "You don't think I spend literally all my time dealing with souls, do you? And with enough time, you can end up learning a lot of things. Sometimes whether you want to or not."

The dish turned out to be delicious, and after the first bite, she forgot about her anxiety and devoured it. Since he cooked, she dealt with the dishes before they continued the tour.

Taking her back to the circular room, he headed right for one of the doors behind the staircase. Saying nothing, he pushed the door open and strode inside. It was a huge room, with two rows of columns leading down the length of it to a dais with a black throne set in the middle of it.

Who knew Death had a throne room? Wasn't that unnecessary if no one was around? Still, she slowly crossed the room, stopping just a few feet in front of the throne. It had a high back and wide seat, but there were no skulls like were rumored to be on the thrones of several death gods. Instead, it was absurdly plain, without any decoration whatsoever. But, like the scythe she'd so recently held, it radiated power. It didn't feel quite the same, but since both belonged to Death, it made sense that they would have different purposes. She had to wonder what magic a throne would need.

"Why a throne room? I haven't seen anyone here but you and Death," she asked as she turned back to Grim and began to walk back to him.

Grim smirked and shrugged. "I know you were probably hoping I'd be your source of info for this place. Maybe we'd become BFFs and all that. And hell, maybe we will. I never was good at telling the future. But if you want to know about Death, maybe you should ask him."

Her eyes narrowed, but she had hoped he'd be her guide to all things Death and Cindatha. "Might be hard to do since he said all I was supposed to do while I was here was stay out of his way."

Chuckling at her, they left the throne room and went back upstairs. "Yeah, well. He's a complicated guy," he said before he pointed to a door. "That's my room." Further down, he stopped at the room she'd gone in before. "This is yours. And don't bother trying to snoop up here. Unless you're invited, the doors won't open to anyone but whoever's staying there."

That explained why none of the other doors had opened. She wondered which door led to Death's bedroom, but had a feeling Grim wouldn't answer. "Thanks. But you didn't tell me what's upstairs."

"No problem. And we'll save upstairs for another time. Until then, if you need me, just holler," he told her before he pulled a Death and disappeared.

"I hate it when they do that," she muttered as she stepped inside and closed the door behind her, leaning against it. Sighing, she looked around the bedroom and missed seeing her things. She missed hearing the sounds of her family outside her door. Hell, she just missed her family, even if she'd only been gone for a little while. With the time she'd spent trying to bring Mira back, she hadn't really interacted with them for a few weeks.

Pushing away from the door, she moved to the wardrobe and opened it, gasping when she saw familiar clothes inside. Just to be sure, she pulled out a shirt and immediately recognized it as one of hers. Putting it back, she checked and was fairly sure all her clothes were in here.

Frowning, she wondered if this was Death's doing, or Grim's. Either way, she appreciated it. She could have wished for more of her things, but there was enough in the library and theater to keep her occupied. And having her own clothes might at least help her feel a little more connected to her old life. Her old self.

Closing the wardrobe, she made her way into the bathroom. It had been a few days since she showered, so she definitely needed one, and if nothing else, it might help relax her. Her shoulders had felt like steel since Death had first made his offer. Except she discovered that whoever had filled her wardrobe had also brought her toiletries over.

Confused, she took a long, hot shower, but while it relaxed her, it also drained the last of her energy. After drying off, she crawled into bed without bothering to get dressed and fell into a deep, dreamless sleep.

Grim didn't go far after he left Blanche, just downstairs, to the room she'd heard music through the door. Death was still there, sprawled lazily on a loveseat, a violin tucked beneath his chin as he started playing again. Though it was played wonderfully, the tone of the song was harsh. It was a jumble of anger, fear, and confusion, but Grim had a feeling it accurately conveyed the emotions of one of the most powerful beings in existence.

He sat in one of the chairs nearby, slouched down and watching his boss play. He didn't say anything until the song came to an end.

"What do you want?" Death asked, setting the violin in his lap, his eyes cool, his voice harsh.

"I just left Blanche," Grim answered as he teleported a beer from the fridge, popped the top and took a long drink.

Death waited a beat, then said, "And?"

Grim couldn't decide if he was looking forward to Death's reaction to the news he had to share, or dreading it. Death wouldn't kill him for it, and he genuinely considered the guy a friend, but he could be seriously scary. Then again, that was half the fun. "She got into the tomb."

Death narrowed his eyes, then shook his head. "You're lying."

Oh yeah, he didn't like that, but Grim had to hide a smile. "Sorry, but she specifically mentioned the tomb, and described it too." Sort of. "I mean, maybe she was making it up since I've never been in there, but it didn't seem to me that she was lying."

"What'd she say?"

"Just that she found a tomb with a sarcophagus in it," Grim answered casually, toying with the coin in his pocket.

Death's body went rigid as he processed those words. They didn't sound like much, but no one but him should know there was a sarcophagus in his castle. The door was kept sealed, much as the bedrooms were. For her to have gotten inside worried him. When he was alone he'd have to recheck the door, but this castle was almost part of him. It was literally his power made physical. So how had she gotten inside?

He realized Grim was staring at him, so he shrugged and lifted the violin to his chin again. "Doesn't matter. Not like she can do anything with a sarcophagus," he told Grim before he set the bow to the strings and began playing again. The reaper might be one of the two people Death actually trusted completely, but that didn't mean he had to share all his secrets.

Though Grim rolled his eyes, he wasn't taking the music as the dismissal it was. "So what are you planning on doing with the girl?" he asked, raising his voice to be clearly heard over the sad sounds of the violin.

"Nothing," Death said in a flat tone.

"It's going to be hard to do nothing with her since she's living here. And, you know, one of only four people here."

Annoyed, the instrument made a sharp, unpleasant sound as Death abruptly lowered it. "If you're so worried about it, then you can deal with her. Entertain her. Fuck, for all I care, you can take her to see the entire realm. She's a necromancer. She'd probably like to see the places she's read about. Just make sure she stays out of my hair. Understood?"

Annoyance turned to simmering anger when Grim smirked. "Understood." He gave a salute that somehow managed to be sarcastic, then disappeared.

Sighing, Death closed his eyes and tried to regain his calm. Not that he'd actually been calm even before Grim's appearance. Blanche wasn't supposed to have taken the deal. When she'd agreed, he should have just told her to shove it and returned home. Or maybe killed her like Abaddon had suggested. He sure as hell shouldn't have brought her back, not just to Cindatha, but to his castle. Although, it would be easy to create her a home outside and bar the front door to her.

With that thought in his mind, he smiled. Now there was an idea. If the little necromancer started to become a thorn in his side, he'd just shove her out of his castle and banish her to a house on the edge of Cindatha. He wouldn't have to worry about her ever again.

Satisfied that he'd come up with a plan, he began to play again. The tones now were less discordant than they'd been, but he didn't notice that the song he played was one of longing.

CHAPTER 5

Blanche wasn't sure how long she'd slept, but she knew she'd slept for entirely too long. She was also well rested for the first time in weeks. It didn't mean she felt good, she wasn't quite to that point, but she felt better than she had since Mira died.

Though she allowed herself to lounge in bed for a little while, she didn't linger too long before she got up, got dressed, cleaned the healing cuts on her hand, then went downstairs. She'd noticed a coffee pot in the kitchen the day before, and rested or not, she was desperate for some caffeine.

It was no surprise when she saw no one on her way to the kitchen, nor when she found the room empty. This morning—or she assumed it was morning, since she hadn't seen a single window—she was happy for the solitude. She'd never been a morning person, and even less so in these circumstances.

The coffee brewed as she poked around to see if there was something palatable for breakfast. Not that she thought the food would be bad, she just wasn't sure what would be easily stomached at the moment. She wasn't feeling the full brunt of her anxiety, but she was feeling a little nervous, which didn't make for a calm belly.

Hearing the soft sound of footsteps, she turned with the fridge door still open and froze. It was the fucking cat again. Rather than abject fear this time, she narrowed her eyes and got annoyed. She refused to be terrorized by Death's house pet. Especially not if she was going to be dealing with him for the next few thousand years.

Trying to keep him in view as much as possible, she rummaged in the fridge until she found some thick slices of ham. It seemed an odd thing to find in Death's kitchen, but then again, so was pasta. Or any food at all.

Shutting the fridge, she turned to Sa as he slowly padded closer to her. "Nice kitty," she murmured, doing her best to ignore her pounding heart. "We're going to be good friends, you and I. Even if I have to skin you to do it," she added in a low mutter.

When the saber-tooth tiger got closer, she tossed a piece of ham at him, unsurprised when he snatched it out of the air. It disappeared as quickly as he caught it, but then he sat, tail lazily swishing behind him. Cocking her head, she tossed a second piece, and he caught that, too.

"Huh. Maybe you really are an overgrown house cat," she murmured, but when she took a step toward him, his ears flicked back and his eyes went to slits. Just as a snarl began to build in his throat, she stepped back. "Okay...maybe not." But, since she had a third slice, she threw it as well.

She studied him as he did the same to her, and considered. While books and movies were entertaining, she had a feeling she'd get tired of them eventually. Maybe she should consider a hobby, and it seemed like figuring out how to gain the affection of this prehistoric beast would be a good—and time consuming—hobby.

"You really shouldn't be feeding him."

Blanche flinched but managed not to yelp in surprise at the voice. Her gaze flicked over to the door and she saw Grim, though he looked more put together than he had the day before. "I figure making friends with him is better than being eaten. Besides, a couple pieces of ham can't hurt him." She cocked her head and gestured to him with the last piece of ham she had. "What's with the preppy look?" she asked before tossing the ham to Sa.

He frowned and looked down at his clothes. "Preppy look? This is how I always dress."

Her expression mirrored his. "No it isn't. Last night you were wearing a tee-shirt."

His face cleared and he shook his head. "Ah. No, that was my brother. I'm Abaddon."

"Oh! Sorry, you look just like him."

He grinned. "It would be more accurate to say he looks like me. I'm older. Just by a few minutes, but it counts. And I'm glad Sa isn't bothering you. He doesn't really warm up to a lot of people. And I've only seen him allow Death to touch him."

"Not sure why most people would want to," she said, giving the long teeth a pointed look.

Abaddon chuckled. "Fair point. I can't say I've ever wanted to. I'm still not sure why Death picked him out of all the animals in Cindatha."

Though Blanche was curious about Sa, she was more curious about Cindatha. She might not be a scholar in underworlds and their rulers like Mira was, but she was still knowledgeable. Except she was clueless when it came to the place she now called home. "What exactly is

Cindatha? Death said it was the realm of souls, but I've never heard of it before."

"Technically, you have. But instead of me just giving you a lecture, would you like to see it?"

"See it? You mean leave the castle?" she asked, unable to decide if she was curious, excited, or just happy to leave what all too closely resembled some weird prison. Sure, her bed was comfortable and she had the freedom to roam, but not being able to leave the realm, much less the castle, made her feel trapped.

"I do," he agreed. "Feel up to it?"

She hadn't actually managed to find food for herself, but since she hadn't been sure she could stomach anything to begin with, she wasn't upset. She did, however, down the rest of her coffee and rinse the mug out. "Absolutely. Lead the way."

Though Abaddon didn't skirt around Sa, Blanche did, but he just watched them leave with a bored look.

"You're a necromancer, correct?" Abaddon said as they walked toward the huge door she'd found the day before. The one that was barred.

"I am."

"So you've heard of Hades, Kur, the Duat, and so on?"

"Of course."

He grinned. "They're all Cindatha."

Her brow furrowed. "Huh?"

"They're all Cindatha," he repeated. "Every underworld or afterlife, anywhere souls go to when they die, they're all Cindatha."

"Okay, I understand the words, but I'm going to need more of them."

"There's only one underworld. Ages ago, Death was the sole ruler of Cindatha, but there were too many souls for one person, even one as powerful as Death. Since there were gods and goddesses who had an affinity for death and souls, he gave them...I won't say ownership of different sections of Cindatha, because Death still rules them all. Think of it more like a long-term lease. So Hades rules the Greek underworld, Osiris the Egyptian, and so on."

Blanche was so stunned she stopped walking. "Are you kidding me? So all these gods, who act like they are the absolute power within their underworlds, are full of shit?"

It took Abaddon a few steps before he realized she wasn't beside him, and he stopped and turned. "I wouldn't say they're full of shit," he said slowly. "For the most part, they are the absolute power in their area. The world has gotten very full. There are more than a hundred thousand deaths every single day. If Death tried to manage all those souls, he'd have to tend to somewhere around a hundred of them every minute. Without reapers, without the various death gods, without their helpers, some of those souls would slip through the cracks. Souls can't travel here without a guide."

Blanche hadn't thought of it that way, and she'd sure as hell never done the math, but he had a point. "So why is the name Cindatha not known by...anyone?"

"Would Hel or Arawn or Yama be as feared or respected if it was known to their worshipers that they weren't actually the highest power for their religion's death?"

"No, probably not," she had to admit as they started walking again. "So is it just reapers and the rulers of each section of Cindatha that know the truth, then?"

"Mmm...Probably not. For instance, Hades would no doubt love to be the only Greek—other than Persephone—who knows, but I would guarantee Zeus, Hera, and a few others know as well." He stopped by the door and glanced at her. "This is the only door that leads out of the castle—unless you can fly, in any case."

"Why just the one?"

He shrugged. "You'd have to ask Death that, because I don't know. However, it's fortunate you're a necromancer, or you wouldn't be able to open the door."

"Why not?"

"Because it's magically locked. It requires a touch of death-related power and the right words to open. Words that most can't speak." She started to ask, but he continued before she could. "I'm told you were able to summon Death, which means you know the sort of words I mean."

She did. She didn't understand it, but she knew what he meant. Words that most couldn't understand. Sounds most couldn't wrap their tongues around. She called it the language of death, at least in her head, but she had no idea what language it actually was.

Abaddon showed her how to open it, spoke the words that sent a chill across the back of her neck, and the heavy doors swung open. "Welcome to Cindatha," he said with a smile, gesturing toward the now visible land beyond.

Blanche was shocked. Other than her brief trip to the doorway of Kur, she'd never been to an underworld, but she'd read hundreds of accounts describing them. None of them had looked like this.

There was a semi-circle of flat stones directly outside the doors, almost like a huge patio, but beyond that there was a clear line separating two very different landscapes. To the left, it was dry and the various shades of tan and red of a desert. Small shrubs and trees dotted the land, along with stones ranging from pebbles to huge boulders. In the distance, she saw a single narrow mountain, like a spear of rock rising from the earth. It was compelling in an odd way. Yet to the right, it was entirely different; green and lush. Tall tropical-looking trees and thick bushes crowded the area so it looked like a single organism. Dots of color betrayed the fact that there were flowers mixed in with the green and brown of the other plants. It was beautiful.

And it was night.

Stepping away from the castle, she looked up. A round moon bathed everything in a soft glow, and millions of pinpricks of light dusted the sky. It was as compelling a view as the jungle, but it made her wonder.

"What time is it?" she asked, looking to Abaddon, who had joined her on the stones.

"Time is tricky here," he admitted. "There is no sun in Cindatha, and the moon never shifts far from where it is now, so it's perpetually night. And since no one here ages, either because they're dead or immortal, we don't worry too much about time. But it's about nine in the morning on the east coast of America, if that's what you mean."

"No sun?" Blanche wasn't exceptionally attached to the sun, but she couldn't deny some regret that she'd never see it again.

"None," he confirmed. "I should clarify that it's only here in Cindatha proper. Some of the claimed sections do have sunlight, a regular cycle of day and night. This section is different. It changes, too. It used to be a great deal more of that desert section, but over the centuries, the green has spread. In another hundred thousand years, it might all be green."

"Interesting," she said, though she was still trying to process it all. "And does anyone live out there? Or are you, Grim, and Death the only living people here?"

"No, there are reapers there, ones who prefer not to live amongst the humans and Arcane. There are the souls, too, so you would probably run into them. But you should be careful."

"Why? Could they possess me?" she asked, hoping he'd say no. Death hadn't exactly answered her the night before.

"Well, I suppose some could, but they could also attack you. Not all die easily, and not all truly adjust to being dead. And there are also animals here."

"Animals? Live ones?"

"No, none of them are alive. They're all like Sa." He paused, considered. "I take that back. A few of the reapers might have pets, but if so, I haven't seen them."

She hadn't known Sa was dead, but realized she should have. His species had been extinct for thousands of years, after all. But it did surprise her that not only did reapers choose to live in the land of the dead, but had brought living animals over to keep as pets. But the fact that animals could live here—actually live—meant she probably was still living herself.

When she didn't say anything for a long moment as she thought about what little she knew of Cindatha, he broke the silence. "Would you like to..." He trailed off and his eyes flicked back to the castle. "Death wants to see you."

"He does? I find that hard to believe," she muttered, but when he turned back to the door, she followed. He led her to the throne room, opening the door and gesturing for her to go ahead. Sighing, she stepped inside.

The faint hint of power she'd felt from the throne the last time she was here was overshadowed this time by the man currently lounging in it. Sa was sprawled out at the base of it, looking like an overgrown, spoiled pet. A pet that stared at her as though remembering the earlier ham and wanting something more substantial to fill his belly. Like her.

"I heard you wanted to see me?" Blanche asked when she was only five feet or so from Sa's swishing tail. She refused to be intimidated by either Death or Sa. Or at least she refused to show it.

Death's cold gaze shifted to Abaddon. "Thank you." It was clearly a dismissal, and Abaddon gave a half bow before he turned and left the room, closing the heavy door behind him. Alone now, Death turned his focus back to her but said nothing for several minutes. Having that intense gaze fixed on her made her want to squirm, but she forced herself to stand still and quiet until he spoke.

"From what I understand, you spoke directly to Brigit and Rune?"

Surprise had her blinking at him. "Yes? Why?"

"You said they didn't have the scythe with them?"

This time she didn't blink, she sighed. "Right. They had hidden it in a forgotten catacomb near Abydos in Egypt."

Death inclined his head slowly. "Full of death magics, I assume?"

"No, full of fucking revenants that swarmed us and killed my sister," she said, unable to keep her bitterness out of her voice.

He only nodded again. "Did they say why they decided to secret it away instead of protecting it themselves?"

Mira might be alive now, but it didn't erase the soul-crushing grief she'd felt for two weeks. Especially since she'd had less than five minutes to see Mira whole and well before she was whisked off to this place. His questions were just adding salt to the wounds. "No, and if you want to know so bad, why don't you just ask them yourself?" she snapped.

"What did they say?" he asked, ignoring her outburst.

"Why does your throne radiate death magic?" she asked instead.

"What did they say?" he repeated, leaning forward on his throne, no longer looking relaxed.

"That they would have given it to you if you'd just asked, but no, instead you preferred to wreck a few lives!"

"I had my reasons!" he yelled, slamming his fist down on the arm of the throne. It was louder than it should be, and even Sa lifted his head to look at Death.

"Your reasons suck!" she yelled back, forgetting in that moment that he was the supreme power when it came to death, forgetting to be afraid of him. Instead, all the anger she'd felt toward them both surged to the front of her mind and she was fully intent on releasing it on him. "If you'd just gotten over your ego and gone to them directly, Mira wouldn't have died and I wouldn't be stuck in the most boring place in all the realms! And you can't even answer some simple fucking questions!"

He shot to his feet, eyes darkening to pewter. "You have no right to ask those questions! And if you and your friends were more competent, your sister never would have died," he sneered.

He was seriously blaming her for Mira's death? If he was anyone but Death, she'd think he had a death wish, and she was sorely tempted to see just how hard it was to kill him.

Before either could react to his harsh words, Sa rose to his feet and let out a roar that filled the room. Both Blanche and Death stilled and looked at him, Death with surprise, and Blanche with wariness. It had the added benefit of calming them both somewhat. Neither was as relaxed as when she'd first walked in, but they also weren't on the verge of attacking either.

Blanche took several deep breaths and looked back to Death. "Did you really just expect me to read and watch movies for the rest of eternity? Isn't there something more I can do around here? Something to actually give me purpose?"

"Are you wanting to reverse our deal? I can send you back to Earth and bring your sister here in your place," he offered in a dry tone.

"No!" she replied instantly. "No," she said more calmly. "I'd much rather have Mira alive. That's worth whatever you do to me."

"Then you can go."

Blanche wanted to argue, but a glance at Sa had her biting back her retort. Instead, she gave Death a tight smile then left, wondering if this was really what the rest of her existence was going to be like. She sure as hell hoped not.

CHAPTER 6

Death watched Blanche leave, then narrowed his eyes at Sa. "And what was that about?" he asked, but the saber-tooth tiger just stared with half-lidded eyes before he laid back down and rested his head on his paws. Annoyed with his long-term companion, he debated what to do with his newest houseguest. The idea of sticking her in a house outside of the castle was still a valid one, but it wouldn't really solve the problem. She'd still be in Cindatha, and she'd still be able to access the tomb.

What he needed was more information. He knew nothing about her beyond that she was a necromancer who had helped recover his scythe. Clearly, she wasn't going to just give him the information he wanted, which meant he'd have to find another way of obtaining it. Making himself invisible and ensuring his power was hidden, he teleported himself to Blanche, finding her in her room. She was pacing and muttering to herself, so he moved to the corner so she wouldn't run into him.

"Boneheaded men. Doesn't matter whether they're human, Arcane, god, or whatever the hell Death is. Why in the hell did he want me here if he's just going to ignore me most of the time?" she asked, throwing her hands in the air before they slapped against her waist and stayed there.

She glared at the bed and drew one foot back slightly. It was clear she was considering kicking it, but thought better of it and huffed in annoyance. "Can't believe I'm stuck here with nothing to do," she said as she dropped onto her back on the bed, staring up at the ceiling. "Seriously, would it kill him to give me *something* to do? Gotta be something to do around here that doesn't violate our deal." She rubbed her hands over her face and gave a deep sigh. "Something to distract me," she added in a voice even he could barely hear.

Since she not only had a point—about part of her ranting, anyway—and her focus seemed to be centered solely on complaining about him, he left. Not just her room, but Cindatha. He appeared in the bedroom in her home—her old home in the living realm—still invisible. He wasn't sure why he was curious about her, but expected it had something to do with figuring out how to limit the impact she'd have on his household. Which is why he did something he was well aware she'd done just the day before. He snooped.

Her bedroom wasn't cluttered, which was both blessing and curse. Less to snoop through, but also less to find. There was a closet, dresser, canopy bed, nightstand, and free-standing mirror, so not a lot of options for him to discover something.

Since he knew Grim had taken pity on her and brought her clothes to Cindatha, Death ignored the closet and wandered to the dresser. The human skull sitting on it had him cocking his head, but he wasn't really surprised. Most necromancers surrounded themselves with death in some fashion. He'd even known a few to actually live in cemeteries or tombs. He wasn't sure why exactly, since neither one tended to be the least bit comfortable, but he was hardly one to judge another's choice of living space.

Opening the first drawer, he found it empty, as was the second. The third had various pieces of jewelry and weapons. He poked through them and quickly concluded that they, too, all had connections to death. Tools of a necromancer's trade. In fact, he recognized one of them in particular. Picking up the mummification knife, he narrowed his eyes at it, certain this very knife was the one she'd used when she'd summoned him the first time.

He really had to find and destroy all copies of that particular spell, but that was for another time. For now, he just replaced the knife and moved on.

The jewelry box on top of the dresser had a mix of what he thought of as normal jewelry, and some Blanche likely only wore when she needed a connection to a specific death deity, as he recognized symbols of Hades, Osiris, and others. Some of it looked nicer, more expensive, and he idly noticed that she tended to favor silver and colored stones over gold and diamonds.

The bookshelf was half-filled with books, but she had some artifacts on the shelves as well. Not all of them, he noted, were ones expected of a necromancer. Sentimental value, he assumed. Or she'd just thought they were pretty, like the small Greek-style vase.

Wandering over to the bed and the nightstand beside it, he opened the single drawer. Two bottles of pills—ibuprofen and an over-the-counter sleep aid—an eye mask, and a small, stoppered vial filled with a golden liquid. He was mildly curious about it, but left it where it was.

Nothing in here really gave him any insight into the woman currently making his castle uncomfortable. Frowning, he focused, and sensed four living beings nearby—and one ghost—and all had some measure of death magic about them. Since they were clustered together, he sent himself to their location.

He ended up in a kitchen and found four people sitting at a table—two women, two men—with the ghost hovering nearby. The men both had blue eyes and red hair, with one looking like a smaller carbon-copy of the other. The women, on the other hand, both looked exceptionally like Blanche. One he recognized as the sister he'd met in the hotel room and had seen lying in Blanche's bed a few days ago. Mira, he thought her name was. The other was likely Blanche's mother as she looked older.

"Are you sure she didn't tell you how she summoned him?" the larger of the two men asked Mira.

"I'm sure, Dad." Mira sounded guilty. "Death whispered it to her, and at the time there didn't seem to be any reason for her to share it. We had no idea I was going to die down there."

"What about the other spell? The first one you told us about?" the second woman pressed. "You helped her do that one."

"I did...But I'm not sure it'll help."

"Why not?" the smaller man demanded. "It worked, didn't it? So summon the bastard and we'll make him bring her back."

Death narrowed his eyes at the man he'd identified as a banshee, but did nothing other than seethe. Their family was wholly alive thanks to him. The ungratefulness they were showing was exactly why he so rarely did favors for anyone. Favors always ended up biting him in the ass in one way or another. Either the recipient betrayed him, or they just made his life hell for a little bit. This family was clearly in the latter category.

Mira closed her eyes and leaned against her father, resting her head on his shoulder. He wrapped his arm around her, though he looked devastated when he spoke. "It sounded like they made a deal, Aidan. Blanche specifically said she chose it, that she begged for it. What do you think he'd do to her if we essentially tried to force her into reneging on the deal?"

"There has to be something we can do!" Aidan shouted, shoving his chair back and starting to pace. Despite his coloring being so different from Blanche's, his mannerisms in this moment were so similar Death temporarily forgot his anger. Instead, he was a little baffled. He'd seen millions of families, and no matter how close they proclaimed to be, both in life and death, he'd rarely seen a family that was actually so close they acted this similar to one another. And very, very few people would have gone up against him to save a family member. This family had at least two. Interesting.

The ghost spoke for the first time, resting his ephemeral hand on the unnamed woman's shoulder. "As Mira said, Blanche chose this. I think we all understand why. I want her back as much as any of you, but I think—at least for now—that we need to respect her wishes." The corners of his mouth tipped up in what tried to be a smile. "At least until we figure out how to contact her and find a way to bring her back. Or she finds a way to come back to us herself. Blanche is a smart, stubborn woman. Do you really think she'll simply give up?"

Once again, Death was surprised. This ghost was several hundred years dead. At that point, all but a rare few ghosts had gone mad in some way. Anger, depression, or just flat out insanity. This ghost seemed as lucid as any of the living in the room. Did it have something to do with the fact that the home he haunted was inhabited by other creatures of death? It wasn't something that happened often, and normally the living did their best to extinguish the dead. However, with this family made up entirely of banshees and necromancers, that could have helped him keep his mind intact.

It was interesting, but still, none of this helped him. Blanche's family being angry wasn't really news to him. Sure, he could give all of them what they wanted, but that set a precedence he really didn't want to set. It was one thing about the death gods he understood. If they allowed everyone to return to life just because a family member had asked, everyone would be asking. Not only was it a waste of time, it violated the natural order and would be devastating to the Earth. No, it was much better to allow the dead to stay dead.

He really should have just killed Blanche when she started nagging him incessantly. It would have saved him more than one headache.

Suddenly annoyed with each and every member of her family, he went some place he swore he wouldn't visit again, but it was time for answers.

Death appeared on the veranda of an estate in Louisiana. An estate he'd sent Blanche and her friends to only a few weeks before. He strode toward the door, which opened in time to allow him to walk through without pausing. He felt both of the people he was searching for, and turned to enter the parlor to find a fire brewing in the hearth, a man sitting in a chair, and a woman perched on the arm of that chair.

The man, Rune, was tall and broad, with brown hair that reached his shoulders, and a slightly darker mustache and beard. His companion, Brigit, wasn't quite as tall or muscular, but looked just as formidable as the viking beside her. Her red hair was done in a single fat braid down her back, and her blue eyes showed absolutely no surprise at having Death enter her home.

"We've been waiting for you," she told him, her voice low and musical.

"I fucking hate when you do that," Death retorted as he crossed the room and stood only feet from them.

Brigit smiled and shrugged at him. "Shouldn't you expect it by now?"

"Doesn't mean I like it," he said, folding his arms over his chest. "Why the hell didn't you just give me the scythe?"

"Why didn't you come and ask us for it?" she replied smoothly. "You could have come and gotten it at any time. No one was trying to keep it from you."

A centuries-old rage burned in his chest and he clenched his hands into fists. "You know good and well why I didn't come here. And don't think that I've forgiven you just because I'm here. I'm here because I want answers, nothing more. Why didn't you give me my scythe?"

Brigit sighed and looked to Rune, who slid his arm around her waist and pulled her onto his lap. She curled into him, soaking up his love and comfort. "You know how visions and fate work. Things had to happen the way they did. It could have been different if you had kept the scythe to begin with, or if you had asked for it back centuries ago, but since you didn't, it had to play out exactly how it has."

He took a step toward them and had to use all his willpower to keep from blasting them both to a deep hole in Cindatha. "Really?" he sneered. "A woman had to die? Another had to make a deal to remain in Cindatha? Forever? It had to happen that way?" A woman had to turn his castle upside down in just a day?

Rune spoke for the first time, but said only, "Yes."

Death narrowed his gaze at the man and kept his answer just as succinct. "Why?"

There was no fear, not even any concern in Rune's eyes as he met Death's cold ones. But it was Brigit who spoke. "Maybe you should get to know your newest houseguest. Perhaps she's important. Perhaps there's a reason why she's there."

"Why? All I wanted was my scythe back. I gave it to you to keep it safe, and instead of keeping it with you like any sane person, you put it in a revenant-filled catacomb? Why?" he repeated.

Brigit drew herself out of Rune's lap and walked to Death without fear, leaning up to kiss his cheek before she smiled. "Do you really think I'm going to tell you the ending?"

"There's a first time for everything."

She laughed, and he hated how sweet the sound was. "Not this time," she assured him. "We'll see you again soon, though," she told him, before both she and Rune disappeared. The instant they were gone, the fire died, the ashes as cold as if they'd never been there at all.

Beyond annoyed, Death flashed back to Cindatha. He wasn't sure what he'd expected of the visit. Neither had ever been particularly forthcoming with him, even when it would have been wiser for them to be. But the fact that they had not only known things would end this way, but seemed to approve of his current situation, concerned him.

Fate was a bitch, and even Death wasn't immune to her.

CHAPTER 7

Blanche didn't see Death for five days after their brief screaming match, but she was far from disappointed at that fact. She could happily never see him again and be content. Sure, he was gorgeous and physically the type she tended to go for, but he was such an arrogant asshole that his looks couldn't make up for it. Not to mention that he seemed to lack any hint of empathy. It both made sense and baffled her. Thousands of years dealing with nothing but death could take a toll on a person—even a god-like being like Death—but wasn't empathy necessary for dealing with the souls of the recently deceased?

Not having to deal with him meant that she had some semblance of peace, though. Yes, she was growing more and more homesick and thinking of her family constantly, but she was able to find distractions and even settle into a loose routine.

Every morning she showered, tended to her hand, then went to the kitchen. As if he timed it, Sa arrived right as her first cup of coffee was ready, and she found something to feed to him. She wasn't sure where the food came from—she couldn't see any of the men in the castle going grocery shopping—but she wasn't about to complain since they didn't cheap out on the food. After they'd both eaten, she'd go to the library and browse, sometimes finding a book to spend a few hours with. After the second day, Sa had followed her and curled up nearby. Not close enough to touch, but it felt like company. Even better, it was company that didn't irritate or anger her, and he never ran his mouth. When her stomach started growling, she'd head back to the kitchen and find at least one of the twins there. Grim more frequently, but Abaddon appeared often enough as well.

After lunch, she'd wander. It took her four days in Cindatha before she finally made her way upstairs. At first she was disappointed to find a hallway just like the one her bedroom was in, with several locked doors and even more empty rooms, but then she found a door which led to a small balcony. That alone was nice, because it meant fresh air without worrying about running into any of the dangerous souls wandering around. But then she discovered the tower. It wasn't much, just a spiral staircase that led up to a small room, but that room had a three hundred and sixty degree view, impeded only by the columns supporting the roof. It had given her the first good view of her new home.

Cindatha was beautiful. Most of it was the sand and rock she'd seen on her one excursion outside, with mountains and hills in the distance, but in the moonlight, even that had its appeal. But the chunk that reminded her of a jungle was what had caught and held her attention. From that height, she could see not just the trees, but tall green mountains and the glittering of what she thought might be a distant lake. There were hints of brown and dashes of color, which added to its beauty.

What she couldn't see were the sections of Cindatha that were held by the various death deities, but she wasn't upset by that. Some were said to be paradises for the dead, but more than a few were hell-realms that she hoped to never visit. Either they were too far from the castle for her to see, or somehow kept separate. Neither answer would surprise her.

At least once a day after that, she spent an hour up there, letting it relax her like nothing else in the castle could.

On the seventh day after she'd arrived, she woke to find things were different. Not vastly, but as soon as her shower had cleared some of the cobwebs, she realized her bedroom had been altered. The bed was the same, except now it had a silvery canopy, just like the one on her bed back on Earth. There was also a mirror standing in the corner. Approaching it slowly, she saw it was almost identical to the one she'd had for a century or so. The wood was a slightly different color, the mirror itself just a little more oval than squared, but at first glance, it could be mistaken for the same one.

Except...where had the mirror and canopy come from? Had someone brought them here, like with the clothes and toiletries? And if they had, why? And how had they gotten in? Hadn't Grim told her that only she could get into her bedroom without permission? Death, she was sure, could get inside with no problem, but why would he? He barely tolerated her, and even that was too strong a word.

Deciding not to try to figure it out before her morning coffee, she went downstairs. This morning, she found Sa already there and waiting by the fridge. She couldn't stop herself from grinning. "I'd like to think you're warming up to me," she told him as she filled the coffee pot with water and got it brewing, "but I think you're just warming up to the spoiling." Crossing to the fridge, she dug around for something special. She found a steak and considered. One of the guys was probably planning for this to be their dinner. They'd probably also be pissed if they found it missing. On the other hand, it could be what tipped Sa from seeing her as a handy source of food to a friend. And she didn't really care if she pissed off Death. Grim and Abaddon? She'd just have to apologize to them if they got upset.

Mind made up, she pulled it out of the fridge and held it up. The moment Sa's gaze landed on it, he licked his lips and sat, more like a well-trained dog than a prehistoric predator. It was cute. "Oh yeah, this is the good stuff, huh?" He allowed her to get closer than usual, but she still tossed it, not wanting her fingers to get caught in those teeth if he tried to snatch it from her hand. "Do they even feed you? I mean, you're dead, so you probably don't actually need to eat, but it's nice, isn't it?"

She went perfectly still when he rose and padded toward her, right before delight and surprise burst in her chest when he headbutted her hip like the overgrown house cat she'd once accused him of being. He even allowed her to touch his head, but only for a second before he turned and walked away.

"Wow," she said under her breath, a little awed by the experience. And surprised her plan was working. Pouring coffee into a cup, she'd just sat down when Death appeared. She stiffened, expecting him to start acting like an ass again. Instead, he got himself some coffee, then sat across from her.

For several minutes, they did nothing but sip at their coffees while Sa sat nearby and watched them. Then Death asked, "What do you think of the castle?"

Of all the things he could have said to her, that was way down on her list of possibilities. He didn't like her, so what did it matter what she thought of the castle? Still, she couldn't refuse to answer, not if she wanted to try to make her stay here bearable. Nor could she answer honestly, since it was pretty bare and lifeless. Not that it was out of place, considering who the owner was. "It's...nice," she decided on. Noncommittal, but also nothing offensive.

He scoffed and shook his head. "Don't try hiding the truth from me. It's impossible."

Her eyes narrowed. "You're what, some sort of human lie detector?"

"I'm not human," he said flatly.

Blanche rolled those eyes now. "Fine, but you get my drift. Besides, do you really want my opinion?"

"Not really," he admitted. "I was just curious how the castle appeared to someone who wasn't a reaper."

"Empty, lifeless, and impersonal," she answered without hesitation, giving up on the idea of being polite about it. If he wanted honesty, she'd give it to him.

Death arched a brow but didn't argue her view. Probably because he couldn't. It was all those things. Just because it was his home didn't change the facts. Of course, arguing would have been more expected than what he actually did. "Maybe I should show you around."

Her first reaction wasn't to accept or decline, it was to get suspicious. "Why? We're not friends. You clearly don't want me here or to spend even five minutes with me."

"If you'd like, I can leave you to just spend the rest of eternity in the library."

"No," she said quickly, hoping that if he showed her around, it might open up some of the empty doors. Give her more to do than read and watch movies. But she still had to wonder why. Death didn't seem like the sort to do anything without a purpose, so what was his purpose in this seemingly friendly gesture?

"Then let's go." He rose and looked to Sa. "You stay here."

Blanche was surprised that she wanted the feline to join them but said nothing as she followed him out of the kitchen. He led them back to the large, round room. And since he was acting so accommodating today, she decided to ask questions while she could. "I have to say...having a saber-tooth tiger for a pet is a little...unusual." She didn't want to say weird, as that tended to have negative connotations, as she well knew from a lifetime of being called weird. Not that she personally thought being weird was bad. Weird just meant you didn't fit into a predefined mold which, in her mind, made you interesting. She'd rather be weird than boring any day.

"So is being Death," he retorted. "Besides, even I occasionally want companionship, and before the reapers, all I had were the souls of the dead. Sa doesn't complain. They do."

His answer almost made her smile, but she forced her mouth into a flat line instead. "How long has he been here?"

"A while."

Okay, so he wasn't completely accommodating. "And why do you have cells?" she asked when they reached the room she was starting to think of as a foyer, even though it wasn't exactly.

"Why wouldn't I? I'm the highest authority when it comes to death. I get the souls no one else can claim, and can claim the souls of anyone I wish. And not everyone has earned a peaceful afterlife."

No, they hadn't. Some people did bad things for good reasons—or desperate ones. Some people did bad things because they enjoyed it. And some people did horrible things for selfish reasons. So why would a mass murderer or something get a peaceful afterlife just because they'd died? Death didn't erase anything. There was no clean slate, not that she was aware of. Reincarnation, maybe, but she wasn't sure that really wiped away the bad karma of heinous acts.

So far he was being cooperative, so she asked the question that had been burning in her mind. Looking down the short hallway, she asked, "Why do you have a tomb in your castle? And who's it for?"

He stopped and followed her gaze, pushing down the sudden rage that tried to boil his blood. He disliked discussing the tomb and its contents. It had been bad enough when Grim had brought it up, but for her to mention it? She had no right. But Grim had said she'd been able to get inside. That had curiosity smothering the anger. Especially since it was the entire point of this little experiment.

Instead of going upstairs, he led her toward the tomb, saying nothing until he'd opened the door. Leaning back against the doorframe, he folded his arms and studied her face closely, refusing to look inside. "What do you sense?" Never before had he opened this door for anyone, but he had to know why she could get in here.

Her gaze was fixed on the sarcophagus and he noted that she'd lost some color in her cheeks. She stopped right beside him, her shoulder brushing his elbow, either unable or unwilling to go any further.

"What do you sense?" he asked again, the last vestiges of his anger fading.

"I...don't have a word for it," she said, her throaty voice little more than a whisper. "The closest I can come is...I don't know. Dark anticipation? But that's not it, not exactly. And I'm not sure why. I've seen hundreds of tombs and coffins. Death and the dead are as normal for me as they can be for anyone...well, who isn't you, I guess. And since I don't feel any power coming from this sarcophagus, I have no rational reason why I'd feel that…whatever it is."

Death had only been partially truthful in the kitchen, when he'd told her she couldn't lie to him. He could sense lies—or any kind of deception—but that didn't mean he could always sense what the truth was. Disguises were easy. He could see through those without even trying. But partial truths that were spoken were more difficult. He knew she wasn't being fully honest with him and considered pressing her, but also sensed he wouldn't get the rest out of her, not yet.

He reached past her and pulled the door shut. She stepped back a few paces so it didn't hit her in the face. The trip to the tomb hadn't given him the answers he was wanting, only more questions. Neither Abaddon nor Grim had ever claimed to sense anything from the tomb, and he wondered if it had something to do with her ability to open it. That was something to consider. It might even be entertaining. It was certainly something new, and he reveled in new.

Life got very boring when you were as old as dirt.

She was quiet as they headed up the stairs. Recovering, he assumed, since what color she had was slowly returning to her face. It wasn't until they were headed up the second set of stairs that he spoke again. "Why did you make the bargain with me? Why is it so important that Mira be alive? You said yourself that death is normal for you, and she can't be the first person in your family to die. You're not young enough for that."

Frowning at him, she shook her head. "No, Mira's not the first I've lost, but she's my baby sister. I'd do anything for her. Besides, she was only in those catacombs because of me. If I hadn't pulled her into all of that, she never would have died to begin with."

"But you're a necromancer," he went on, wanting to understand how mortals thought. "A strong one, too. She might have left a ghost you could speak to. Or you could have waited until you died as well and joined her in…" He paused, head cocked as his powers brushed against her soul. Normally he could feel which part of Cindatha a person's soul was bound to, but he could sense that her soul had a connection to multiple underworlds. Interesting. That didn't happen often, and on the few occasions it did, it was only ever just two. Often a result of one half of the family worshiping one pantheon, and the other worshiping another, or a change of faith midlife. "The afterlife," he finished instead.

"She also might not have left a ghost," she pointed out as they climbed the stairs to the top of the tower. "And you should know better than I that we might not have found each other in the underworld. You may be the supreme authority over death, but you don't strike me as a micromanager. Which means you probably know that some of the lords and ladies are kind of…petty."

Death laughed, the sound shocking him more than her. He couldn't remember the last time he'd laughed, but she was right. Quite a few of the deities who resided in Cindatha were petty with their power. He could replace them, he supposed, but the system largely worked. And didn't mortals have a saying about if it wasn't broke? Besides, replacing them would mean finding the replacements, and he had neither the time nor inclination to deal with that.

"That's a valid concern," he agreed after schooling his face back to its normal impassive state.

They reached the top of the tower and he looked out at the divide between green and tan. This view was one of the few things that gave him pleasure. It had always relaxed him, and might just do the same for her so he could figure out her mysteries. Unfortunately, it had been a few thousand years since he'd really interacted with mortals—other than a few reapers—so he wasn't exactly sure how to go about it. He knew torture was rarely as effective as people would like, as most would say whatever they thought the torturer wanted to hear just to make the pain stop. Badgering her was also unlikely to be effective. He might not know her well, but the three days he'd spent with a headache had proven just how fucking stubborn she could be. No, he might have to make friends with her. Not a prospect he looked forward to, but it was what had the highest chance of success.

"Did someone explain Cindatha to you?" he asked as he leaned his forearms on the stone railing and watched the darkened landscape.

"How all underworlds are just part of Cindatha? Yeah. It's a little...hard to wrap my head around."

"Why?" he asked, genuinely wanting to hear the answer.

She blew out a breath and mirrored his pose. "All my life you hear about the different pantheons. Each has different people who rule over the dead or the underworld. Some of them are connected, but they're all presented as completely separate realms. But if Kur and Hades and Valhalla are all the same place, then what else is really the same?"

"They're not the same place," he corrected with a shake of his head. "Not anymore than your United States are the same as Greece or Australia. They're all in the same realm, the same planet, but they're separate places. It's the same for the underworlds. Thing of them as just different kingdoms on the same planet."

"That helps, actually. I hadn't thought of it like that." She looked at him and cocked her head. "Why give up control over those parts of your realm, though? Why let people think that those gods are the authorities over the dead? That you don't exist?"

"I didn't just allow it, I made sure it happened. Think about it. Everyone dies. Sure, some take longer than others like the gods, but eventually, everyone's soul will come to Cindatha. There's about eight billion people on Earth right now. That's just the ones alive now. There have been more than ten times that who were alive. Would you want to deal with each and every one of those souls? Listen to them whining? Begging for a second chance? Putting people where they're meant to go? Choosing who is allowed to reincarnate and begin the cycle again?"

Her nose wrinkled and shook her head. "Good point. That sounds like a special kind of hell."

"Exactly. It wasn't bad when there were only a couple million people alive. But now? No. I needed help. Giving those gods and goddesses who had some power over death a sliver of Cindatha meant I had that help."

"Then what about—"

Abaddon appeared just a few feet away, his shoulders tense, his mouth tight. As soon as Death's eyes landed on him, he spoke, his tone dire. "You're needed in the throne room."

CHAPTER 8

Death knew that tone and didn't hesitate to teleport down to the throne room. In his haste, he brought not just Abaddon with him, but Blanche as well. Too late for that, and once he saw what was waiting for him, he forgot about her presence.

Grim was there, along with two of his reapers—Darius and Antonia. Darius was from ancient Sumer, with the golden skin and black hair that had been common enough in the region. He had a beard and mustache that were kept trimmed, and wore jeans and a tee-shirt. Honestly, he looked like he could be brother to both Abaddon and Grim—especially Grim. Antonia had been a Roman woman, though she'd adopted a goth style when it had become fashionable in the last few decades. Her chocolate colored hair was in its habitual braid, left to hang to her hips.

And on the floor in front of them was the body of Bjorn. Another of his reapers, one who had been a viking, and still acted and dressed like the culture he'd been born into. And now he lie there, bloodied, beaten, and dead, apparently thanks to a deep gash across his throat.

"What happened to him?" he demanded as he crouched by the body.

Darius spoke, his fists clenched tight, his mouth a thin line. He tried to act calm, but the accent of his home was present, which proved just how upset he was. "I hadn't seen or heard from Bjorn in a few days, so Antonia and I went to check on him. We…" He shook his head, gaze flicking to the body, then quickly up again.

"We found him like this," Antonia said, her voice steady, but she looked no happier than Darius. "Right there in his house. It was trashed, though it looked like it was from a fight, not someone ransacking it. And whoever was responsible just left him on the floor like he was nothing."

"A fight shouldn't have killed him. Nor should a slit throat," Death said, unable to believe that one of his reapers had actually been killed. He laid a hand on Bjorn's arm, ignoring the blood on it. Such a touch should have allowed him to see the final moments of Bjorn's life, to see who had killed him, and how, but he saw nothing but the room around him.

Furious, and more than a little concerned, he rose and fixed his gaze on the four living reapers. "Has his soul been found?"

Grim and Antonia exchanged a look, then the latter spoke. "I looked, while Darius was bringing his body here. And Grim checked again when Abaddon was looking for you. We haven't sensed him. Not in his house, not in Valhalla, and not here in Cindatha," she admitted.

Though the fury remained, Death was now more worried than angry. There weren't that many ways to kill a reaper, much less a soul. He could do it, of course, and a few of the death deities could, but beyond that? It took either an exceptionally powerful necromancer, or an even more rare weapon. Neither had been seen in thousands of years.

"Deal with the body, but don't destroy it yet," he ordered, before disappearing to search for Bjorn's soul himself.

Blanche stood back, not wanting to intrude. It was clear Bjorn had been friend to these reapers, and it was equally as obvious that they didn't often lose one of their own.

Abaddon and Darius picked up Bjorn's body, moving him gently, though he was beyond feeling anything. They carried him out of the throne room, with Antonia right behind them. Blanche wasn't sure if she should follow, but Grim motioned for her, waiting until she was beside him before he, too, followed Abaddon and Darius.

"I take it you guys don't die that often?" she asked Grim quietly, hoping the others couldn't hear her.

"No, it isn't. I was one of the first, and I've only known of a few to ever die," he replied, keeping his voice down as well. "We're not as powerful as Death, but we're damn hard to kill. And blood loss isn't one of the ways we can die."

She had to wonder how reapers could die, but knew better than to ask. Not that she had any intention of killing one, but it wasn't likely they'd want to share that information with anyone, especially right now. "Do you guys have a lot of enemies?"

He shot her an incredulous look. "Are you kidding? We're pretty much considered enemies to everyone who's breathing."

That had been kind of a dumb question and just as obvious answer, so she only nodded.

On the second floor, they opened the door to one of the bedrooms and laid Bjorn's body on the bed. When Abaddon and Darius stepped back, Grim started asking questions. "Had he been acting off or any-thing the last time either of you talked to him?"

Darius shook his head, the motion jerky. "No. We got drunk. We joked around. He didn't say anything was bothering him, and he didn't act like it, either."

"I didn't notice anything the last few times we spoke," Antonia said, leaning against the wall, her eyes closing before she rubbed her fingers over them.

"To the best of my knowledge, he didn't have issues with any other reapers either, correct?" Abaddon asked.

"Fuck no," Darius shouted, scowling at Abaddon. "He was a hot-head, sure, but he was also the kind who always had your back, and would happily take a fist to the face, then lift a beer with you."

"I didn't think he did, I was just wanting to confirm," Abaddon soothed.

Death reappeared and Blanche had to fight to keep her feet planted where they were at the coldly furious look on his face and the power pumping off of him.

"Did you find him?" Darius asked.

"No. I'll keep looking, but right now...it doesn't look good." His jaw clenched as he looked at the body on the bed. "Where was Bjorn's favorite place?"

"His home," Antonia said wearily. "It was built on the land his family owned back when he was mortal. He loved it and hoped he'd always be able to stay there, though he was getting a little worried people were starting to notice he wasn't aging."

Death nodded and manifested a ceramic jar. He removed the lid and Bjorn's body crumbled to dust within a few seconds. An instant after that, the dust swirled into the air, flowed toward Death, then into the jar. When all of what had once been Bjorn was in the jar, he closed the lid and rested his hand on top of it.

Darius took a step toward Death. "Please...can Antonia and I scatter his ashes? He was my best fucking friend. I want to do at least that much for him."

"Of course." Death offered the jar and Blanche noticed Darius took it with reverence. "I'll continue to look into his murder. We'll find out what happened to him."

"Thank you," Darius said before he disappeared. An instant later, Antonia did as well.

Death drew in a deep breath and turned to the twins. "I don't want you two reaping until this is solved. This is the highest priority. If someone's out there killing my people, I want to know who," he said in a voice that promised retribution. "Find out what you can. I don't care what methods you have to employ, but I don't want this getting out."

Almost in unison, they bowed their heads, then disappeared.

He stared at the bed, with only the rumpling of the bedding to show anyone had ever been there. It seemed he'd forgotten about Blanche, and she was reluctant to remind him. Yes, she may have risked angering him for Mira, but there was nothing to be gained now. Besides, she wasn't so cold as to make light of someone's grief, even if it was someone she didn't particularly like.

Minutes passed, and she just stood there, doing her best to be as unobtrusive as possible, but when he turned to leave, he spotted her and frowned.

No, she didn't particularly like him, but she understood what he was feeling. "I'm sorry about Bjorn," she told him, and she meant it.

"People die. It's what literally everyone does," he said, but the empty tone didn't match his eyes.

"Maybe they do, but I'm still sorry."

He cocked his head, staring at her like he could root around in her head. And for all she knew, he could. "You really mean that."

"I do."

"Then you can help Grim and Abaddon figure out who killed him, and how."

How the hell was she supposed to do that? She was a necromancer, not a detective. Still, it was something to do, and she was coming to like Grim and Abaddon, so helping them out wouldn't be a bad thing. And she did hate murderers. "Okay...but how am I supposed to figure out anything if I'm stuck here? I don't have your powers, after all."

He shrugged. "I doubt you can," he admitted in a blunt tone. "But anything is possible, I suppose."

Yeah, she definitely wasn't helping for him. "If I'm going to help, I'm going to need some information."

One dark brow arched. "Such as?" he asked, a warning in his voice. She had to ignore it though, because she couldn't work blind, and all she knew about reapers were stories.

"Like what can kill a reaper."

There was a long pause. No doubt he was deciding what to tell her, if anything. "Not much. Myself, of course. My scythe. Reapers could technically harm one another as well. There are a few gods who could manage it, and a few rare weapons."

Reapers could kill reapers? She really hoped that fact didn't turn out to be significant, or he'd be even more of a pain to live with. Instead, she focused on the other things he'd said. "Do you know where your scythe is?" If someone had stolen it, then they'd have a bigger problem than one dead reaper.

He scowled at her, but held a hand out, his scythe appearing in it. It didn't look as it had when she'd first seen it—dull and ordinary—but was sharp, bright, and covered in symbols. And it was radiating power. Pure, unadulterated death magic. Though she kept talking and tried to take her mind off it, her eyes were fixed firmly on the scythe.

"It seemed like death was working as it should when the scythe was in the catacombs, so why did you send us to get it?" she asked. "You clearly don't need it to keep the whole life and death cycle running."

His eyes darkened. "You really should mind your own business," he warned. But when he shifted and the scythe moved, her gaze followed it. He seemed to notice. "Why are you staring at my scythe? It's not the first time you've seen it."

"It's not, but it doesn't feel like it did last time. Before, it was kind of...ignorable. Now? I could be blind and deaf and find it from a mile away." She blinked and managed to shift her gaze to meet his. "Besides, I'm a necromancer. My whole life has revolved around death. Of course I'd be curious about it."

He made a low, thoughtful sound, but nodded and vanished the scythe. The moment he did, she was able to relax. "Do you trust all of your reapers?"

The frown was back, but she ignored it. "Of course I do. Even the newest reaper to accept my bargain is a few centuries old, and I know all of them. Grim and Abaddon know them even better than I do, but they're my right and left hands. They'd let me know if there was a problem."

"Bargain?" She wasn't aware of any bargain reapers made, but again, there was little truly known about them. The only thing she could confirm at this point was that they existed.

He sighed in annoyance. "Yes, bargain. All reapers are born mortal, with limited powers. When they agree to become true reapers, to ferry souls to Cindatha, they become immortal and their true powers—which come from me—are unlocked."

Blanche could only stare at him. Not just at the news that reapers had once been mortal—though she hadn't expected that—but because he had actually offered her information. She wasn't sure why, but she appreciated it. Of course, she also wanted to know more, but now wasn't the time. Even if Bjorn hadn't been a friend and was just one of Death's reapers, his murder clearly affected Death. It might just be that someone had killed a person he considered to be his, but the result was essentially the same. But he'd also inadvertently answered another question she had. Reapers could kill each other because their power was part of Death's power. You couldn't defend from yourself.

"Oh," she said after a long moment. "Thank you." Getting back to the topic at hand, she asked, "Can you think of any reason why someone would want to kill a reaper? I mean, does that actually help anyone in any way?" If she was going to play detective, she did need *some* information.

"No," he said firmly. "Yes, people have tried to kill or trap reapers in the past, hoping it'll prevent their deaths, but reapers are, again, hard to kill, and equally hard to trap for long. Besides, reapers don't actually kill anyone, they just bring the souls to whichever part of Cindatha they're bound for."

Blanche nodded slowly as she tried to piece together the few facts they had. Then she remembered Death had said he couldn't find Bjorn's soul. If anyone could, it would be him. She was certain he could locate any soul anywhere in Cindatha, which sparked a terrifying idea. "Is it...possible to kill a soul?" she asked, sure he was going to tell her off or disappear.

His jaw clenched, but he nodded once. "It is, but it's even harder to do than killing a reaper."

"What could do it?" she asked hesitantly.

His cold gaze fixed on her. "Not much," was all he said, and she knew the moment of sharing was over.

Wanting to give him some time alone to mourn—or whatever Death did when he lost someone—she nodded and slipped quietly out of the room.

Alone, Death stared at the empty bed, though his eyes didn't truly see it. He was searching the entirety of his realm for Bjorn's missing soul. Normally such a thing was as easy as blinking for him. He could find any soul at any time, and was especially connected to his reapers, but Bjorn was just...gone. It made him wonder if Blanche wasn't onto something with her question about killing souls. It truly was something nearly impossible to accomplish, but it was possible.

But soul or no soul, he could see no way that someone could have hidden the truth of Bjorn's death from him. Never before had he ever touched a body and not seen the moment of their death, felt the truth of it. No murderer had ever been able to hide from him...until now. *No one* had ever been able to hide from him before, not even those who had made him what he was today, and they were without equal in power.

So how in the hell was someone managing it now? Why had they killed Bjorn? He didn't need to ask why they would have killed his soul, not with the rest of it. If they hadn't, then Bjorn could have simply told Death what had occurred, who had killed him. It was smart, but whoever was responsible had made one very large mistake.

Death had eternity to search for them, and would not stop until he had found them and torn their soul to shreds, dooming them to oblivion. Just as they'd doomed Bjorn.

Blanche didn't retreat to her room, though it might have been the safer option with Death so angry. But she was curious now, and it was something more to do than just reading and watching movies. Would she find who had killed Bjorn? Very unlikely, but it felt like something useful to do, which was enough for now.

Stepping into the library, she blew out a breath and looked around the massive room. She knew from her time here that it was only loosely organized. Fiction and non-fiction were separated, but beyond that, it was hit or miss whether she'd find genres or subjects grouped together. Even if it had been properly sorted, she was doubtful there would have been a section about reapers or souls. Then again, maybe there was, and she just hadn't found it. She had been primarily focused on novels until now.

A soft sound made her glance over her shoulder, but she wasn't surprised when she saw Sa enter the library. It seemed to be where he spent most of his time when he wasn't begging for food. "No ham right now, but don't eat me and I'll give you a double serving later," she told him. He didn't answer, of course, just walked over to a couch, hopped up, then stretched out, blinking at her. Good enough.

Heading up to the second level, where she'd found most of the non-fiction, she started skimming the spines, looking for something that might be helpful. After an hour, she'd found only a single book on reapers. It definitely wasn't helpful for the current situation, as it was a journal written by a reaper over the span of a century. It confirmed what Death had said about the bargain, but beyond that was filled more with what the reaper had done and felt rather than any secrets about his kind.

There were tons of books on magic, but they were either generalized and offered few specifics, or were so specialized that they didn't apply to the situation. While she might take some time to read some of them later, knowing more about vampiric or elemental powers didn't help now.

Then she came across a book on sorcery. She knew what it was, of course. All of the Arcane knew of the spells that anyone—even humans—could learn and perform, but she'd never had a reason to delve into it herself. She was a witch, after all, but it did get the gears turning in her head.

Most of the Arcane looked down on sorcery and sorcerers, feeling that their natural powers—often limited natural powers—were superior. Some even felt that sorcerers should be killed and sorcery made as illegal as sharing their existence with humans.

Blanche disagreed.

Sorcery was extremely versatile and, while not as powerful as god magic, could still be very effective. The spell she'd first used to summon Death a month ago, before he'd taught her the less rude method, was sorcery. It had to be. A spoken spell, a ritual...It couldn't be anything else. And if it could summon Death, one of the most powerful beings in all of existence, then could it be adapted to summon a soul? It made sense once she thought about it. Ghosts could be summoned, and she'd personally summoned a wraith, so why not a soul? Especially since she was currently in the realm of souls.

Fortunately, the spell wasn't complicated and didn't need a lot, but she was trapped here and was missing an object of death. Last time she'd used a mummification knife, but it was back in her bedroom. A place she was never going to see again.

She shoved that thought as far back in her mind as she could and left the library. She needed to think and wanted the tower—and its view—for that. This time she was surprised because Sa left his spot on the couch and padded along beside her. He didn't let her touch him again, but she thought he was softening toward her.

At least someone in this castle was.

On the second floor, she ran into Abaddon. He looked as happy as Death had, though not quite as unapproachable.

"Any luck?" she asked, though she doubted it.

"No," he said, running a hand over his hair. "It's as if the killer simply disappeared with Bjorn's soul."

He sounded so dejected she laid a hand on his arm. "Hey," she said, rubbing comfortingly, "you'll find whoever did this."

He smiled faintly, but didn't look certain of that fact.

"Death said you and Grim know the reapers better than he does," she continued.

"I mean...I suppose we do? We tend to handle smaller problems and handle teaching new reapers what they need to know. It does tend to lead toward a certain familiarity with them. Why?"

"So you knew Bjorn pretty well, then?"

"Not as well as Darius and Antonia, but fairly well, yes."

"Can you think of any reapers who had something against him? Some rivalry or hatred or whatever?"

The question made him think for a moment before he shook his head. "I can't think of anyone offhand, no. Darius seemed to right about that. Reapers, as a rule, only really interact with a handful of other reapers on a regular basis. Sometimes there are issues, of course, but when those occur, we simply shift people around. As solitary a job as this is, we try to make sure reapers are sort of grouped together, so they have at least a few people to lean on. Solitude can drive a person mad, you know, especially with jobs like we have." He paused and scratched thoughtfully at his beard. "Darius and my memory could be wrong, however. I think I'll do some checking. Thank you, Blanche."

He smiled at her and disappeared before she could stop him. Huffing, she realized she should have asked him about the object of death. Certainly a reaper would have one. Too late for that now, she thought, as she continued up the stairs.

Staring out at the moon-brightened landscape, she tried to think of a solution. And wondered if Grim and Abaddon would stand in for her group, or if she'd be the one driven mad.

CHAPTER 9

Three days. It had been three days since Blanche had seen a single person. Oh, Sa had stuck fairly close, but talking to him was almost as helpful and entertaining as talking to a wall. He might give her the occasional ear flick or tail swish, but he was far from the world's best communicator.

It wasn't that the guys weren't around, either. She'd heard voices in the throne room every day, and often more than just the three of them. But every single time she'd tried the door, it had been sealed tight. She had enough sense of self-preservation that she'd refrained from banging on the door or calling out, but it left her feeling extremely alone, just like the reapers Abaddon had mentioned days ago. She could very easily see how someone could go mad from solitude. Sure, some might like it, but she wasn't one of them, especially not if she hadn't chosen the solitude.

She'd spent most of her time either in the tower thinking, or in the library searching for something to help. She had toyed with the idea that anything in the castle might be considered an object of death considering it was all owned by the actual Death, but it wasn't something she could really confirm. And it might be possible to try the spell without confirmation, but if she did and it failed, she wouldn't have any way of knowing if it was because she had the wrong object or because the spell couldn't summon a soul. Better to wait until she could get the right item to use or one of the guys nearby to verify one way or another.

That morning, she showered and went down to get something to eat. To her delight, Sa curled up beside her and basically ate from her hand. No, she wasn't quite brave enough to truly feed him directly, but tossing the food from just a foot away basically counted, right?

It wasn't until she'd left the kitchen and heard muted shouts from the throne room that it truly hit her that she hadn't spoken to anyone but Sa in days. She'd never gone this long without some sort of interaction. The worries she'd felt after her last conversation with Abaddon shoved right to the front of her mind, followed by a sudden panic. Gasping, she stumbled against the wall, her hand clawing at her chest, where she could feel her heart trying to break free of her chest.

Struggling to breathe, she slid down the wall until her butt hit the floor, and she closed her eyes, trying to do her breathing exercises. Here in Cindatha, there would be no annoying but loving older brother to talk her through it. No warm hugs from her mom or sweet singing from her dad. Nothing but herself to pull her out of yet another panic attack.

She wasn't enough. She couldn't be enough, she thought as tears stained her cheeks. Not for this, not for finding what had happened to Bjorn. She was never going to tame Sa or find out if Grim really would become her BFF. The mysteries of Death would remain mysteries. If she couldn't even breathe properly, there was no way she was going to manage any of it.

Something wet and rough slid over the entire left half of her face, making her jerk as her eyes shot open. She had to close them again quickly when Sa delivered another lick, this time to the right side of her face.

"Sa, stop it," she protested, trying to shove the smilodon away, but she was far from strong enough to move almost a thousand pounds of feline unless he wanted to be moved. This one didn't.

And yet the licking did what she hadn't been able to do by herself. It distracted her mind from her loneliness, reminded her that she wasn't completely alone. The panic disappeared in the wake of the cat grooming her. Or it could have been disgust at having her face covered in cat slobber. Either way, she was calming down.

"Okay, okay! I'm okay!" she told him as she tried to shield her face against another lap of that tongue. To her relief, he did stop licking her and instead flopped down across her lap. Her eyes widened as her legs were essentially crushed, but she didn't really care about that because Sa was in actually her lap and he was purring! She hadn't known any of the big cats could do that, but there was no mistaking the sound or the vibration now running through her. Hesitantly, she lifted a hand, but Sa didn't make any move to stop her or shift off her lap as she stroked her hand between his ears and down his neck. Fresh tears flowed as she realized what she was doing, but it didn't stop her from repeating the caress over his surprisingly soft fur.

"You're really a sweetie, aren't you?" she asked in a whisper as he lowered his head and his eyes closed in pleasure. She eyed his long teeth cautiously, but he kept them away from her soft flesh, so she didn't try to move him. Not that she was going to forget they were there. "Were you actually going to eat me that first day? I bet you were just being a jackass to the new girl, weren't you?"

Though her legs quickly fell asleep, she stayed that way for quite some time, taking comfort from the huge predator. It was stranger to her than ghosts and wraiths—even stranger than living in Death's castle. Now, she couldn't say she'd ever had a 'normal' pet, or wanted one—though she did kind of miss her sister's snake—but she'd also never felt drawn to the soft, helpless animals so many people chose.

Blanche couldn't have said how long she sat there petting Sa, not with it being the most relaxed she'd been since before Mira had died. But then she heard violin music again. It was just as beautiful as before, but the tone had changed. Instead of sorrow, she heard conflicting emotions. Wild ones.

It had to be Abaddon playing. If it was Grim, he would have gone for guitar and angry rock. And Death? Well, she couldn't see him doing something as ordinary as playing music.

"Hey, you need to move," she told Sa, shoving at him, but until he yawned and lifted his bulk off her, she didn't manage to budge him. "Come on," she whispered as she crept down the hallway, unsurprised to find the music coming from the same room as before. Though she would have wagered money on the door being locked again, this time the handle turned. Excited to be getting into one of the rooms previously blocked to her, she carefully eased the door open, relieved when none of the hinges creaked. In an effort to prevent herself from being noticed, she only cracked the door enough to peek inside.

Blanche had to cover her mouth to hide her gasp. The wonderful, hauntingly wonderful music actually was coming from Death. He was mostly turned away from her, but she could see his profile. The black leather pants he seemed to prefer showcased his butt and thighs to perfection, and even the equally dark tee-shirt helped show off the muscles of his back as his arm moved, sliding the bow across the strings of the violin.

Entranced, she left the door partially open and leaned against the frame so she could watch him and let the music seep into her. Never before had she heard anyone play who was so talented, and she'd heard several Arcane musicians, all who had studied their instrument for centuries.

But where she was content to listen without letting Death know she was there, Sa had other ideas. He pushed past her, simultaneously shoving the door wide open and knocking her into the room. Blanche tried to keep herself from falling, but though she prevented a painful—and embarrassing—faceplant, she landed on her hands and knees.

The music was gone and she slowly lifted her head, expecting the worst. Her eyes met Death's icy blue ones and she could see his irritation. It didn't disappear even when Sa walked over to him and rubbed against his legs. But when Sa moved back to her and headbutted her shoulder, shock replaced it.

Using Sa as a support, Blanche rose to her feet. "Sorry," she mumbled. "Didn't mean to interrupt."

Death stared as Sa remained by Blanche's side. In the entire time Sa had lived in the castle, he had let precisely one person other than Death touch him, though 'let' was a strong word. If Grim wasn't what he was, he would still bear the scars of that attempted bit of affection.

Thoughts of Sa's surprising fondness toward Blanche didn't linger long in his mind, though. Not when they still hadn't found anything on Bjorn's killer. They didn't even know if it was a one-off—something specific to Bjorn—or if someone was going after his reapers. And if it was the latter, then others might die if he didn't find something. And if he didn't find something soon, he was seriously considering going to the Anunnaki. Not that he truly expected any help from them.

Blanche shifted, reminding him that he wasn't alone, and his gaze narrowed on her. "What are you doing here?"

She hesitated, then lifted her chin. "I had an idea, but I need help to make it work—if it can work—but I haven't seen you, Abaddon, or Grim in three days."

Partial truth, but he let it pass. "And what is this idea?" he asked, tapping the wood of the bow against his leg, the violin gently resting against his other thigh.

Another hesitation, and this time she looked uncomfortable. "The spell I used to summon you...the first time, I mean. I was thinking, if it was powerful enough to summon you, then maybe it could be adjusted to summon Bjorn's soul. If ghosts and wraiths can be summoned, then I can't see why a soul couldn't, especially not here."

It was an interesting proposition, he could admit that. And her theory had merit, but he wasn't sure if it was as simple as she was making it out to be. Still, while his own methods to locate or summon souls hadn't worked, he wasn't against trying anything if it meant they could fix this problem.

He didn't voice his doubts, instead asking, "What is it you need to do this spell?"

"An object of death," she answered. "All of my equipment is back...not here."

Death's lips twitched. "Can you be more specific? Or would my toothbrush qualify?"

"Doubtful," she said flatly. "Last time I used a mummification knife, if that helps."

He did remember seeing her with that implement when he'd first met her and her friends, and since he'd seen it in her bedroom, he knew exactly where it was. Since he did, it was easy enough to summon it, and he offered it to her. "Anything else?"

Blanche took the knife, and he was surprised to see her brush her fingers over the hilt in a way he could only describe as loving. "Something to draw blood with," she told him when she looked back up at him.

That was even easier, and he offered her a knife a moment later.

Blanche took it and sat down on the sofa—the only furniture in the room. Everything else was instrumental in some way, from the guitars to the stool in front of the drum set. He watched as she set the mummification knife across her lap and used the other to slice her palm. She let several drops of blood land on the mummification knife, then she gripped it in her uninjured hand and closed her eyes.

"Soul of Bjorn, reaper, come to me. Come tell Death what happened to you. We seek the truth. Come to us, Bjorn." Her words were quiet, but he could feel the power building around her, proving that she was doing something. He didn't sense any new souls, though.

Minutes passed before she opened her eyes and frowned at him.

"I take it I'd arrived by now?" he asked dryly. When she nodded, he considered. "Try another, just so we can verify whether the spell is defective or not."

"Makes sense. Have anyone in mind?"

He considered for a moment, felt for a nearby soul. "Eugene Washington."

She nodded and repeated the spell, calling for Eugene instead. This time, the summoning worked and the soul of a confused older man appeared in front of her. Though she looked a little startled, Death stepped in and took over.

"You're okay, Eugene," he soothed, laying a hand on the man's shoulder.

Instantly, he calmed. "What's going on?"

"We needed to test something, and I'm afraid you were nearby. But not to worry, I'm sending you back now," he promised. And, with a wave of his hand, he did just that. But the simple fact that Blanche's spell had worked...

"Bjorn's soul is gone, isn't it?" Blanche asked, her thoughts mirroring his own.

"Almost certainly," he agreed. "As you said, that spell summoned me, and I'm not a weak-willed god to be unable to resist such things." And he was beyond furious that someone would not only kill one of his reapers, but destroy their soul. That was something even he was unable to undo. Bjorn could never rest in the afterlife, never be reborn. He had ceased to exist. It wasn't a fate Death would wish for anyone but the most heinous of people, but especially not a man who had done a vital job admirably for centuries.

Blanche couldn't say she liked Death, even if he was responsible for Mira being alive. She definitely couldn't say they were friends, or even friendly, but she saw the grief and anger on his face and could sympathize. Hadn't she done absolutely everything to bring Mira back? Hadn't she slaughtered the revenants who had killed her? She'd even stood up to Death.

Sa bumped against her knee, reminding her that she had both knives still in her hands. Silently, she offered the sharp knife back to Death, but the mummification knife got slid into one of her cargo pockets. It was hers, after all. No reason for her not to keep it.

Brushing her hand over Sa's head once more, she rose, ignoring the throbbing in her injured hand. She had no skill with healing, but it was a shallow enough cut. It would heal in time, just as the wounds from summoning Death repeatedly had. And right now, she had bigger priorities.

"You need a break," she told Death.

His gaze narrowed at her. "A break?" he repeated.

"A break," she confirmed. "Look, anyone—even a stranger—can see you're stressed as fuck. You don't seem to have any new leads, and you just found out one of your people was killed. *Really* killed. So yeah, you need a break."

"A break isn't going to find Bjorn's killer," he argued in a dismissive tone.

"It might," she said, shrugging and crossing her arms over her chest.

"Explain."

She sighed. "Have you never heard about letting your mind focus on something new, so whatever you're worried about cooks in the back of your mind? Or changing your perspective?"

He mirrored her pose, his muscular arms folding over his chest. "And say I did agree. What exactly would you suggest I do for this break?"

She hadn't thought that far ahead, but it only took her a moment to think of something that would benefit them both. "Show me some sights." It was clear he was about to protest, so hurried on. "Look, I haven't been out of the castle since I got here, except to step literally ten feet outside with Abaddon on my second day here. I want out and you need a distraction, so...show me your favorite place here in Cindatha, or the local reaper hangout, or anything." Sa bumped into her again and she rolled her eyes. "And we could take Sa with us. I get the feeling he doesn't get out too much, either."

Blanche didn't really hold out much hope that he'd agree, but she realized she was dying to see more of Cindatha. She'd seen plenty from the tower, sure, but it had made her curious about what it looked like from the ground. Silently, she tried to will him into saying yes, but could only wait as he thought it over.

"Fine. But first I want to know why you haven't just left the castle," he said as he placed the violin on a stand, then started for the door. Except his legs were longer than hers and he didn't seem to be a man to meander when he could power walk. So it wasn't until they were outside the castle with the door closing behind them that she got a chance to answer.

"Two reasons," she said, happy he'd stopped, even for a moment. Hopefully, he'd slow down now that they were outside. "First, Abaddon told me that there are the souls of animals here, not just people, and made it sound like there were predators as well, like Sa. And while Sa might have taken a liking to me, I really don't want to get mauled. And more importantly...I think I told you I'm a receptacle. I have to work—hard—to avoid being possessed, and since I'm not exactly sure how that all works when it's souls rather than ghosts, I really didn't want to risk it. Spending the rest of eternity with a soul camped out in my body is definitely not my idea of a good time."

Death said nothing for a long moment, just studied her. Then his hand lifted toward her. Though she wanted to flinch away, she forced herself to hold still. If he wanted to kill her, she was pretty sure he wouldn't need to touch her to do it, so best to just wait and see what he intended.

What he intended was to touch the tip of his finger between her brows. There was a faint warmth that spread outward, then flowed down her body before disappearing when he drew his hand back. "You no longer have to fear possession. Any ghosts—or souls—who wish to take over your body will need to have permission from you, freely given."

One of her hands lifted, and she touched trembling fingers to the same spot his finger had brushed. "Seriously? I'm immune to forced possession now?" she asked in a hushed voice.

"Didn't I just say as much?" he asked impatiently.

She never had to worry about ghosts again? She could just be a necromancer? Learn from ghosts, help them, but she didn't have to constantly stress about which ghost would be the one to get past her defenses? Even when she was a child it had been a concern for her and her family. She never would have made it to adulthood without constant vigilance from both her and her mother. This was huge.

She felt her eyes grow warm as tears pricked at them, but she ignored that. Crying was allowed after receiving a gift like this. It was life changing, even if that life was to be spent here.

Without thinking, she threw her arms around Death's neck and gave him a crushing hug. He stiffened but didn't push her away. Even better, he didn't strike her down for the audacity of touching him in such a way. "Thank you," she whispered against his shoulder. "I've spent centuries always having to make sure I was protected. I always knew I'd have to be in the underworld to be free of that fear, but I didn't realize I'd be alive when it happened."

Death sighed and his arms lifted slowly before he returned the hug awkwardly. It made her wonder how long it had been since he'd been hugged, but on the heels of that thought came another.

Had he ever been hugged?

Blanche didn't let go immediately, unable not to notice just how good he felt. Death may be portrayed as an old man or skeletal in essentially every bit of myth or lore, but if what she was feeling was accurate, then he was absolutely built. Maybe swinging the scythe was a good workout? It certainly couldn't be the violin playing.

Not quite certain why her thoughts had gone in that direction, she drew back and smiled at him, aware it probably looked forced. "Thank you," she said again.

He stepped back and nodded. "You're welcome. As for the animal souls, they shouldn't be an issue, but you can always take Sa with you when you leave the castle."

Sa agreed in his own way, by leaning against Blanche's side and shoving her off balance...and right into Death. He caught her before she could fall, and for a few seconds, they stared at each other.

This close, she could see that his eyes weren't just pale blue, they also had a pale ring around them that looked more lavender than blue. While they were definitely otherworldly, even eerie at first, after more study, they were...beautiful.

Oddly, all of Death was beautiful. Masculine for certain, but beautiful.

Righting herself, she glared at Sa, certain the little shit was doing this on purpose. She wasn't sure why, but if a saber-tooth tiger could laugh, this one would be. She was certain of it.

"So...you need to relax, and I need to see more of Cindatha than what's visible from the tower. Show me someplace you like going? Maybe your favorite place?" she prompted, hoping to move past the weirdness that was only partially caused by Sa.

"As you wish."

With nothing more than a thought, the three of them disappeared, and when she saw what he thought of his as his favorite place, she could only gasp.

CHAPTER 10

It was easy to see why this was Death's favorite place. A single glance and Blanche thought it might be hers as well. It looked like something out of a fairy tale set in a tropical paradise. They were surrounded by green, putting them in the jungle side of Cindatha, and when Blanche turned in a slow circle, she was just stunned by the beauty of it. But the amazing plant life was overshadowed by the water.

Towering in front of her was a waterfall, one that fell over multiple tiers, spreading out then narrowing again to spill into a small lake. It had to be nearly a hundred feet from the top to the lake, and all that water meant she was surrounded with a low roar.

She was drawn toward the lake and let out a second gasp when she stood on a flat stone at the edge of the bank. The water was perfectly clear, so she could see the bottom. More than that, she could see the colorful fish that swam about, and the rainbow of coral and aquatic plants that covered the floor of the lake. The light of the moon sparkled on the surface, beckoning her closer still.

"Please tell me this is close to the castle," she said, unable to stop staring at the water.

"Not if you're walking, no," Death told her as he joined her at the edge of the lake.

Shaking her head, she sighed. There went her plans to visit here daily. "Well, I can understand why this is your favorite place. It's just become mine, too, so long as those fish aren't piranhas in disguise."

"No, they're harmless enough, even for you."

"How often do you come here?" she asked, debating the wisdom of stripping down to her underwear and jumping in. She'd never been a huge swimmer, but there was just something so alluring about this spot. Only the fact that she wasn't alone made her resist.

"I actually haven't been here in centuries."

Surprised, as she was already planning to come back as soon as possible, she looked up at him. "You should, especially if you're always dealing with a shitload of stress."

Death could only stare at her. This was so odd. He hadn't left the castle for those centuries except for work—or to deal with Blanche. And while he considered Grim and Abaddon friends, they also didn't spend too much time just talking like he was doing now with Blanche. And they'd definitely never hugged him. So why was he allowing it now? What was it about this woman that had him doing things out of character for him? Taking breaks? Inviting the living into his castle? Hugging? He didn't even like her, so it made no sense.

"It normally isn't this bad," he told her, frowning at the water.

"You're Death. You can't tell me there isn't stress involved in every single one of your days."

"No, I can't," he admitted.

"So why—"

He missed whatever she was going to say because Sa knocked hard into the back of his legs and he fell directly into the lake, unable to regain his balance in time. It only took him a few strokes to surface, but Sa had chosen that moment to dive in himself, splashing Death right in the face.

Oh, he was going to get that cat. This was not how he'd planned to spend the day, even with Blanche wheedling him into coming out here.

The first thing he saw when he blinked the water from his eyes was Blanche down on one knee, her arms wrapped around her belly as she laughed so hard he wouldn't be surprised if she was crying.

Treading water, he cocked his head, then his lips started to twitch. He couldn't blame her. It probably was pretty damn funny from her end. But he couldn't let her get away without any repercussions.

Using his power more than his body, he scooped his hand through the water and sent a small wave to wash over Blanche, leaving her as soaked as he was.

She sputtered for a second, blinked at him, then the laughter resumed. Not content to simply laugh at him, he felt her magic gather as well, before he was splashed a second time. And though playing was an alien concept to him, he found himself engaged in a magical splash battle. It was...fun. He couldn't remember the last time he'd had fun. Once he solved Bjorn's murder, he might have to indulge in it more often.

Sa wasn't content to just swim or watch. Right after Death had sent another wave of water toward Blanche, he felt huge paws on his shoulders, which shoved him under the surface for a few seconds before the weight disappeared. Kicking back to the surface, he was just in time to see Sa bite Blanche's shirt, then tug back until they both joined him in the water with a squeal from the necromancer and a loud splash from both.

Blanche surfaced for a moment, sputtering, before she dipped back under the water. It took Death a moment to realize that she was having difficulty, though he wasn't sure if it was because she was a poor swimmer or because of some other reason—like being fully clothed and surprised.

Cursing, he swam over to her and slid beneath the water, wrapping one arm around her chest before he pulled them both to the surface. She clung to him as she sucked in a large breath. He almost let them both dip back under the water, but caught them just before her mouth got submerged.

The movement brought her eyes up so they met his while her hands remained fisted in his shirt. For the second time in one night, he was struck by the nearly forgotten feel of a woman pressed against him. He was no innocent, but it had been...hell, he wasn't even sure how long it had been since he'd bothered to indulge in something as frivolous as sex. A few thousand years at least, but it could be more. And while it could be just his memory dulling over those long years, he didn't recall that woman feeling quite this good. Blanche was thin, yes, though she'd filled out some during her time here, and she still had that softness that said female to him.

And for the first time in centuries, he felt his body hardening. It was an inconvenient time for him to rediscover lust, but he was reluctant to shove her away. Besides, hadn't she told him he needed a break? To think about something else for a while? So why not this aggravating, stubborn, tempting necromancer?

Blanche's gaze dropped to his lips, her own parting slightly. He took that as a sign from fate—though he normally ignored her—and drew her in tighter to his body. When her legs bumped his, which were still kicking to keep them afloat, she wrapped them around his hips. He stifled a groan at the brush of her body against his rigid cock. To prevent the sound from escaping, he bent his head and kissed her.

It was nothing like their first kiss, the one where he'd given her an ability he never should have given to anyone—and had never granted before. This one wasn't done out of anger and necessity, but desire. It also wasn't brief or painful, but lingering and sweet.

Her eyes drifted closed and she moaned against his lips. His tongue teased hers until she opened further for him. Tilting his head, he deepened the kiss and couldn't contain the groan any longer when he got his first taste of her. There was something familiar about it, but that thought was pushed to the back of his mind. Instead, he lost himself in the taste of her, the feel of her wrapped around him, the press of her center to his aching groin. Even without being inside her, even with them both fully clothed, it was still the most pleasure he'd had for the whole of recorded history.

Her legs tightened, putting more sweet pressure against his cock, and he momentarily forgot to keep his legs moving. They slipped under the water, but it took a few seconds for either of them to realize it.

Her eyes opened with shock and mild panic, and he mentally cursed as he kicked them back to the surface. But the moment was broken. He carried her over to the bank and lifted her out and onto the rock. When he was sure her footing was good, he pulled himself out as well.

Silently, careful not to look at each other, they started to wring their clothes out. It wasn't all that effective, but it helped. At least until Sa climbed out and shook his fur out, covering them with more water.

"Sa isn't a normal saber-tooth tiger, is he?" Blanche asked as she eyed the feline with both amusement and annoyance.

Not for the first time, Death cursed his lack of actual god powers and yanked his shirt off. He hated being in wet clothes, so continued wringing it out. But while he was powerful, and could do more than deal with souls and cause death, he'd never had the ability to instantly dry his clothes. He'd have to complain to his creators. "For the most part, he is, but he has been with me for thousands of years. Any animal can start to act more like a person after that long."

Blanche barely heard anything he said after he took his shirt off. She blamed the train of her thoughts on the kiss, because she couldn't help but stare at his chest. It was broad, muscled, and covered in those black and silver swirls and symbols that she'd seen on his arms. There was only the faintest dusting of hair, leading from his belly button and disappearing into his pants. Oh yeah, Death was hot. Why did all the best looking ones have to be assholes as well?

Assholes and fantastic kissers.

No, she wouldn't think about that, though she was kind of happy that her pants were wet. It hid her body's reaction to the kiss and the way he'd felt when she'd been wrapped around him like a freaking monkey.

Gods. Of all people she had to be attracted to in Cindatha, why did it have to be her captor and not someone relatively safe like Abaddon?

"Blanche?"

Oh shit. He'd been talking to her, and now had an expectant look on his face. "Sorry, tired. What'd you say?"

"I asked if you were ready to head back to the castle."

"Oh. Yeah, sure."

He gave her a curious look but nodded and teleported them back into the round room at the base of the stairs. She grimaced, because all three of them were now dripping water all over the floor, but she supposed it wouldn't hurt the stone they stood on.

"Thanks. For showing that to me. And..." She laughed and rubbed over her heart. "And for making it so I don't have to fear ghosts anymore."

"You're welcome," he said, and she wondered at the stiffness in his voice. "Good night."

He disappeared and without him there, her mind went back to the sight of his chest, of that six-pack. Without meaning to, she pressed her lips together, trying to retain the taste of him, though most of it had been washed away when they'd been dunked. Just enough lingered to make her sigh in frustration. That, she knew, was never going to happen again. She just wished she knew why that thought filled her with so much regret.

Blanche tossed and turned for hours before she was finally able to drift off. Almost immediately, she slipped into a dream.

The land looked nothing like what she was used to. There were no trees, no green, just shades of brown, from a tan that was indistinguishable from white, to a deep, almost black tone. And while there were structures, the buildings were all small, single stories, and made of sand, straw, and mud. Yet for the moment, it felt like home.

Walking into one of the homes, she smiled at the back of the man who sat on a stone stool, hunched over as he worked on something. He wore nothing but a loincloth and sandals made of leather and sinew. To combat the heat, he'd tied his black hair up at the nape of his neck. And oh, she loved how he looked, how he dressed during the summer months, putting all his tanned skin on view. If they were lucky, they'd harvest enough crops and preserve enough meat that the winter months would be lazy. Lazy months were the best for spending time in bed with her husband.

Crossing to him, she bent and kissed his shoulder before resting her chin on the same spot. "What are you doing, love?" she murmured. The part of her mind that wasn't fully involved in the dream noted that she wasn't speaking English, or any other language she had ever heard, but she understood each word.

He leaned his head against hers and lifted the piece of wood in one hand. It was starting to resemble a creature she thought was a mammoth—though those were further north, so she'd never seen one herself—but he still had a lot of work to do. "Carving a toy."

She laughed and straightened so she could move around him and settle herself in his lap. "A little early for that, isn't it? I don't think there's any chance we could be pregnant yet."

Her husband set the carving and flint knife he'd been using aside, and wrapped his arms around her waist. He smiled at her and she traced a finger down his cheek, along his jaw, then over those soft lips, all while staring into his beautiful brown eyes. "Maybe not," he agreed, "but if I start now, then by the time our child is old enough for such things, he or she will have plenty to play with." A grin replaced the easy smile. "Besides, I'm committed to trying as often as possible."

She laughed and kissed him lightly, because she was just as eager to try whenever they could. While she loved her life, there was nothing better than the time she spent in their bed with his body joined with hers.

"Why don't we try now?" she asked, shifting to straddle his lap, which made her skirt shift to reveal her thighs, the skin just as tanned as his.

"I do love the way you think," he murmured, sliding a hand into her hair and drawing her in for a kiss.

Their lips connected as he reached down to shift their clothes out of the way. Rising up, she angled her hips, then started to slide down onto him, moaning.

And it was on a real moan that a banging on the door dragged her sharply from sleep.

CHAPTER 11

The room around her wasn't right. Blanche fully expected to see the mud house around her, feel her body stretching around her husband's, but instead she lie in a plush bed, with a canopy above her and no one there but her. A fact that her body deeply regretted, as it was thoroughly primed for lovemaking. And instead of the halter-style top and skirt, she wore panties and a tee-shirt.

Everything about that dream had seemed so real. And that man...It was so weird. It had just been a dream, but she could still feel an echo of the love she'd felt for him. Even stranger, other than the lack of tattoos, the color of his eyes, and the length of his hair, he'd looked exactly like Death. But Death had never smiled like that. And she sure as hell couldn't see him carving toys for a baby.

Somehow, though, she could see him as a father.

Another loud banging on the door jerked her upright and pushed thoughts of the dream to the side for now. "What is it?" she called as she pulled herself out of bed.

"It's Abaddon. Death wants us," he called through the door.

Groaning, she went to the wardrobe and pulled out a pair of pajama pants and robe, slipping both on. Only then did she open the door to see Abaddon dressed in his usual attire, looking impeccable. "What's going on?" she asked.

"Not sure," he admitted, cocking an arm toward her. Yawning, she slid her hand through it and they walked downstairs. Instead of the throne room, they headed to the kitchen. She said nothing until she'd gotten a cup of coffee and sat at the table, with Grim on her right, Abaddon on her left, and Death across from her. To her delight, Sa sat beside her and leaned against her side. Though she gave him an absent stroke—and saw both Grim and Abaddon gape in surprise—she gave Death her attention. That seemed to be some kind of signal, because he began speaking.

"With Blanche's help, we figured out why I was unable to locate Bjorn's soul."

Both brothers looked at her, the surprise from Sa's affection fading as they braced for the news and turned back to Death. "Where is he?" Grim asked.

Death's lips thinned as he pressed them together. "Dead. Body and soul."

"How certain are you?" Abaddon asked, looking no more pleased than Death was.

"As certain as I can be without having seen his soul extinguished myself."

"Shit," Grim breathed, rubbing a hand over his face.

"How is that possible?" Abaddon breathed, a hand gripping the edge of the table.

"Since I know I didn't kill him and unless Bjorn managed to anger a powerful god, then the only feasible option is that another reaper killed him. No idea how they managed to kill his soul."

Silence filled the kitchen. Even Sa didn't make a sound as Grim and Abaddon processed the news. Blanche was quiet out of respect for their loss, yes, but also because she felt like something was off about Death's statement. A god or Death was the only way to kill a soul? With what she knew of souls and magic, she doubted that, but she didn't say anything. If there was a third way and Death was keeping it from his two most trusted reapers, there had to be a reason. And as terrible as it was, her mind wasn't really on this. She knew everything Death was saying already, and the dream Abaddon had woken her from was playing in her mind, pushing everything else to one side.

Why had Death been in her dream? And looking so different from how he did now? And why in the hell had she been dreaming about sex with Death? Not only was she not prone to sex dreams, the few she'd experienced had always featured someone she'd liked. While yes, the kiss with Death the day before had been hot, she still really couldn't say she liked the man. But the weirdest thing was that it hadn't been all sex. She'd *felt* for the version of Death that had been there with her. The feelings of love were fortunately fading, but it made her wonder what her subconscious was trying to tell her.

Still, it wasn't the biggest priority right now, not with a reaper out there killing other reapers.

"Do you really think one of us killed Bjorn?" Abaddon asked, his voice tight, choked.

"Not the two of you, no, but unfortunately, I do think it's a reaper," Death answered without hesitation. "I'm going to go look into this—discreetly—but while I'm gone, I want you two to stay here. I need someone here in case more dead reapers are brought in. But if others arrive for normal business, I don't want a word of this getting out. Not yet. We don't need anyone panicking if there's no reason."

"At least some have probably heard about Bjorn's death," Grim pointed out.

"Undoubtedly," Death agreed. "If they ask, you can tell them we're investigating, but I don't want any hint that we know his soul was killed or that another reaper is responsible. I don't want to start a panic. Am I clear?"

"Clear," Abaddon said as Grim nodded.

Then Death looked at Blanche and arched a brow. She scoffed and shook her head. "I'm not telling anyone jack shit. Besides, no reaper's going to believe me about anything. I'm a mortal outsider."

"Probably true, yes, but still better not to put the idea in anyone's head," Death told her.

"Fair enough. My lips are sealed." She doubted she was going to see any other reapers in any case.

He gave her another long look, and she wished she knew what was going on in his head. After a long moment, he disappeared. With him gone, she looked to the remaining two reapers. "How likely is it that Bjorn just pissed off a god?"

The twins shared a glance before Abaddon spoke, sounding just as unhappy about the situation as Death had looked. "Unlikely. I won't say Bjorn was a saint by any stretch of the imagination, as he was crude, impulsive, and a bit of..." He trailed off and glanced at his brother.

"A slut. He liked sex but hated commitment," Grim filled in. "And I'm not one to slut shame—do what you want with your body—but not all of the women he slept with were okay with being casual."

"Could he have slept with a goddess who got pissed at being a one night stand?" Blanche asked. "Doesn't seem like the sort of thing many—if any—goddesses would tolerate."

"Also unlikely, but anything is possible. But for them to have killed him...." Abaddon sighed. "Death meant it about a powerful god being necessary. Just like not every god can resurrect the dead, not all gods—even death gods—can harm a soul that completely. And to be able to kill Bjorn's soul, the god would have to be able to kill Bjorn to begin with, then destroy his soul."

"I've never met a god I was scared of, though that could be because we're just that awesome," Grim added. "That said, I know other reapers who have gotten on the bad side of a god or two and lived to tell us what happened. And if those gods could have killed them completely, I think they would have."

Abaddon pulled out his phone, frowning as his thumb moved over the screen. Blanche's breath caught at the sight of the first form of communication she'd seen since she got here. If she could get her hands on a phone, she could contact her family. She could make sure Mira really was okay. No, she didn't think Death would have let her be brought back wrong, but she didn't really want to take a chance with her baby sister. Then Abaddon started speaking, and she forced herself to focus on the here and now, while promising herself she'd keep an eye out for an opportunity to borrow a phone.

"What concerns me is the soul being gone, to be honest. I know I said a powerful god could do it, but it's just theory. There are definitely gods who can manipulate souls—stealing them, moving them, that sort of thing—but I've never heard of anyone but Death being able to destroy one." He paused, glanced at her briefly. "At least, nothing I could confirm," he said before looking back to his phone.

"That's a good point," Grim murmured as he pushed back his chair. "I'll be back in a few. I want to check on something," he said as he strode quickly out of the kitchen.

Blowing out a breath, Blanche glanced at Sa and scratched behind one of his ears, giving Abaddon a minute to finish whatever he was doing. "Do you think there are going to be more dead reapers?"

Abaddon made a low sound of displeasure and slid his phone back into his pocket. "I really couldn't say," he admitted. "It all depends on who killed Bjorn and why. If it was a reaper, then it likely was a personal attack—though again, I don't know how a reaper would be able to snuff out his soul. But if this was some grievance between Bjorn and his killer, then it's more likely that he will be the only victim. And, unlikely as it seems, I hope that's the case."

"Fair enough. I hope that's the case, too. I mean, I didn't know Bjorn, but I know how much it sucks to lose a friend." Which, of course, made her mind go to her sister. No, Mira wasn't dead any longer, but Blanche hadn't gotten but a minute to soak that in before she'd been whisked off to Cindatha. Gods, she wished she'd been able to spend some time with Mira before leaving, but this was still better than the alternative.

He must have noticed the tension and sadness on her face, because he reached across the table to rest his hand over hers. "Would you like to go to the theater? Relax a little and try to forget about all this for a while?" he asked with an understanding smile.

"I'd love that," she told him as she pushed back her chair and rose.

"I'll even let you choose the movie," he promised as they started for the theater.

A man appeared in a dimly lit stone room and quickly noted the faces of the others already gathered. A few immediately noticed his arrival, but others continued their conversations, oblivious.

"Listen up," he said, pitching his voice to fill the room. He waited until the voices died off and every face was turned toward him. "Death is onto us." The immediate shouts of concern were expected, and he said nothing for a minute, letting them get it out. "Enough!" he said after a few minutes, and this time, silence filled the room more quickly. "We planned for this, remember? We've got a man on the inside, and he was able to warn us. Death is investigating reapers. All reapers. So we need to be careful. We need to be vigilant. Make no move that isn't in line with your normal routine. Only come here if necessary unless our contact calls us. Try not to interact with each other too often. We need to do *nothing* that could turn his suspicion to us directly."

A man stood, called out. "And what if Death comes to question us directly?"

"We've hidden before. We've tested the gifts from our contact. They work. Use them. Keep them on you at all times, and make sure you can use them as soon as Death shows up." He paused, meeting each and every pair of eyes before he spoke again. "We can't mess this up. If we screw up—if even one of us screws up—then we're all dead.

There's no way we can achieve our goals unless we can make our next move without Death seeing it coming."

It was a woman who spoke this time. "Should we risk contacting those who aren't here?"

He grimaced but nodded. "We have to. They need to be warned before Death reaches them. But do it discreetly. Figure out who is the most logical person to call or visit, someone Death won't see as out of the ordinary. And, until further notice, I'm the point of contact. We can't risk having our inside man discovered." He paused, then asked, "Any further questions?" No one spoke, so he nodded. "Get to it. And be very, very careful. We can't fail."

Almost as one, they disappeared until only he and the woman who'd spoken up remained. "Are we positive this can work?"

He nodded. "This plan has not been put together hastily. Besides," he said, smiling tightly, "at this point, we can't really back out, now can we?"

"No, I suppose not," she said before disappearing.

Drawing in a deep breath, he teleported home, and hoped that their leader was right. He didn't relish being on Death's bad side.

CHAPTER 12

Grim joined Blanche and Abaddon while they were picking out a movie. He dropped down beside Blanche, so she was sitting between the brothers. He had to be careful not to step on Sa, and was curious as to why the decidedly unfriendly tiger had decided to befriend the necromancer. Not that she wasn't a good and interesting person, but in all the centuries since Grim had been in Death's castle, he had only seen Sa act affectionately with one person—Death. Perhaps it just spoke of Blanche's character, because both he and his brother had taken easily to the woman, and they tended to be a little more standoffish than most of the reapers.

But then, they'd been around the longest.

"So, what are we watching?" Grim asked as he slouched down and got comfortable, slinging an arm over the back of the couch.

"Not sure. I'm normally okay with whatever, but it seems cold to watch something with death in it, but that narrows the choices down to...almost nothing," Blanche admitted as she stared at the wall of movies.

"And I told you, there's no need to go that far," Abaddon told her. "True, it might be considered insensitive to watch a horror movie, but even movies for children often mention death. Just choose what will take our minds off things for a little while."

Grumbling, she did, sticking a disc in the player before she plopped back down between them. To Grim's shock, she rested her feet on Sa's side, and the smilodon didn't so much as twitch an ear.

The movie played, but he wondered more about Blanche for a little while rather than watching. She wasn't what he'd expected her to be, not when his first glimpse of her was when she'd given Death a headache. But he liked her. She was a little standoffish, but that could be because of circumstances. There was something unusual about her, and he couldn't put his finger on it. The tomb was the least of it, he thought, but he didn't have time to dig into the rest for now.

Thoughts of what was occupying his mind meant that, inevitably, his thoughts turned back to Bjorn. On the other side of the couch, Abaddon's thoughts went in the same direction. It had been centuries since a reaper had died, and the last time it had been at the hands of another reaper, it'd been a matter of impulse. Not to mention the soul had remained intact. This whole incident was a first, not just for him, but for everyone. And Death...he would be relentless until the culprit was found, that he was certain of.

A shiver went through him and both he and Grim sat up and their heads turned toward the door. That sensation could only mean a reaper was in the throne room and calling for them.

"Want to meet another reaper?" Grim asked as he got to his feet.

"Uh...sure?" Blanche said as she rose. "Who?"

"We're not sure yet. We only know someone's here," Abaddon answered. "Just remember Death's warning."

"No mentioning Bjorn's soul got killed. Check," she agreed, nodding and following them out of the theater.

They were silent as they made their way to the throne room. A man was standing there, wearing loose, cream-colored linen pants, a brown vest, and sandals. About six feet, he was obviously muscular, with a smooth, bald head, golden skin, and green eyes. The outside of one wrist held a tattoo of an ankh, while the other had a scythe.

"Imhotep. What brings you here?" Abaddon asked as they approached the man. He didn't realize Blanche had stopped until she made a sound suspiciously close to a muffled squeal. Turning, he gave her a concerned look. "Are you okay?"

"Imhotep?" she asked, her tone oddly reverent. "Like—"

"I am *not* a walking mummy, nor have I ever been, nor will I ever be," Imhotep said, sounding aggrieved. "I certainly never betrayed my pharaoh."

"No, no, no," Blanche quickly said as she started walking again. "I mean, don't get me wrong, I love that movie, but I was going to say like the genius who designed Djoser's step pyramid and was a master of a dozen different things."

Imhotep visibly relaxed. "Oh. Then, yes, I'm that Imhotep. Sorry, I don't meet too many people who aren't reapers, and they all immediately associate my name with those movies."

"This is so fucking cool," Blanche breathed, and Abaddon fought against the uncharacteristic urge to roll his eyes. Most reapers had a history, and a few had made it into the history books. Some were even known of by humans, even if they tended to think it was all myth and folklore. Though he did have to admit Imhotep was one of the better known ones. He wasn't entirely certain why.

"And who are you, other than a woman of exquisite taste?" Imhotep asked, giving her a wide, flirtatious smile.

"A necromancer who made a deal with Death. Also known as Blanche."

Imhotep took her hand and bowed over it, kissing her knuckles lightly. "A pleasure to meet you, Blanche."

She only grinned at him, looking star-struck.

Grim cleared his throat. "You came here for a reason?"

"Hmm? Oh!" He straightened, winked at Blanche, then gave Abaddon and Grim his attention. "Nothing I really needed, other than to let you know that a few of the gods are complaining about how few souls they're receiving lately." He glanced to Blanche briefly, before returning his focus to the twins. "Can I speak freely?"

"You can," Abaddon agreed. "And the gods are always complaining. It isn't our fault that more people are no longer believing in all the gods or the afterlife."

"Yes, well, I'll let Death or one of you two explain that to them. They won't want to hear it from me." He drew in a breath, blew it out slowly. "It seems like there are more souls needing reaped the last few days. Or I should say, the same number of souls, but fewer of us to reap them."

He was clearly fishing, and even Blanche could hear it, stunned as she was to meet a man who was one of her heroes. He might not be a necromancer in the sense that she was, but the Egyptian priests had known secrets of death she never thought she'd learn until she came here.

"I assume you've heard about Bjorn," Abaddon said, voice tight, and she fought the urge to rub his arm soothingly.

"So it's true?"

"It is," Grim confirmed.

Imhotep cursed and Blanche would have loved to know what language he was using, but it sounded pretty cool. "I was hoping it was just a rumor."

"I'm afraid not," Abaddon said, shaking his head. "We're looking into it."

Imhotep clenched his jaw. "Are you planning on letting us all know when you figure out what happened?"

"We are."

He nodded sharply. "Then I'll leave you to it." Once again he looked to Blanche, and while he didn't smile, some of the hardness eased. "It was a pleasure meeting you, little necromancer," he said before he disappeared.

"I can't believe I just met Imhotep," Blanche breathed.

"Just wait until she meets some of the other reapers," Grim said as he turned her back toward the door.

"What? Why? Who else is a reaper? Though his being one does explain why they haven't found a tomb."

Grim grinned. "You'll just have to wait and see."

They returned to the theater after a quick stop to the kitchen for snacks, and this time, all three were at least somewhat focused on the movie. Blanche was the most distracted. Meeting Imhotep should have boosted her spirits, but she felt them sinking instead. Worse, despite the gift Death had given her—freedom from possession—she felt the beginnings of an anxiety attack trying to stir in her chest. She was entirely too used to both panic and anxiety attacks, and while she tended to associate both with ghosts, that wasn't the case now. Was it the stress of being separated from her family? Bjorn's murder? The memory of that kiss with Death?

She wasn't sure, but her heart was quickening and she felt the need to squirm on the couch. No, to stand up and pace. Movement would be a good thing, regardless of how she managed it.

Just as Blanche started to push up from the couch, Death walked into the room. All four of them immediately focused on him. For a moment, Blanche was able to ignore the building attack and note the tightness of his eyes and mouth, the tense set of his shoulder.

"Did you find anything?" Grim asked after pausing the movie.

Death shook his head. "Nothing suspicious, no. And neither Darius nor Antonia had any idea of who might have had an issue with Bjorn."

He didn't sound happy at all, but she couldn't blame him. And it would have been too much to hope that he would have found the killer so quickly. Anyone who could kill a soul was likely someone both smart and powerful. Blanche had no doubt Death was extremely powerful—maybe even one of the most powerful beings to have ever existed—but no one was infallible.

Abaddon made a low sound then asked, "No leads, either?"

"None. Did anything happen while I was gone?"

"Imhotep showed up," Abaddon answered. "While he said he wanted to let us know he was having some issues with a couple of the gods, it seemed like the true reason for his visit was to ask about Bjorn."

"Not unexpected," Death said, sighing and running his hand over his head. "You told him nothing, correct?"

"Correct."

"Good. I want you both to be vigilant when you deal with any other reapers. Let me know if anyone says or does anything that even remotely seems suspicious to you," he ordered. "None of my reapers are stupid—the ones who are don't get the offer—but that means that whoever is responsible isn't going to make a big mistake. We need to focus on the little ones."

"Understood," Abaddon said, his answer echoed by his twin.

Grim added, "We'll figure out who did this, and how. You know none of the reapers will tolerate something like this. Most of us only have other reapers, so we're family."

Most only had other reapers? It didn't sound like they were forbidden from interacting with humans or the Arcane, but more like it didn't happen often. Thinking of Suni, the witch who had made herself immortal, she realized she understood. Not as much as the reapers or Suni, of course, but it had to be difficult to bond with people who had limited lives when you would live forever. Because if Imhotep was still alive and looking like he was in his thirties, then reapers had to be immortal. It made her wonder how often they were allowed to interact with the souls in the various realms of Cindatha, or if they truly only had each other for lasting company.

Death nodded and glanced at the paused movie, then Blanche, before ignoring her in favor of the twins. "Keep me updated," he said before he turned and walked out.

"Damn," Grim muttered. "I was hoping he'd have good news."

"As did I," Abaddon agreed. "But he had a point. None of us are stupid. True, few of us are as smart as people like Imhotep, but he does refuse the offer to those without the wits to do the job properly."

"Can you tell me more about the offer?" she asked. Death had mentioned it, of course, but she wondered if there was more to it than the little bit he'd given her before.

The twins exchanged a look and appeared to have a silent conversation before Abaddon shrugged, then nodded. Grim nodded as well, then turned to Blanche. "Reapers are...unique. Barring a few exceptions I won't get into, they have to be born, and are only born to humans. They have powers from birth, the powers of a reaper, but they're mostly dormant. They might be able to see souls or something, but can't do things like teleport here to Cindatha or reap souls."

"If they're born to humans, though, wouldn't they be human?"

"Basically, yeah," Grim confirmed. "Without interference, they'll live a human lifespan, never gain the full range of reaper powers, and die. They probably won't ever even figure out what they are."

"So how do they get to be immortal? At least I assume immortal, because if I remember right, Imhotep is something like four or five thousand years old."

"That's the offer," Grim said with a smile. "Occasionally, Death will go to one of those baby reapers and make them an offer. They can come and be a true reaper like Imhotep and us, or remain as they are. If they accept, the rest of their powers are unlocked and they stop aging. That's why you'll see that reapers all look different ages. It all depends on how old they were when they accepted Death's offer."

This was insane and fascinating. Blanche immediately wanted to tell Mira about it because it was the sort of thing her sister would have loved. And that thought made the pressure in her chest increase. Fun. Distraction hadn't derailed the anxiety attack, she thought as she rubbed at her chest, only delayed it.

"Are you all right?" Abaddon asked.

She smiled faintly and nodded. "Yeah. And it's cool, hearing about the reapers. I had no idea, but you guys are myths, even to the Arcane."

"Not as much as we'd like, to be honest," Grim admitted. "Even if we don't actually kill anyone, a lot of people think we do, thanks to those myths about reapers. And Death's the only one with a scythe." He grinned then corrected, "Well, the only one with a scythe that's magic, anyway."

"What do you mean?"

"Well, some of the reapers like to play pretend."

Her hand stilled. "Are you telling me reapers cosplay Death?"

"Yep," he said, grin widening.

"That is...I can't decide if that's awesome or not." Blanche shook her head. "I think I'm going to skip the rest of the movie, though."

"Let one of us know if you need anything," Abaddon said as she rose.

"I will. Thanks."

She made her way upstairs, but stopped just before opening her door. A shower might help, but she didn't think she could go to bed just yet. Instead, she started knocking on doors, hoping to find Death's room. It was time to take her own advice and find a better distraction.

CHAPTER 13

Death had to fight not to slam the door to his room. Not only had he discovered absolutely nothing, when he'd returned, it had pissed him off to find Blanche sitting between the brothers and relaxing. He wasn't even sure why. Yes, he'd kissed her, but he didn't even like the woman. She had badgered him into bringing her sister back, then not done the wise thing when he'd offered her the absurd deal. He sure as hell didn't want her here...did he?

Growling under his breath, he sat on the edge of his bed and rubbed at his eyes before swiping his hands over his face. That wasn't important, especially not now. An irritating woman was nothing compared to the annihilation of someone who shouldn't be killable.

Tapping his fingers on his knee, he brought what he knew of Bjorn to mind. He knew each and every reaper—he had to, as only he could grant them the full access to their powers—but he had to admit he knew the younger ones a great deal less than he did those who were thousands of years old. Back then, they'd had to work together more, coordinate to ensure all the souls were dealt with in a timely and respectful manner. Now? The older reapers tended to train the younger ones, and he only dealt with them when issues appeared. Issues didn't crop up often, either. The most common complaint he heard was the same that Imhotep had voiced in his absence. Underworld and death gods complaining. They all knew they weren't the top of the food chain when it came to death and souls, but several of them didn't like that fact, even if Death kept his existence largely a secret. He was a silent partner. Well, more like a hands off boss, but still.

But all of that boiled down to the fact that he didn't know Bjorn well. He'd been a viking, and a vicious one at that, but Death knew he'd transitioned surprisingly well to the role of reaper. Often, he was the one claiming the souls of warriors, as he could identify with them better than most reapers. But other than Darius and Antonia, he wasn't sure who he'd been close to, and neither of them could name another reaper that he had spent time with. Apparently on his off time, he'd spent time with humans and the Arcane. 'King of the One Night Stands,' Antonia had called him.

This wasn't even something that could be considered an accident, either. The fight? Okay, he could see that. Reapers were known to brawl from time to time, but that had almost zero chance of ever being lethal. A slit throat? That was intentional. Even if the culprit hadn't known that would truly kill another reaper, the fact that Bjorn's soul had been extinguished said everything.

Blanche had been right to ask if he trusted his reapers that first day. He hated it, but she'd been right. Which made him wonder if he had a single traitor in the ranks, or if there were others. Was this just something that dealt with Bjorn, or something bigger?

He needed to visit each and every reaper, but wasn't sure that was the way to find Bjorn's murderer. Which meant tomorrow, he'd have to do something unexpected. Something that might help draw the killer out.

A knock on his door derailed his thoughts, and he frowned at it. When it came again, he scowled and rose to answer it. On the other side stood Blanche, because of course it was her. He couldn't escape her.

"What?" he asked, voice harsh.

She cocked her head and arched a brow, and something about the motion teased at his memory. "Can I come in?"

Having her in his bedroom was the last thing he wanted, but he knew firsthand how persistent she was. Though stubborn as fuck might be a more accurate term. He could say no, shut the door in her face, but he doubted she'd go away. And, for some reason, he still didn't want to kill her and banish her soul to another part of Cindatha, far away from his home.

Silently, he moved back and pulled the door open. She stepped inside and he noted she was rubbing her chest. Instead of speaking immediately, she looked around then frowned. It brought the scowl back to his face as he did the same, then he mentally cursed. Her room mirrored his own. It hadn't been a conscious decision, but it was done and he couldn't go back and change it now.

"What do you want?" he prompted as he closed the door, hoping this would be a quick visit.

Turning toward him, her fingers remained on her chest, and he realized she was breathing a little too quickly. "You seemed pretty pissed downstairs. I wanted to make sure it was just Bjorn's death and not something else that had happened."

His brows lifted. "Why?"

She hesitated, then shrugged. "I guess I was worried. Fuck if I know why, since you're not exactly the easiest person to get to know or like, but..." She trailed off and shrugged again.

"Isn't the fact that one of my reapers killed another reason enough for me to be pissed?" he countered, unwilling to admit the unwanted stab of jealousy he'd felt when he'd found her hanging out with Grim and Abaddon.

"It is," she agreed. "Like I said, I just wanted to..." She paused, drew in a breath, and blew it out slowly. "Just wanted to make sure that was it."

He frowned as he watched her. She was paler than normal and seemed jittery. Here she was claiming to be worried about him, but something was clearly wrong with her. "Are you okay?"

Blanche smiled, but it was weak and only surface deep. "Okay is a stretch, but I will be."

"What's wrong?"

Her gaze flicked to the door and she took a step toward it. "Nothing. I should go."

He caught her arm before she could reach the door and she made a sound he could only describe as a whimper. "Blanche, what is it?"

She went still and closed her eyes, breathing in through her nose and out through her mouth. After doing that a few times, she answered, her voice shaky and full of...shame? "Anxiety attack."

Death had no experience with anxiety attacks. None of the reapers had ever had one around him, and he'd never had one himself. Which meant he wasn't sure what to do to help her, though he *had* to help her. He wasn't sure why, and he was starting to get pissed at the confusion when it came to this woman.

Impulsively, he scooped her up and moved to the bed, placing her on it. She wasn't sick, but laying down helped with most everything, didn't it? And if this was caused by anxiety, then he just needed to calm her down, right? It couldn't hurt, in any case. Except that also wasn't his forte.

He studied her as she rolled onto her side and drew her knees up, her eyes still closed. "Sorry," she mumbled, and he felt a spurt of annoyance. Why the hell was she apologizing for something she clearly had no control over? He walked into his bathroom and grabbed a washcloth, wetting it with cold water. After returning to her, he sat on the bed and placed the cloth on the back of her neck. "This happen often?"

"Too often," she whispered.

That filled him with an irrational anger, but again, he wasn't sure why. She was an unwanted houseguest. Why would he care if she suffered from these attacks, even if they happened daily? But he did. He didn't want her to deal with this.

Before he could realize what he was doing, he stroked a hand over her hair, keeping the touch light. Then he did it again and found that the repeated caress was soothing him, even if it wasn't doing anything for her. But the tightness around her eyes didn't seem quite as pronounced as it had been, so he kept it up.

"Do you know that places like the waterfall aren't uncommon in Cindatha?" he asked as he continued to touch her. She shook her head a bit, but that was her only answer. "That's the most beautiful, in my opinion, but Cindatha is full of beautiful spots. Waterfalls and pools, clearings filled with flowers, trees with bark every color of the rainbow. Even the side that looks like desert at first glance has some amazing spots. Colored arches. Snow-capped mountains. There's even a cave that has crystals covering its walls. If you take a torch in there, they shimmer and reflect colored light over the floor of the cave. You wouldn't want to lean against the wall, but if you want a peaceful place to just sit and look, it's great."

Her eyes opened and shifted up to meet his face. "What kind of crystals?" she asked. Her voice still wasn't steady, but it was better than it had been.

Death lifted the washcloth, turned it over, and placed it again on her neck before he resumed petting her hair. "Sapphires, though they're not all blue. If it were Earth, it would be the richest sapphire mine in the world, but I've forbidden anyone from chipping off a single stone. Beauty like that is meant to be appreciated, not selfishly taken."

"I'd like to see that," she admitted quietly.

He didn't mean to do it, but his mouth formed the words before his brain registered the thought. "I'll take you sometime." He cursed himself mentally but didn't take the offer back, even though he withdrew his hand. "How are you feeling?"

She breathed slowly, her eyes fixed on his as she took stock of her body. "Not fantastic," she decided, "but a hell of a lot better than I did five minutes ago." Pushing herself up on her elbows, she kept eye contact. "Thank you."

"You're welcome," he said as he got to his feet and moved to the door. Getting rid of her was safest. Getting rid of her meant he didn't have to see how good she looked stretched out on his bed. A bed which had never had anyone in it but for him.

It was a dismissal and she clearly recognized it as such. Part of her wanted to protest, and not because she still felt a little off. She was on the other side of the anxiety attack, so couldn't claim she needed more time. But she liked being in his bed, and it was that thought that had her sitting up and getting to her feet.

"Let me know if there's anything I can do to help," she told him as she stepped past him and opened the door. Before she left the room, she added, "Or if you need another distraction."

A scowl was his only response, which perversely had her smiling as she shut the door behind her. Maybe she should poke at him more often. He likely wasn't used to anyone arguing with him or teasing him, which meant it was good for him. Plus, it was fun, now that she was fairly confident he wasn't going to kill her.

She crossed the hall to the door directly across from Death's and entered her bedroom. When she closed the door behind her, she frowned. The room had changed again. It still wasn't a huge change, but there was a dresser that hadn't been there before, and it looked just like the one she had back home, including the mirror above it.

This couldn't be Death's doing. He hadn't had time, even if he'd been willing to try. So where had it come from? She crossed the room and her frown deepened. It didn't just look like her dresser, it was identical, right down to the imperfection on the top. Curious, she opened a drawer, but found it empty. Whoever had brought her dresser hadn't thought to bring her things. Odd.

Wanting to make this room at least a little hers, she moved to the trunk at the foot of the bed and retrieved the mummification knife she'd placed there the day before. After setting it on the dresser, she took a shower, letting the warm water help ease the last of her anxiety. By the time she was done, she felt drained, and happily crawled into bed, falling into sleep within minutes.

DANCE WITH DEATH

And that night, she again dreamed of the brown-eyed Death.

CHAPTER 14

The next morning started off as normal—or as normal as a day in the realm of souls could get. She had her usual breakfast with Sa, though Abaddon joined her this time. Then, shortly after finishing his coffee, Abaddon stiffened.

"What's wrong?" Blanche asked.

"Death's summoning us," he answered as he got to his feet.

"Us?" she asked, though she rose as well.

"The reapers. *All* the reapers," he said as he strode out of the room.

All the reapers? In one place? No way was she going to miss that. She hurried after him, only dimly realizing that Sa kept pace with her as they headed to the throne room. There were already several dozen people there, and as she walked toward the throne so she'd have the best view, she noticed that reapers were the most diverse group she'd ever seen. She saw reapers of every race that had ever lived, and none of them were dressed the same. She saw the expected goths, and the preps like Abaddon. There were also punks, cowboys, someone who looked like they didn't know disco was dead, and one man who was dressed in a freaking tuxedo with tails. Maybe he'd been at some fancy event when he got summoned? Because who the hell wore a tuxedo unless they had to?

But it was the man standing in front of the throne that took everyone's attention, including her own. Death's face was set in stern lines, his eyes cool and serious as he watched more and more reapers appear. Within minutes, Blanche could see why the throne room was so large. If there weren't more than a thousand people in it now, she'd eat one of Abaddon's tailored shirts.

All the gathered reapers looked either confused or curious. Though Blanche knew why they were all there, she didn't see anyone who looked guilty or was acting suspicious. Not that she expected it would be that easy.

And still Death waited. Even when no one else seemed to be arriving, he waited, until people started fidgeting and shifting from one foot to another. Either he was pissed, or he wanted people to feel uncomfortable. Uncomfortable people were more likely to make mistakes or say something they didn't mean to, right? But then she felt something she hadn't consciously noticed at first. Death wasn't just standing there, he was filling the room with his power. It was a gradual thing, and she'd gotten used to feeling death energy around her, which was why it took her so long to notice it. And he didn't stop until it was thick enough she felt she could swim through it—or be crushed by it.

She didn't see him losing control to this extent, so whatever the reason, it had to be intentional. Was this another way of putting the reapers off guard? Or was it something more devious than that? There was so much she didn't know about Death and his powers, so she couldn't even hazard a guess.

The one thing she did know was that she didn't feel the least bit intimidated by the display of power. Instead, she found it oddly sexy. Who knew she'd have a thing for powerful, dominant men? Especially when it wasn't their only setting. She couldn't help but remember how he'd helped her with the anxiety attack. How he'd pulled her out of the water and kissed her. He'd been more human then, almost tender. And though it was a completely inappropriate moment to be daydreaming about such things, she felt a tendril of desire coiling in her belly. But as soon as she realized she was getting turned on by Death of all people, she shoved those thoughts aside and tried to focus.

"Bjorn is dead," Death said flatly, his gaze skimming the gathered reapers as several of them murmured to each other. "Many of you knew this already. Many of you have been wondering how that's possible, when it's no easy feat to kill you. What most of you don't know is that he was murdered." The conversations picked up and Blanche watched as faces reflected shock, outrage, and fear. She could understand all that, but she was hoping to see one face that looked just a little shifty. Someone trying a little too hard to match the emotions of the reapers around them. There were too many crowded into the throne room for her to see everyone, though.

Death didn't lift a hand or call for silence, just let his power pulse. It was enough to have every reaper going silent again, as that pulse was strong enough to be almost painful. "The only person we've found who might be responsible...is standing in this room."

Reapers gave each other suspicious looks, but Death blasted them with power again. This time it didn't immediately ebb, but remained wrapped around them all. The reapers showed a range of reactions from discomfort to pain, with one reaper actually doubling over. Blanche didn't feel anything like that, just an ache from the press of his power, so could only assume it was directed solely at the reapers.

Death saw the doubled-over man as well. He stepped down from the dais and strode directly to the man, the other reapers parting to allow him to pass by. As he walked, the other reapers were freed from whatever he'd been doing to them, while the man groaned and went down to one knee.

A minute passed as Death looked down at the man, and for the first time, Blanche was truly afraid of him. There was no trace of anything human on his face, just a cold, deadly rage. He made a lazy upward gesture with his hand, and the reaper was yanked off the floor to hover, eye to eye, in front of him.

"I didn't kill him," the man protested, his voice more groan than anything else.

Cocking his head, Death studied the reaper before shaking his head. "No, you didn't kill Bjorn," he confirmed. "You are far from guiltless, though." He stepped closer, until he was in the man's face, and his voice grew harsher. "I have given every reaper immortality and the means to live well for that eternity. I don't ask much of you in return, but there are a few things I cannot, *will not* condone, and you seem to be using those things as a personal checklist. A depraved bucket list. Or did you think I would never discover the things you do when you aren't ferrying souls? Did you think I wouldn't care what you've done to women? To children? Being a reaper doesn't give you carte blanche."

"No! I didn't! I..."

The man's arguments trailed off as Death gave him a withering look and wrapped his hand around the reaper's throat. And there was power behind that look, in that touch, because the light in the man's eyes faded. A minute later, Death loosened his hand and the now lifeless body dropped to the floor, leaving behind a soul, still caught in the air by Death's magic.

Reapers gasped and murmured at the unexpected death of one of their own, and even Blanche's eyes widened with surprise. But it was when he grabbed the soul by the throat that she made a low sound of her own. He leaned in, whispering something to the soul, before his hand squeezed and the man's soul disintegrated, not even leave behind ashes or dust like Bjorn's body had. Dropping his hand, Death looked to the body, and it crumbled just as cleanly.

He turned and strode back to the dais before he spoke again. "You are all my children and I will protect you to the best of my ability, but I will *not* tolerate anyone abusing their power. You were not given your longevity and powers so you could rape, murder, or otherwise harm those weaker than you. Accidents happen, I understand that, but if any of you step out of line, I will end you, too. You are reapers. You are meant to be compassionate and carry souls to their resting places, to guard and tend to them. You are not monsters to indulge your every fantasy."

No one made a sound, not even a scrape of a shoe on the stone floor.

"Now...As I said before, Bjorn was killed by a reaper. This is also something I won't tolerate. Again, I know accidents happen, and quite a few of you have been warriors all your life and enjoy sparring, but there is a vast difference between an accident while fighting, and cold-blooded murder. One can be forgiven, the other cannot. You are all brothers and sisters. Family. You're meant to protect one another. So if any of you know *anything*, no matter how small or insignificant it might be, then tell me. Stay behind when everyone else leaves, come and find me later…I don't care, just tell me in the next twenty-four hours. Because if anyone knows who killed Bjorn and neglects to tell me, then they will be considered just as guilty as the one whose hand wielded the knife. If they come forward by the end of the day, I'll be lenient. Am I clear?"

A thousand voices all murmured their assent in a variety of languages, and Death nodded. "Dismissed. And be careful."

The reapers began disappearing just like they'd appeared, the room slowly emptying. Blanche half expected to see at least one reaper stay behind, but after a few minutes, only Death, the twins, Sa, and herself remained. A glance at Death's face showed he expected someone to stay as well, and she felt a pang for the disappointment she saw there. He might not be a traditional father, but he clearly cared for these reapers, and expected more from them than he was seeing.

Before she could decide what to say or do, he stalked off, so she just sighed and turned to the twins. "That went well," she said dryly.

"I don't think he was expecting to find another…monster…amongst his reapers," Abaddon said quietly.

"No, none of us were," Grim agreed. "I had no idea Ralph was…" He trailed off, unable to find the words.

"None of us did."

"Does that happen often? Him executing a reaper? And out of the blue?" Blanche asked.

"No, not often," Abaddon said. "There isn't normally a need for it. I can think of…what, three?"

Grim nodded. "Three sounds right. Well, four, including Ralph. And it's never for minor things, either. He might punish a reaper for overstepping, but they have to do something pretty fucking bad for him to just execute them, especially when he kills their soul as well. But there's never a trial, if that's what you mean."

Horrified, she shook her head. "He just gets it in his head that they're guilty and kills them?"

Abaddon shook his head, pulling a coin from his pocket and setting it to walk across his knuckles. It looked like the one she'd occasionally seen Grim toy with, and almost smiled because the twins fidgeted the same, even if they didn't dress the same. "He doesn't just get it in his head," he corrected. "Remember that reapers are Death's. Our power comes from his. It *is* his, in a way, it's just sectioned off and in our bodies. When we're in the same room as him, he can use that power to get in our heads. That's how he knew what Ralph had done. He saw it from Ralph's own mind. Ralph condemned himself with his actions and thoughts."

Good. She wasn't sure what she'd have done if Death was the kill first, ask questions later type. Though she was glad she wasn't a reaper so he couldn't get in her head. Although, was it still possible because she was a necromancer and most of her magic revolved around death? Could her magic come from him like it did for the reapers? Now that was a terrifying thought, especially if he'd caught her remembering their kiss.

"Do you think anyone's going to come forward?" she asked, to get her mind onto another, safer topic.

"Hell if I know," Grim said on a sigh. "I think if they were going to, they probably would have just stayed behind. But it could be they're worried about getting killed themselves, and are waiting until they're positive the castle is empty so no one knows they're the one who came forward."

"It does seem logical," Abaddon said, nodding slowly. "If I was one of those reapers, and I knew who killed Bjorn, I think that's how I'd do it. Wait an hour or two, then come back. Or maybe summon Death to them, so even we're guaranteed not to be around."

"I hope someone does. I don't think he's going to be easy to live with until he knows who and why," Blanche said.

"No, probably not," Abaddon agreed.

And that pesky need to comfort Death was back. She could try to ignore it, but he'd helped her through her anxiety attack the night before, so it was the least she could do. As she told the brothers bye and went in search of Death, she tried to convince herself that the dreams of Death had nothing to do with it. She knew she was lying to herself.

CHAPTER 15

Death was actually in the first place Blanche looked. She wasn't sure whether that was a testament to how well she was coming to know him, or how predictable he was. But since it came with him playing music again, she didn't care at the moment.

She opened the door to the music room and slipped inside, closing the door before Sa could intrude like he had last time. Which meant Death didn't notice her right off, so she had a chance to enjoy the music—and the sight of him playing.

He was sprawled on the couch, his eyes closed as he played. It wasn't violin today, but guitar, and instead of haunting or sad, this music was angry. He didn't sing, but the melody sounded vaguely familiar.

Blanche let the sounds wrap around her as she studied his face, the frustration and fury on it. It made her want to trail her fingers over the lines around his eyes and mouth, to smooth them away. The impulse had her curling her hands into fists, then changing her mind and shoving them into her back pockets. Better to leave him be. Music, she knew, could be cathartic for some people, and if this was helping him deal with the betrayal of one of his reapers—no, two of them—then she'd wait until he was done.

After that song, he played another, then a third, never opening his eyes, and she was astonished by his skill. The violin had been impressive enough, but adding in the very different songs he'd played tonight? He was one of the most skilled musicians she'd ever heard. She only had to hope she'd eventually hear him play the other instruments in the room, because he had a good two dozen different types spread around, including a grand piano at the far end.

At the end of the third song, he sighed and his arms relaxed, his eyes opening. They narrowed when they spotted her, but she just gave an apologetic smile. "How long have you been standing there?"

"Not that long."

"Liar."

She shook her head. "Fine. About fifteen minutes."

"What do you want?"

She walked to the couch and sat on the opposite end from him. "You helped me last night. I wanted to return the favor."

"Unless you can tell me who killed Bjorn, or somehow make it so he isn't dead, then there isn't really any way you can help me."

"Now who's the liar?"

His brows shot up and she almost laughed at the shocked look on his face. "Pardon me?"

"Are you trying to say I didn't help you the other day? You seemed to be less murdery after we got back from the waterfall. I'd say that's help."

"That's your solution now? Go swimming again? Somehow, I don't think it's going to make me forget that I just had to kill one of my own reapers for being a murderer and rapist."

"No," she admitted, "it won't, but my suggestion isn't swimming. And what I do have in mind won't make you forget either, but you need an outlet or you're going to go crazy. And this may just be me, but an insane Death doesn't sound like a good thing for anyone, and especially not people who are stuck in Cindatha for the rest of eternity."

He scoffed and ran his fingers across the strings, making a sound that caused her to wince. "What is this brilliant suggestion of yours?"

"Honestly? Nothing you weren't already doing. As they say, music has charms to soothe the savage breast," she said, nodding to the guitar.

"It wasn't really working," he said flatly.

"Then you need more of a distraction." Not that she had any idea what that distraction could be. He wasn't into going to the waterfall again, and just playing wasn't doing it.

Again he strummed the strings, though the sound was more pleasant this time. It matched the expression on his face, which was thoughtful now. Since he seemed to actually be considering her suggestion, she said nothing, just waited, despite the intense look he was giving her.

Rising, he put the guitar on a stand, then stepped back. A moment later, a different guitar—an acoustic, she thought—started playing without being held. It surprised her enough that it took her a minute to register the melody. She didn't recognize it, but it was a slow song, sensual. Beautiful.

While she'd been staring at the guitar, Death had walked over to her. She only noticed when his hand appeared in front of her. Blinking, she looked at it, then up to his face. He arched a brow and gave her a slight smile. Seconds more passed before it clicked that he was asking her to dance, and that immediately brought her latest dream to mind. Where the first one had been flirting and the start of making love, the last one had been dancing at some festival beneath the moonlight. The music had been drums then, and the dancing wild and free. It was entirely different, but still felt the same.

As she placed her hand in his, her heartbeat quickened. She couldn't pretend this time. She was clearly reacting to him specifically. Odd, since she didn't normally dance, but the thought of this dance, with the dream teasing at her mind, had her anticipating every second.

He gently pulled her into him, so their bodies were touching. Part of her ached to press closer, but she resisted the urge as she lifted her free arm until her hand rested on his shoulder. Then, he started to move, drawing her along with him. And even with as little skill as she had, there was something so natural about dancing with him. It should be ridiculous, slow dancing with Death in the underworld, but it felt good. It felt right.

Death hadn't danced in thousands of years. He'd never wanted to, but when Blanche had suggested music, the thought had forced its way into the front of his mind and refused to leave. This was probably a mistake, just as the kiss at the waterfall had been, but this aggravating woman was getting under his skin. And if he was going to make a mistake, he was damn sure going to enjoy it, and he was definitely enjoying the feel of her body against his.

As he stared down at her, into the eyes that were only shades darker than his own, he found himself pulling her tighter against him. When she didn't protest, just moved easily into him, he went a step further, releasing her hand so he could slide that arm around her as well.

She was so small for such a force of personality—and such temptation. Most people—even other necromancers—wouldn't be holding up so well to being drawn into Cindatha so abruptly. Then again, most people would never have dared to badger him into resurrecting a loved one. He reluctantly admitted to himself that he admired that about her. She was bold and brave, determined to push forward no matter what stood in her way. It was what would have made her a good warrior. Or a fierce queen.

He slid his hand slowly up her back, causing them to press more firmly together. Though his power kept the music playing, the dancing soon devolved into little more than swaying together, close enough that he could feel her heart pounding in her chest.

When her eyes dropped a few inches, he gave in to the temptation and bent his head, laying his lips against hers. Her body softened further against his as she opened for him. Still moving to the oddly erotic song—something he tried to tell himself was accidental—he fell into the kiss. His tongue lazily teased hers, exploring her reactions. The sigh had his arms tightening around her. The soft moan made him kiss her more deeply. And when her hand slid up to the back of his head, gripping his hair? It took all his self-control to avoid lifting her so she'd wrap those long legs around his hips. Except he wasn't willing to fall into bed with her, especially not with everything going on. She'd be the ultimate distraction, which would certainly improve his mood, but he couldn't afford distractions right now.

But oh, she might be the best mistake he'd ever made.

Dimly, he realized the music had stopped and kissed her once more, lightly, before releasing her and drawing back. If he was pleased that her eyes looked a little dazed, it was only natural. He was a man, after all, and having that effect on another person was always nice. But he promised himself that it wasn't going to happen again.

She took the few steps to the couch and sank down onto it, and he had to fight back a smile when he realized her legs weren't quite steady. Then again, he was hard as a rock, so maybe he shouldn't be so smug.

"Um…" she said before pressing her lips together and rubbing her hands over her thighs. "Since that keeps happening…it seems like I should know something about you other than your job description."

"Such as?" he asked, leaning a shoulder against the wall. He really wasn't prepared to sit down in tight pants with a hard on.

"I don't know…Favorite food? Movie? Best Friend? Did you ever have a family? Wife? Kids? Siblings?"

That erased every bit of desire he felt and spoiled what had become a pretty fucking good mood. He scowled and was aware he was leaking power, much like he had only an hour ago in the throne room. Too unsure of what would come out of his mouth if he spoke again, he opted for discretion and transported himself to his bedroom. Right now, solitude was the wisest course of action, but he sincerely regretted losing the moment he'd just shared with Blanche.

And that was something he definitely wasn't going to think about too hard.

Death's abrupt departure baffled Blanche, and the possible reasons for it bounced around in the back of her mind for the rest of the day. Even when she was reading or talking with one of the twins, it lingered in the back of her mind. And when she climbed into bed, it was the last thought on her mind.

Her dreams began as odd, disjointed flashes. Memories at first. The moment in the catacombs when Mira had been killed by revenants. The one when she'd been dragged into the pool at the base of the waterfall and had trouble surfacing. The harsh kiss when Death had given her the ability to resurrect her sister. Then they changed. She was running from a huge feline that looked similar to Sa, her heart pounding as she tried to figure out how to escape the beast. Next, she was sitting around a campfire with several other people, laughing at a story one of them had told.

Then, surrounded by the darkness of night, she held the body of someone. She rocked them as her heart broke and she screamed her rage and grief to the moon above her. Her hands were wet with blood, but nothing mattered but for the fact that the body in her lap didn't move. Would never move again. And she couldn't understand why. Nothing like this had ever existed in her universe before, and she simply couldn't process it now.

When she woke, her cheeks were damp, proving she'd truly been crying, and not just in the dream. She stumbled into the bathroom and splashed cool water on her face, trying to remember who she'd been holding. They'd been dead, she was sure of that, but didn't know why she'd cared, or why it had felt like so foreign a concept to her. She'd understood death by the time she was a toddler. She'd summoned her first ghost at four, and experienced her first possession before she'd hit puberty.

Something about being in Cindatha was affecting her dreams, and she was hoping tonight would be the worst one she'd experience here.

The other dreams hadn't been bad. In fact, they'd been pleasant, if a little confusing. And yes, the first one had left her feeling horny, but it hadn't left her feeling like this. Like her world was falling apart.

She didn't like it.

Knowing she wouldn't be able to get back to sleep now, she changed and went down to the theater. Her mind was too unfocused for her to be able to read, so she hunted through the available movies until she found one she'd seen a dozen times before. Putting it on, she curled up on the couch, and let the familiar characters and lines comfort her. But though she dozed, she didn't sleep again.

CHAPTER 16

Death spent his morning teleporting from reaper to reaper, invisible as he watched the ones he deemed most likely to either have run into Bjorn fairly regularly or do something like commit murder in the heat of passion. It was tedious and he wasn't seeing anything that was suspicious. A few of his reapers had some unusual habits, and a few even he would classify as weird, but nothing he considered immoral. Certainly none that were murderous.

By midday, Death was regretting how he'd left Blanche the day before. Yes, he wanted more emotional distance between them, but she had no way of knowing that family was a sore spot for him. Did he want to talk about it? No, absolutely not. But he could have simply told her so and changed the subject. It would have been the rational thing to do. Which meant he was feeling the annoying urge to make it up to her. The problem was, he wasn't used to doing things like making apologies or amends, which meant he wasn't sure what to do.

It took another hour of spying before the idea came to him. She'd showed interest in the sapphire cave. It wasn't something he advertised as existing, and to his knowledge, only a few reapers or souls had ever located it. That had to be good enough for this, right? Besides, she kept saying he needed distractions, and after the fruitless day he'd had, he could use one now.

Taking himself back to the castle, he checked in with both Abaddon and Grim, but was unsurprised when neither had any news for him beyond the expected. Upset reapers and no clues as to who Bjorn's killer was. That done, he felt for Blanche, locating her in the theater.

Sa was actually curled up on the couch beside her, his huge head in her lap, her hand resting between his ears. It took a moment to recognize the movie, but he was amused to find she was watching *The Goonies*. Not a bad choice, he thought as he strode further into the room. "How involved in the movie are you?" he asked.

Sa's gaze flicked over to him, but he didn't otherwise move. Part of him was annoyed that she was stealing his tiger's affections, but the rest was pleased they both had the company.

Blanche reacted more than the feline, jumping slightly before she turned her head to look at him. There was wariness on her face, but he couldn't blame her. "Um, I mean, it's a good movie, but I've seen it a couple dozen times, so if there's something you need me for..."

"You seemed interested in the sapphire cave the other night. Would you care to see it now?"

She straightened and turned more fully toward him. "If you're fucking with me, I'll figure out a way of paying you back. You might be able to smack me down for it, but I'll do it," she warned. "If you're not, then I say hell yes."

He chuckled and walked over to her. "No, I'm not fucking with you," he confirmed. "But it does mean you'll have to get that lazy beast off you first."

Blanche immediately gave Sa's side a light slap. "Come on, Sa! Up! Mama's gotta go see some pretty things," she told him before giving him a shove. It wasn't effective, as Sa weighed several times what Blanche did, but when she kept badgering him, he yawned and half-rose, half-rolled off the couch, looking as though it was his idea the whole time. The second he was off her lap, Blanche got up, though she groaned and took a moment to stretch. "He always makes my legs go to sleep," she complained, lightly stomping her left foot on the floor in a clear attempt to wake it up. "Okay, let's go," she said, smiling at him. Since it was a genuine smile, he deduced that this was, in fact, the perfect thing to make amends with.

He teleported them to the cave, offering nothing for a moment to supply light, which meant they were in absolute darkness. It didn't bother him, but she gasped and her arms shot out until she was able to grab hold of his forearm. He bit back a laugh and waited, but didn't need to wait long.

It was only a minute before she huffed. "You do know that I can't actually *see* any of the sapphires at the moment, don't you?" she pointed out, her voice echoing until it was ten times louder.

"You can't?" he asked, careful to keep his voice soft as he feigned surprise. "My apologies." He manifested a light in the center of the chamber, bright enough to send it refracting through the crystals, but not so bright as to take away from the cave's beauty.

It was chilly in the cavern, but as soon as her sight was restored, she forgot about the mild discomfort. Blanche gasped as the full splendor of the place was revealed, her hand tightening on his arm. He'd said it was beautiful, but he'd vastly understated it. She'd also been extremely wrong when she'd tried to imagine what it might look like.

The cave was every bit as big as the throne room, though some sections were twice as tall. The floor was packed dirt and stone like every other cave she'd seen, but that was where the similarities ended. Every inch of the walls and ceiling were covered in sapphires. Most were small, a foot long, tops, while a fair number were a little bigger—up to maybe five feet long. A few stretched to a good ten feet in length, spearing into the air. And when Death had said they weren't all blue, he hadn't been kidding. Blue was definitely there, in various shades from sky blue to teal to a deep navy, but she saw every color except for red, including a few black and clear crystals. And with the light hitting them like it was, it turned the ground into a chaotic, fantastic rainbow.

Releasing Death's arm, Blanche walked toward the closest wall and a patch of crystals that had an ombre effect that she'd never seen in a gemstone before. The blue faded to purple, then to pink, and when she held her arm out, she was strangely delighted to see it covered with bands of color. She moved her arm back and forth, just to watch the light play over her pale skin.

Looking over her shoulder back at Death, she asked, "Can I touch one?" She wanted to see if it would feel cold like most crystals, or if it would be warm. This cave felt oddly alive, despite there being nothing organic here but for her and Death, so she wouldn't be surprised if the crystals felt alive as well.

He nodded. "These crystals have been here for longer than humans have had writing. I don't think one necromancer touching them is going to hurt them in the least."

She held his gaze for a moment, again wondering why he'd disappeared the night before. Had it been her question? Or the kiss? He did seem to be uncomfortable or annoyed every single time they kissed, so it was a toss up which had been responsible.

Shaking her head, she turned back to the crystals. Spotting one that was a pale, pale blue, almost a match for Death's eyes, she lifted her hand and rested it against the flat side. It was as chilly as the cave, but she didn't care. She'd never touched a crystal this large. Ones the humans found were mere shards, and even the Arcane rarely found any of substantial size. There were a handful of crystal caves, she knew, but pictures she'd seen paled compared to the grandeur of this one. She could see why he was so protective of this place.

Blanche walked slowly around the outside of the cave, marveling at the crystals—and stroking her fingers over the ones she found appealed to her the most, including the ones with spears of pale color within them. But though she'd begun ignoring the cold, a tee-shirt wasn't the best thing for a chilled cave. Reluctantly, she drew herself away from the crystals and made her way back to Death. He'd been quiet other than giving her permission to touch the stones, and she wondered at his patience. He didn't seem the sort to indulge these sorts of frivolous things, so she wasn't sure why he'd done this for her, or why he'd simply stood there while she enjoyed herself.

She also wasn't stupid enough to take it for granted.

It wasn't until she'd reached him that she stopped and wrapped her arms around him in a hug. "Thank you," she told him, the words just as sincere as she'd been when she thanked him for making her invulnerable to possession. "I loved the waterfall, and do want to go back and see it at some point, but this? It's...absolutely unique. I've never seen anything even close to it."

He sighed, but he returned the hug, though she noticed he didn't pull her in as close as he had when they were dancing. "It is," he agreed. "And hopefully you can see why I've protected this place."

"I do. A greedy reaper could easily lop off even a fraction of one of these crystals and be set for life back on Earth," she said as she stepped back, putting a few feet between them.

"And while the reapers are generally decent people, it's human nature to want to live a comfortable life, and they started as humans."

It was the nature of pretty much any sentient species, so Blanche nodded. "All the more reason to thank you for letting me see it."

Death inclined his head, accepting her gratitude. "Are you ready to go back?"

She cast one last look around the cave before she nodded. "I am."

He took them back to the castle, right to where he'd found her in the theater. Sa was still there, but so was Abaddon. Death nodded to Abaddon before disappearing once more.

Blanche stared at the spot where he'd stood for a moment before she flopped onto the couch between Abaddon and the large cat.

"Everything okay?" Abaddon asked, pausing the movie he'd been watching.

"Yeah, it's fine," she said as she half leaned against Sa, almost smiling when he started to purr.

"Where were you?"

She wanted to tell him. In the weeks she'd been here, she'd come to think of both him and Grim as friends, and had realized that they were Death's right and left hands, but it had seemed like Death didn't want the cave becoming common knowledge. Now, odds were he'd told them already, but on the off chance he hadn't, she wasn't going to spill that secret. "He was just showing me some spots in Cindatha," she told him, pleased it was true enough, even if it wasn't the whole truth. "It's kind of funny. People don't tend to think of the underworld as being beautiful. I mean, sure, there are heavens and all that, but they aren't exactly the things people think of first."

He smiled. "It does have some truly stunning views, doesn't it? But I'm glad you've been getting out of the castle. It's not good for anyone's mental health to stay cooped up in one place for too long. Do you have a favorite so far?"

That was a difficult choice. Rainbow of gemstones, or the shimmering beauty of a waterfall? "One of the waterfalls," she decided, because while the sapphire cave had been gorgeous, the waterfall was a place where she could relax and spend hours.

"Ahh...Yes, they are gorgeous," he agreed. "Mine is the volcano to the northeast."

She frowned in surprise. "A volcano? But aren't they just...gray rock and occasional lava? Doesn't really sound like a photo-worthy view."

Abaddon laughed and shook his head. "No. Some resemble that, yes, but this isn't *Lord of the Rings*. A lot of volcanoes—even those on Earth—are green and gorgeous, just like any other mountain. You are aware that every Hawaiian island is or was a volcano at some point, aren't you? And isn't that considered one of the most beautiful places on Earth?"

He had a point, and though she was aware of Hawaii's volcanic past, it wasn't the first thing she thought of when she brought the islands to mind. "But isn't the northeast in the desert part of Cindatha?" she asked.

"It is," he allowed, "but it's not entirely desert. And even those tend to have at least some vegetation. But there's beauty to be found even in the desert." He smiled. "If you look hard enough, you can find beauty in anything."

"Now that I'll argue with. Some things are just horrible, no matter how you look at it."

"Oh?" he asked, obviously intrigued by her statement. "Do you have an example?"

"Torture," she said without hesitation.

He lifted a hand, index finger lifted. "Ah, but some would say there's even a beauty in that. Not the torture itself," he was quick to add when she started to argue, "but in the strength of the victim. The ability to withstand such horrors and come out the other side."

"And what about the victims who break? The ones who die? You can't honestly say there's a beauty in that."

Sighing, he shook his head. "No, I can't," he conceded. "And I'd like to clarify that I wasn't condoning torture by any means. But the strength of the human—or Arcane—spirit really is something spectacular. What can be endured, even overcome, is astonishing. Often unbelievable."

"Maybe it is, but some things should never have to be endured," she murmured, but it wasn't the sight of her sister's death that came to mind as she spoke. It was the dead man from her dream. Frowning inwardly, she decided to change the focus of her thoughts as well as the conversation.

"How long have you and Grim been reapers?" she asked, shifting to face him and leaning back against Sa. He made a good backrest, though not a perfectly stationary one.

The question made him laugh. "Grim and I were the first two reapers created, actually."

It wasn't quite the answer to her question, but it was interesting nonetheless. Except now she was confused. "Created? Do you mean the first that accepted the offer?"

He wiggled his head back and forth for a second. "Eh...yes and no? While almost all reapers were born human then accepted Death's offer, the first seven were different."

"Different how?" she wondered, loving how she was learning so much truth about death and all that it entailed. Mira would have been thrilled.

"As I said, we were created, but likely not in the sense you're thinking of. We weren't created from nothing, but rather transformed. One day we were something else, then we accepted Death's bargain and became reapers. After that, all reapers were born human, then ascended—so to speak—to what they are now."

"Huh. So were you guys like the test to make sure he had it right, or the seven to help him stem the tide until the other reapers could be born and grow up?" she wondered.

It took him a few seconds to answer, which made her think she might have inadvertently hit a sore spot. She was getting good at that.

"I believe the latter, but as you are surely aware, Death doesn't always reveal his motivations, even to Grim or myself," he answered.

"Really? Thousands of years and he keeps himself that isolated?" No wonder he'd acted so surprised when she'd hugged him the first time.

"Really," he confirmed. "I don't imagine it's easy being what he is, much less managing so many reapers. Even if he has help, both from us and the death deities, it's still quite the burden."

"Yeah, it must be," she agreed absently. But had he isolated himself because he felt he had to because of those burdens, or had something happened to make it his only option?

"Hey," he said gently, laying the tips of his fingers against her knee. "Enough serious stuff. Why don't we put on something funny and forget about burdens and all that for a little bit?"

She smiled and nodded. "That sounds like a good idea."

And for a little while, she was able to set aside all those concerns as they laughed at the on-screen antics.

CHAPTER 17

When Blanche woke the next morning, she was determined to find a way to borrow a phone. She wasn't positive, but she had a feeling Death still wouldn't approve of her calling home, so just asking one of the twins to borrow theirs was out. Which meant she'd need to be sneaky. Sadly, that wasn't her best thing, but she had to try. She owed her family that.

She had breakfast with Grim, but never caught a glimpse of his phone. Abaddon showed up right before Grim disappeared, but his phone was equally as hidden. There was no chance for the next few hours, either, but finally, when both twins showed up to share lunch with her, she saw her opportunity.

When Abaddon bent over to grab something out of the fridge, she saw the corner of his phone. She glanced at Grim to make sure he wasn't paying attention, then bit her lip. Using her telekinesis, she carefully eased the phone upward, trying to go slow enough that he wouldn't register its movement. She had to stop once when he paused, certain he'd noticed, but he quickly went back to what he was doing. Breathing out a quiet breath, she drew the phone the rest of the way out of his pocket and quickly brought it to her hand. Sliding it into her own pocket, she rose. "I'll be right back. Don't wait up on me," she told them with a smile before she left the kitchen, careful not to walk too fast.

Once she was out of view, and sure they wouldn't hear her footsteps, she ran up the stairs and to her room—the one place she was sure they couldn't just walk in.

Leaning back against the door, she drew the phone out and mentally crossed her fingers. If he locked his phone, she was screwed, but either Abaddon was one of those who had only partially adjusted to technology, or he had no fear of people doing exactly what she was doing now.

She wasn't sure whether to laugh or cry when it only required her to swipe a finger across the screen to unlock it. It opened to a text message, and though she didn't mean to, she caught the last part of the conversation.

Banshee: *When are you coming? I need you.*

Abaddon: *I can't get away right now.*

Abaddon: *I'll get there as soon as I can. Promise.*

Banshee: *Hurry.*

Blanche had no idea who Banshee was and wondered if it was a reaper or an actual banshee. Since it sounded like someone he was close to, she was leaning toward a nickname, because it was considered rude to refer to someone by their species.

Minimizing the messenger, she pulled up the phone app and dialed her sister's number, happy she actually remembered it. Now she just had to hope that Abaddon's cell service could make it from Cindatha to Earth.

"Hello?"

Mira's voice was curious, but Blanche had no idea what had popped up on caller ID. Right now she didn't care, not when it was the first time she'd heard Mira's voice in weeks. Closing her eyes, she smiled as a tear slid down her cheek. "Mira...It's me."

"Blanche?" Mira asked, shocked now rather than curious. "Is that really you?"

"Yeah, it's me. Are you okay? I mean, nothing went wrong when you came back? You're...you?"

"I'm me. I'm fine. I didn't come back wrong," Mira quickly assured her before she pulled the phone away from her ear to yell for the others. "Mom! Dad! It's Blanche! Get Aidan!" With the phone back to her face, she continued to speak rapidly. "What the hell happened? I was dead, then I woke up, and then you were fucking gone. And Death was there? What the hell did you do?"

"I couldn't let you stay dead, Mira," Blanche said, ignoring the tears that kept sliding down her skin. "I just couldn't. You shouldn't have been in the catacombs with me, and none of the gods were giving me the time of day, and I even went to Kur, but I couldn't get in the front door, so the only thing—"

"Kur? You went to Kur?" Mira asked, her voice rising in pitch. "How the fuck did you get to the Sumerian underworld and how did you get back? Scratch that. Tell me later. I want to know why Death was there and what he had to do with it. Did you trade yourself for me?"

"Where's Blanche?" Blanche's father's voice was hard to make out at first, then Mira must have put her on speakerphone, because she could hear them both clearly after that.

"Mom and Dad are here," Mira offered helpfully.

"Blanche?" her brother asked breathlessly.

"So is Aidan," she added. "So you can tell us all what you did."

There was no way she was getting out of this, but she had to try. "Look, I've only got a minute. I'm not really supposed to have contact with...anyone...but I had to make sure you were okay."

"When are you coming home?" her mom asked.

Blanche winced. "I'm not," she answered softly.

"What do you mean you're not?" her brother demanded.

"That was the deal. I'm alive. I'm okay. I'm not being tortured or anything—other than occasional boredom, anyway. But if I wanted Mira brought back, that was the deal."

"The deal? What, are you Death's slave or something?" Aidan asked suspiciously.

"No!" She rubbed at her face. "I'm just...here. Like a permanent houseguest."

"In...Death's house," Mira said slowly.

"Pretty much?" None of them said anything for a long moment. "I really don't have long. I just wanted to make sure you were all okay and make sure you knew I was okay. You don't have to worry about me." And if she was lucky, the separation wouldn't even be forever. She'd see them in a few hundred years when they joined her in Cindatha naturally. Except...they might not end up in this part of Cindatha. Her father and brother tended to worship the Celtic gods, her mother the Greek, and Mira death deities, so they could end up spread out.

"I wish you hadn't done it," Mira said, her voice quiet enough Blanche had to strain to make it out. "It was my time. You could have lived the rest of your life."

"What life could I have had? I'm the reason you were in that situation. I'm the reason you were surrounded by revenants. Which means ultimately, I'm the reason you died."

That had changed and Blanche wasn't sure when. She used to blame both herself and Death, but at some point she'd shifted the entire guilt to herself. Death hadn't made her go, hadn't made her take her sister. And it didn't sound like he'd had a choice in where the scythe had been kept, so why blame him? Or maybe she'd given up blaming him at the same time she'd stopped hating him.

She knew if she let the phone call go on that they'd argue with her, and the longer that went on, the better the chance Abaddon would notice his phone missing. "I have to go. I'll try to call again, but seriously, I'm okay. Don't call this number back or you'll get me in trouble. I love you," she said, trying to ignore how her voice broke.

Pressing the end call button was one of the hardest things she'd ever done. Sniffling, she quickly erased the call from the history, closed the app, and opened the message app again. She took a quick minute to wash her face before she went back downstairs.

Grim frowned when she walked in. "Blanche? What's wrong? Have you been crying?"

Dammit. With her pale complexion, her face tended to get red when she cried, especially her eyes. She'd momentarily forgotten that. Smiling weakly, she decided to play it off. "Little bit, yeah. Just...I miss my family, you know? Sometimes it just sort of hits me," she told them truthfully as she retook her seat. Now she just had to figure out how to return the phone before Abaddon noticed it was missing. Abaddon didn't make it easy as he stayed in his seat for a while. He finally rose, but Grim was facing her.

Sa might be the soul of a long-extinct saber-tooth tiger, but part of Blanche was convinced he was psychic. He always seemed to know what she needed, and he proved it once again when he got between the two brothers and let out a small roar. It had both men looking at him, and she took the opportunity to slip the phone back into Abaddon's pocket. He glanced at her, but she just shrugged. "Don't look at me. I don't speak cat," she said, feigning ignorance of what the look—possibly—meant.

"Neither do I. Unfortunately," he said before giving Sa a piece of the chicken he'd prepared. She noted he tossed it rather than feeding it directly, and she smiled. Somehow, Sa apparently trusted her more than the twins, who had been here for far, far longer than she had.

They'd made her a plate too, and while it looked delicious, the emotional conversation with her family had wiped out all traces of appetite. Friendship had her taking a few bites, but though the food objectively tasted good, it settled like stones in her belly.

"Sorry guys," she said, truly meaning it, "but I'm just not hungry anymore."

"I get it," Grim said. "You didn't exactly come here under the best of circumstances."

"No, I didn't," she agreed as she got to her feet. So the food wouldn't go to waste, she handed Sa the rest of her chicken, feeding him directly. The stunned looks on the brothers' faces improved her mood slightly.

"How the hell do you do that?" Grim asked.

"What can I say? I just have a likable personality," she said, rather than admit she'd bribed her way into the feline's good graces. Grim just rolled his eyes.

"Feel better, Blanche," Abaddon offered as she left the kitchen. And just before she was out of earshot she heard Grim's baffled, "Why the hell do you let her do that, but I can't even touch you, huh?" It was enough to lift her spirits a little.

Now she wasn't sure what to do with herself. She wasn't in the mood for reading or movies, but she also didn't want to hide in her room. The music room was an option, but she didn't know how to play any instruments. So she ended up wandering. Down one hallway, up some stairs, down another hallway and back, down the stairs.

Hours passed as she simply drifted through the castle, somehow not managing to run into anyone, even Sa. The solitude wasn't unwelcome, not now. She had a lot on her mind. Missing her family was top of the list, of course, but it wasn't alone. Then there was Bjorn's death. She'd been asked to help investigate, but her resources for doing so were beyond limited. Other than attempting to summon his soul, she didn't have anything else. She didn't know the reapers, and she wasn't free to travel like the others were. It would be nice if she could, though. To be able to just think about it and, say, teleport herself to, say, the tower when she needed a good spot to think and relax.

The world shifted around her and she stumbled. Her hands flew out to catch herself, but rather than smacking against a wall, they landed on the railing of the tower. Dizziness threatened to send her to her knees, so she gripped the stone railing tightly as she fought to stay upright.

What in the fuck had just happened?

She had just been in the hallway outside the library, she was sure of it, so how had she managed to end up here? She had *never* been able to teleport, and she'd tried for a full century to figure out how after Mira had started doing it. Now she'd just thought about doing it and…had? It made no sense. There was nothing that would have just granted her that ability. Maybe she hadn't teleported. It could be she'd just walked up here on autopilot and not remembered the time between here and there. That was a more likely scenario.

The dizziness slowly passed, and she breathed out a breath, leaning fully against the railing. Seriously, what was going on with her? Weird dreams? Lost time? What was next? Would she randomly turn into a purple-suckered monster? Would her clothes disappear in front of large crowds?

She heard footsteps on the stone stairs behind her and turned. Grim stopped when he spotted her and shoved something into his back pocket. Cocking her head, she wondered at the guilty look on his face. What the hell had he just hidden from her, and why did he look like she'd caught him dipping his hand in the till?

"Sorry. Didn't know anyone was up here. I'll leave you alone," he said before she could speak, and disappeared just as quickly.

That was definitely suspicious. And as much as she liked both twins, she could only think of one thing at the moment that would make anyone in this castle look guilty. But as easily as that thought slid into her mind, it was harder to push it out.

Looking back at the jungle side of Cindatha, she debated what to do. She didn't want to say anything to Death. Not yet, anyway. She'd seen what he'd done to that one reaper—Ralph, wasn't it? Okay, so he had proof that Ralph had been guilty, but while Death was looking for justice for Bjorn, she was well aware of how quickly a search for justice could turn into a witch hunt. The last thing she wanted was for Grim to die because she'd jumped to conclusions.

Why the hell did everything have to be so complicated here? And why the hell did the reapers have to be so damn human? In all honesty, they weren't anything like she'd expected. Not their origins, not the way they acted, not how they organized. Not that any of it was necessarily bad, but everything in her world had been flipped upside down and she felt like she was never going to find her footing.

Shaking her head, she decided she needed to get out of the castle for a bit. Now that she didn't have to worry about the souls, she thought a walk with Sa at her side was just the thing she needed.

If only all her problems were so easily solved.

While Blanche was agonizing over her family and Grim's suspicious activity, Death was back at work spying on his reapers. It had started to feel wrong, like he didn't trust them, but he couldn't afford to let affection for their species—or for specific individuals—make him miss the killer.

He bounced around the world—and Cindatha—watching them as they worked, as they relaxed, as they spent time with humans, Arcane, and other reapers. Once more, he learned about his reapers, and mostly, he was happy for that fact. Antonia apparently had been dating a jinn for a while, though he wasn't sure if she'd been honest about being a reaper or not. It didn't matter too much to him. He wasn't about to restrict them from revealing themselves to loved ones like that. Keeping their existence secret was largely just a matter of convenience, not necessity.

Then there was the threesome he'd accidentally popped in on. He could have done without knowing firsthand that three of his reapers were in an intimate relationship, and quickly teleported elsewhere.

One of his reapers was doing some moonlighting as a cat burglar, and Death made a note to have words with him later, but a little crime was a much lower priority at the moment.

He'd been at it for most of the day when he teleported to Chris's house. The man lived in a secluded home that most would term a mansion. A small one, to be sure, but still a mansion. He stood in the kitchen, preparing a drink and talking to himself. No, Death realized, he was using one of those earpieces that had become so common on Earth.

"No, he doesn't know anything. Uh uh. No, just that it's one of us." He paused to shake whatever drink he was making, oblivious to the fact that Death was only feet away, his anger starting to build. "Yeah, he said he destroyed the knife as soon as it was done, so there's nothing to lead any of us back to Bjorn's death." Chris laughed and shook his head as he poured the cocktail into a glass, unaware that his free, extremely cushy life was about to end.

Fuck, there wasn't just one killer. He had a conspiracy brewing right under his nose.

Death moved closer but didn't reveal himself right away, waiting until Chris hung up, not wanting to give further warning to the other traitors.

As soon as the phone was disconnected, Death dropped his invisibility. At the same time, he grabbed Chris by the throat. The glass slipped from the reaper's fingers, shattering on the stone tile floor. It was gratifying to see the man's eyes widen and his face pale with shock.

A face that soon turned red when Death lifted him off his feet by his throat, cutting off his air supply.

"I don't know anything, do I?" Death asked in a silky, dangerous tone.

"Death," Chris choked out, but Death's hand tightened and cut off further words.

"You know your life is forfeit now, don't you?" He smiled darkly and cocked his head. "But if you cooperate—and weren't the one to slice Bjorn's throat yourself—then your soul might escape. I somehow doubt it, though."

Without another word, he brought them both to the castle and directly into one of the cells. They were impossible to escape from, as the doors only opened from the outside and he was the only one who could teleport from them. Once they were inside, he threw Chris from him, not minding one bit when the reaper hit the wall then collapsed against the floor. He stayed there, sucking in breaths as one of his hands went to his throat. He was scared, Death could see that clearly enough, but there was more than fear in his eyes. There was anger.

Death folded his arms over his chest and shook his head as he studied the man who had lost all right to the gifts he'd been given four hundred years ago when he'd accepted Death's offer. "Why? Why kill Bjorn? From all accounts, the man never did any lasting harm to anyone."

Chris was either braver—or dumber—than Death thought, because he got to his feet and stood defiantly, his chin lifted as though proud of his actions. "Because he was a weak, selfish bastard who thought of nothing but the next fight, next pint, and next pussy."

Death scoffed. "That's hardly a reason to kill someone. Do you know how many people—and I'm including humans, Arcane, and reapers in that—who feel the same? As long as they don't hurt anyone, what does it matter? It's their life. Let them live it."

"Yeah, you'd say that," Chris muttered. "He didn't deserve to be a reaper."

"Neither do you. And after today, you'll never be one again."

That chin lifted a little higher. "Maybe not. But you'll never find out anything from me."

"You forget who I am," Death warned, his power starting to creep out and toward Chris.

Chris smirked and crossed his arms as well. He didn't seem worried, though it was hardly a secret that Death could slip into the minds of the reapers. And that worried *him*. "And you are too arrogant to see what's right in front of your face."

It took only seconds for Death to understand why Chris showed no fear of the intrusion of his mind. Because Death was finding nothing. Not a single thought, which should be impossible. No one—*no one*—should be able to hide from him. Even worse, Death's magic didn't seem to touch him. Reapers were made up of his magic. There shouldn't be any way that any of them would be invulnerable to him. Hell, even *gods* were susceptible to his powers.

"What have you done?" he asked, masking his apprehension with a cool facade.

Chris only smiled and leaned back against the wall of the cell.

"Don't think you'll be escaping this cell ever again," Death warned as he strode out of the cell and slammed the door. On the other side of the thick wood and metal, he heard Chris laughing, and for the first time that he could remember, felt fear.

CHAPTER 18

Blanche was getting sick of these weird dreams. As she drank her first cup of coffee and hand fed Sa his morning snack, she decided she was going to spend her day distracting herself. No more wandering aimlessly, no more watching movies, no stressing about investigating something she wasn't equipped to investigate. She could explore the area around the castle again, but that would just be another type of wandering.

No, she realized, there was something here in the castle she was curious about. Something she'd found the first day and hadn't quite gotten out of her head. The tomb.

She'd avoided going near that hallway since Death had taken her there, knowing she'd feel drawn to it again, which was a little weird even for her. Being comfortable with death, being familiar with it, was very different from being pulled to a tomb. So maybe if she investigated it, figured out who had been laid to rest there and what the symbols on the sarcophagus were, then she could put it behind her.

A few days ago she'd spotted some empty notebooks in the library, and she went there now to retrieve one along with a pencil. Sa, of course, followed along, but when she entered the hallway the tomb was in, he stopped and sat, letting out a pitiful sound better suited to a house cat than a tiger.

"Sa?" She moved back to him, running a hand over his head. "What's wrong?" He butted his head against her stomach, but that was the only response she got. "It's okay. I'll be back in a bit," she told him. Though such acts of affection weren't really her thing, she bent and kissed his head before she walked down the hallway to the tomb. The room Grim had acted so oddly about. She got the feeling he didn't know much about it, but he was acting odd about several things. It was part of why she needed a distraction. The thought that one of her only friends here might be a murderer was not one she wanted living in her brain.

Blanche pressed her hand against the door and felt magic surrounding it, but it just felt like Death's power. The same power that infused every inch of the castle. It was strong, of course, but that power didn't hide the pull she still felt, or the near dread she felt emanating from the room.

Curiosity won out over her instinct to run and she pushed the door open, stepping inside. Nothing had changed in the weeks since she'd been here, but she hadn't really expected it to. It was still just the two torches and stone platform with the ceramic sarcophagus set atop it. For a few minutes, she did nothing but study it from the doorway. Why the hell did this one tomb freak her out? She'd been in half-collapsed catacombs. Had opened cursed caskets. Hell, she'd spent several days in the Paris catacombs putting ghosts to rest. But this single, apparently harmless sarcophagus gave her the creeps. It was time to find out why.

She opened the notebook and moved closer, her eyes moving over the writing on the lid. Each symbol—or they could be letters, she supposed—was precise and as clear as if they'd been drawn into the clay only yesterday. On the plus side, it meant she wouldn't have to struggle to figure out what anything was, just what they meant.

Very carefully she begin to draw the symbols in the notebook, making note of where each line or image was located. It was a pretty alphabet, regardless of what language it was. Every single letter was made up of swirls, straight lines, or both. There were a few pictographs, too, though they could have just been crude pictures. Hard to tell, so she'd copy them as best she could. She was hardly an artist, but she took her time, even if she wished she had her phone so she could just take pictures. Though once, when an image was giving her trouble, she set an empty page against the lid and carefully rubbed the flat of the tip of the pencil over it, making a negative of the picture.

After the lid, she moved to the sides, but it only took a few minutes of doing the first side before she sat her ass on the ground. No way was she going to crouch or kneel for as long as it would take to copy everything. Even her body had limits, and this thing was a good six feet long and three feet high.

When she was done copying every symbol, she'd return to the library and see if there was a book on whatever language this was. Her guess was it was extremely old, because while she was hardly a linguist, she'd been in enough burial sites to have seen dozens of ancient languages, and she'd never seen one quite like this one. Since languages tended to be remembered for far longer for the Arcane than they did humans, that said a lot.

The process of copying the writing became soothing somehow. She could still feel the off-putting aura the place seemed to give out, but for the first time in weeks, her mind was actually calming. Oh, she wasn't at peace by any stretch of the imagination, but better. And she hadn't thought of Bjorn's death or Grim's odd behavior in more than an hour. Okay, so her back was starting to ache, and her butt had gone numb from the hard stone, but she could handle physical discomfort.

She was still sitting on the floor, working on the second side, when Death found her.

He hadn't seen her in two days and couldn't prevent himself from seeking her out again. She made this whole Bjorn situation easier. Not good, but she was definitely onto something with the whole distraction thing. It made things more bearable. That was before he'd realized she was in the tomb. He'd immediately teleported himself there, invisible at first so he could see what she was doing.

As he watched her painstakingly draw the letters onto the notepad, he frowned. Not because of what she was doing, but because he'd expected to be angry—furious even—for finding her in here. But for some reason, he just wasn't. Instead, he leaned against the wall and took the opportunity to watch her when she believed herself to be alone. With her guard down, her face was subtly different. Gone was the wariness in her eyes, the stiff set of her shoulders that was a physical manifestation of her stubbornness. In fact, other than her eyes being bright and clear, she looked as relaxed as she had after they'd kissed.

She intrigued him, and he couldn't say he particularly liked the fact, but could admit that it was true enough. Nor could he say it was just her appearance that drew his interest. She was lovely, of course. The dark hair, fair skin, and those eyes filled with intelligence were absolutely pleasing to the eye. Her body—at least what he could tell of it—was equally enticing. He'd felt some of those soft curves for himself, but knew there was strength in those slim limbs as well. Even her voice, with the lightly roughened, husky quality was appealing. But there were other women just as beautiful physically, if not more so.

He liked how she wasn't afraid of him. It wasn't something he was used to. Even Grim and Abaddon had a healthy dose of respect for him, and they'd lived in the castle for what felt like an eternity. But not Blanche. She would pester, she would ask for things others would never dare, and she didn't seem to do anything halfway. But again, she couldn't be the only woman in the world with those qualities, so what was it about her that made her...special?

Blanche set the notebook in her lap and straightened, pressing her hand against the small of her back as she stretched out stiff muscles. He took that as a sign to reveal his presence.

"You won't find anything on that language in the library, if translating it is your intention."

To her credit, while her back went rigid, she didn't jump. Turning her head to bring him into her line of sight, she arched a brow. "Why not?"

"Because pretty much everything that language was written on has long since been destroyed or worn away. Only a few texts remain, and they aren't in my library." They were in his workshop and bedroom, but she didn't need to know that.

Her nose wrinkled in disappointment as she glanced down at the pages she must have spent a good two or three hours filling. "Well fuck." She sighed and flipped the notebook closed before she set it on the floor and stood. "Can't blame me for trying, though, can you?"

"No," he decided, "I suppose I can't. Everyone needs a hobby, and yours does seem to be harassing me."

That actually made her grin. "I'm pretty good at it, though. And it's good for you. All work and no play, right? Except instead of making Death a dull boy, it makes you the ultimate serious one, which isn't good for anyone."

He arched a brow. "You don't think death and the afterlife should be serious?"

She made a thoughtful noise in her throat. "To an extent? But isn't the afterlife just a second life? And one with no time limit on it? Aside from reincarnation, anyway, right?" she said, and he nearly smiled. It was clear she was fishing on that last statement, and he decided to throw her a bone.

"No time limits, no. Not everyone is given the opportunity to reincarnate, and in the other parts of Cindatha I tend to let the god or gods in charge decide who gets the chance, but it generally comes when someone is ready or needs it. Their slate is wiped clean, their memory is wiped clean, and they get a chance at a second, brand new life."

It seemed like she'd been thinking that was the case, because she looked entirely too pleased at his answer. Of course, she then had to do some of that harassing he'd accused her of making her hobby.

"So what's up with this tomb, anyway? Who's in here?" she asked, laying her hand over the lid. Curiously, she didn't actually touch it, but hovered just an inch above it.

"No one you need to worry about," he said, his tone stern enough he hoped she'd drop the subject. She did, but dove directly into another sensitive subject.

"Can you tell me about your scythe, then? It's kind of iconic, and there are all sorts of rumors about it. Of course, there are all sorts of rumors about you, too." She smiled mischievously. "I was almost disappointed the first time I saw you when you weren't a skeleton or old as fuck man."

"Those rumors came because reaping and drunkenness don't go together. And no," he added as she opened her mouth, "I was not the one drunkenly reaping."

"Pity. But yes, your scythe?"

He debated for a moment, but there wasn't really anything she could learn about the scythe that would cause him any trouble, and it was a safer option to discuss than the occupant of the sarcophagus.

Summoning the scythe, he brushed his thumb over the smooth wood. "This was a gift, a long, long time ago."

Blanche shifted from one foot to another as the death energy in the room increased. It still wasn't uncomfortable, but she wanted to get her hands back on that scythe. She'd held it once, but back then it hadn't radiated anywhere near the power it did now. It was like being in Death's possession had charged it or something. "From who?"

His finger tapped against the wood for a moment. "How about I tell you the story, and if you have any questions when I'm done, then you can ask." Smirking, he added, "Though I don't promise I'll answer them."

"Of course you don't," she said dryly. "But yeah, that sounds fair."

"I didn't always have the reapers. At one point, I was the only one bringing the souls to Cindatha. Then I recruited the gods and gave them pieces of the realm. For a time, it was enough. The world's population back then was small enough that we could handle the number of deaths that occurred each day. But as both humans and Arcane continued to fill the Earth, there were soon more souls than there were people able to ferry them from Earth to here. The problem was, I didn't have any real way of getting help. I could have given other gods the ability to travel between the various realms within Cindatha, but that's a tricky process as gods can't always be trusted—as I'm sure you know. And the Arcane? Too many of you have a lust for immortality, power, and knowledge, so you weren't much better. Which left humans. Except they have a very limited lifespan, and being gifted powers like that doesn't generally work out well. Their bodies or minds tend to reject the power in some way."

Blanche already had questions, but bit her tongue. Not because she really wanted to obey his suggestion, but because she was afraid if she interrupted, he'd stop, and she wanted to know more about the scythe. She'd suffered too much because of that thing.

"You may or may not know that each and every species of the Arcane was created by one group of gods or another. The Lemurians created witches like yourself. The Celts created the banshees, the Greeks the vampires, and so on."

Blanche had absolutely *not* known that, and was dying to know more, but remained silent.

"Doing that was probably my best bet, but the problem," he said with a wry smile, "is that my powers revolve around death. I can create anything here in my realm, but I can't create sentient life. And while

I could have asked one of the gods to help, that would have imbued reapers with their power, not just mine, which was not acceptable. Not only did reapers need my powers in order to do the job intended, I also didn't want another god having a hold on them." He shook his head. "It's hard enough listening to some of the gods complaining that reapers can just come and go in their realms as they like, and without that god's permission."

"Sounds annoying," she agreed. "Especially since all their realms are your realm."

"Mmhmm. So I went to the only ones I believed could provide me with an answer, and they gave me the scythe. With it, I *can* create life. I transformed the first seven, to make sure my new reapers could do what was needed and to give me immediate help, then I used the scythe to..." He took a moment to search for the words. "I suppose the easiest way to explain it would be placing a magical gene in humanity. A recessive one. The rare human would be born as more. They'd be born as a reaper—or a potential one, in any case. Able to handle the powers needed, both physically and mentally."

Blanche should have realized that was what he was leading up to, or at least had an inkling, but she'd been so interested in the rest of what he was saying that she was a little blindsided. "Wait a sec. So you're telling me that Death's scythe...probably the most feared weapon in the world, the one rumored to be instant death to any it touches, the one that can claim souls...is an instrument of life and *not* a weapon?" she asked, her brain trying to short-circuit.

He chuckled and shook his head. "Isn't a scalpel both a tool of healing and a weapon? Very few things in any world are only one thing, and my scythe is no different. It can absolutely kill, it can snare and hold souls, it just also has the ability to allow me to create life."

She was getting information that any necromancer—and a lot of other Arcane—would kill to get, but there were two things that she couldn't quite figure out. "Who had the power to be able to create something like that, though?"

Death sighed and leaned the scythe against his shoulder, careful to aim the point away from him. "Have you heard of the Anunnaki?"

"Yeah...either they're a group of some sort of Mesopotamian gods, or aliens who came here to teach humans or something."

A startled laugh burst out of Death and she stared at him in shock. She'd heard him laugh, but never an uncontrolled one like that. She just didn't get what was so funny about it.

"They're not aliens. And while several Mesopotamian cultures tried to claim them, they're not Mesopotamian."

"Then who are they?" There was actually an amused glint in his eye, which made her brace.

"They are the three beings who created everything. And when I say everything, I mean literally everything. The universe, Earth, the gods, the humans, the animals. Cindatha. They are the creators."

Her brow furrowed. "Wait, what? But what about the stories about how the Earth and all that got created?" Every culture had one, and a few of them shared extremely similar stories about it. Then there was the scientific theory.

He shrugged and twisted the shaft of the scythe so the blade swung lightly back and forth. "They're just that; stories. Gods are generally extremely egotistical, and since they rely on worship to maintain their powers, they want their worshipers to believe they are the reason everything exists. Trust me, though. It's all a lie. Just like it's a lie that Hades, Hel, and all the others are the supreme powers over death."

That did honestly explain a few things. A dozen vastly different stories about the creation of the Earth couldn't all be correct, after all. But had it really been created by three people who were barely known?

"Okay, so you know these...Anunnaki, and you just went and asked and they gave you this scythe?"

"Essentially, yes."

"So I'm guessing it's more powerful than you're really letting on?"

"I don't know about that. Being able to kill, create a new race, and gather souls seems fairly potent to me."

Which brought her to her other question. "Then why did Brigit and Rune have it? Why would you ever let it out of your sight? And if you did, why not give it back to these Anunnaki?"

"The Anunnaki? They are...not like other gods. They are the three primal forces. And I do mean primal forces. Not like gods of the sea or wind or anything like that. I mean the very things needed to create life, to create a universe. They are Time, Fate, and Chaos, the very building blocks of our universe. Without those, then there couldn't be the sea or wind, there couldn't be life or anything else. And it's not always a simple matter to deal with them. Brigit and Rune were two people I trusted to keep it safe, but we ended up having a...falling out, we'll say."

She would not say that Mira had died because he was having a fight with his friends. She would not get angry with him about that. But she'd damn sure think about it later, when her mind had stopped spinning. That, and she'd learned to read his facial expressions well, and something about this conversation had upset him. And bringing up the recent past wouldn't help either of them. Especially not when she found she wanted to comfort him. She was starting to hate that reaction, even as it grew stronger. He had so much on his mind, and she just wanted to ease it for a while.

The thought had no sooner occurred to her than the tomb around them disappeared, and she found herself in her bedroom. With Death.

CHAPTER 19

Eyes narrowed, Blanche looked at Death, not immediately catching the surprise on his face. "Why did you bring us here?"

He shook his head as he looked around the room. "I didn't."

She rolled her eyes and crossed her arms over her chest. "Right. So we're just randomly teleporting around the castle?"

Rather than answering her, he asked, "Where did the dresser and canopy come from?"

His tone was too serious for a question like that, and banked her annoyance. She'd thought he'd done it, but if he hadn't, she needed to know. "I don't know. I thought someone was trying to be nice, making the place more homey. Grim or Abaddon, maybe?"

"No, it wasn't them. They can't enter your room without your express permission—or mine."

She didn't think he was lying, but if it hadn't been him, and it hadn't been the only two other people in the castle, then how had it happened?

Death sent the scythe back to wherever he stored it and moved closer to her. "I take it teleporting isn't one of your powers?" Wordlessly, she shook her head. "And have you teleported before? Here in the castle, I mean?"

She started to say she'd never done it at all, but remembered how she'd gone from the library hallway to the tower. With what had just happened, she had to wonder if maybe it hadn't just been autopilot and lost time. "Once," she said in a small voice, "I think."

He scrubbed his hands over his face before sighing. "I didn't make any changes to your room, and I didn't bring us here to your bedroom. You did."

Blanche stumbled over to the bed and let gravity pull her down onto it, a hand holding onto the post to keep her in a sitting position. "Okay, the teleporting…maybe. A new power manifesting after a couple of centuries is totally possible." Though highly unlikely. "But how in the hell could I possibly change my room? That's like…manifestation or something, isn't it? That's a god ability."

"Not always," he murmured, but he was just as concerned as she was. Things were not adding up when it came to this necromancer. First she could get into a tomb that literally no one but him had ever been able to open, and now she was popping around his castle and changing it? Even Abaddon and Grim couldn't affect his castle like that, and they were the two most powerful reapers alive. They could teleport within the castle, but only because he'd specifically given them that ability.

He also didn't like how her skin was now a pale grayish shade. Had this been one too many shocks? While the Arcane tended to be able to handle things better than a majority of humans, everyone had a limit, and he was worried she'd just reached hers. At least it didn't seem like she was having another one of those attacks, but shock wasn't really any better.

Crossing to her, he sat on the bed beside her. Doing the only thing he could think of, he slid an arm around her shoulders and pulled her in against his side. She accepted the comfort easily, but it didn't seem to be enough. "Distract me?" she asked.

That was something he knew well how to do, and her soft plea lit a need within him. Without hesitation, he lifted her onto his lap. With his other hand, he tilted her face up, then crushed his mouth to hers. She met him full force, her hands fisting in his shirt as her lips parted. Their tongues didn't stroke or explore so much as they dueled, both of them seeking relief from all the things that had been weighing on their minds. Before, their kisses had been...not timid, but soft, like they'd been learning each other. Those kisses hadn't been expected, hadn't been intentional, and neither had even been certain they liked each other. This one put all those doubts behind them.

His hand dropped from her chin to grab her ass, pulling her in tight against him. She showed her approval by both moaning and squirming on his lap. Since that rubbed her over his instantly hard dick, it brought out a groan of his own. It had the additional effect of making him forget every reason why he hadn't touched a woman in so long he'd all but forgotten what it felt like.

Blanche was fully on board with his form of distraction and reached down, grabbed his shirt, and pulled it up. Their lips parted just long enough for the fabric to be tugged over his head before they were diving back into the kiss. Right now, he wanted her more than he wanted to find Bjorn's murderer, so unless she said no, he wasn't stopping. He was past pretending that he wasn't drawn to her, and with the way she felt at the moment, he didn't even care about any possible consequences. She just needed to say yes.

He fisted his hand in her hair and drew her back just enough so they could truly look at one another. "Either tell me to stop now, or it doesn't end until I'm buried inside you," he warned.

Her answer was silent and unmistakable. With her eyes fixed on his, she tugged her own shirt up and, once he released her hair, got it off and tossed it carelessly to the side. Even better, she wasn't currently wearing a bra.

Death had known she'd be sexy beneath her clothes, but the sight of her breasts, the nipples already tightened with arousal, undid him. He growled low in his throat and lifted her higher so his mouth could tease one of those taut peaks. She moaned and grabbed his hair with both hands, holding him against her. He sucked, he teased, he even gently bit, and she made the most amazing sounds. Sounds that had his cock throbbing in his confining pants.

He used to be a skilled lover. He'd had finesse and patience, had known how to play a woman's body as easily as he now played the violin. The skill might still be there, but the patience had evaporated the moment he'd seen all that fair skin on display, had heard her whimper with need.

Using his magic, he vanished her pants and panties. He left his on, knowing he'd never be able to wait if they were both naked, and while he might be impatient, he refused to be selfish. With her nude and on his lap, he needed to touch her, to make sure she was as ready as he was. He might be Death, but the last thing he wanted to do was hurt her in his rush to have her.

He repositioned her so she was on her knees, straddling his thighs. It put her at the perfect height for him to give her other breast the same attention the first had received, but also spread her legs. His resolve was sorely tested, as she was only inches from his cock, but he ignored his demanding body to focus on hers. Sliding his fingers between her thighs, he groaned against her skin at how wet she was. Gathering that moisture on his finger, he pressed it firmly against her clit and drew harder on her nipple. She gasped and her hips jerked toward his hand.

Her body was ready for this, for him. He could fuck her now and they'd absolutely both enjoy it, but something held him back. There was a desire to make her come first, to let him watch her as she found that release. He could only thank the universe that she was so damn responsive to him. At this point, he wanted her so badly it was physically painful, and it was killing him to hold back.

When his hand shifted down, he slid one long finger inside her while the heel of his hand rubbed against her clit and she cried out. Yanking his head back, she bent hers forward to claim his mouth for another kiss. All too willing to oblige, he kissed her like he was never going to stop, and right then, he wasn't sure he would. His hand rocked against her, into her, pushing her body closer and closer to release. He loved the way she reacted, moving against his hand, kissing him harder as she clung to his hair and her body started to tighten.

When the climax hit, when he felt her clench around his finger, felt the fine trembling of her body, he couldn't stand anymore of the torment. If he wasn't inside her now, he was going to lose all traces of control. Sliding an arm around her, he stood and turned to press her back against the thick post of her bed, relieved it was smooth and rounded so it wouldn't hurt her.

Death made all his clothes disappear as he shifted his grip so he was supporting her by her hips, and she cooperated by sliding those legs around him. He looked into her eyes, saw that content look he immediately loved seeing on her, then drove into her, stopping only when she'd taken all of him. Her sharp cry drowned out his low groan as her body sheathed him so perfectly. He could feel the aftershocks of her orgasm, and his fingers tightened on her hips as he fought his body's instincts, that desire to come instantly. This may have started as a way to distract her, but it had become something more. Something important. He wasn't going to act like a teenage boy with his first girl. No, he wanted to brand this moment in his mind, on her body. On their souls. And he tended to get what he wanted.

Few could resist Death, he just hadn't had any idea how much he'd love it when he and Blanche stopped resisting each other.

When he was sure he wouldn't embarrass himself, he started to move. There was nothing slow, gentle, or tame about how he took her. He slammed into her hard, over and over again, savoring the way she felt moving over his sensitive flesh. It was fortunate she didn't seem to mind him being rough, because he didn't think he had any other way in him at the moment. With each thrust, she gave him delicious moans and gasps, her hips bucking to meet his, to drive him deeper, harder within her.

It was when she wound her arms around his neck and kissed him hard, kissed him like he was a person and not just a convenient dick—not just the ruler of death—that he lost it. Making a sound that was barely human, his thrusts quickened as his mind emptied of everything but her. Her hips would probably be bruised in the morning, but he couldn't make himself loosen his grip at all. Couldn't stop pressing her against the post.

Then he felt her starting to flutter around his cock and his power swelled and began to fill the room. When he came, it was with a roar of satisfaction he'd long since forgotten he could feel. Shoving his hips forward, he ground his pelvis against hers, not caring that his power had probably just blasted through most—if not all—of the castle. How could he, when the pressure against her clit had pushed her over to the edge? He couldn't remember a single thing that had ever felt so sweet as her clamping down around him while he poured himself deep into her body.

Dropping his head to her shoulder, he breathed heavily as he tried to recover. Not an easy task, as even his legs didn't quite feel steady. Unwilling to do something embarrassing like drop her, he managed to take one step to the side, then fall forward onto the bed, catching his weight with one hand.

"Gotta unwrap your legs if you want me off you," he mumbled. He was tired now, but felt better than he had in...Hell. Even the gods probably couldn't remember back that far. He certainly couldn't.

"Don't wanna," she protested, tightening her legs.

Chuckling weakly, he patted her thigh. "I need to lie down, too," he reminded her.

Wrinkling her nose to show how much she disliked the idea, she loosened her legs and let them slide over his hips and to the bed.

Slowly drawing out of her, he gritted his teeth because he wanted to do that all again. Instead, he dropped onto his back beside her. He hadn't shown any control before, but he could now. No matter how good she'd felt, how right being inside her had felt, he wouldn't be ruled by his cock.

For a few minutes, they both just lie there, staring up at the canopy as their bodies recovered from the brief, intense round of sex.

"That...was not what I expected when I asked for a distraction," Blanche admitted, voice still breathless.

Death let out a short laugh. "Not what I was expecting to use for a distraction," he said, "but it worked, didn't it?"

"Definitely." She went quiet for a minute. "Are things going to get weird now?" she asked.

It was a good question. The problem was, he didn't have an answer. At this exact moment he didn't think so, but he wasn't sure if it was because he was still riding the endorphins, or if it was what he truly thought.

"I don't know," he finally said. "I'd like to say no, but my powers are all related to death, not telling the future."

She nodded like she'd expected that answer. "Be right back," she said, pushing herself out of bed. Her legs were a little shaky yet, and he didn't bother to hide his smile as she made her way into the bathroom.

By the time she returned, he was sitting up and had put his pants back on, though he hadn't picked his shirt up yet. As she walked toward him, he noticed something he hadn't before. Something that made him feel sick and as though jagged shards of ice were running through his veins.

Reaching out, he drew her closer and turned her slightly. "What's this?" he asked, tracing the mark high up on her thigh, almost to her hip. It was distinct, a small circle with two little arcs coming off it, almost like the symbol humans used for hurricanes. No bigger than a penny, he doubted most people would have paid much attention to it.

Blanche looked down and shrugged. "Just a birthmark. Literally been there since I was born. Why?" she asked, frowning lightly at him.

He forced himself to smile as he shook his head. "Just curious," he lied, and to further distract her, he leaned in to press a kiss against her belly. When she made a tiny sound, he almost pulled her onto the bed for a second round, but that birthmark...

"I've got to go. I still need to find out who killed Bjorn," he told her as he got to his feet. His fingers brushed over her hip—over that birthmark—before he made himself release her.

"No, I get it. It's important," she agreed, and he was oddly relieved that she sounded like she understood. "Good luck. I hope you find the bastard, because he deserves everything you'll do to him."

"That he does." And because it seemed wrong not to, he kissed her—gently this time—before disappearing. But he didn't go back to the prisoner or the search. It was to his room. He needed to figure out what that mark meant—if anything—before something worse than the death of a reaper happened.

Several hours later, when Blanche slept, it was fitfully. She didn't remember the entirety of the dream she had, but she remembered the grief, then an unexpected joy, followed by a feeling of utter shock and betrayal. After that, all she remembered was blackness. Nothing more than that, just complete and total blackness, with no sound, no sensation. Yet, rather than being terrifying, it was rather peaceful.

Yet, when she woke, it was with confusion. One day, she hoped she'd understand these dreams, but until then, she'd just chalk it up to an overactive imagination.

CHAPTER 20

Death hadn't done a damn thing to try to find Bjorn's murderer. In fact, he hadn't done much of anything since he'd woken this morning. Though he'd been well rested—good sex did that—his mind had been anything but peaceful.

He'd left his room early that morning, not wanting Blanche to easily find him while he tried to sort out his thoughts. Then again, if she was able to teleport around the castle and subconsciously alter it to suit herself, it might not matter if he was in his throne room, bedroom, or his workshop. Still, he hid himself away in his workshop and tried to figure out what it meant that Blanche had that particular birthmark.

Though it took a large amount of the right kind of alcohol for him to get drunk—something he often considered a waste of time—he'd been working on reaching that state all day. After five hours and six bottles, he was finally getting close.

There was a knock on his door and he frowned at it. "Come in." His mind was just fuzzy enough for him to need a minute to remember that the door would only open to his hand. Pushing to his feet with a sigh, he moved to the door and opened it, frowning at the man standing on the other side. "Abaddon? Is something wrong?"

"I was going to ask you that, actually," he admitted. "I called for you a few times, and you've never not responded, even if it took you a little while."

Death shook his head and walked back to his chair, dropping into it and reaching for the glass half full of divine liquor. "Maybe? I mean, it could be, but I don't know." He grimaced and tossed back a healthy swallow of the alcohol. "Could just be a coincidence, but it's kind of an unusual birthmark. Not sure what the odds of that are."

Abaddon stepped inside and shut the door behind him, shaking his head in confusion. "I don't understand. What birthmark? Whose? And why would a birthmark be a problem?"

Death stared into his glass for a while, but the issue weighed heavily on him. He couldn't tell Blanche, but he needed to get it out. Who better than his second in command? Of course, the alcohol was probably loosening his tongue more than he might have liked, but did it matter? He gestured with his glass to the only other chair in the room. "Did I ever tell you I had a wife once? Centuries ago, of course. Long before the reapers ever existed."

Abaddon's jaw went slack, his eyes widening slightly. "I had no idea," he admitted as he took the seat. "What happened to her?"

"I killed her," Death admitted flatly before downing the rest of his glass. "Right after I gained my powers."

It took Abaddon a few tries before any words came out. "I'm not sure what to say. I think you regret that, but without more information..."

"It was an accident," Death confirmed, setting the glass on the table and glaring at it. "I never would have harmed her if I'd had a choice. I loved her."

Abaddon nodded slowly. "Why didn't you resurrect her, then? It's a simple enough task for you, and you said it happened after you had your powers."

Death laughed, but it held zero humor. "Because her soul disappeared when she died. I've always thought I managed to kill both her and her soul at the same time. No real way to confirm that, of course, but I never found a trace of her soul anywhere on Earth or in Cindatha." Though he also wasn't sure he'd recognize it if he had. The one brief moment he'd encountered it, he hadn't understood what he was, what he could do. Hers would have been the first soul he'd encountered, if he had actually interacted with it in any way.

"I'm so sorry, Death. I can't even imagine how horrible and traumatic it must have been for you," Abaddon murmured.

"That's an understatement. I'd just died, just became Death, then killed my wife. Nearly drove me crazy."

"I think it would have done the same for anyone. I don't understand why you're telling me, though. Or what that has to do with a birthmark."

"My wife had a birthmark," Death said as he picked up the bottle, but set it down again instead of pouring more. "A very distinctive one. Last night...I noticed that Blanche has the very same birthmark, in the very same location."

"I...you said you thought you had killed your wife's soul. With Blanche having the same birthmark, are you thinking it was just waiting to be reincarnated instead?"

"It's the most likely scenario, even if I don't understand how. If her soul hadn't died, then I should have been able to find it. You know there isn't a soul in Cindatha I can't find, but I was never able to find hers."

Abaddon nodded slowly, like he was trying to understand everything. Death wished him luck, because he didn't. "Did you tell her?" he asked.

Death shook his head and leaned back, lightly pounding the side of his fist on the arm of his chair. "No. I couldn't. How would that conversation have gone? 'Oh, by the way, I think you might just be my dead wife reincarnated. Want to pick up where we left off?' I doubt that would have gone well."

"No, probably not," Abaddon had to admit. "Is there not a way you can confirm your suspicions? You can read souls as easily as others read a sign."

"Not sure," Death said with a shrug. "Normally, sure, that's not an issue. But with this? It's not exactly a situation I've been in before."

"So what are you going to do?"

"I have no fucking idea. The smart thing would be to just ignore it, especially since Bjorn's killer is still running around. That has to take priority over a possibility all based on a birthmark."

"I'll do what I can to help with that," Abaddon promised. "You have Grim and myself for a reason. Let us deal with that investigation while you try to figure out what's going on with Blanche." He gave Death a tiny smile. "It's not like you've taken a personal day in a few thousand years. I think you're entitled to at least one, don't you?"

"Maybe you're right. Thanks, Abaddon."

"You're welcome." He rose, but touched Death's shoulder for just an instant before he left the room, shutting the door behind him.

Alone again, Death once more considered the remaining alcohol in the bottle, but wasn't sure it was the answer. Unfortunately, he had a feeling he knew what the answer was, and he didn't like it.

It wasn't fair to keep Blanche trapped here in Cindatha. She was alive, and the living—reapers and gods aside—didn't belong here. Perhaps more importantly, it seemed that Bjorn's death was part of a conspiracy, and that meant it was dangerous for her to be here. If she was his wife—and he strongly suspected she was—then he couldn't bear to see her die again. Yes, she would die at some point since she was mortal, but dying of old age after a long, full life was vastly different from dying as a result of murder or an accident.

And nothing said that he couldn't find her once she'd returned to Cindatha in the normal manner. Though quite a bit could happen—could change—in a few hundred years. Not just for her, but for him as well. His attraction to her could simply be because she was a novelty. The first living woman in his castle, the first person to stand up to him. The first person to treat him like he was a normal person. Nevermind that he hadn't touched a woman in a few thousand years. He hadn't been completely celibate since his wife, but he'd lost interest after a few partners. For the most part, the women who made advances had only wanted to sleep with him because of *what* he was, rather than who. Blanche saw him.

No, she wasn't a novelty, even if she wasn't his wife reborn. And truthfully, it was entirely possible she wasn't. Yes, she shared the same birthmark, and now that he was letting himself remember his wife, he realized their appearances were remarkably similar, but Blanche could simply be a descendant of one of his wife's relatives. That could potentially account for those similarities. Especially since their personalities were vastly different. His wife had been full of laughter and joy, always willing to help people, happy to compromise. But she hadn't been a pushover, oh no. She'd had a temper on her, she just hadn't released it except in rare circumstances and usually on someone else's behalf.

And he'd loved her so very, very much. Which was why he couldn't take the chance. If there was even the slightest chance Blanche might be her, then she had to go back to Earth, back home where it was safe. Just...not yet. Tomorrow. Tomorrow he'd send her home.

He picked up the bottle and took a healthy swallow, knowing it was going to be one of the hardest things he'd done.

Blanche was surprised when she hadn't seen Death by mid-afternoon. True, he wasn't a typical guy, and this was far from a typical situation, but she'd still expected to at least see him for a few minutes after one of the hottest bouts of sex she'd ever experienced. On the other hand, he wasn't the most social of people, and he was dealing with a murderer, so she tried not to take it personally. Mostly, she failed.

Besides, she finally had something to investigate. Okay, so Grim acting a little suspicious wasn't a lot, but it was the first real hint of anything she had to go on. And even if he wasn't involved in the whole Bjorn situation, he was still hiding something. So what was it? Was it something personal? Embarrassing? Against Death's rules? Or did he really have a hand in Bjorn's murder?

Gods, she hoped not. She really liked the guy. Abaddon, too, but Grim was just more laid back, which meant he was a bit more fun. But fun, she knew, didn't mean he wasn't hiding an evil streak.

She started to go in search of him, but was reminded of the conversation she'd had with Death right before their clothes had come off. If he was being truthful, she had been the one to teleport them. Which meant she could do it now...if she could figure out how. So why not try to kill two birds with one stone? Teleport directly to Grim, eliminating the need for a search and proving Death's theory. Except, if Grim was guilty, she didn't really want him knowing she could teleport. Which meant she needed to be careful.

Closing her eyes, she tried to remember what she'd done or thought right before she'd teleported. The only thing she could think of was a desire to be in the place she'd ended up. Thinking that she wanted to be right outside where Grim was, she cracked an eye open. Nope, she was still in front of her bedroom door.

Blowing out an annoyed breath, she closed her eyes and tried again, this time *pushing* her magic into the thought. There was a slight sense of vertigo, which made her eyes pop open, and she grinned broadly.

She'd moved! Now she was standing in the hallway, just outside the kitchen. Peeking in the open doorway, she saw Grim standing by the coffee pot, his phone out, a grimace on his face. His other hand was fisted around something, but she couldn't tell what it was. There was a flash of gold, but that was all she could see.

"Everything okay?" she asked, keeping her voice friendly and as normal as possible as she stepped inside. No reason to let on that she suspected anything.

His head jerked up, and he quickly shoved the object into his pocket. His phone followed a moment later. "Yeah. Well, as okay as it can be with a murderer on the loose, anyway," he said with a weak smile.

"Still haven't heard anything?" she asked as she joined him at the coffeepot and poured a cup for herself.

"Nope. Not from the reapers or Death."

"I really would have thought someone would know something," she said, turning and leaning back against the counter, sipping her coffee. "Do you think the murderer really covered their tracks that well? Or do you think they could have scared anyone who might know something that much? I mean, they've already proven they not only can, but will kill reapers."

He pulled his coin out and started rubbing his thumb over it as he thought. "I'm not sure. Don't cops say that there's no such thing as a perfect murder? Of course, they deal with human culprits, and reapers have a lot of tricks up their sleeves that humans don't. Hell, they have some they Arcane don't have."

Blanche wasn't entirely sure about that, but she didn't know enough about what reapers could or couldn't do, so didn't argue, just let him continue his train of thought.

"Reapers also don't tend to be timid or passive. Even the ones who weren't warriors prior to accepting Death's deal all have a spine. He doesn't make the offer to those who can't do the job. Which means I don't think a reaper would be scared of another reaper." He frowned. "Or they might be, but even if that was the case, they could have appeared instantly in the castle, and you've seen how quickly Death can neutralize a reaper who's gone...bad."

Unfortunately, that all made sense to her...unless the reaper they were scared of lived in the castle. Then she could see someone being hesitant to drop by. What if a reaper had shown up, but Grim had found them before Death had arrived?

"Do reapers have family? Or even close friends, perhaps who aren't reapers?" she asked.

"A lot of new reapers try for relationships, even marry or have children, but it rarely lasts," he admitted. "And before you ask, it's not the job, it's the immortality. They end up watching their family die of old age, then have to see them here in Cindatha. A few reapers have gotten involved with other reapers for that reason, because it's safer. They know reapers won't die on them. But all that said? Yes, some reapers have family, and some of those families aren't reapers themselves. Why?"

"Because there's one thing guaranteed to make someone do something stupid, and that's protecting or saving someone they love." She gave him a crooked smile. "I'm living proof of that. It's how I got here, remember? I just wanted to save my sister, and I was willing to go up against Death to do it."

Understanding hit him and he nodded. "So someone might have seen something, but is saying nothing because they might make it here, but they may not get to their family to protect them before the killer does. Yeah, that might do it. Problem is, we can't definitely guarantee the safety of any family, if that's even the case."

"Why not? You said Death could handle the reapers."

"And he can, but think about it. The witness would have to get here to the castle, call Death, explain what's going on, then get back to his family. That leaves at least a few minutes where the killer could get to the family. And it only takes a moment to slit someone's throat, which seems to be the killer's preferred method."

More logic, but it unfortunately was more reason why it could be Grim. The instant any witness showed up, he could go to their family and be back before Death could show up. It also didn't prove anything.

"No one has any idea why Bjorn would be killed, either? Wouldn't knowing the why lead to the who?"

"It would," he agreed, "but we don't have any way of learning that. And before you ask, yes, we've searched Bjorn's house. Myself, Abaddon, and Death have all been there. I think even Darius checked it out."

Blanche took another drink and wished she was better at this. She had no idea what questions would lead to him slipping up—or proving his innocence. Hell, she wasn't sure why she was trying. She was equipped for dealing with ghosts and tombs, not living murderers.

"How have you been doing?" he asked, still toying with the coin. "It seems like you've gone from one upheaval to another. Getting brought here, then all of us dealing with Bjorn's death. Must seem like everything is kinda crazy around here."

She couldn't argue with that. "Bouts of insanity, yeah. Not sure I can say I've really settled since things have to...be normal, I guess, for someone to settle. But I'm starting to get the hang of most of it, I guess." More than just getting the hang of it, but this conversation hadn't made her feel any better about him knowing about her new-found power. Which meant continuing to keep a secret. "And there are definitely parts of Cindatha that are beautiful. I really should leave the castle more, but with a murderer on the loose..."

"Mmm. Yeah, I think I'd be a little wary of doing that, too. The castle has protections on it, but Cindatha? Outside the castle, any reaper can wander as they like. And unarmed, untrained in fighting, it wouldn't be a fair fight."

"I'm not exactly untrained," she protested, but she knew that compared to the warriors he'd mentioned, she was a rank novice. Like most of the Arcane, she had trained enough to let her fend off human attackers, but the Arcane not only had magic tricks up their sleeves—literally—the ones who were serious about it had longer to train. Centuries instead of decades.

He seemed to guess her train of thought because he only smiled. "Just be safe. No need for unnecessary risks."

"I won't. In fact, I think I'm going to grab a book from the library and go back to my nice, safe room and read a bit." Because it sounded like the safest place to be in the castle if she wasn't with Death.

"Enjoy. And let me know if you want to hang out and watch another movie."

She made herself smile. "I will." Setting her coffee cup in the sink, she did just as she said, but it wasn't a novel she selected from the library, but the journal of the reaper she'd spotted days before. It was the only thing she could think of to give her insight into reapers without asking someone who might be guilty of murder. And the only thing that might distract her from thinking too hard about what it had been like the night before. But she sincerely doubted it.

CHAPTER 21

Blanche read for a while, showered, then curled up in bed once more with the book. When she reached the end of the journal, she admitted to herself that it hadn't really helped her with the current issue, but she did understand reapers a bit more. Unlike the Arcane, whose powers varied greatly even within the same race, the reapers all had the same powers. Some were more powerful than others, but the powers themselves didn't vary.

They could all travel between Earth and Cindatha at will, regardless of where in Cindatha. Not even the gods could prevent a reaper from entering their realms—which included not just those in Cindatha, but the divine realms like Valhalla and Olympus. Then, of course, they could see and collect souls, even pulling them from a body. None of that was really news to her, though she did find it interesting that they could sense other reapers. What did surprise her was that they could feel nearby deaths. Not just sense them, but literally feel them. The sensations were muted, according to the journal, but she didn't imagine even a muted slice to the throat or gunshot to the gut would feel good.

While it was hard for Blanche to deal with the ghosts death left behind, she thought it was far better than the deal reapers had. Especially since she wasn't worried about possession any longer.

After setting the journal aside, she snuggled down into the bed and sighed. She had to hand it to Death, the beds here were extremely comfortable. Even when she was in hers alone. Still, mind full or not, she was able to drift off without too much trouble.

Hours later, she began to slowly come back to consciousness. The first thing she noticed was a warm, hard body lightly pressed against the front of hers. The second was that a finger was tenderly tracing over her face. Sliding from her forehead, down to her cheek, along her jaw, then finally, across her lower lip.

She gave a sleepy smile as she opened her eyes and met Death's pale blue ones. "Hey," she murmured.

"Hey," he echoed, letting his thumb brush lightly over her lips once more before he slid his arm around her.

She scooted closer to him as he ran his hand up and down her back, making her sigh in contentment. It had been too long since she'd enjoyed this kind of affection from a man, but she didn't think it had felt this...meaningful. Because it did now, and because she wanted more, she leaned in and pressed her lips to his. He groaned and teased the seam of her lips until she opened for him. And his kiss...Gods, she could kiss this man for hours and never get tired of it or him. And though she'd only had him inside her once, she had a feeling she could quickly become addicted to the way he felt. The way he made her feel.

Just the kiss, nothing more, managed to speed her heart and she could feel herself going damp with desire. But as much as she wanted more, she'd almost be satisfied just to do this. Almost.

His hand then slid down beneath her shirt. The feel of his rough fingers sliding over her belly made her sigh, but when those calloused fingers brushed her nipple, she moaned. He didn't let up, but continued to kiss her like he'd never stop while he teased her breast.

"Death," she whispered, pressing into his hand.

He made a low noise to show he'd heard her, but didn't respond verbally. He didn't need to. Instead, he rolled her onto her back and used his powers to strip them both of their clothes. When he slid over her, she whimpered at the sweet friction of skin on skin, but he didn't immediately join his body with hers. Rather, he opted to either tease her or enjoy her for a little longer. She both loved it and hated it, but couldn't resist rubbing against him, reveling in the feel of his hard body and warm skin.

After kissing her again, his mouth trailed along her jaw toward the sensitive spot just behind her ear. She shivered and slid her arms around him as he nuzzled, then slid a little further down to gently bite her neck. Goosebumps broke out over her skin, but he wasn't done. He continued to work his way down until he reached her breast. He sighed as he brushed his lips across her nipple, one of his hands dropping to her hip. His tongue slid over the tight peak, then he gently blew on it. At the same time, his hand slid between her thighs and his finger brushed over her clit. She gasped and her hands curled, pressing her nails against his back. He growled softly against her breast before he slid his finger deep into her.

"I want it all, Blanche," he whispered before taking her nipple into his mouth and drawing firmly on it, right as his finger curled, hitting just the right spot. The combination of the two made her hips buck against his hand. And he didn't stop. He added a second finger to the first and she started to rock, unable to keep herself still while he was playing her body more skillfully than he'd played the violin. Somehow, this man who literally embodied death knew more about giving her pleasure than anyone else she'd been with. It didn't make sense, but she wasn't going to think too hard about it.

Her body began to tense as her climax approached, and though he lifted his head, his fingers didn't stop. Meeting her gaze, he smiled, a softer, more human expression than she'd ever seen on him. "That's it, *arami*, come for me," he breathed.

The strange word felt so familiar and sparked an emotion in her she couldn't identify at the moment. It also pushed her body into that first orgasm. Arching, clenching around his fingers, she cried out, unable to look away from him as her body trembled. She gripped him tightly, unable to make herself release him as she spasmed around his fingers. Gasping, she moved against his hand, trying to make the feeling last as long as possible.

A minute later, when the climax began to fade, she expected him to replace his fingers with his cock, but to her delight, he opted to slide further down her body. He kissed his way down her chest and over her belly, making her breathing quicken with anticipation. The fact that he didn't look away from her as he worked his way down somehow made the moment that much more intimate. Even her skin seemed more sensitive just because of that.

When his head was above her pelvis, she found herself holding her breath in anticipation. His tongue stroked across her folds and she had to fight her body's urge to let her eyes drift closed. She couldn't bear to miss this, couldn't bear not to hold his gaze when he started to tease her clit. When his tongue delved into her, causing her to arch against his mouth, she gave a soft cry.

"Give in," he murmured. "I meant it. I want it all." Though the caress of his mouth remained tender, he was also merciless. He teased, he plunged his tongue into her, he tormented her clit, until she had come twice more and was a writhing ball of need and ecstasy, on the verge of begging him to stop. But he didn't, not until he'd wrung one more orgasm from her deliciously abused body.

He kissed her belly and gave her a moment—just one—to recover before he moved back up her body until his cock was pressed against her entrance. He waited until she was able to lift her eyes to his before he pushed into her slowly. The feel of him sliding into her was the most exquisite thing she'd ever felt. And she'd never felt more connected to anyone in her life than she did when she was fully joined with him.

He whispered her name, his hand resting on her cheek. His thumb brushed across her skin before he drew his hips back, then surged forward. In that moment she saw stars, though she'd always thought such things existed only in romance novels. "Death," she moaned, lifting a hand to the back of his head so she could pull him down for another kiss, wanting them to be connected as much as possible. Nothing seemed more important in that moment than doing her best to become one with this man who wasn't truly a man.

Death took her mouth hungrily as he thrust into her, slow, hard, and deep. Each stroke threatened to steal her breath, but she didn't dare ask him to stop. Not when it felt like each one was bringing her closer and closer to the most intense pleasure she'd ever felt. More, it felt like she was easing closer to something infinitely more important, she just wasn't sure what. But whatever it was, she wanted it desperately.

Their bodies moved together in a way that felt utterly natural. As if this wasn't the second time they'd been together, but the hundredth. The thousandth. And while she might have expected such skill from some men, it was surprising from a man as cold and controlled as Death. Apparently, that stoicism masked an extremely passionate man. No one else had ever touched her like she mattered quite like he was. And she realized in that moment that she was starting to fall in love with him.

The thought was swept away as he quickened his pace, his body tensing as he started to get close to his own climax. He pulled his mouth from hers and stared down into her eyes as he pounded into her, driving her body crazy with the things he was making her feel.

"One more, Blanche. Give me one more," he said, the tone of his words a tender counterpoint to the clear demand.

"Death," she gasped, as her body tightened, then detonated. Her world went black as an overwhelming pleasure poured through every cell of her body, temporarily rendering her blind. Not that it mattered. She could focus only on the sensations as he pumped into her a few more times, then groaned her name as he joined her in that moment of ecstasy.

He ground against her as his body released inside her own, then collapsed over her, with only one elbow keeping the bulk of his weight from crushing her. Though admittedly, she couldn't have cared less at the moment. For a few minutes, it was doubtful she would have noticed anything but the sensation of his body pressed to hers.

It took a little while longer before he had the presence of mind to move off her, but it seemed he wasn't willing to give her up entirely, because when he rolled, he drew her along so she was stretched across his body. Smiling, she rubbed her cheek against his chest and sighed in absolute satisfaction.

"I see you were doing a bit of light reading before bed," he said, his voice hushed.

It took her a moment to remember what he was talking about, then she nodded. "A bit. I want to understand more."

"Did it help?" he asked, sliding the tips of his fingers along her back.

"A little," she admitted. "Answered some questions about your reapers. Not a lot about you."

His hand stilled, then slid down to her backside, gently squeezing. "Is there something specific you want to know?"

There was quite a bit she wanted to know, but in her sex-addled state, she could only think of one thing that didn't involve her. Under normal circumstances, she probably would never have dared ask, but at the moment she felt like she could ask him anything.

"Were you always Death? I mean, were you born as Death, like the gods were born?"

He sighed and tightened his hand for a moment before he reached over to draw the covers over her. It was such a thoughtful gesture that she smiled.

"No, I wasn't always Death," he admitted as she shifted a little to rest her hands on his chest, with her chin atop them. "I was human once."

Her head lifted sharply, all traces of fog washing away with shock. "How did a human become Death?"

He smiled sadly and brushed her hair back from her face. "It's not a happy story. Are you sure you want to hear it?"

For a man who had just gotten laid, his words had an ominous ring to them. Yet she couldn't find it in herself to choose the safe route. She wanted to understand him. To understand why he was the way he was. "I do," she said quietly.

He nodded, but urged her head back down to his chest. She could only conclude that this was a tale easier to tell without eyes on him. "I was one of the first people to ever live. Not the first, but one of. There were a few thousand of us, living in different settlements of a few dozen to a few hundred. We weren't as primitive as history portrays us, because we were close to the gods and the Anunnaki. We were, for all intents and purposes, the ancestors of the Sumerians and most everyone else. But we were normal people. We hunted, we farmed, we lived, and we loved." He drew in a slow breath, released it on a sigh. "But for all we knew, all the knowledge we'd learned from the gods, there were things we didn't know. Couldn't know."

"Like what?" she asked, her voice a bare whisper.

"Like death. You see, none of us had ever died, so we didn't know we could. The concept was just...alien to us. We hunted animals, as I said, but we didn't understand that animals were alive, just as we were."

She didn't like the sound of that, though a world without death sounded like both a paradise and a hell. But since she knew people died now, their ignorance couldn't have lasted long.

"We didn't know death, but we did know injury," he went on. "One day, I was out hunting. I thought I was alone, but a man I'd believed to be my friend followed me. When we were away from our village, he stabbed me with his spear. I didn't understand back then, but he had to have hit something vital. All I knew then was that I was in pain, getting colder and colder, and my vision was going black. I was scared and confused."

"Then what happened?" she asked when he stopped.

His thumb brushed over her cheek. "Then...I died," he said simply. "Except I found myself in nothingness, as no being had ever been in Cindatha before, so it was just empty. I'm still not sure why I came here automatically, since every soul since had to be carried here. Either way, I had the dubious honor of being the first person not just to die, but to be murdered."

"That must have been terrifying," she murmured as she tried to imagine what it must have felt like.

"It was. I had no idea what had happened to me, where I was, or why my friend had betrayed me. But I wasn't there for long. Not alone, anyway."

"Did someone die right after you?"

He shook his head. "It took a bit longer before anyone else had died. No, I was joined by the Anunnaki. All three of them. And they all apologized for what had happened to me. Ananke for not foreseeing it, Chronos for not being able to take it back, and Tiamat for the chaos that had inspired it all."

Blanche frowned as she heard the names. "Wait, I know two of those names. Chronos is a Greek god—or titan—and Tiamat is a Sumerian goddess, right?"

His lips curved. "Don't you remember how I told you the Mesopotamians claimed the Anunnaki as their own, but that they weren't actually Mesopotamian?"

"Yeah..."

"Well, Chronos and Ananke—who the Greeks claimed as their goddess of inevitability—aren't Greek, and Tiamat isn't Sumerian. They're all the Anunnaki. The creators of the gods. I do believe they're the parents of a few, too. Not just the creators, but the actual parents. Regardless, they apologized and wanted to make it right. They couldn't undo it or bring me back, not without breaking their own laws, but they realized that being the first person in Cindatha had done something, to both me and Cindatha."

"Did being the first one make you into Death?" she asked, lifting her head. It seemed a little too easy and kind of anticlimactic, so she couldn't quite believe that was it.

"No, but it bonded me to Cindatha in a way they hadn't expected. Which left two options. They could leave me alone, to linger there by myself until others died, or they could build on what Cindatha had done to me. They decided to give me power over Cindatha and the souls that would come here. Their way of making amends, they said. Because back then, they were very involved in the lives of humanity and the gods, so they knew me and they felt true remorse."

"It's hard to imagine gods—though I know they aren't really gods—being like that," she admitted.

"Even the gods you know of as cold or callous weren't always that way," he explained. "The Arcane live for a about a thousand years—with a few exceptions, of course. A few of the gods you know of are older than I am. We all change with time, and the millennia can wear on a person and alter them drastically. Back then, the Anunnaki were already old, but they had a sort of renewed vigor with the creation of beings to share the universe with them. They'd found, for lack of a better term, their humanity. Or it might be that they'd found their purpose."

"So you were murdered and the creators of everything made you the ultimate power over death as an apology?" she summed up.

"Essentially yes."

"That's a hell of an apology." And a little terrifying. Didn't that mean that Death was as dead as the souls who resided here? Or had he been able to resurrect himself? It could also be that he was essentially the prototype, different from those who came after. It seemed like a cold question to ask, especially with his body so warm under hers, and the sensations he'd made her feel still echoing through her body.

"I suppose you could say that."

There was something sad in his eyes and she was sorry she'd brought it up, though she was happy he'd shared that with her. Not just because it showed a level of trust in her, but because she wanted to know about the man she'd just shared a bed with.

Wanting to erase the sorrow, she shifted over him. Her knees settled on either side of his hips and she leaned up to kiss him, a brief, sweet kiss. "Thank you for telling me," she whispered before deepening the kiss. He hesitated a moment before he returned it, and she was sorry for that. Determined to erase the bad memories, if only for a moment, she braced her weight on one hand, and used the other to stroke over his chest.

She wasn't sure if his body had been frozen in its prime when he'd been killed or if he worked out now, but she loved it. Toned, muscled, delicious. Her fingers trailed down over his stomach and she felt the muscles twitch.

They continued to move further down his body, until her hand brushed against his hardening shaft. The simple touch made it stiffen, and when she wrapped her fingers around him, he groaned and arched into her grip.

Seeing no point in delaying, in denying them both what they wanted, she eased herself down onto him and they gave mutual moans of pleasure. Since she wasn't prepared to give up his mouth, she could only rock against him, but it was enough. His arms came around her, holding her tight as they moved in the dim light. Their first time had been frantic, intense. Their last time had been tender but still intense. This? This was more like coming home. The goal wasn't to give pleasure, but to share it. To share themselves. This time, when she came, it was like a sigh sweeping through her. A gentle wave that lifted her up, then eased her down.

When she stilled above him, both of them breathing a little harder, she didn't make any move to shift off him. She simply rested her head on his shoulder and drifted off to sleep. And for the first night in a week, she didn't dream.

CHAPTER 22

When Blanche woke, she expected to find Death gone, but he was still beneath her, his lids heavy, but his eyes open. A hand lazily slid up and down her back, and she sighed in contentment.

"Morning," she murmured, nuzzling the side of his neck, reluctant to get up and lose whatever this was.

"Morning," he answered.

A few minutes later, her body forced her to leave the bed. She dealt with her morning necessities before joining him, tossing on a tee-shirt before she sat on the bed. He was sitting up and had redressed. His expression was also serious, sending a flood of apprehension through her.

"Is everything okay?"

"I'm breaking our deal."

She wasn't quite awake enough for this. "Deal?"

"The deal we made when I agreed to give you the means to bring your sister back to life."

A cold shiver went down her back. "Are you going to kill Mira?"

"No!" He shook his head. "No, my end of the deal will remain intact. Your sister will live until she's meant to die. Naturally. What I meant was your end. I'm sending you home."

Her fear for Mira's life morphed and grew infinitely more complicated. She wanted home, wanted her family. She'd been dreaming of ways she could manage this very thing, and now he was just giving it to her. But she was torn. Part of her wanted to stay, and not just because of last night. Not even wholly because of him. The parts of Cindatha she'd seen were gorgeous, and she'd become friends with Grim, Abaddon, and Sa. She wanted to see out the investigation into Bjorn's death.

And she very much wanted to see where this thing with Death went, if it went anywhere. If it *could* go anywhere.

Then there was the timing. Why was he doing this right after they'd slept together? It hadn't been bad, she was certain of that, so...why? Did he regret it? Did he see it as nothing more than a mistake?

"Why?"

"You were never supposed to accept the deal, Blanche. I didn't want you here. When I came to you, made the offer, I was completely expecting you to refuse it. It seemed insane to even consider that anyone would have accepted. You should have refused and left me in peace. The living don't belong in Cindatha. They certainly don't belong in my castle. *You* don't belong in my castle."

"You say you didn't want me here, but then why...last night..."

He got to his feet and looked down at her, his eyes as cool and distant as they'd been when she first met him. "You may not have noticed, but there are no other women in the castle, and the reapers may as well be my children."

She had just been a convenient hole for him to stick his dick in? Seriously? Yeah, some guys were like that, but she'd honestly expected more from him. She wasn't sure why, but she had. And the fact that he'd used her made her royally pissed.

"You've got to be fucking kidding me," she muttered as she shoved off the bed and went to the wardrobe, grabbing out a pair of black pants. She yanked them on before she turned back to him, but she stayed where she was. If she got too close, she might do something unwise. Like punch Death or set him on fire. He might have given her some leeway in the past, and sure, they'd slept together, but she didn't know if he'd forgive a literal attack. "I thought you were better than the mortal assholes who will do or say anything to get a woman in their beds. But no, you're just another fucking piece of shit."

The asshole merely shrugged and folded his arms over his chest. "You're the one who nagged and begged until I gave you what you asked for. Now I'm just removing an annoyance from my life."

Her eyes narrowed, but he was done with the conversation. Before her mouth could open to release a torrent of angry words, she felt an instant of vertigo before she found herself back in her bedroom on Earth. A second after that, the mummification knife appeared on her dresser. No doubt the rest of her things were back where they belonged as well, but she was too pissed to check.

"That rat fucking bastard!" She wanted to throw something. She wanted to hit something. But since she was back at home, surrounded by her own things, it wouldn't do anything but further piss her off. It didn't stop her from pacing as she vented her hurt and rage with every insult she could think of. To think she'd started to trust him. To like him. To fucking start to *love* him. But no, he was just another jackass. And what had she expected from a man who'd shown absolutely no remorse when his laziness had resulted in the death of an innocent woman?

Her stream of profanity attracted attention, and a few minutes after she arrived, her bedroom door opened. Aidan's face appeared in the crack of the door before he let out a curse of his own. Ducking back out of the bedroom, he shouted, "Blanche is home!" He shoved the door open and half ran across the room until he could scoop her up in a tight embrace, lifting her clear off her feet. "You're back! You're alive!" he said, hugging her so tightly she was genuinely worried he was going to break something. Not that she told him to stop. It was too good to see her family again, even if it was Aidan, who was the champion of annoying her. But that's what big brothers were for.

"I'm fine, I'm good," she promised as she hugged him back.

He set her on her feet only for another pair of arms to grab her, whirling her around then pulling her into a solid chest. Her eyes filled as she looked up into the beaming, tear-filled expression of her father. "Hi, Dad," she whispered as she pressed her face against his chest and let her anger flow away. Death might be an asshole, but Mira was alive and Blanche was with her family. It was everything she'd wanted a few weeks ago when she'd first summoned Death.

So why was there sadness lingering under the other emotions? Why did she want to cry?

It wasn't long until Mira and her mom found them, but Elliot refused to let her go, so Blanche found herself in the middle of a slightly uncomfortable group hug. She loved it.

"Let the girl go, Elliot," her mom finally told her dad, rubbing his back, though her other hand was clasped in Blanche's.

Reluctantly, he obliged. "Where the hell have you been?" he demanded, wiping his damp cheeks without a hint of shame. "I know you said Death's house, but...where?"

"If I told you Cindatha, would any of you know what I meant?" Blanche asked, the question a genuine one rather than a deflection.

The expressions on their faces told her they were all as clueless as she'd been. Blowing out a breath, she sat on the edge of the bed, resigned to the fact that her mom wasn't going to release her hand anytime soon. "Apparently all underworlds, afterlives, and all that are actually one realm, just split up into sections. The name for the place as a whole is Cindatha. It's also the name of the...area...that is solely under Death's control. That's where I was, in his castle," she explained.

"Why did he take you to his castle?" Aidan asked suspiciously.

"I told you before, I wasn't his slave," Blanche told him. "Look, he didn't want to bring Mira back, so he made me an offer he was positive I'd refuse. Mira gets brought back, but I have to leave here and never return." Her gaze slid to Mira's face. "He underestimated how much I love my sister. Even when she's a pain in my ass."

"Love you, too," Mira said dryly, but she was smiling.

"If that was the deal, why are you back? How are you back?" her mom asked.

The last thing she wanted to tell any of her family—much less her parents—was that she'd fallen into bed with Death, then gotten kicked out of his house. And despite being pissed at him, she didn't really want to betray his trust by telling them about Bjorn's death—and how she suspected one of Death's top reapers of being the killer. But she had to tell them something.

"Like I said, he didn't really want me there. After dealing with a mortal in his castle for a few weeks, he decided to send me home." It was truth, even if it wasn't the whole truth.

"So you're back for good?" her father asked.

"I'm back for good," she confirmed.

"Did you at least find out anything cool while you were there?" Mira asked, bending down as her snake entered the room and slithered over to her. As a hand was offered, the serpent slid up Mira's arm and coiled about it before Mira straightened. It made Blanche think of Sa again, and she felt another pang of sadness. She pushed it away and focused on Mira's question.

"How about confirmation reapers are real?" Blanche asked, a smile sliding over her lips. She didn't want to betray Death, but that was just too good to keep to herself.

"Are you shitting me?" Aidan asked at the same time Marguerite gasped and Mira said, "Seriously?"

Their reactions were no less than Blanche had expected and made her laugh. "I met a couple of them. Including...Imhotep," she said, gaze settling on her sister.

"Imhotep? Like *the* Imhotep? The Egyptian priest and genius?" Mira asked in awe.

"The Imhotep," Blanche confirmed. "He's kind of a flirt once he makes sure you're not picturing him as a mummy. And turns out? They're all born mortal. Human, actually. Well," she corrected, "basically human. Until they accept a deal with Death to become immortal ferrymen of souls."

For the next hour, she ended up answering questions about reapers—and Imhotep specifically. She didn't mind, though. Her family was as involved with death as the man himself was, so to be able to share information like this was their form of family bonding. It also helped her forget, at least for a little while, the last conversation she'd had with Death.

She needed it, because she knew the reprieve wouldn't last.

Hours later, after Elliot had insisted on feeding her and Blanche had showered and changed into comfy clothes, she found herself sitting cross-legged on her bed, the mummification knife in her hands. It was forever linked in her mind now with Death. She'd used it to summon him, and later to help him. Which meant she needed to decide whether to keep it, sell it, or give it away.

Someone knocked on her door. Though part of her just wanted to be left alone, to sleep and try to forget the last few weeks had happened, she called, "Come in."

Mira stepped inside and closed the door behind her. Like Blanche, she'd changed into a pair of cotton pants and a tank top, and didn't hesitate to walk over to the bed and sit on it across from Blanche.

"What's up?" Blanche asked, leaning over to set the knife on the nightstand.

"A lot," Mira said with a faint smile. "Starting with me wanting to tear you a new one for trading your life for mine and ending with what you didn't want to say around Mom and Dad."

"I didn't trade my life," Blanche argued, hoping she could distract Mira from the second half of her comment. "I mean, here I am, just two weeks later. And I didn't die, I just...spent a vacation in the underworld. It actually has some gorgeous spots, you know?"

"I'm sure it does, and you can tell me about it later, but you won't distract me," Mira said firmly. "You had no idea you'd be back here. You thought you were signing up for an eternity in that place. Cindatha, right?"

"Yeah, Cindatha."

"So, for all intents and purposes, you were bringing me back for a few hundred years in exchange for millions of years in that place."

Blanche sighed and slumped back against her pillows. She was getting tired of being reamed out for that. It was done, and she'd argued her point several times. Doing it again served no purpose. "First, we're all going to be there in a few centuries and be there for millions of years unless we reincarnate. Second, if our positions had been reversed, can you look me in the eye and honestly tell me you wouldn't have done the same thing? Would you really have just let me remain dead?"

Mira hesitated. "I don't know. I do see your point, and don't get me wrong, I'm thrilled not to be dead, but it's going to take some time for me to get over it, you know?"

Since she did, Blanche nodded. "Yeah, I know."

"Then we'll table this for a while, but I do still want to know what you were holding back. Because I *know* you were holding back something. And if you try to deny it, I'll sic a couple of ghosts on you."

There was one thing Blanche had forgotten to share, and maybe it would be enough for her to keep Death out of this conversation. "Sic away. I did pick up one little trick while I was there." She smiled and had no doubt it was a broad, cat-ate-the-canary smile. "I can't be forcibly possessed anymore. I have to allow them in before they do anything to me."

Mira's eyes widened and she leaned forward, gripping Blanche's ankle. "Are you serious? How? Are you sure?"

This was part of why she'd missed her family so much. Mira knew exactly how hard Blanche's life had been, how many times she'd been possessed without her permission. And she knew, without question, without needing to think about it, just how much it meant for Blanche to finally be free of that threat. It might not eliminate the panic attacks, but it definitely eliminated part of the reason for that panic.

"I'm sure." Death may have misled her about some things, but she found she didn't doubt him one bit on whether he'd done as promised. "I can still deal with ghosts, but I don't have to fear them anymore."

"That's...I don't even have words for how awesome that is! I'm so happy for you!" she said, her smile filled with the same joy Blanche had felt. Then her gaze turned calculating. "And you're trying to distract me. Spill, or I'll do what I can to poke around in your brain."

Blanche winced. Mira's telepathy was far from refined, and she knew from experience that her mental probes hurt. A lot. "I don't want to go into it too much, but...I kind of had a fling with him."

"Him? With Death?" Mira asked in a voice several notes higher than her last words. "Are you fucking kidding me? You get snatched away by Death and you decide it's a good idea to fuck him? Death? The actual Death?"

"Shh," Blanche hissed, glancing to the door and hoping no one else had heard the outburst. "And I didn't just decide. I couldn't stand the guy at first. Yes, he's hot, but he was kind of a dick—still is kind of a dick—but that's not all he is," she admitted, preferring to keep this conversation to everything that had happened before today. "Besides, it's over. I'm back here, and I don't see Death, do you?"

"No, I guess not."

"Well, there you go. But look, I'm tired. It's been a long ass day."

Mira nodded and gave Blanche's ankle a squeeze before she slid off the bed. "All right. I'll give you a pass today." She smiled. "I'm happy you're back."

"Me too." She watched Mira shut off the light and leave the room, then climbed under the covers. Her words hadn't been a lie. The day had been long and trying, so as soon as she found a comfortable position, she fell asleep and into dreams.

She was back in the dark, holding the still figure in her arms, sobbing, but this time, she wasn't alone. Pinpricks of light grew larger, and she recognized them as torches. People were approaching, drawn by her screams. Like her, they were confused, then scared when they realized the man wasn't moving.

Hands pulled her away from the body, though she screamed and fought to hold on to him. She saw others lift his body, even as she was slung over someone's shoulder, and both were carried back to their village. After that, it became hazy, like she was experiencing everything through a fog.

Time passed, though she couldn't have said how long, until she was sitting in her home, staring at the bed she had shared with her husband. The bed that was now empty. That would somehow always be empty. She didn't understand it, but she knew it, without a shred of doubt.

But a miracle happened. He appeared before her, looking as he had the last time she'd seen him when he was warm and moving. His eyes met hers, relief in them, though they were now light rather than dark. Crying out, she stood so quickly her chair was knocked back, and ran to him.

"Arami," he breathed as he met her halfway and reached for her. But rather than the joy she should have felt when his arms came around her, she felt the sharp edge of pain slicing through her. She had only an instant to see horror flash through his eyes before everything slipped away. The sight of him. The feel of his arms around her.

The last thought she had before death claimed its second victim was that she couldn't believe she'd lost her husband then herself—and the baby that had just begun to flutter in her belly.

She woke sharply, trying to shake off the remnants of the dream as she sobbed into the darkened room, her hands covering her flat belly protectively. That had been the brown-eyed Death again. Rolling onto her side, she shoved her face into the pillow and tried to slow her breathing, to push past the sorrow she'd felt so keenly in the dream. She'd never thought about having children before, but the way the end of that dream had felt? Gods...even losing Mira hadn't felt like that. For the first time, she truly understood what people meant when they said something was soul-crushing. Nothing had ever hurt as much, and she doubted anything ever could. And this was just a baby in dreams. It wasn't real.

The tears kept flowing as she curled her body around her belly. Even knowing there wasn't a baby—surely there couldn't be—she felt that loss.

What in the hell were these dreams trying to tell her? And how did she make them stop? She needed to move on from Death, not see him over and over again every time she closed her eyes. More, she needed to stop feeling these intense emotions that had no basis in reality.

Now if she could just get her subconscious to cooperate.

CHAPTER 23

Death lasted twenty-four hours before he had to go check on Blanche. A large chunk of why he'd sent her away had been shock and grief, the rest a desire to protect her. It had been thousands of years since he'd become Death and had accidentally killed his wife and child, but some things were, apparently, impossible to get over. Though he'd honestly believed he had until Blanche had bulldozed her way into his life.

There'd been something about her from the moment he'd first seen her, when she'd nearly passed out after summoning him. It was why he'd been so gentle when he'd caught her and set her on the couch. And that kiss? It had awakened things in him that he'd thought were as dead as he was.

Which was why he was currently in her bedroom in the early hours of the morning, invisible, watching as she dug through her dresser. He wasn't sure what she was looking for, but she was getting more and more frustrated as it continued to elude her.

"If that bastard left it in Cindatha, I'm going to make his life a living hell as soon as I die," she muttered as she shoved the clothes haphazardly back into the drawer, then slammed it. Straightening, she put her hands on her hips as she glared at the dresser. Stomping over to the closet, she yanked the door open and started sorting through those.

He was curious about what she was looking for, especially since he'd sent everything in her room here. Okay, he amended, *mostly* everything. The shirt she'd been wearing when he'd come to her that last time was currently in his bedroom. It smelled like her, and while he was determined to do everything he could to forget about her so she could live out her life, he hadn't been able to give up everything. And, as much as he hoped she'd forget him, he'd been equally as unable to leave her without anything. Though if he was lucky, she wouldn't find the memento he'd hidden for her, not yet. Especially since he'd done his best to make her start to hate him. He wanted to make this as easy on her as he could.

It was the most difficult thing he'd ever done.

But, of course, things rarely went the way he intended. He may have power that most would kill to have, but it was also limited, and foresight was not something he'd ever been gifted with.

As Blanche hunted for whatever she was searching for, she ended up grabbing a dress to move it out of the way. But she must have grabbed it in such a way to feel the hard object in the small pocket of the dress because she stopped and frowned at it. The dress wasn't something that looked like her style—it was lavender and she was definitely a woman who didn't go for pastels—so he'd thought it would be quite some time before she even touched it.

Frustration turned into confusion as she used a finger to pull the pocket open so she could look inside. Still not understanding, she reached in and pulled the object out. She let it rest on her palm as she stared at it. It was a rounded, oblong stone, a good two inches across at the widest point, and an inch at the narrowest. The gem was a dark, dark blue that appeared black outside of direct light, and had a bluish-white starburst on the top. Unlike most star sapphires which only had six rays on the star, this one had twelve. It was rare to find one like it of any size, but it had made him think of her.

Death had seen just how much she'd enjoyed the sapphire cave, and though he'd never before allowed anyone—himself included—to take a single crystal from that cave, he'd felt compelled to give her a piece of it. Maybe he was secretly wanting her to think of him until she returned to Cindatha.

Blanche ran a finger along one of the rays as she frowned at the stone. It was clear the moment she realized what it was because her face cleared and she wrapped her fingers around the sapphire as she dropped her head back and closed her eyes. "That fucking idiot," she breathed, but there wasn't any anger or hatred in the words. She took a few breaths before opening her hand to look at the stone again. "He did it on purpose." Her eyes narrowed and she looked up at the ceiling. "Death, you're lucky you never told me how to contact you without actually summoning you," she called to what she clearly thought was an empty room, "or I'd burn your ears before kicking your ass. Just a convenient fuck, huh? Bet you thought you were protecting me from something, didn't you? Though I have no fucking idea from what."

He watched her walk to the bed and drop onto it and wanted, more than anything, to go to her. To draw her into his arms and tell her she was right. But the fact that she'd found him out in only a day didn't change anything. He'd already killed her once. Yes, he had control of his powers now, had proven he could safely touch her, but the past haunted even him. And Bjorn's murderer was still able to hide, even from Death.

After she was done venting about him being a good intentioned moron, she turned her attention to the sapphire again. Cocking her head, she studied it for a moment, then got up and moved to her dresser with the brisk movements of a woman on a mission. Curious, he followed her. She opened her jewelry box, and though he expected her to put the stone inside and close it, instead she used her free hand to dig around until she found what she was searching for. It was a wide silver cuff bracelet with some kind of knotwork etched the surface.

After studying it closely for a minute, she nodded and he felt her power direct itself at the bracelet. He saw the silver heat, then draw apart in the middle, until it formed a void just a little smaller than the sapphire. Quickly, she pressed the stone against the bracelet, then seemed to use her magic to cool it until the stone was set in the cuff. She tested it for a minute, ensuring the sapphire wasn't going anywhere, then hesitated before she slid the cuff onto her wrist.

He loved seeing his gift on her arm and smiled despite himself. But as much as he'd love to stay with her, he still had a murderer to find. Sighing silently, he took himself back to the castle, and was immediately met by the roar of an annoyed tiger.

Sa had been waiting for him in the throne room, and now that he was back, rose and stalked toward him. The damn tiger had been pouting since he'd sent Blanche home. She really had stolen his companion. For all he knew, she'd stolen his second and third in command, too. Yet he couldn't resent her for that, not really.

"It was for her own good," he told Sa as he briskly rubbed a hand between the cat's eyes. "I'm sure you'll see her again in a few centuries."

Sa didn't look appeased at that, but since Death felt the same way, he couldn't blame him. "You want to come with me?" he offered. "I have a prisoner to question. It's been a few days, so he might be bored enough, hungry enough, or tired enough to slip up."

He wasn't surprised when Sa fell into step beside him. They left the throne room and returned to the cell he'd left Chris in. When he opened the door, his jaw clenched so tightly he was surprised he didn't crack a tooth.

His one lead was dead.

Chris was lying in the corner of the cell, his eyes open and filmed over, a deep gash crossing his throat. While Death wasn't an investigator, he was the expert on death and killing blows. It was painfully obvious that the wound wasn't self-inflicted. Somehow, Bjorn's murderer had figured out he had Chris, gotten out of the throne room, and broken into the cell to kill his co-conspirator. Something else that shouldn't have been possible.

He had a feeling he knew what he'd see, but he still stomped into the cell and bent to rest a hand on Chris's skin. Just like Bjorn, the moment of his death was hidden from him, and he felt no trace of Chris's soul anywhere in Cindatha.

Death let out a roar of absolute fury as he stalked back to the door of the cell, punching the stone wall hard enough to crack it. Sa shrank back, making himself as small as possible. Abaddon and Grim appeared only seconds later.

"What's happened?" Abaddon asked, staying several feet away from Death. Both he and his twin looked leery, but they weren't turning tail and running.

Death pointed into the cell. "I had a prisoner," he said, well aware he was snapping at them, but he was too far gone to care. "He was working with the person who killed Bjorn. I told no one I'd found him, much less that he was locked up here, but somehow, someone knew, got into his cell, and killed him. His soul is gone, too."

Grim started forward first, with Abaddon only a step behind him, and they both looked into the cell. Grim's mouth tightened into a line, giving him an expression that matched his name. Abaddon simply went pale.

"I haven't seen anyone in the castle today but us," Grim told him, staring at the body. "I haven't even seen Blanche."

"There were a couple of reapers yesterday, but no one left the throne room. I saw them leave myself," Abaddon added.

"Even if a hundred reapers were here yesterday, it isn't possible for any but the two of you to leave the throne room without an escort," Death said, wondering if he'd been betrayed by one—or both—of the two people he trusted most.

Grim now went as pale as his brother and shook his head. "I swear, I had no idea he was even here. And if I did, I wouldn't have had any reason to kill him!"

"Neither of us would have," Abaddon insisted. "We've both been doing everything possible to help *find* Bjorn's killer. Why would we do something like this? We've been at your side for most of our lives. Betraying you would be...unthinkable. Like betraying each other."

"Then do either of you care to explain how another reaper was able to bypass *my* security measures and wander the castle without an escort?" he challenged, and in that moment, he almost wanted to wipe all the reapers out of existence and start fresh with those he trusted.

Except, that was essentially what he'd done to begin with, and now he'd been betrayed by at least two of them. That fact would make it difficult for him to trust anyone.

"I have no fucking idea," Grim admitted. "But I also didn't think it was possible for there to be a death you couldn't see. And I've been racking my brain trying to figure out how that was possible, but I haven't thought of anything even remotely viable."

"Nor have I," Abaddon added, and Death had to admit they both sounded earnest. More, he didn't feel any trace of a lie from either of them.

"And you're positive, one hundred percent positive, that you didn't see anyone acting suspicious or anywhere in the castle they shouldn't be?" Death asked.

"Absolutely positive," Abaddon confirmed. "I would have notified you immediately."

"Same here," Grim said. "I've got nothing, Death. I wish I did. Bjorn didn't deserve this. Chris might have if he was in on Bjorn's death, but not Bjorn. And sure as hell not you. You're a good boss."

The absolute sincerity in the words made Death relax, but only slightly. He still couldn't guarantee anything, but they were right. They'd been his reapers long enough for him to give them the benefit of several doubts.

"Very well." He flicked his fingers at Chris's body, and it dissolved to dust. "Let me know if you see or hear anything out of place," he told them before disappearing.

If Bjorn's killer had one accomplice, there might be more. Which meant it was time to spy on more of his once trusted reapers.

CHAPTER 24

Since Blanche had left her room that morning, her family had been hovering. She got it, she did, but she was far from used to having people constantly around her, even when she was at home. Yes, they did things together, but they also spent plenty of time doing their own thing. Apparently, her family had forgotten that fact while she'd been gone.

She managed to deal with it until just after four, then she had to escape. Nowhere in the house would be safe, not with the ghosts and powers of her mom and sister, so she snuck out and disappeared in the woods behind her house. No one in her family was very outdoorsy, so it should be safe for a bit. Which was good, because she had something to do. If Death thought she'd just forget everything that had happened, then he didn't know her very well. And he definitely shouldn't have given her the sapphire.

Her fingers stroked over the bracelet for a moment before she pulled out her phone. There was someone she was sure could help her, but the problem was, she didn't know their name or how to contact them. But she knew the woman who did.

"Hi Blanche. Is everything okay?" Suni asked when she answered the phone.

The concern in her voice reminded Blanche that Suni likely had no idea Mira was alive again. Since she was aware that Suni blamed herself for Mira's death, she forced herself to take a minute to clear her conscience. "Oh, no. I'm good. Um...Mira's alive."

"What?" Suni asked in a shocked voice. "How? When?"

"A couple of weeks ago. I couldn't tell you because...let's just say it was a whole thing. And the how, let's just say I made one more deal with Death."

There was a long moment of silence, but Blanche let it ride. It wasn't everyday someone came back from the dead, so Suni probably needed the time to process.

"I'm not even sure what to say other than I'm happy for you," Suni said when she got her mouth working again. "I know how much Mira means to you."

"She does. And she's okay. Back to normal."

"That's great! Tell her I'm happy she's okay now, and that I'm so sorry she got hurt in the first place."

Blanche shook her head. "She doesn't blame you, Suni. Neither did I."

"I know, but I'm still sorry. You were both helping me get the formula for mithridate. But I don't think that's the reason you called me, was it?"

"No. I was hoping you could tell me who you got those summoning spells from, and put me in contact with them."

The silence this time went on longer. "I can't give you his name, Blanche. I'm sorry, but he needs to be kept anonymous. It's important to the work he does."

Suni sounded like she meant it, but Blanche needed help. Someone was killing reapers, and she needed to prove or disprove Grim's innocence. It would drive her nuts not knowing. And she felt like she owed it to Death to do what she could.

"I got that impression when we were in Egypt, but it's important, Suni. Like literally life and death serious. I can't give you all the specifics, but a good man was murdered, and there's some kind of really obscure magic keeping a friend from finding out who did it. And when I say obscure, I mean they're doing things that shouldn't be possible." There was no immediate answer, so she went on. The longer she spoke to Suni, the more important it became for her to do this. "Please Suni. I can't say I'll do anything, but I'll do a lot."

"I don't know..." But she was softening, Blanche was sure of it.

Her family's reaction to the information about the reapers came back to her and she smiled. She might have a bargaining chip. "This person, they sounded kind of like Julian. Like they enjoy learning things? Especially magical things that are super fucking rare or haven't been known in centuries?"

Suni laughed softly. "Yes. I actually think he's worse than Julian in a lot of ways."

"Then can you just ask him if he'll talk to me? If he agrees, I can give him some information I'm almost positive he's never heard, and I can guarantee its accuracy."

Suni sighed and Blanche bit back a cheer. "I can't promise anything, but I'll give him a call and see what he says. He's kept some of my secrets, so I have to keep his unless he gives me permission."

"I respect that. But if he knew the summoning for Death and wraiths, then just tell him I know about reapers. It should be enough to get him on the phone with me."

"I'll call him as soon as I hang up. And Blanche?"

"Yeah?"

"I'm glad both you and Mira are all right. And that your family can stop mourning."

Suni was the most empathetic person Blanche had ever met. And while she was a little too hippy for Blanche to normally be friends with her, she genuinely liked the witch. "Thanks, Suni."

When she hung up, she felt something she hadn't in weeks. Hope.

"How's Blanche doing?" Evane asked as he walked back into the room. He'd left when he heard Blanche's name, giving Suni some privacy, but now he settled on the couch next to her and slung his arm around her shoulders.

Suni gave a half laugh as she leaned her head against his shoulder. "Considering she got Death to bring Mira back to life? Pretty well, I'd say."

"She did what?" He was just as surprised as she'd been, but after a few seconds he chuckled. "Good for her. He owed her."

"I think she'd agree with you."

"Is that why she was calling?"

"It that why she was calling?"

She shook her head. "No, she wants Erasmus's number."

His brow furrowed. "For what?"

"Not exactly sure. But it sounds like she's got some good information to trade, and whatever the reason, it sounded extremely important to her." Could it be part of that deal with Death that she mentioned? For Blanche's sake, she hoped not. The last deal hadn't exactly gone well. Technically, Suni had gotten what she needed, but the cost had been much higher than she would have chosen to pay.

"So what are you going to do?"

"Call Erasmus and see if he's willing to talk to her."

He nodded. "I'm sure he will. Information is like a drug to him."

It was, so she only smiled as she selected his contact and listened to the phone ring.

"*Parakalo?*"

"Hi Erasmus. Do you have a minute?"

"For my second favorite healer? Of course!"

She grinned. "Just your second favorite?" she teased.

"Well, Sergei lives in the Athenaeum with me, and is generally the one on hand, so if I didn't name him as my favorite, he wouldn't be too pleased, now would he?"

Though his tone was as jovial as ever, there was something off in his voice. Not duress or stress, but a slight tremor that hadn't been there any of the times she'd spoken with him. She had to wonder if he was overworking or had just woken up. And it was silly of her to worry. Sergei was an extremely capable healer, so if there was something wrong, the man was likely already on it. More, Erasmus knew she would be all too happy to help if there was something wrong. Still, she made a note that if he sounded like this the next time she spoke to him, she'd pry. "That's a fair point."

"Most of my points are! But what can I do for you?"

"I have a…request to pass on."

"Oh?" he asked, the single word filled with curiosity.

"A friend of mine just called and asked for the number of the person I got the wraith and Death summoning spells from. Said she's working on something that's life or death and it sounded like she needed information."

Erasmus made a thoughtful sound. "I don't normally just pass out information to just anyone. While I am a librarian of sorts, you know most of the information here isn't anything we want to get out into the world," he said, voice uncertain.

"I know, and after hearing some about what's there, I get that. I even applaud it. But I honestly don't believe she's wanting information for any kind of insidious reasons." She blew out a breath then added, "I should also add that she's the necromancer who summoned both a wraith and Death himself. She also said she could trade information on reapers?"

Her words had flipped a switch and Erasmus went from wary to excited. "She is? And she can? I have found very little about reapers, and after you asked for those summonings, I may have spent a week or so on related topics, including reapers. They're essentially a myth, even to us! And I'd love to speak with the necromancer who was able to summon Death. *Nai*, absolutely I will talk to her. Send me her phone number and I'll call her right now."

His enthusiasm was contagious and she smiled. "I will. And Erasmus?"

"Mmhmm?"

"She said she could guarantee the accuracy of whatever information it is she's going to give you."

He laughed with delight. "Then what are you still doing on the phone? Send me her name and number! And thank you, Suni. You get me such interesting information."

"You're very welcome," she told him before they hung up. She took a moment to text him Blanche's information, then just smiled as she shifted into Evane's lap. "Speaking with that man never fails to lift my mood," she told him.

"Oh yeah? I bet I can lift it even more," he promised, before cupping the back of her head and drawing her in for a kiss. And in the next hour, he made good on that promise.

While Blanche waited to hear back from Suni, she debated calling Julian. He was a smart guy, but from everything she'd heard and witnessed, his expertise was in demons and fighting, not Death and reapers. But if Suni's mystery guy refused to talk to her, she'd give him a shot. Because there was something very weird going on in Cindatha, and the longer it continued, the more invested she became in finding out what it was.

Her phone rang and she glanced at the screen, surprised when it didn't show Suni's name. Instead, it said the number was blocked. Odd. She answered and lifted it to her ear. "Hello?"

"Hello! Is this Blanche?"

The voice was of an older man, cheerful but kind of tired. He had a faint accent she identified as somewhere in Eastern Europe, but she wasn't positive which country. "It is..."

"Wonderful! I'm Erasmus. Suni called and told me you need-ed some information. Are you really the woman who summoned Death?"

"I do, and I am. Thank you for agreeing to talk to me."

"Of course I agreed. When I found that spell for Suni, I wasn't sure it was possible, so you have already done me a great service by confirming its accuracy. I am not about to refuse the information she mentioned on reapers, though. I have very little in my library about them. Just enough for me to be convinced they exist, but not much more."

Blanche had already decided how much she was going to tell him, but she had to make sure it wasn't going to end up shared with all the Arcane. "I do, and I'm willing to share it, but I have to know that you'll be discreet. They've kept themselves largely hidden for a reason."

He laughed, but the sound morphed into a harsh coughing that made her frown. When he got control, he said, "I assure you, there are few on the planet who are as discreet as I am. My mouth is sealed and my mind is a vault. I will document what you tell me, *nai*, but that information will remain secure in my library."

Suni would have warned her if Erasmus had loose lips, so Blanche nodded. "Reapers are definitely real. I've met several of them. And here's something you likely don't have...They were all born human. Human lifespan, very little powers—if any. They only become reapers as you think of them when they accept a deal to work for Death, taking souls to the underworld."

She heard the soft tapping of a keyboard for just a moment be-fore he spoke again, excited now. "They're all human? Never Arcane? You're certain?"

"Heard it from a reaper's own lips," she promised him. "It sounds like accepting the deal unlocks all their reaper powers and longevity. And they come from all over and are definitely immortal." Because he sounded so delighted and so damn affable, she added, "You should also know that every single underworld, afterlife, heaven, or hell is connected. They're like regions of a larger place. Like how Michigan and Vermont are all states in the United States, Hades and Kur and the rest are just regions in *the* underworld."

The sound he made now was incomprehensible, but overjoyed. "That both answers a lot of questions and creates quite a few more," he admitted. "But I am a fair man and you have already given me much to research, which means it's time for me to uphold my end of the bargain. Though I will say that if, at any point, you want to talk to me about anything else regarding this, I will always answer my phone for you. And I don't mean simply you giving me information, either. I'm not a selfish man, even if I am greedy for information. I mean discussing it. This is all so fascinating!"

"I'll keep that in mind," Blanche told him, unable to keep the smile off her face. "And I'm really hoping you'll be able to help me."

"I'll do my best. What is it you need, my dear?"

This was where it got tricky. She'd have to be careful to tread the line between giving him enough information that he could help her, or too much and betraying Death.

"I can't be as open as I'd like, which might make this difficult," she admitted.

"That's not a problem. You tell me what you can, and we'll see what we can figure out," he said kindly.

"It's actually two things I'm trying to figure out. I know they are possible, but I'm not sure how. First..." Blanche closed her eyes and just went with what had been bugging her the longest. "How is it possible to kill a soul? Are there relics? Spells? I know some gods can do it, but I'm not sure what would allow someone who isn't divine to do that."

"That...I can certainly research that," he began slowly, "but I have to be assured that you aren't planning to actually use the information I may or may not find."

Blanche liked him better for that concern. "I'm not. And maybe I should take a step back and explain a bit more of what's going on. A man was killed a week or so ago. I can't give you any details there other than to say that it wasn't just his body killed, it was his soul as well. All signs point to this not being a divine murder, and it was committed by someone who is able to hide what he's done from someone who should be able to read through any lie, see any death."

That was as good as she could get without revealing too much, but she had underestimated just how freaking smart Erasmus was.

"Are you saying that this murderer has hidden his actions from either the reapers or Death himself?"

Blanche let out a short laugh and nodded. "Yeah, I am. And it really shouldn't be possible. So I'm trying to figure out how they killed this man's soul, and how they're hiding themselves from capture."

"Mmm. I can see why it was urgent enough for you to offer up unknown information on the reapers. This could potentially be a very dangerous situation. But I have to ask...are you safe?"

What was it with Blanche meeting people the last few months who actually gave a damn about complete strangers? She was used to apathy, people who only wanted to focus on them and their family. Suni and Erasmus were changing her expectations. Even Grim and Abaddon had, which made her suspicions of Grim that much worse.

"I am," she promised him. "Do you know of anything offhand that would allow either of those things?"

"I don't," Erasmus admitted, "but I am very curious myself. I don't have anything pressing at the moment to tend to, so I'm going to do some research and see if I can come up with something. Is there a time frame you need this information in?"

"As soon as possible. And anything you can find will be more than I have now, so don't hesitate to call, no matter the time."

He chuckled. "I wouldn't worry about that. When I get involved in a deep research project, I tend to forget things like time, meals, sleep...My whole world narrows down to whatever I happen to be involved in at the moment."

She smiled. "Sounds perfect. And thank you, Erasmus. I owe you."

"You have already given me plenty. Be well, Blanche. And I'll speak with you soon."

"You too. Bye, Erasmus."

She hung up feeling better. No, she didn't have anything new, not really, but if this man had been able to find spells to do two things previously thought impossible, then she had to believe he could find her what she needed.

"Blanche!"

Her dad had found her. They'd all been so clingy since she got back, it shouldn't surprise her that they'd gone looking outside the house. And she didn't really mind—it just meant they loved her and were worried—but it was a little smothering.

"I'm here," she called as she walked toward his voice.

"Ah! Come, dinner's ready. You need a few good meals," he said, wrapping his arm around her shoulders and giving her a squeeze. He kept his arm there as they started back toward the house.

"I'm fine. I've been eating. I just needed to get away for a few."

Elliot sighed and nodded. "I get that. Everyone needs some time alone, but do try to see it from our perspective. First we lost Mira, then you were determined that we not bury her, and then, out of the blue, she was alive and you were gone. Your mother and I essentially lost both our daughters in the span of just a few weeks."

Guilt sliced through her. "I know, and I'm sorry for that."

"No, don't be sorry," he said firmly. "Mira wasn't your fault, and you brought her back to us. But can you really blame us for hovering a bit now that we have you both back, alive and well?"

"Not really," she admitted. "It's just an adjustment. You two were never the kind to be up our asses all the time, and yeah, I get why you are now, but I just need to breathe sometimes."

"And we get that," he promised. "Just give us a few days to do our own adjustment. Though if Aidan goes off and does something stupid or disappears, both your mom and I might lose our minds."

"If he does, I'll hold him down while you two use the rubber hoses," she promised.

He laughed and gave her another squeeze. "That's my girl."

His words lingered in her mind, and she pushed her need for solitude aside and enjoyed not just a nice family meal, but also hung out with them that night. But she kept her phone close, just in case Erasmus found what she needed.

CHAPTER 25

Blanche didn't hear from Erasmus that night, or the next. By the day after that, she was doubting he was going to be able to come through. Oh, she didn't doubt his sincerity in that he'd do everything he could, but since he'd mentioned research, there just might not be any references in existence that could help.

And she missed Death. Now that she'd realized he'd intentionally tried to make her hate him, she couldn't be angry with him. Well, not much. She was still pissed he hadn't explained anything or even given her a choice. And she was surprised that if he had, there was a chance she might have stayed. Yes, she would have wanted a way to be able to travel back to Earth to see her family and friends, but once she'd adjusted, she liked Cindatha. She liked the castle, loved the land, and missed the damn man-eating tiger. Just not as much as she missed the man himself.

How in the hell was Death such a thoughtful man and skilled lover? He could even be tender, which seemed to be completely at odds with everything else about him. The man looked like a badass biker and had total control over life and death. He ruled over all of Cindatha and was technically the boss of even the most powerful death gods...but he'd taken her to see a waterfall and cave full of sapphires. He'd touched her like she was someone who mattered. He'd even done his best to make their parting easier on her. And he'd given her a given her a gift that was worth literal millions. Whatever his role as Death had done to him, it hadn't removed all his humanity.

She'd just gotten dressed after a shower and was debating if there were any other avenues for her to explore when her phone rang. Her heart sped up when she saw the same blocked number message on the screen and rushed to answer it. "Hi Erasmus."

"I think I've found something," was his greeting, but she didn't mind.

"About the soul being killed or the hiding?"

"The hiding. Now, I can't say anything for certain," he warned, "as my information tends to come from old documents, and like with the summoning spells I gave Suni, they don't always come with notes, and are sometimes incomplete—just fragments, you know?—but it looks promising."

"Nothing in life is guaranteed, so I'll take what I can get at this point. What did you find?"

"I found a scroll which spoke about a group of twenty-one identical relics. It says that these relics were supposed to be able to hide the truth from literally anyone, and it alludes to including the gods in that."

Death wasn't a god in the truest sense of the word, but that sounded like something that might still work on him. It was definitely better than anything else she had. "Does it give any details? Like how they worked, or what kind of truth they could hide?"

"The notes are actually good compared to some from this time period, but they aren't as thorough as I know you'd prefer. However, they do say that if one of these relics is in someone's possession, their minds are impossible to read, lies are impossible to detect, and any illusions they cast are impenetrable. It really hides truths the user wants to keep hidden, it sounds like. Now, since I'm not sure how the person you referred to sees a person's death, I can't say for certain, but it sounds like they might fit what you were looking for."

"That they might," she murmured. She also wasn't sure how Death saw how a person died, but she could see how a relic like this could potentially prevent it. It would also have prevented him from delving into the murderer's mind. "Does it say what form these relics are in? I know you said identical, but what were they?"

"Coins. Silver coins, similar to those used in ancient Greece or Rome."

"Holy shit," she breathed. "Anything else? A description, a picture, anything about what they specifically looked like?"

"There is, yes. Can I take it that you've seen a coin like this recently?" he asked as the sound of his voice changed. "I'm sending you a picture of the drawing," he added, and she realized he'd put her on speakerphone.

She did the same and waited for the message to come through. Her finger hesitated a moment before she tapped on the image to enlarge it and wanted to curse or cry or rage when she recognized the design. It looked like the same coin she'd seen both twins playing with from time to time. Heavy, with a face on one side, an owl on the other. "Shit, shit, shit. Fuck!" She kicked her dresser and barely felt the immediate pain that shot through her foot.

"You've seen one of these recently," he said, the words a clear statement, not a question.

"Yes, I have," she said darkly. "I've got to go, but thank you, Erasmus. This helps immensely." She hung up and dropped her phone on the bed. This wasn't exactly concrete proof, but what were the odds that both Abaddon and Grim would have the coins and not be involved? Especially since they were uniquely positioned to know everything going on in the castle. They were the first point of contact for all the reapers, and since they were the first reapers made, they surely knew more about Death than most. If anyone was going to be able to find a way to kill a soul or hide from Death, it would be them. Which meant she needed to warn Death that he had two very dangerous foxes in his hen house.

Blanche whispered the summoning Death had taught her, but after several long moments with no answer, she went for the harder to ignore option. She retrieved her mummification knife and grabbed a sharper blade. Without hesitation, she cut her hand and dripped seven drops of blood on the mummification knife. "Death, please, for the love of all the gods, don't ignore me. I *need* to tell you what I've found. You've got to come to me. You need to pay attention. It's Grim and Abaddon. C'mon Death...Please, please listen to me," she breathed, putting everything she had into the words. She wished she had another way of contacting him, but she'd never seen him use a phone, and while she had some skill with telepathy, it wasn't anywhere near powerful enough to reach into Cindatha. The problem was that she wasn't sure if he actually heard the message, or if the words just triggered a pull which would summon him.

But no matter how long she called or which summoning she used, Death didn't respond. She wasn't sure if he was ignoring her or somehow incapacitated, but neither idea calmed her racing heart. So she called until the cut on her hand began to clot and the blood on the knife had dried.

One way or another, she'd find a way to warn him. It may be that neither of the twins could actually harm Death, but that wasn't a chance she was prepared to take.

She was calling him again. It couldn't be about her sister again, he knew that. Death felt every time a soul was brought into his realm, and since he'd been in their presence, he knew the souls of her family and none of them had arrived. Likely she was searching for an explanation, and he just couldn't give that to her. Finding the sapphire had given her some idea he was sure, but he couldn't confirm whatever it was she was thinking.

He hated it. He did want her back in Cindatha with him, alive and well, but it wasn't safe for her here. Maybe, once he found the murderer and had routed out any other betrayal, he could invite her back, but not now.

Shaking his head, he pushed her repeated calls out of his mind and focused on the task at hand. Never before would he have thought he'd regret having so many reapers to help ferry souls into Cindatha, but now it meant he had more than a thousand people to vet. Even for him it would take a while. So far, he'd visited almost two hundred, and had only been able to verify for certain that a hundred and eighty-three were completely innocent. Another twelve were far from upstanding citizens, but not guilty of betrayal, nor guilty of anything worthy of death. But two he suspected might be involved for the simple fact that he was unable to get a read on them, just like with Chris. They hadn't said or done anything suspicious while he was watching them, but considering how little time he was able to spend with each one, it wasn't enough to rule them out. Which meant he'd be visiting them again soon.

On the whole, he was pleased with what he'd seen. All of the reapers worked hard, and while he'd seen a few who could stand to show a little more compassion to the souls they were carrying to Cindatha, none were actually cruel. And outside of their jobs, he saw little sign that any were truly unhappy. Reaping was a job he knew could weigh on a person—that he'd learned firsthand when people had begun dying—but he did his best to ensure no one burned out. Every reaper worked in an area with at least two other reapers so they weren't alone. They had a network of friends to commiserate with and who could pick up the slack if someone needed a day off. He didn't bar them from relationships or mortal jobs, and if they used what they learned from souls to make a little extra money to make their lives easier, he was okay with that. Even mortals knew they couldn't take their wealth to the underworld with them, so why would he complain about reapers taking wealth that would otherwise be forgotten?

He spent the next several hours visiting other reapers. Imhotep still spent most of his time in Egypt, and though the man was serious even in Death's opinion, he seemed content. When Death had been there, he'd been holed up in the basement library he'd been building for the last few centuries, writing another book. It was amusing, in a way. Imhotep was constantly studying and writing, but to Death's knowledge, he hadn't made any of his works public, not since he'd become a reaper. But it made the man happy, so who was Death to tell him it was pointless?

Banshee was the next reaper Death found, but she was working. He watched for a little while, but he saw nothing but a compassionate woman carrying a soul to Elysium, another to Annwn. She was gentle with the man and child she carried, and he was prepared to move on, crossing her off his list of suspects, but like the other two he was suspicious of, he was unable to get into her mind.

Why were there reapers he couldn't read? Was it some magical accident? Or had they intentionally done something to block him? What was worrying was that it was possible at all, regardless of the method. The Anunnaki might be able to manage it—and that was a big might—but unless one of them was helping the reapers, it just shouldn't be possible. And the idea that the Anunnaki might now be working against him was terrifying, even to him.

Making a note to revisit Banshee later, he returned to his castle. There were two reapers in the throne room, along with Abaddon, and he remained invisible, observing.

The reapers—Cheng and Niall—were concerned after Bjorn's death and the group meeting he'd had days ago. Understandable, and the fact that he could instantly read them meant he listened for just a few minutes before he teleported to his workshop. At this point, anyone he could read could be considered innocent, but he now had three people who might be part of whatever plot was going on. He just wished he knew what that was. What had Bjorn's death accomplished? It wouldn't make the entire system of souls and reaping fall apart. There were too many reapers for that. So what was the point? He just couldn't see it, and it was pissing him off. How could he be one of the oldest living beings and be ignorant of that one single fact? Worse, how had he misjudged his reapers so badly?

The wisest course of action might be to just imprison or kill the reapers he couldn't read, but they might not be alone. If he took those pieces off the board, the others might simply go into hiding or find another way of hiding from him. Something he couldn't detect. No, for now, he simply needed to watch them until he was sure he had every stinking rat on his sinking ship.

Then he would act, and no reaper would ever dare betray him like this again.

CHAPTER 26

It had been almost thirty-six hours since Blanche had received the picture from Erasmus and started trying to summon Death. Her left hand was now a mess of cuts and she was fairly certain at least one of them was trying to get infected, but it was to be expected since she'd attempted to summon Death a good dozen times with that method.

If only necromancers could also be good healers.

When she hadn't been able to get Death to respond by ten this morning, she'd called Erasmus again. If summoning Death wasn't working, she hoped there'd been a way to just contact him. Send a message, something. Unfortunately, all Erasmus had been able to find so far was a way of sending a message to a relative who had died. Useful, sure, but not in this case. She had no blood link to Death, and that was one requirement of that particular spell. Erasmus promised to keep looking though, and she realized she was going to owe him far more than just the scant information about the reapers she'd already given him.

In the meantime, she had to keep trying. Last time she'd simply worn Death down until he'd come to bargain with her. At this point, she didn't care if he showed up because he missed her, was annoyed by her, or because she'd given him a migraine. It didn't matter. If he showed up, she could tell him about Abaddon and Grim. Hopefully before it was too late.

Blanche looked at her left hand and grimaced. There weren't any unmarked spots for her to cut, which meant she was going to need to reopen one of the other wounds. Wincing, she drew the point of her knife across her hand and started to drip the blood on the mummification knife, but after the first drop landed on the metal, three reapers appeared in her bedroom.

She was so surprised she nearly dropped the knife, but when she saw Abaddon was one of the three, her grip tightened. She tried to keep her anger toward him off her face and smiled instead, putting confusion into it. "Abaddon? What are you doing here?" she asked, looking at the two reapers with him. "And who are they?"

One was a woman a little shorter than Blanche, with olive skin and beautiful silky black hair. The other was a man a few inches taller than her, with short, curly brown hair, tanned skin, and a lanky frame. Neither looked happy, but Abaddon had a smile on his lips.

"What am I doing here?" Abaddon asked, stepping over to her door and locking it. "What do you think I'm doing here?"

"If I knew, I wouldn't ask, would I?" Blanche retorted with a laugh, but even to her ears it sounded forced. "Where's Grim?" she asked, shifting in an attempt to make sure she had a wall behind her. The last thing she needed was a reaper to teleport in behind her and grab her before she knew they were there.

"My brother? Probably giving Death's boots a shine with his tongue," he said, and Blanche was shocked at both the animosity in the words, and the cadence of them. Abaddon had always spoken like he'd had an upper class upbringing, but now the tone and choice of words was more casual. They sounded more like something Grim would say.

"I don't understand," she said honestly, as she'd never caught any whiff of friction between the twins.

"Doesn't matter if you do or not." Abaddon glanced to the woman, then gave a little jerk of his head toward Blanche. The woman smiled and pulled a curved knife with a ring at the end of the handle from a sheath at her belt. Armed, she moved swiftly toward Blanche, weapon raised. It was pure defensive reaction that had Blanche's hand lashing out just as the woman reached her. Her knife ended up completely buried in the woman's belly, the reaper's own momentum helping the weapon slide deep. Her blade slashed over Blanche's arm, but it was forgotten when her eyes widened and she glanced down to the blade in her gut.

"What the fuck are you waiting for?" Abaddon asked as he strolled across the room, and Blanche realized he couldn't see what had happened. For that matter, she wasn't sure what had just happened, either. Death himself had told her how hard it was to kill a reaper. Since she wasn't a god or a reaper, and was armed only with a mundane weapon, she shouldn't be able to do any lasting damage to the woman, despite how she'd reacted. Blanche wasn't going to take any chances though, and twisted the knife, angling it in an attempt to hit something vital. But even that wouldn't be enough. There were three of them and only one of her, and she would lay down and die before she called her family and put them in danger. Which meant she was vastly outnumbered.

The woman took a staggering step back and Blanche yanked the knife out then slashed as deeply as she could at the woman's throat, hoping like hell that she hit the right spot. Unwilling to appear weak, or to go down without a fight, she used her powers to shove the woman back, sending her flying toward Abaddon. He frowned and sidestepped, so the woman collided with the lanky man and both went down as blood poured from the wounds.

Abaddon clearly didn't see Blanche as a threat because he turned and looked at his two companions. The man looked shocked and shoved the woman off him. "She's fucking dying," he snapped at Abaddon. "How? Who the hell is this broad?"

"It isn't the who that's important," Abaddon mused as he looked back to Blanche, his expression one of mild interest. "It seems like Death has been busier than I realized." He smiled and shook his head. "But it won't save you."

He summoned a weapon that looked eerily similar to Death's scythe, but she could tell instantly that it was a pale imitation at best. She'd held the true scythe, been in its presence when fully powered, and this one didn't have the same oomph of the real thing. That didn't make it any less deadly.

Abaddon teleported just in front of her and swung the razor-sharp blade. She tried to dodge, she tried to block it with her knife, but while she'd had a bit of fight training in her two hundred years of life, he'd been doing this for thousands of years. He was faster, stronger, and infinitely more skilled than she was. The knife was knocked from her hand, and she shoved at the scythe with her magic, but it just kept coming, until he delivered what seemed to be his signature blow and one she'd accidentally mimicked; a deep slash to her throat.

Pain on par with what she'd felt when Mira died erupted through her, and her hands clasped her throat as she tried to suck in air. Nothing seemed to be reaching her lungs and she fell to her knees as she stared up at the man she'd considered a friend. She mouthed the word "Why" up at him as she felt her own blood pouring through her fingers. Death was something she knew, and she had only minutes left at best. And she needed to know why he'd done this.

Using the end of the scythe, he shoved at her until she fell over, already too weak to resist the blow. He pinned her to the floor with it as he stared down at her, his face full of hatred and disdain. "You should have let your sister stay dead. Should have forgotten Bjorn ever existed. Your soul might have lived if you had."

Oh fuck. Her mind was going fuzzy, but even now she could process what he meant. He was going to do to her exactly what he'd done to Bjorn. Kill not just her body, but her soul. Otherwise, she'd end up in Cindatha and would just tell Death what he'd done. It would all be over for him.

She couldn't allow that to happen, but knew she only had a few seconds before she lost consciousness. Fortunately, she had one trick up her sleeve. It was the same trick that had allowed her to save Mira's soul in her locket. She'd never used it on herself, never had reason to, but reached deep to be able to do it now. She just had to hope that it would work. Since she wasn't a reaper, there was no guarantee it would.

Blanche yanked her soul free of her body and thought of the castle, of Cindatha, and shoved it, as hard as she could, toward the underworld. With her last thought, she prayed to Death that it arrived safely in his realm.

The second her soul was gone, her body went limp, her unseeing eyes fixed on Abaddon's face. But as her soul flew through the cosmos, whatever consciousness she still had slipped away.

Back in her bedroom, Abaddon dropped to one knee beside her body and slammed his hand into the center of her chest. He immediately knew what she'd done, because her soul was no longer in her body. Which meant he didn't have much time to finalize his plans and do what needed done. If he was lucky, with the way her soul had been ripped out, it would take years to make it to Cindatha. If he wasn't, she could be there already.

Fighting back the scream of rage that wanted to escape, he straightened and walked to his companions. It took only a glance to see Banshee was truly dead. How had that bitch managed that? Even if Death was right about Blanche being his reincarnated wife, that wife had been human. Blanche in this life had just been a witch.

Unwilling to allow Banshee's incompetence and Blanche's surprising abilities to spoil everything he'd worked for, he drew Banshee's soul from her body and held it with a hand around her throat.

"What are you doing?" Dean asked, taking a step back.

"I don't know how Blanche killed her, but you know that we can't let her soul return to Cindatha," he answered, vanishing his scythe and replacing it with a knife he'd owned since before he was a reaper. A knife only a trusted few knew existed. A knife he now plunged into the center of Banshee's soul, causing it to implode with little more than a soft gasping sound. "Grab her body. We don't want any sign we were here," he ordered before he disappeared.

Uneasy with the way this had gone, Dean picked up Banshee's body. Before he teleported out, he looked to the body of the woman they had come to kill. While he wasn't sure he agreed with Abaddon's decision to destroy Banshee's soul, he couldn't say he wasn't relieved to have a mortal who could kill them out of the way.

Blanche couldn't say how long she'd been out, but when she came to, she was lying on the ground. Working her eyes open, she struggled to figure out where she was. From her vantage point, all she could see was green and dark brown, but she could tell it was nighttime.

Pushing herself into a sitting position, she looked around. She was in a...jungle? The plants didn't look right for a forest. There was too much life, and the leaves were just wrong for anything but some kind of jungle. But which jungle? And how had she gotten here?

She took stock of her body, but didn't feel like anything was wrong. For her memory to be this fuzzy, she'd expect some kind of head injury, but she didn't have even a trace of a headache, and when her fingers ran over her scalp, she didn't feel any tender spots or bumps. Something traumatic maybe? No, that was likely to come with some sort of injury as well, but she physically felt as good as she'd ever felt. Which meant it had to be something magical, and that presented a whole other set of questions.

Getting to her feet, she brushed dirt off the butt of her pants and turned in a slow circle. She didn't see any signs of buildings or civiliza-tion, which sucked, because being in the middle of a jungle at night wasn't a place she wanted to be. There was no telling what dangers were around.

She patted her pockets and didn't find her phone, but there was a bracelet on her left wrist that looked only partially familiar. The silver cuff had been a birthday present years ago, but she didn't recognize the stone set in it. It was pretty, but where had it come from? She didn't feel any magic in it, which meant it was a problem for later, after she'd found her way home. And the only way to do that was to start walking.

Here was hoping she didn't run into some kind of jungle predator.

Back on Earth, Death watched as two of his reapers hung out, drinking and watching TV. It was a normal enough sight, even though he was aware most people wouldn't think of reapers doing anything so mundane.

So far, they hadn't done anything suspicious, which meant Death's mind had a chance to wander. He realized it had been a good six hours since Blanche had last attempted to summon him. It was a good sign. Other than a five-hour gap when she'd likely been sleeping, she'd been attempting to summon him every two hours like clockwork. Maybe this meant she was moving on. It was the best possible outcome for her. She'd get to live her life. Hopefully, a full and happy life. That was partly why he'd given her the gift he had. He couldn't change the future or affect free will, but while money couldn't buy happiness, it could make life a great deal easier for mortals. If she needed to, she could sell the sapphire and live comfortably for quite some time.

But though he wanted her to have a good life, he selfishly hoped it would be one that didn't include a husband.

The movie ended and one of the reapers left, leaving just Malcolm. Malcolm was one of the younger reapers, just a hundred years old or so. He wasn't likely to have the power needed to do the things that had been done, but Death wasn't going to rule anyone out without evidence.

Just as he was about to do his compulsory check, Malcolm's phone rang. Curious and completely unashamed of eavesdropping, Death waited.

"How'd it go?" Malcolm straightened in his seat and frowned. "What do you mean Banshee's dead?"

Another of his reapers had died? True, Banshee had been on his short list, but he hadn't confirmed anything yet, which meant he was now pissed.

"That's impossible," Malcolm continued. "No, it's fucking impossible. Shit. Yeah, it does move up our timeline. Death's suspicious enough as it is. I don't want to be the next reaper he executes in front of a crowd." He scoffed. "No, we need to get this done before we all end up dead. Okay, yeah. I'll be careful. Business as usual until I hear from you. Thanks for the heads up."

When Malcolm hung up, Death acted. The reaper had said enough to earn him a death sentence, but he didn't go straight to killing. He grabbed Malcolm by the throat and lifted him off the couch at the same moment he dropped his invisibility. "Care to share what you meant by that?" he asked coolly.

Malcolm's eyes widened as he clawed futilely at Death's hand. "Didn't say anything," he gasped.

"I was here for the entire conversation, Malcolm, so try again. Or do you want to die for people who likely wouldn't give you the same courtesy?"

"Can't. They'll do worse than kill me," Malcolm said, still trying to pull Death's hand off him.

Death surrounded Malcolm with his power, unsurprised when the man read as a void to him. Which meant he'd probably be just as talkative as Chris had been. But Death had learned from that particular failure. Malcolm wasn't going to see the inside of a cell, but he also wasn't going to go free.

Death brought his scythe to his hand, which made Malcolm thrash in his grip. It didn't save him. With a thought, Death killed Malcolm, then touched the scythe to his soul, drawing it into the weapon. Not wanting to leave any evidence for the other traitors to find, he disintegrated Malcolm's body.

Teleporting directly to his workshop, Death selected one of the bottles sitting on a shelf and transferred Malcolm's soul from the scythe to the bottle. The reaper would still be aware in there, unable to escape or sleep. A few days like that would certainly help to loosen up his tongue, because Death was done playing around. Too many reapers had died already for this fucking plot. Bjorn, Chris, Banshee, Malcolm. He was determined that Malcolm would be the last.

CHAPTER 27

Blanche wasn't sure how long she'd been walking through the jungle. Hours, certainly, but how many was impossible to tell. There was a moon, and it had moved, but not much. It sort of just circled around the same spot. And though she'd expected to see a sun begin to rise at some point, there wasn't even a hint that dawn was approaching. She could have been here for a few hours or a full day at this point, and she'd have no way of knowing.

She'd paused once at a stream barely four feet across, sipping at the water, which was surprisingly cool despite the humid heat of the jungle. It had tasted clean and had quenched her thirst more completely than anything she'd ever drank. Something she'd needed, as this place was a mix of eerie and soothing. It felt like home, despite a tingle of uncertainty she'd felt when she realized there were none of the usual sounds of life. No birds, no insects, not even the distant roars and screeches of predators. All she could hear was the rustling of leaves and occasional sounds of running water.

After she'd left the first stream, she'd just kept walking until she came to a larger river. Deciding that people would likely live near fresh water, she followed it upstream. It was better than wandering aimlessly. At least this was a plan. A weak one, but still a plan. The only downside was that it left her mind plenty of time to think.

She still couldn't remember what had happened before she woke up...wherever she was. In fact, the only things she could remember felt like they were distant. Her childhood was as clear as expected—which meant a little fuzzy, with impressions more than real memories—and she was good up until around her two hundredth birthday, but the rest blurred together until she couldn't quite put things in order.

Since trying to force the memories gave her a hell of a headache, she took stock of herself while she walked. Physically, she felt fine. No wounds, not even a bruise or paper cut, and she didn't look like she'd dropped weight, so she couldn't have been out for that long. Mentally, there was the memory loss, but otherwise she didn't think there was anything wrong. Magically...well, there weren't any ghosts around—or so she thought—so she had no way of judging her necromancy. She was able to summon a small flame above her palm and shoot a fist-sized rock against the trunk of a tree, so at least she had her powers. If she did run into any predators—or predatory people—she wasn't defenseless.

The sound of water was growing louder and Blanche moved closer to the edge of the river, looking upstream. She couldn't see anything from her current vantage point, not with the trees growing so close together. Eager to see what was ahead, she quickened her pace as much as she was able, but unless she got into the water, she was forced to make her way around massive trees and dense brush. So it took time until she found the source of what she realized was the roar of a waterfall.

When she finally stepped out of the trees and was able to see it, she gasped and let her eyes move upward over the various levels of the waterfall, then back down to the pool it emptied into. It was absolutely fucking gorgeous...and felt so familiar it was scary. She couldn't remember ever being in a jungle, so how could a waterfall in the jungle be familiar?

No, no overthinking. This place felt warm and safe and was as good a place as any to rest. Maybe she could even find a place to sleep. There might be an endless night here, but she still needed sleep. But first, she needed a bath. She may not have been running through the jungle, but she had still gotten dirty, and there was little as relaxing as a bath.

As she kicked her shoes off, she realized that she didn't actually need to relax at the moment. Odd, since she'd had anxiety issues since she was a child, but there hadn't even been a hint of a panic attack since she woke up. If anything should have triggered one, being alone, lost, and without her memory should have done it.

Shaking her head, she decided not to question that either. If something was giving her a reprieve from her issues, she was going to accept it with a smile.

Stripping and placing her clothes on a flat rock at the edge of the water, she circled the pool until she found a spot that looked relatively shallow. While she could swim, she wasn't very good at it, and she just wanted to get clean. Stepping in, she sighed at the feel of the cool water and sank down to dunk herself. When she surfaced, she realized she wasn't alone in the pool, but there was no fear, only delight. Brightly colored fish swam about, and one even came to investigate her hand, but darted away when her fingers moved.

Blanche had no idea where the hell she was, but at this exact moment, it felt like paradise.

Death was as close to drunk as he could possibly get, and steadily drinking more.

Grim had never seen Death like this, and he wasn't sure if it was because of Bjorn and Chris, or because of Blanche. His best guess was fifty percent each, because Blanche had disappeared from the castle a few days ago and Death refused to discuss her. Grim had a feeling Death had sent her home and was now missing her.

Good for him. It was about time the grumpy fucker found something to live for other than dealing with Cindatha and the reapers.

He was currently in the music room, sitting in a chair, while Death sat on one end of the couch, Abaddon on the other, with Sa curled up on the floor nearby. They all had glasses in hand, but only Abaddon and Death were drinking. Grim was content to swirl his as he and his brother tried to get Death to relax, or at least to open up.

It was definitely not an easy job.

"There are at least three people involved, and I'm almost certain there are more, but even three is three too many," Death said, shaking his head. "I just don't know what would cause any of the reapers to rebel like this." He took a long drink, looked to Grim, then to Abaddon. "Neither of you have heard anything—even a whisper—about them being this unhappy?"

Abaddon shook his head. "I haven't," he admitted. "I've been thinking since we first realized Bjorn had been killed by one of our own, analyzing nearly every conversation I've had with a reaper, and I can't think of a single instance where they sounded unhappy. Frustrated at times, certainly, or furious because they transported a soul who didn't deserve to be dead, but that's all normal."

Grim had to agree. "There are going to be days like that for all the reapers—hell, we've all had them—but I can't think of anyone who just seems pissed. And I may not be as good as you at telling when someone's lying, but I'm still damn good at it. I also take my position seriously, even if I don't act like it. When reapers show up acting like Abaddon mentioned, I follow up." He shrugged and gave the amber liquid in his glass another swirl. "They always just need some time. Maybe to get drunk one night, or to themselves in someone's body. Just some sort of stress release, you know?"

"Then why in the hell are they doing this? I've got multiple dead reapers and not a single reason for it," Death grumbled.

"Trust me, if I knew, I would have told you immediately," Grim promised. And it was true. He'd been thinking about what could have possessed anyone to start killing reapers, and had rejected every idea that had crossed his mind. Revenge? Okay, possible, but it wouldn't have created a conspiracy. Nor could he think of anything Bjorn might have had that anyone would have killed for. Yes, he'd had money, but pretty much every reaper did. He might have had some relics from his time as a human, but again, a lot of reapers did. Hell, some of them picked up relics as the centuries went by. Reapers could get places even some gods couldn't, so they were excellent treasure hunters—if they cared to bother, which most honestly didn't.

So what could have possibly been important enough for some-one to risk Death's wrath? There really wasn't anything stupider than angering Death. Even the gods could—and had—fallen to Death. Literally no one was more lethal than he was.

"As would I," Abaddon said with a nod. "There's nothing logical about it, though."

"Right? It's like someone cooked up some stupid ass plan and didn't actually think it through," Grim agreed, surprised when Abaddon frowned. What the hell was up with his brother? He didn't have time to think too hard on it, because Death tossed back the last of his drink and pushed to his feet, starting to pace.

Death was definitely acting weird, too, but that just amused the hell out of Grim. "You know, you're not going to be able to completely focus on finding out what's going on if you're focused on missing Blanche."

Death stopped and glared at Grim, but he just smiled. Death wouldn't kill him, not for this. "I told you I don't want to discuss her. She's gone. End of story."

"And why is she gone? Wasn't that the deal? She gets her sister alive and stays here for eternity?" That was the one thing he couldn't figure. Why had Death sent her elsewhere? Even if he had gone stupid over her, didn't it make more sense to keep her here? Seduce her into wanting to stay? Grim had a feeling she wouldn't have minded.

There was a tightening of Death's features that had Grim's body tensing, and when he looked to Abaddon, Grim knew he was missing something important.

"Death had a wife when he was human," Abaddon said quietly after Death had nodded to him. "She died, just after he became Death. He has reason to believe that Blanche is the reincarnation of that wife."

Grim's fingers nearly lost their grip on his glass. Abaddon could have told him he was Bjorn's killer and he wouldn't have been more surprised. "How sure are you?"

Death gave a tight, unhappy smile. "Almost positive."

"Then why the fuck did you send her away? Did you tell her any of this?"

"No," was the only response he got, so he looked to Abaddon, giving him a questioning look. Abaddon could only shrug.

"Right..." Damn, Grim now wanted to go to Earth and check on Blanche. To see if she had any idea. Reincarnations were far from an exact science, even for reapers. Sometimes they lived their entire life without ever knowing who they'd once been. Most often they got glimpses, dreams, but were never able to really confirm anything. Then there was one tribe that had lived a few thousand years ago who had somehow managed to get blessed—or cursed, depending on how you looked at it—to reincarnate over and over, regaining the full memories of their past lives. Now and again that happened naturally, but it was most definitely the exception rather than the norm. Which meant odds were that Blanche had no idea who she'd once been, or what she'd been to Death. And didn't she have a right to know?

His gaze slid to Death, who had resumed his pacing. Then again, it wasn't really his place to be the one to say anything. Which meant that until Bjorn's killer was caught, Death was going to be hell to live with.

CHAPTER 28

I t had been a few days since Blanche had found the waterfall, and
for some reason, she hadn't left. Every time she thought about
leaving to find people, to figure out how to get home, something had
stopped her. It was as though she was meant to be exactly where she
was. Though it didn't make sense, she couldn't argue with a feeling
that strong, that certain. So she'd stayed at the waterfall, which was far
from a hardship.

She'd spent her time swimming, exploring the area around the pool,
and laying on the flat stone where she'd first set her clothes. And
it hadn't just been relaxing, it had been exciting. One of the times
she'd been exploring, she noticed something odd behind the curtain
of water. It had taken some time—and more than a few slips that
had resulted in her falling into the water or onto the rocks—but she'd
finally found that there was a cave behind the waterfall. It was like
something out of a movie, and she was delighted despite it not being
very big. The main chamber was only about fifteen feet long, maybe
ten wide, and went from just five feet high to what looked like twenty
at the tallest. There was a smaller cave off that, just long enough to
accommodate a person lying down and wide enough for two. If they
stayed very, very close.

After being inside the cave, she'd seen an easier way to get in and out, which meant she'd spent her time both inside and out, thoroughly enjoying both. And while she hadn't felt hunger since she'd woken, she had occasionally gotten tired, and had taken to sleeping in that smaller chamber. After she'd added some leaves to cushion the stone, it had actually been surprisingly comfortable, and certainly more protected than the area around the pool. Though she still hadn't seen any sign of animals or people beyond the pool's fish.

On what she estimated was the second or third day she'd been there, she was sitting on the flat rock, one leg tucked beneath her, while her other foot dangled in the water. She'd expected to be bored by now with no one to talk to and nothing to do, but it felt like a much needed vacation.

Which, of course, meant something had to spoil the serenity.

For the first time, she heard the sound of life in this place, and it had to be the roar of a predator. Only a minute later, she saw that very predator. A huge cat with big ass fangs, specifically. What in the hell was an extinct animal doing in the jungle? Or anywhere outside of a museum, for that matter?

Blanche froze, as the single thing she knew when faced with something like this was not to run. That didn't necessarily mean that moving slow was wise, either. Her eyes flicked to the waterfall, and she wondered if she could make it there before the tiger noticed her. Deciding she had to try, she slowly pulled her foot out of the water and eased into a standing position. Except that brought the cat's attention directly to her.

Her heart pounded in her chest as she watched and waited to see what the tiger's reaction would be. But when her eyes met its, there was another flash of that same familiarity she'd felt when she first saw the waterfall. She decided to not focus on it right now, not when faced with those huge teeth. The waterfall was a passive thing, but the tiger? It could chase her down and kill her. When it started running for her, she knew that was exactly what it had decided to do.

She stumbled back a step, but that was as far as she'd gotten when the tiger shocked her by sliding to a stop and headbutting her in the stomach. It was relatively gentle, but it left her just as confused as she was freaked out. It purred as it rubbed its head against her and she could only stare down at the huge tawny head. A head which lifted, then tilted as the purring stopped. If she didn't know better, she'd say it looked just as confused as she felt.

What she wasn't expecting was for it to gently bite her shirt before it dove into the water, pulling Blanche with it. She only had the chance to gasp before she went under, but when she was submerged, fully clothed, with a saber-tooth tiger, the recreation of a previous experience made her memories come rushing back so fast her head hurt.

Mira's death. Her resurrection. Cindatha. The waterfall. The twins. Sa. Death.

Everything returned to her, including the knowledge of where she was and how she'd gotten there. And with that knowledge came the mess of emotions that went with them. The sorrow over Mira, the growing love for Death, and the absolute fury that had come after that.

Abaddon had fucking killed her, and she was all too keen to return the favor.

The last few days had fortunately strengthened her meager swimming skills, and she managed to break the surface and pull herself out. Sa joined her a few seconds later and gave her a curious look. Had he known he could trigger her memories like that? There were moments where he seemed more intelligent than any normal animal. But even if he hadn't intentionally helped her, she owed the tiger, big time.

Bending, she threw her arms around him, pressed her cheek to his wet fur, and held him tight. "I am so fucking happy to see you right now, Sa," she murmured to him. "And I really hope you know how to get back to the castle."

The words were no sooner out of her mouth than she felt the vertigo she'd experienced only a few times before. It didn't truly surprise her when she lifted her head and saw the round room of the castle around them. Good, now she just had to hope Death was home and that she could find him before she ran into Abaddon.

Blanche's first stop was the music room. It was the only place she had really seen Death on this floor, but the instruments were all silent and the room was empty. She hurried back, dripping water as she went while Sa stuck close to her. Half-running, she went up the stairs to check Death's room, but she'd made it only a few steps down the hallway before the twins came out of Grim's room and turned toward her.

"Blanche? What are you doing back here? How did you get back here?" Grim asked, stopping when he caught sight of her. Abaddon stopped as well, but rather than surprise, his jaw was clenched and his eyes had gone a mix of black and red swirled together. Oh, he wasn't happy to see her at all.

Good.

All her intentions, all the reasons why she should avoid Abaddon, disappeared. Her anger flared, as did her powers. Eyes narrowing, her power crackled around her, the strands of her hair that had dried lifting like she was full of static electricity. The doors nearest her rattled in their frames, and even Sa reacted to her emotions, his fur fluffing up as a low growl rumbled in his throat.

"Blanche?" Grim said again, his eyes shifting from Blanche to Sa and back, uncertain now. Not afraid, but she knew this was out of character for both her and the tiger. Except for today. Except when faced with a murderous asshole.

"You fucking bastard," Blanche said, her voice low, her eyes fixed firmly on Abaddon. He'd all but confirmed his brother had nothing to do with Bjorn or her own death, which meant right now she cared only about the one twin. The one who had fooled them all.

She had no weapons, only her mind and her magic, and she used them now, unwilling to let Abaddon escape and continue to murder indiscriminately. Shoving her hand toward him, she hit him hard with her telekinesis. He flew back several feet before his body slammed into the floor. Before she could pin him there, Grim stepped between them, eyes wide with shock.

"What the fuck, Blanche? Stop it!"

"Your piece of shit brother killed me!" she screamed, tiny flames tickling over her fingers, her magic itching to get out. "I intend to return the favor."

"You're insane," Abaddon yelled at her, and she was darkly pleased to hear he was a little breathless from his contact with the stone floor.

Denial had Grim shaking his head. "Of course he didn't. You're standing right here. Besides, you can't kill a reaper."

Blanche felt the smile spreading over her lips and knew it wasn't a pleasant expression. "Oh, but I did. Ask your brother what I did to that bitch he brought with him. After you check and see that I'm just a soul. A soul he tried to kill."

Grim shook his head again as he helped his brother to his feet. "Something's wrong," he muttered before calling out, "Death! Got an emergency!"

Some of Blanche's anger faded when Death appeared between her and the brothers, then burned higher, brighter. This was the man Abaddon had betrayed. He was going to be crushed when he found out, and she had to be the one to do that to him. She hated Abaddon even more for that.

"What is it?" Death asked, his back to Blanche.

"Not entirely sure," Grim admitted, looking past Death. "She just attacked Abaddon, saying something about killing him. Why didn't you tell us she was back?"

"What do you mean? Who's back?" Death asked, turning his head to see who he meant. "Blanche?" he whispered, his shoulders tensing when he caught sight of her. She caught longing mixed in with the shock, before her currently unalive state registered. "No." Long steps carried him to her and he ignored the fire and waves of telekinesis, scooping her off her feet and into his arms. Never before had she been hugged with so much emotion, and despite the anger, she couldn't help but return the embrace. Nor could she take her eyes off Abaddon, who looked like he was trying to figure out how the hell he was going to get out of this. There was no way he could prevent her from telling Death what had happened now.

Death put her back on her feet and cupped her face, studying every feature. "What happened? You were supposed to be safe!"

"Abaddon is a betraying piece of shit," she told him, side-stepping so she could watch the reaper. "He and two other reapers showed up at my house."

"That's a lie," Abaddon protested. "I've never been to her house. Why would I?"

"Bullshit!" she screamed as she lunged toward him, but Death caught her. He held her against his side as he turned so he could see the brothers. Grim looked absolutely baffled and was quickly glancing between his brother and Blanche. "You showed up, insulted your brother, and told that bitch who was with you to kill me." She smirked and put every bit of smug disdain in her voice that she could manage. "Didn't work so well for her now, did it?"

"She's gone insane," Abaddon insisted. "This isn't making any sense."

"What do you mean it didn't go well for her?" Death asked. His voice was deceptively calm, but his power was leaking out again, and though she'd heard the term vibrating with rage before, she'd never witnessed it before. She was now. He was absolutely livid.

"I mean, I had a knife in my hand and killed her before she could kill me."

Grim and Death both paused. "What kind of knife?" the former asked.

Blanche shrugged. "Nothing special, just a knife. And no, I have no idea how the hell I managed it. Besides, it didn't do any good. When she failed, Abaddon summoned a scythe and killed me. Pretty damn sure his plan was to kill my soul, too, so I couldn't do exactly what I'm doing now."

"Is that so?" Death murmured as he released Blanche. He didn't get the chance to do anything before Abaddon cursed and disappeared. No doubt running before he could be captured—or killed. Coward.

Grim stepped backwards until he hit the wall, shaking his head. "No." He looked to Blanche. "No, it can't be true. It had to be someone else. You must be mistaken."

Blanche felt for him. "I'm sorry, Grim, but I'm not wrong," she said, her voice as gentle as she could manage at the moment. Unfortunately, it wasn't very gentle. "It *was* Abaddon. Abaddon, a man, and a woman. And he all but admitted to killing Bjorn, too. Said if I had left my sister dead and not worried about Bjorn, that I wouldn't have died, too."

Death's eyes were narrowed on Grim and his hand shot out, pinning the reaper to the wall with his magic. No doubt he was preventing him from disappearing as well. "Did you know any of this? Were you a part of it?" he demanded.

Blanche was pretty damn sure Grim was innocent, but wasn't as certain Death would take her word on it. Then again, he had taken her word about Abaddon killing her. But then she recalled what she'd been trying to summon Death to tell him. "There are relics," she said, touching his arm.

"What do you mean relics?" he asked without releasing Grim.

"Just because you shoved me back to Earth didn't mean I was going to stop meddling," she answered with a shrug, dropping her hand to Sa's head when he forced his way between her and Death. "I got in touch with a researcher who told me about these relics. Twenty-one identical coins that were said to be able to hide the truth from anyone, even the gods. They look just like the coins I've seen the brothers playing with."

"What? They're relics?" The shock on Grim's face was impossible to fake. Death must have thought the same, because his hand lowered, allowing the reaper to move. Grim fished the coin out of his pocket, staring at it like it was a spider about to bite him. "Here," he said, shoving it toward Death.

The coin was taken and Death held it up to study the innocuous-looking piece of silver. After a minute, he nodded. "It is a relic, and a subtle one. I couldn't sense it until it was in my hand." He glanced down to Blanche. "But it sounds like that was its intended purpose."

"Exactly," Blanche agreed. "So ask him now. I'm pretty sure Abaddon didn't let him in on any of this, but now you can ask him and get a real answer."

Death didn't say a word, just looked at Grim and arched a brow.

"I'm not saying Abaddon had anything to let me in on because I don't believe my brother's a murderer, but I swear I had no part in Bjorn's death or Blanche's," Grim insisted. "I'm a reaper, not a fucking murderer, and neither is my brother."

"And Chris? Do you know who killed him?"

Grim shook his head. "I didn't even know he was in the castle until you called us and showed us his body."

Death nodded slowly and turned the coin around in his fingers. "And this? How did you come by it?"

Grim's answer took a few moments, and when it came, it was reluctant. "Abaddon gave it to me a few centuries ago. Said he found a couple of them when he was reaping and thought they were interesting," he admitted.

"You said a few. How many?"

"I don't know. I only saw the two, but I guess there could have been more."

Nothing more was said for several minutes as the two men stared at each other. Grim never looked guilty, just stubborn and slightly ill, but Blanche could understand that. If someone had told her Mira was a murderer, she wouldn't believe it either, and if she'd been confronted with proof, she'd feel sick, too.

"Very well, I believe you," Death said, relaxing a little. "But I also believe Blanche. If anyone would know who killed them, it would be her."

"I'm sorry, Grim," Blanche said again, and she meant it. He didn't deserve this anymore than Death did. Or Bjorn had.

"There's got to be another answer," Grim argued. "I know my brother, and he's...he's got a stick up his ass! He's all proper and contained and not at all a murderer. He couldn't do this. I'm going to find out who did." With that, he too disappeared.

Once they were alone but for the now purring saber-tooth tiger, Death turned to her and lifted her back into his arms. "I'm so sorry, Blanche. I had no idea Abaddon had anything to do with this," he murmured against her hair.

"I know," she told him, closing her eyes and soaking in the feel of him. "And I tried to warn you. That's why I was summoning you. I wanted to tell you about the coins, that it was one or both of the twins."

He cursed, too low for her to make out the exact word, but the tone was clear enough. "I'm sorry I ignored you." He set her back on her feet but didn't release her.

She reached up, laying a hand on his cheek. "I know you sent me back to protect me. Kind of figured that out when I found the sapphire, but I just don't know why. Yeah, we slept together, but you don't strike me as the love at first sight type. Or I guess it would have been love at first fuck, but whatever."

His somber eyes remained on hers as he dropped a hand to a spot on her inner hip. He drew in a breath, released it on a sigh. "I think there's something I should show you."

Blanche didn't like his tone. It was ominous and gave her chills, but she only nodded and rested her hand in his when he offered it. They disappeared, only to reappear—without Sa—in front of the door of the tomb.

CHAPTER 29

"Why are we here?" Blanche asked, feeling the tug of the room more intensely than she had in the past. It was strong enough now that she rubbed the heel of her hand between her breasts, trying to relieve the ache that had formed. And she had to say that was bullshit. After dying, there shouldn't be any aches or pains.

"Because I can't keep the truth from you anymore, or deny it myself," he said, opening the door and stepping inside. "Did you know that until you arrived, no one had been in this room but me? That no one could even open the door?"

"I didn't," she admitted, following him, though she lagged a few steps behind. The tomb hadn't bothered her this much before, but it was almost unbearable now. She really wished she'd gotten a chance to translate the writing on the sarcophagus. "Who's in there?" she asked.

"My wife," he answered, resting his hand on the ceramic. "And I think you need to see her."

It shouldn't scare her. The way he acted, any wife he'd had would have been dead for ages, which meant there was likely nothing more than bones inside. Bones were a normal part of her life. Hell, she'd kept a skull on her dresser back on Earth. But she really, really didn't want him to open the sarcophagus. And she couldn't even begin to form the words to beg him to stop.

The lid lifted and levitated to the wall, where it came to rest, leaving the remains within uncovered. All she had to do was step forward and look inside, yet everything inside her rebelled at the thought. She did *not* want to see the body lying inside, and felt her heart start to race, her hands begin to tremble. Instead of breathing normally, she was aware that she was getting dangerously close to panting. All because of a freaking skeleton. Why? And how the hell was she having an anxiety attack when she was dead? Shouldn't things like that have disappeared the moment her body had? Wasn't she formless now? But such questions didn't really matter, not now, and the answers wouldn't change anything.

She shook her head and stumbled back, pressing herself against the wall. Her palms flattened against it, paying attention to the rough texture, the cool temperature, in a bid to let her mind focus on something else. "No," she said, or tried to, but though her lips formed the word, no sound came out. She closed her eyes and forced herself to breathe in through her nose, out through her mouth. It didn't really help, but after a minute she was able to say, "I don't want to."

When she opened her eyes, Death's chest hurt at the fear and misery in them. It was doubtful she knew of his suspicions, but her reaction now only confirmed his theory for him. He'd seen her room on Earth, her family's home. Hell, he'd even caught her in here before, so the only reason he could think of for her to be having this kind of reaction was that her soul recognized its former home. Very few could look upon their own lifeless bodies without a reaction, even if it was a body they hadn't inhabited in thousands of years.

The anger that had banked after Abaddon had left his sight rekindled at what he was putting her through. What he needed to put her through. Hiding this from her just wasn't an option, not anymore.

Moving slowly, he approached her and gently grasped her upper arms. When she didn't resist, he pulled her against him, urging her cheek against his chest. Stroking her hair, he sighed softly. "I'm sorry, *arami*," he murmured. "I'm sure you don't. But I honestly think you need to. And I wouldn't insist if I didn't think it was important."

Her arms crept around him, her hands fisting in the back of his shirt. "What's that mean? *Arami,* I mean. What language is it?"

She was trying to distract herself, and he allowed it for the moment, but she needed to know. "The language doesn't have a real name," he explained as his hand continued to move in slow, soothing strokes. "It's the language we spoke when people were first created. We had no need to name it because at the time, it was the only language we knew of. Oh, there were the languages of the gods, but people? Mortals? We all spoke the same language. And while we learned to write, very few examples survived."

"Like the sarcophagus?" Blanche whispered.

"Like the sarcophagus," he agreed.

"But there's nothing in your library?"

Ah, yes. He'd told her about the writing before. He'd forgotten. There'd been so much else on his mind. "Not in the library, no, but I have some in my private rooms. I'll show you later, if you want."

"I'd like that."

Her hands were starting to loosen, and while her breathing was still too quick and there was a tremor running through her body, it was starting to ease. "As for what the word means..." He wasn't sure if he should tell her now, before she'd seen inside the sarcophagus, but he was also tired of hiding it. The first time he'd called her that, it had slipped out. A habit long forgotten, nothing more. This time, though, he realized he'd meant it. Somehow, she'd made him feel things he hadn't felt in all of recorded history. "It means love."

Blanche's head tilted back so she could look up at him, her eyes full of surprise and something warmer. "Like...a pet name?"

"To some, yes," he said, careful not to confirm it wasn't how he'd meant it. "Do you think you can look in the sarcophagus now?" he asked gently.

Those blue-gray eyes flicked to the sarcophagus and she bit her lip, hands tightening once more, but she slowly nodded. His heart clenched when she stepped away and caught his hand with her own. He squeezed it as they stepped forward, but he noted she kept her eyes fixed on the wall across from them until they were directly beside the sarcophagus.

She took a deep breath and fought not to grip Death's hand tight enough to grind bone. After closing her eyes for a moment as she gathered her courage, she looked down at the body. Part of her was completely unsurprised by what she saw, but that didn't stop her from releasing a little sob.

It might be her lying in the ceramic box. The body of the woman was perfectly preserved, so it looked as though she'd died only yesterday. Like Blanche, she had black hair, though hers reached her hips, with little braids here and there. Though the woman's skin was tanned, the features on her face were nearly identical to her own. In fact, this woman looked more like her sister than Mira did. A quick scan of the woman's body told Blanche she'd probably be about the same height as well. And she had a sick feeling that the woman's eyes would be the same shade as her own.

The clothes she wore made Blanche think of ancient deserts—and recent dreams. She wore a thin, pale brown leather split skirt that reached her knees and was open on the outsides. Her upper body was covered by another piece of leather, this one bone white. It was a halter-style that left her slightly rounded belly bare. Sandals covered her feet, the laces wrapping halfway up her calves.

"I don't understand," she whispered, unable to take her eyes off the woman's body.

Death's reply was silent as he leaned in and shifted an edge of the skirt to the side. Blanche's free hand slapped against her hip, the same spot Death had touched right before he'd brought her here. The woman had the exact same birthmark in the exact same location.

"As I said...this was my wife. I told you how I became Death, but what I didn't tell you was that I went back to see my wife," he said as he straightened. He didn't pull his hand from hers, but left it loose. Like, she realized, he was expecting *her* to pull away. Noticing that, she paid attention to the tone of his voice and heard the intense remorse in it. "It was lonely here back then, since no one else had died and there hadn't been anyone to carry the souls of the animals here. That and I missed her. I...wanted to see if she'd join me here. Live with me. But I didn't know how to control my power back then. They were new, untested. I don't even think the Anunnaki fully understood them."

Blanche's stomach rolled as she got an idea of where he was going with this. Her hand flexed, but she couldn't bring herself to pull away from him. She did, however, drag her gaze from the body of his wife to his face. He was watching her as he talked, and she'd never seen such guilt on anyone in her life. She started to shake her head, wanting him to stop, because saying it would make it real, but he continued.

"She saw me and ran to me, and I to her, but when I touched her...I killed her instantly." A tear slid down the cheek of this strong, cold, powerful man, and her heart twisted. "Her and the baby she was carrying."

Blanche's free hand covered her mouth as her eyes widened. There was more horror than that, she was sure, though that would have been too much on its own. To have accidentally killed his wife and unborn child? It was something that would have destroyed most men. She wasn't entirely sure it hadn't destroyed him. Her free hand dropped to her flat stomach, and she felt an echo of the grief for a baby who had never lived. But he wasn't done.

"As I said, I didn't understand my powers or how to use them. At the time, I just thought I killed her. Later, I was convinced I'd killed her soul as well, because I never found her here in Cindatha. And I looked. Oh, I looked. For her and our child. I found the child's soul, ensured it was reincarnated, protected, but never her. And then a woman—a mortal—dared to summon me. She was relentless. And I gave her an offer I was absolutely positive she'd refuse, but she accepted. Somehow, she managed to touch a part of me that no one had reached since I'd killed my wife. And for the first time since my death, I connected with another person, only to find the same unique birthmark my wife had, and in the same place. And once I started thinking about it, she looked like my wife's twin."

It was instinct to protest. How could she be his wife? If his wife's soul hadn't been in Cindatha, then where could it have been before being reborn? Didn't that mean she was a new soul? Except...the dreams. Most of them didn't really confirm what he was saying, but they gave his story weight. And then there was the one, the one that had left her mourning a baby she'd never had. That one lined up exactly with what he'd said. More, there was no way she could have possibly known any of that unless her soul was the same as his wife's. But she had to know for sure.

She couldn't dispel the grief over the baby, but realized that knowing he'd ensured it had been born again helped. Letting her hand drop from her belly, she asked, "Did...did you carve? Before you died?"

Death nodded, a corner of his mouth twitching in remembered joy. "I did. Not well, but I was carving a toy. I started before we were sure you—she—was pregnant yet, but I wanted time to get it right. It was supposed to be a mammoth."

Dammit. That, too, coincided with her dreams. "And did we dance? At some sort of festival?"

"At all the festivals," he confirmed. "You loved to dance."

She didn't now. Was that coincidence? Or had her soul remembered and refused to dance with anyone but him?

He lifted the hand not clasped in hers and used his thumb to wipe a tear from her cheek. She hadn't even realized she'd been crying. "What...what was my name?" she whispered.

"You believe me, then?"

"I've been having dreams," she admitted, "ever since we kissed by the waterfall. I thought it was just my subconscious fucking with me, because you were in them, but you had brown eyes and no tattoos."

"That's the color they were before I died," he confirmed. "And you were named very appropriately, in my opinion. You were Ara. To us, it meant loved one."

She repeated the name silently. There was a sense of familiarity about it, but it didn't feel like her. Maybe because she'd spent so long as Blanche? Or because it had been so long since she'd been Ara? "What was your name?"

"I honestly don't remember. It's been so long, and my name didn't really matter. I had become Death, and it was what I was as much as who."

"Were...were we happy? We seemed happy in my dreams." She didn't know why, but she really wanted them to have been happy. Maybe because this life had been full of so much trauma and sadness.

"It's why I went back for you. I mean, we fought now and again, as any couple does, but nothing major."

Blanche nodded slowly and looked at their clasped hands. "I accept that I was once her, once Ara, but you know I'm not her, right?" She looked back up at him. It was difficult, but she wanted to make sure he paid attention to what she was saying. "If you're thinking I'm her, that I'm just going to become her again—"

"No," he cut in, shaking his head firmly. "You're not, I know that. Believe me, I understand that better than anyone else. With a few exceptions, reincarnation results in a completely different person. And while you're physically the same, as far as your personality?" Humor actually slid over his face and he smiled. "Ara was a lot less sarcastic and a bit more...proper, we'll say. And while you're steeped in death, she was all about life. She had a wonderful hand with plants, whether she was tending to crops or a pretty patch of flowers she'd taken a liking to." The smile dimmed. "But I do want to make something clear. I had no idea whatsoever that you were Ara reincarnated when we slept together the first time. And when I came to your bed the next night, it was Blanche I was wanting, not Ara. I loved my wife, deeply and completely. I always will. What I feel for you is different."

He didn't say he loved her now as Blanche, but she didn't want him to. This was emotional for both of them, and a declaration of love at the moment would just be wrong. She wouldn't be sure if she could believe it. But that didn't mean she didn't feel something for him, or that she didn't want to have him touch her and make her forget—just for a little while—that she had been betrayed and killed by someone they'd both considered a friend.

"Good. Then, if you're sure you want me and not her...take me to your room? Show me?" She wanted to forget, but more than that, she wanted to know for certain that he wasn't wishing she'd act more like Ara.

He pulled her toward him and slid his other arm around her waist. "I'd like nothing more," he told her, before teleporting them away from the past.

CHAPTER 30

Death brought them to his bedroom, beside the heavy wooden bed that had only had one person in it before her arrival. Since his wife had died—since he'd killed her—he hadn't wanted another woman in his bed. The few women he'd been with in all the years between then and Blanche, he'd gone to their beds, or hotel beds. Never his. They'd never even been in his castle. Blanche was the only woman who had been here other than his reapers and the occasional goddess.

They stared at each other, the air around them heavy with anticipation and a rapidly building need. It went beyond the physical, though his body ached for her and his cock pressed painfully against his pants. This was, in a very literal sense, spiritual. He'd suspected who she was the last time they were together, but this time, there were no secrets between them. Or at least none that mattered. And though he knew she was worried he was confusing her with Ara, he honestly wasn't. He had loved Ara, who had been sweet, intelligent, and extremely giving, but he was a different man than he'd been when he was human. A woman like Ara had been couldn't handle who he was now. But Blanche? She was still intelligent, but she was also stubborn and powerful—physically, mentally, and magically. What he was didn't frighten her, and she'd managed to befriend Sa, something even Grim hadn't been able to manage. And she fought so hard for those she loved. Just look at the lengths she'd gone to for her sister. She was a woman who fit who he was, not who he used to be.

He lifted a hand and brushed his fingers across her cheek, his thumb drawing lightly over her lower lip. "Tell me you're sure. Tell me you want me. Who I am, not what I am."

One corner of her mouth turned up and she stepped closer, so her breasts lightly pressed against his chest. "I wish you could remember the name you used to have," she admitted as she slid her fingers beneath his shirt and into the waistband of his pants. "I know you're not human anymore, but when you make me come, I want to scream your name, not your title. I don't want you doubting that I want the man, not Death."

Death felt the truth of her words and dropped his hand, grabbing her shirt and tugging it upward. She helped so he could remove it, then toss it aside. He wanted inside her more than he wanted anything else at the moment—including Abaddon's head on a plate—but he refused to rush this. This time, he wanted to savor the fact that she knew *who* he was and what they had once been to each other. And for some reason, it now felt extremely important for him to remember his name. But once again, she surprised him.

She went up on her tiptoes and wrapped her arms around his neck so she could kiss him. It was chaste as far as kisses went, but enough to have his pulse quickening and all the blood in his body rushing to his groin. He groaned at the sweet touch of her lips, but she drew back before he was ready.

"I told you I've been having dreams," she murmured, her fingers brushing over the back of his neck.

"You did," he agreed, undoing the button of her pants, but that was all he did before his hands settled on her hips and drew them in snug against him.

"They were all dreams of you. Of us," she corrected, "from back then. I remembered those things I asked you about. And I..." Her brows drew down as she struggled with something. The memories, maybe? Or finding the right word, perhaps. Either way, he was content to wait, to let her process whatever was on her mind. They had all the time in the world. Literally.

Her hands slid down his chest. Though one dropped to his waist and beneath his shirt, the other stopped over his heart. "A lot of what I remember is kind of vague. Emotions more than anything. But since you showed me...well, me...down there, more is starting to trickle back, and a name is beginning to form in my head. It might just be wishful thinking, though."

He covered the hand on his chest with one of his own. "What name?" he prompted quietly, his control slipping just enough to have her bra disappearing. She gasped and looked down at her naked breasts, but then giggled and let her gaze lift to meet his.

"Was that necessary?" she asked, though he noted her voice had gone throatier than normal. He certainly wasn't going to complain when she pressed herself just a little closer to him.

"You're lucky we're not both completely naked and flat on the bed with me buried inside you," he answered honestly. "So yes, it was. I want to give you the time you need. I want us both to take our time, but my patience will only hold so long."

"Zirin," she said, her hand dropping from his chest to unlace his pants. "Does that sound familiar?" she asked as her thumbs hooked in his waistband and started to ease the leather over his hips. He could have made them disappear as easily as her shirt had, but he found he loved the sensation of her undressing him. It was the same reason why his shirt remained on. He wanted her to remove his clothing, one article at a time. It didn't even matter if she pulled them off, ripped them off, or used her own magic to make them disappear.

Her hands paused and she grinned up at him. "Are you trying to remember if Zirin sounds like your name, or are you focused on the fact that your ass is bare now?" she teased, one hand sliding around to give his butt a squeeze.

In all honesty, it wasn't his ass sticking out that had his mind wandering, but the feel of her pressed against his cock, with only her pants between them. "Distracted," he admitted before he did focus on the name. It was difficult for him to think back that far, especially for something that had become as unimportant as his name. Since then, he'd just been known by various monikers and had become accustomed to that. Death was simply the most common of them all. Her name had been easy to remember, especially as he'd had it etched into the sarcophagus, but there had been nothing to keep his original name in his mind. But a memory slid to the surface of his mind, probably triggered by her desire to be able to scream his real name. Him with his wife, their bodies wrapped around one another, and her head thrown back as she screamed. And it was now very clear what she had screamed.

"Yes, I do think that's it," he said, a smile creeping onto his lips. "I remember it, and it...feels right."

"Good." In a sharp motion, she shoved his pants down as far as she could reach, leaving him bare from hips to knees. She abandoned his pants and yanked his shirt up and off. Not wanting to fumble with the leather, he made the pants and boots vanish, leaving him bare. Her hands cupped his face and she kissed him. Nothing innocent this time. No, she was demanding, and threatening to make him lose control like a virgin touching his first woman. Part of that could be her delicious body pressed to his, but the kiss certainly wasn't helping.

His hands gripped her hips tight as she turned them until his back was toward the bed. She moved forward until his legs hit the bed, then pushed a little more. He could have kept his balance, but was inclined to give her what she wanted. She'd died. He'd lost her again. He'd give her anything she wanted right now.

Death sprawled on the bed and stared up at her, still dressed from the waist down. But by all the gods, she was so beautiful. Yes, she was slender, but there was a softness to her hips and breasts. His fingers flexed once as he ached to get his hands on them, but made himself remain still, to let her stay in control. For now.

The smile she gave him was enough to make him groan as she kicked her shoes off, then pushed her pants down until she could step out of them. Now as nude as he was, she stepped closer, easing his legs apart before she sank to her knees. Unwilling to give up the sight of her, he pushed up to his elbows and watched as she slid her hands up his thighs and leaned in. He groaned when she bent her head and he felt her warm breath against his already stiff length. Shifting his weight to one elbow, he used his other hand to reach down, brushing her hair behind her ear so he could see her face clearly. She smiled at him, and for an instant he saw both Blanche and Ara, then she took the head of his shaft between her lips and he saw no one but her.

Her cheeks hollowed lightly as she sucked, then began to slowly draw him further into her mouth until he throbbed with the need for release. He held onto every bit of restraint he had, unwilling to let this end so soon. As good as her mouth felt, he wouldn't be satisfied until they were joined and she was screaming his name. His real name. Not just because she was the only one who knew it now, but because it was further proof she was with *him* and not Death.

Blanche tormented him so sweetly, taking her time to taste and explore him with her mouth. That alone was enough to cause his fingers to curl, gripping her hair firmly. But he didn't use the hold on her to direct her movements, all too content to enjoy every second. Then she set a hand on his belly and let it wander up until it rested over his chest, her fingers brushing over his nipple. At the same time, she pressed her mouth down until her lips were wrapped around the base of his cock. His hips jerked involuntarily and he growled, his hand tightening in her hair. Her eyes shined with heat and mischievous delight as she drew back with aching slowness. That was all he could take.

Death pulled her off him as he pushed himself upright. Keeping his hold on her hair, he used his other arm to yank her into his lap so she straddled him, her arms coming around him automatically. Angling her head upward, he fastened his mouth to hers and his tongue dove between her lips to duel with hers. She closed her eyes, moaning, and he swallowed it down, his arm a steel band around her, keeping her tight against his body. The position had her core rubbing against his cock and he ground up against her, ensuring he pressed against her clit.

The shiver that ran through her made him throb and want to smile with satisfaction. He was going to love her so thoroughly that when he was done with her, she wouldn't be able to lift her head.

Without breaking the kiss, he twisted and laid her on the bed with his body covering hers. He lazily rubbed his shaft over her, brushing against her clit, before he lifted his head. Her eyes opened and he smiled at the dazed look in them. "Blanche," he murmured, drawing his fingers down her cheek, over the sensitive skin of her throat. Shifting his body to put just a little space between them, he continued to move his hand down her body. A finger circled one taut nipple, making her breath catch. Then lower, over her stomach, the muscles twitching in reaction. He took his time, letting anticipation build for both of them before his hand slid between her thighs. While he groaned at how ready she was for him, she gave a throaty moan and pressed against his fingers, trying to get them inside her.

"Not yet, *arami*," he whispered as his thumb rubbed over her clit, his touch too gentle to give her what she needed.

"Please," she begged, hips twisting in a desperate attempt to get more friction, more pressure, more *something*. Anything to give her the orgasm her body was primed for. When he refused, kept teasing her, her nails pressed into the muscles of his back as she arched and whimpered. The slight sting of pain made him hiss and his cock jerked against her. "Please," she repeated, "I need to come. I need you to make me come."

"Soon," he promised from between gritted teeth. Holding back was killing him, but he knew the longer he made her wait, the more intense the orgasm would be. Then, and only then, would he give her what they both truly wanted. Him buried balls deep inside her, riding her until they were both exhausted.

When the sounds she was making became frantic, he slid two fingers into her and curled them. She gasped, her channel flexing around his fingers as her hands tightened on his back. "More," she panted.

Smiling, he watched her face as his fingers moved again. At the same time, he pressed the heel of his hand firmly against her clit. Her eyes widened, but it wasn't quite enough to send her over the edge, leaving her teetering, straining for that one brush of his hand that would have her toppling. Now willing to give it to her, he pumped his fingers into her, his chest brushing against her sensitive nipples.

Blanche's hands grabbed his head, yanking him down for a hard, needy kiss. It only lasted a few moments before the movement of his hand finally gave her the release she was craving. Her head fell back as she cried out wordlessly, her hips bucking in small, sharp motions against his hand as she rode out the climax.

There was something so painfully erotic about watching this woman lose control. It was all he could do not to withdraw his fingers and thrust into her, but this moment needed more than a quick, hard fuck.

Death's fingers slid free of her body and he peppered kisses along her jaw and throat as he waited for her to come back down. When she had, his arm slid around her and he rolled them so she was atop him, once again straddling him, though this time he was flat on his back.

Blanche tried to recover her breath, but being flipped over made it catch again. She didn't mind though, since it meant she was draped over him like a blanket. But she wasn't done. The orgasm had been nice—great, even—but it wasn't enough. His mind seemed to work on the same thought, because he shifted her effortlessly, moving her until the head of his cock pressed against her entrance. He didn't wait before he slid smoothly inside her.

She moaned and gave her hips a testing roll, loving the way it felt. From the way he flexed inside her, she knew he agreed. For a minute she stayed like that, chest to chest, only her hips moving, but as wonderful as it felt, as intimate as it was, she wanted more than his eyes on hers. Cradling the back of his head, she urged him to lift it so they could kiss again. It was tender and lazy, more than an exploration, as it felt like they knew each other's bodies as well as their own. They simply couldn't get enough of touching one another, and she finally recognized what she'd felt the moment she'd first seen him. They were connected by more than just his body inside hers. She might not be Ara anymore, but her soul knew his, and she'd waited for all of history to be right where she was. Where she belonged.

Her hands rested on his chest and she pushed herself upright, working him deeper into her. Her breathing caught at the added sensation as she stared down at him. The weight all those years apart had put on him was visible to her, but so was the joy at having her now, and the desire that went far deeper than physical.

Smiling, she arched against him and sighed in pleasure. She continued to roll and twist her hips, every movement slow, languid. His hands rested on her knees, then slid up her thighs to her waist, but he followed her lead, rocking into her rather than thrusting. Biting her lip, she took one of his hands, brought it to her breast. He brushed his thumb over her nipple before he kneaded the soft flesh. Though her head wanted to drop back, her eyes wanted to close, she refused to lose the sight of this supremely powerful man as he lost himself in her.

It was likely she was the only one to ever see him this unguarded, this soft, and that twisted something in her chest. She alone had that effect on him, and it made her feel so special, so honored.

So loved.

Moaning as the pressure within her built quickly toward another orgasm, she kept her hand over the one on her breast. Her other hand slid over his chest, his arm, his hip. The feel of his skin was like a drug and she was addicted to it. From the calloused skin of his fingers to the soft flesh at the crease of his hip, she wanted to touch it all.

Her first orgasm had been like a race; a desperate rush followed by a quick, hard finish. This one built like a tsunami, the pleasure building, building, building, and when it hit, it swamped her, over-whelming her system with pure ecstasy. "Zirin!" she cried, her hips snapping downward and grinding against him while she trembled and her body clamped down on him.

Death groaned and his hands grabbed her hips, holding her in place as he thrust into her just once more before she felt him release deep inside her. And like her, he said nothing but her name, and the part of her that had twisted earlier now melted when she realized it was *her* name, not that of the life she'd lived thousands of years ago.

He was with her, not his former wife, and that meant everything to her.

Collapsing forward onto his chest, she felt his hand slide into her hair and gently tilt her head so he could kiss her gently while her body continued to shiver with the aftershocks of pleasure.

"*Arami,*" he said in a quiet voice as she rested her head on his shoulder. "My memories of my human life...they're fuzzy. Little more than dreams now. But I can't even begin to remember anything like that," he admitted.

"Neither can I." Not her memories of him, or the men she'd been with prior to meeting him in this life. And as she drifted off to sleep with him beneath her, she thought that now that she had him, she wasn't sure she could ever let him go. Yes, she might be dead, but that was hardly an obstacle when she was in the bed of Death. And maybe even in his heart.

CHAPTER 31

When Death woke, Blanche was still atop him, which meant he started the day with a smile, despite everything going on with Abaddon and the other reapers. They took the time to shower—where he'd taken her against the wall—before going downstairs. There was no one else in the castle but them and Sa, who was waiting for them in the kitchen. Death was happy to see the tiger was no longer pouting, but he'd had to catch Blanche when the big cat had happily pounced on her and almost knocked her off her feet.

He made them coffee while she found breakfast for herself, and had smiled when she hand fed Sa. When he'd offered her that deal, he'd had no idea how much she'd change things in his castle, but he could hardly complain.

Once they were sitting down and she was enjoying her first cup of coffee, he had to burst the bubble they'd put themselves in. He needed to know what had happened and stop Abaddon before he could hurt anyone else.

"Something that I've been wondering…How did you get into the castle? It shouldn't have been possible."

"Remember how I accidentally teleported us that once? And I told you I'd done it a couple of times before?" He nodded. "That's how.

See, after I died, I didn't remember it. Not my death, not coming to Cindatha, nothing for a while back. I wandered until I found that waterfall you took me to." She smiled at Sa and reached out to scratch beneath his chin. "After a couple of days, Sa found me and it brought it all back. I thought about how I needed to get back here, to warn you, and then I was just here," she explained.

Which still didn't make sense. Though witches did occasionally have the ability to teleport, even his reapers couldn't teleport within the castle except to the throne room. Everyone—gods included—had to be given permission to teleport within Cindatha. It had always been that way, and to his knowledge, she was the only exception. The same for the powers she'd displayed when confronting Abaddon. Almost all souls lost access to their powers upon death. A few exceptionally strong Arcane and gods managed it, but they, too, were the exception.

"Can you tell me the rest? I know you said you were trying to summon me to warn me, but what did you know? How'd you figure it out?" he asked, resting a hand on her leg and absently stroking his thumb across it.

Blanche blew out a breath and leaned her head against his shoulder. "Luck, honestly. Managed to get in touch with the guy who gave us your summoning ritual." Good. She knew who he needed to visit to have that wiped from existence. But she wasn't done. "Asked him if he knew of any way to hide stuff. He came back with the coins. I realized I'd seen both the twins with them." Her lips tightened. "Of course, before that, I suspected Grim," she confessed. "Never would have thought it would be Abaddon instead."

"I'm sorry I ignored you," he said, picking up her hand and lifting it so he could press a kiss to her knuckles. As he did, he gifted her with the same ability his reapers had. The ability to mentally send him a message when they needed. If she'd had it before, she might never had died. "Hopefully you won't need it, but in the future, simply call for me, think at me, and I'll hear your message."

"Oh, so you mean when you've pissed me off, I can harass you even from another realm?" she asked, and he was pleased to see her lips tipping upward.

"If you must," he said, feigning resignation.

She grinned fully at that before turning sober again. "Back when you offered me the deal, why did you gift me the power to resurrect the dead instead of doing it yourself? Isn't that like, against the god code or something?"

"First, I'm not a god. I'm...other. Second..." He shrugged. "I have no idea. It's not something I've ever done before. Even Grim and Abaddon were never given that power, and they've been my reapers longer than anyone." He paused, scowled. "Or Grim has, in any case. But there wasn't any reason for me to do it before. Hell, there isn't often a reason for me to bring anyone back. Hades has probably done it more, and I'm sure you know how rarely he allows a soul to go free. It just...felt right. Maybe because I recognized your soul, even if I didn't understand it at the time."

"Are you going to take it back?" she wondered.

"No," he said without hesitation. "I know some who would use it irresponsibly or wield it like a weapon, but I don't think you would. And not just because you're a necromancer."

"No, I wouldn't," she agreed. "I probably shouldn't have reacted like I did with Mira, but—"

He cut her off, shaking his head. "I get it. If I could have brought Ara back, I would have, but it didn't work for some reason. At the time, I was sure I'd killed your soul."

"Wait," she said, gripping his hand, "so my soul wasn't here the whole time? Before I was born as Blanche, I mean?"

He shook his head again. "No. Until I saw your birthmark, I had no idea your soul still lived." She nodded but looked troubled. Death didn't blame her, as he was as well. Though it didn't truly matter now, he wanted to find out where her soul had been in all the millennia between her death and rebirth. But that would have to wait.

He pressed a kiss to her hair. "I am sorry for what happened. I sent you away to protect you and ended up leaving you unprotected."

"It's not your fault. Though I won't deny I'd love five minutes alone with Abaddon right now."

She might love it, but the idea terrified him. Blanche was formidable in her own way, but he knew exactly how skilled Abaddon was. He didn't know what he'd do if the traitor managed to kill her soul. Although...

"Do you want to be alive again?" he asked, his hand stilling on hers. He knew of few who would turn down the offer, but so much hadn't been in her control lately, so he wanted to give her what he could.

When she didn't answer immediately, he went cold, wondering if she was an exception in this case, too, but she finally nodded. "I do, but...if I'm alive, will you just send me back to Earth again?"

Ah, that was her concern. Everything in him loosened a bit as he smiled. "No. You can stay here. I'll even insist on it, but this time you can visit your family whenever you want. You won't be a prisoner or bound to an agreement. You can just...live here. With me." As his equal. Hell, most would see her as the queen of Cindatha, though he'd never seen himself as a king. He wouldn't correct any who treated her with the deference, though.

She grinned and his eyes went unfocused as he searched for her body. While doing so, he caught a glimpse of her death, and his jaw clenched. Abaddon had much to answer for, as did Banshee and Dean. Pushing it aside, he brought her body through the realms and to Cindatha, reuniting body and soul. Her parents and siblings would have a shock to find her body missing, as he'd found it in their home. He felt a momentary pang of guilt, but didn't think they'd mind too much when she went to visit and was alive.

The moment she took a breath—one she actually needed, rather than one taken out of habit—her eyes widened and he smiled at her. "Better?"

In answer, she grabbed his face and pressed her mouth to his. This slender, maddening, stubborn, wonderful woman literally threw herself at him and kissed him brainless, and all he could do was hold on and ride the wave of heat.

"The first time I saw you, I knew you weren't as cold and heartless as you came off," she murmured against his lips before kissing them again lightly. "Thank you, Zirin."

"That name sounds so weird now," he admitted as he pulled her completely into his lap. "I kind of like it, but it might take me some time to get used to."

She laughed. "I can keep calling you Death if you like."

"Except in bed."

"Except in bed," she agreed.

Sa's head lifted and he let out a low sound that wasn't quite a growl. They twisted toward the door as Grim walked in. It looked like he hadn't slept since they'd last seen him. His eyes were bloodshot and hair was falling free of his man bun, giving him a messy appearance. He might be the casual twin, but he was never messy.

As much as Death wanted to find and execute Abaddon, he felt for his old friend. It couldn't be easy knowing his own brother had betrayed everything they'd both worked for. Or knowing that his twin was now marked for death.

"Grim," Blanche said, climbing off Death's lap and crossing to the reaper. She wrapped her arms around him, and though he leaned into her, he didn't return the hug.

"I haven't been able to find him," he said in a lifeless voice. "I've looked everywhere I can think of, all the places here and on Earth I know he liked to visit, but there wasn't any sign of him."

Blanche pulled back, leaving one arm around his waist as she led him to the table, urging him into a seat. While she got him a cup of coffee, Death studied his face. He could give Grim time to come to terms with what had happened, but it was better to finish it quickly. Better for Grim, and better for all the other people Abaddon could kill if they delayed. "Do you know why he would do this? Kill Bjorn and Blanche?"

Grim took the coffee when Blanche handed it to him, drinking deeply though it had to scorch his tongue. "I don't know. I'm still having trouble believing he did any of it at all. But if I had to guess—and I do mean guess, this could be out in left field—I'd say maybe he's tired of being a reaper? Could be he misses being a god."

"Wait, hold up and rewind a sec," Blanche said, gripping his shoulder firmly. "Misses being a god?" she repeated slowly. "You two were gods? How do you go from being a god to a reaper?"

Grim's gaze met Death's, silently begging him to explain. "Before the Anunnaki gave me my scythe and I created the reapers, Grim and Abaddon were twin Sumerian gods. When it was time for me to create the first reapers, they volunteered, as the Sumerian pantheon was beginning to lose worshipers, which meant they were losing power. It seemed to be a win for all of us."

"You might know me better as Meslamtaea, and Abaddon as Lugalirra," Grim added quietly. "Twin underworld gods."

Death almost laughed at the look on Blanche's face. When she'd first met him, there had been no shock, no surprise, no awe, but she now looked like someone had smacked her upside the head with a two by four. "Are you shitting me?" She threw her hands in the air and turned, stomping several feet away before whirling and stomping back. "All this time and you couldn't mention that?"

"Would you mention someone you weren't any longer?"

"Yes! Because doesn't that explain how he might have been able to kill souls? Not something normal reapers can do, right? And I'm guessing you two still have some of your god powers, even though you're reapers, too?"

Death froze and he saw Grim do the same. "Yes, we do," the latter said slowly. "And he used to have a knife that could kill disembodied souls." He looked to Death, apology written all over his face. "I'd all but forgotten. I haven't seen that knife since we became reapers."

"I'd forgotten as well," Death admitted. "You two have been reapers far longer than you were gods, and I only knew you for what, a century or so before you became reapers?"

"About that, yeah."

Death sighed and ran his hand over his hair. "Could Abaddon be in your old temple in Kur?"

Blanche surprised them both a second time when she burst out laughing. Not just laughing, she was gripping the back of the chair in one hand, her other resting on her stomach.

"Dare I ask what's so funny?" Death asked, grabbing her arm to steady her when she looked like she might fall over.

"Kur? It had to be Kur. It feels like all of this started in Kur!" Blanche said, grinning at them.

"What do you mean? Did Death take you to Kur or something?" Grim asked.

"Nope. Before I summoned Death to try to bring Mira back, I tried every death god I could think of. When that didn't work, I took a flying leap into Kur. Asshole gatekeeper—didn't catch his name—turned me away. That was the last straw, and what inspired me to try summoning Death."

Grim's lips twitched, and Death just shook his head. "You threw yourself in the so-called Pit to Hell?" He wished he could say he was surprised, but it actually sounded exactly like something she'd do, though he was aware most of the Arcane believed the pit to be nothing but folklore.

She shrugged and sat beside Death. "Didn't have a lot of options. I was determined to bring Mira back one way or another."

The grin that slid over Grim's face made Death feel a bit better about what he was about to do. "Only you, Blanche," he said, reaching over to playfully punch her arm.

"Gotta do what you gotta do," she said, shrugging again, then she turned to Grim. "So I have to ask. Before Death sent me back to Earth, you were acting a little weird. Looked like you were hiding something, too. What was that all about?"

Death was surprised when Grim looked like a deer in the headlights. If he wasn't mistaken, his cheeks were even a little pink. "Grim?" he asked, expecting the worst after what had come to light about Abaddon.

Grim blew out a breath and ran a hand over his hair, which only mussed it further. "I found something and wasn't sure what to do with it. Wasn't even sure what it was at first."

"What do you mean something?" Blanche asked.

He hesitated, then leaned back, reached into his pocket, and pulled something out. Extending his hand, he uncurled his fingers to show a small gold disc, no bigger than Death's thumbnail. The workmanship was crude, but there was something engraved into the surface.

Blanche leaned forward for a better look. "What is that?"

Death didn't need to ask. He knew. And if this had surfaced twenty-four hours ago, he would have gone into a cold rage. "Where did you find that?" he asked instead as he took the disc from Grim's hand and rubbed his thumb over the warm surface.

"Outside the tomb," Grim admitted. "The day Blanche arrived, she mentioned the tomb. After I showed her to her room, and talked to you, I went to check it out. I...was curious. Figured maybe the magic sealing it had worn off or something, and wanted to make sure it was secure. It was, but..." He trailed off and inclined his head toward the disc. "That was right outside the door."

"Outside the tomb?" Blanche asked, her voice soft. "But how? I didn't see it there."

"It was there," Death confirmed. "Except I'm not sure how it got outside the sarcophagus." He slid his arm around her, rubbing his free hand against her bicep. "It was yours. A pendant. The little piece with the hole in it for threading a string through broke, so it was just inside."

She leaned into him and tentatively took the pendant from him. "That's so weird," she whispered, "but I can't think about it now." She slid it into her pocket and gave Grim a faint smile. "Thank you."

"You're welcome," he said, looking uncomfortable.

Death got it. This was an odd situation. But Blanche had a point. "As much as I hate to bring us back to the present," he said honestly, "I'm going to go check your old temple."

"I'm going with you," Blanche said, lifting her chin slightly like she knew he was going to argue.

"And me," Grim added. "If my brother is there, I want to know why he'd do this. I want proof he did this."

Death arched a brow at them both. "You are aware that reapers can kill other reapers, right? And you've already died once, Blanche."

"And you're aware that I killed the woman he told to kill me, right?" Blanche shot back.

"You were serious about that?" Grim asked, frowning at her.

"As serious as...well," she said, trailing off with a flick of her eyes toward Death. "No fucking idea how, but she came at me, I stabbed her with my knife—an ordinary blade, mind you—and killed her."

Scowling as well, Death asked, "You killed Banshee?"

"Banshee? Shit. Her and Abaddon were occasionally sleeping to-gether," Grim said in a tone that matched his voice.

"If that's her name. I didn't exactly get introduced to her or the guy with them," Blanche said, shrugging. "But yeah, I killed her. Any idea how?" she asked Death.

He took her hand and focused not on her body, but her soul, her powers. The strong necromancy was expected, as few could have summoned him using the original spell she'd used. But there was more than that, more than the ability to resurrect the dead. There was part of *him* within her. Part of his powers resided within her, and it didn't feel like a recent addition. But how? Then he realized there was only one way it could be even remotely possible. All those years ago when he'd first touched Ara with nothing to shield his powers, he must have not just killed her, but given her some of what made him Death. It must have embedded itself into her soul, so when she reincarnated, she didn't just have the necromancy that was so common in her family, but something *more*. And if that was true, it explained almost everything else about her that he'd been wondering about; how she could open the tomb, alter the castle, and teleport inside it. All things he could do. He even thought he knew why those powers had only recently manifested.

Which only left the question of where her soul had been for all that time.

"Um, I'm fairly certain I know how you killed her, as well as how you were teleporting around the castle."

Blanche leaned forward expectantly, but Grim had to butt in first. "You were teleporting around the castle? And you didn't tell me?"

"Sorry," she told him sincerely. "I just wasn't sure who to trust."

"I'm going to apologize too, because I ended up sharing this next bit recently with your brother." Shit. He had shared it, which meant Blanche's death was partly his responsibility. His eyes darkened and he felt his power trying to slip free. "Which explains why he went after you, Blanche."

"What? Why?" Grim asked.

"In Blanche's first life, she was my wife. The wife I had when I was human. I told you that much. What I didn't say was that right after I became Death, I accidentally killed her." Grim's mouth dropped open but Death went on, looking at Blanche now. "My theory is that when I touched you—touched Ara—that first time after I died, that because I didn't have a handle on my powers, I accidentally gave you some of my abilities. And I'm fairly certain that when I kissed you to give you the ability to resurrect your sister, that I unlocked their full potential."

"Oh," Blanche said softly. "That...yeah, that would explain a few things," she agreed.

"Including how you were still able to use your magic when you were dead," Death said with a nod. "Most can't."

"Dude. No, I can't handle anymore of this. Can we just go check the temple?" Grim asked, rubbing his forehead.

Death was aware there wasn't any way for him to ensure they didn't follow him—they were both too sneaky and stubborn for that—so resigned himself to the fact that they were coming with him. But before they stepped foot out of the castle, there were a few things he wanted to take care of first. "Grim, arm up. And get some weapons for Blanche. We're not taking any chances. We know others are working with him."

Grim nodded and disappeared to do just that. Once they were alone, Death grabbed Blanche's hand and pulled her back into his lap. "You're going to be careful," he told her, and it was not a request. But just to be certain, he did the one thing he swore he would never do. He did the same thing to her that had been done to him by the Anunnaki. The very thing that had made him hate them, that had caused a deep rift between him and the trio that had become both parents and best friends to him.

He just hoped he didn't come to regret it.

CHAPTER 32

Grim returned, armed with a sword of a style she wasn't familiar with, two daggers, and twin double-sided blades for Blanche. After Death was satisfied, the castle dissolved around them and they reappeared in a structure made of sandstone. It wasn't a temple he'd been in often, but there wasn't anywhere in Cindatha that was completely foreign to him. He knew every inch of his territory.

Abaddon stood in the center of the large main room, a fanatical and slightly insane expression on his face. And he wasn't alone. There were around thirty other reapers scattered around the room, some sitting, some standing or leaning against the walls, all paying attention to whatever Abaddon had been saying when they arrived. Dean, he'd expected, but some of the faces here were ones he never would have thought would be involved in the murder of one of their own. If he was lucky, they weren't. They could be gathered for some other reason. It was a slim hope, but he clung to it. Otherwise, the hurt and fury would overtake him.

"What's going on?" he asked with deceptive casualness, his gaze searching the faces of the reapers with Abaddon.

Several of the sitting reapers rose, all of them moving slowly. He wasn't sure if they were trying not to provoke him, or hoped that by moving slowly he wouldn't notice them. It didn't matter. He noticed them all, and he was already well past provoked. Another thing he noticed was how most of them shifted closer to Abaddon. Fools. Abaddon couldn't protect them. By the end of the day, he'd be dead, as would any who stood with him.

Death shook his head before any of them could answer. "Never-mind that. It's clear enough." His gaze fixed on Abaddon. "Why?"

Abaddon smirked, looking confident with the small army of reapers with him. "Did you really think we'd be content to be under your thumb for all eternity, Death?" he asked, tone mocking. "You treat us like your servants, doing all the work that should be yours. And what do you do?" he asked, strolling forward a few steps. He really didn't seem to have any fear of Death. Maybe because he used to be a god, maybe because of the men and women around him, but they'd all forgotten exactly where they were, and who he was. *What* he was. "You wander around your castle, more dead than any of the souls in Cindatha. You don't care. About us, Cindatha, or the souls. You're just going through the motions. So we," he said, spreading his arms wide to indicate the reapers around him, "have decided it's time for a new Death."

That was not what Death had expected him to say. Not exactly. Rebellions were often had for the sake of power, but he never would have dreamed Abaddon wanted to actually become Death. Power, sure, that made sense, but the rest was just illogical.

He shook his head. "So you gathered all these reapers to help you? To...what? Become your inner circle?" His voice dropped with skepticism thick enough that a few reapers exchanged looks. "You do realize this is a fool's errand, don't you? First, you can't just steal my power."

Though apparently it could be given, at least to an extent, if Blanche was any example. "Second, even if you could, you'd have to kill me, and that's literally an impossible task. I can't be killed, not by my reapers, not by the gods, and not by any relics you may have managed to dig up."

Abaddon scoffed and another smug smirk curved his lips. "Until recently, you didn't think anyone could hide from you either, though. You may be old as fucking dirt, but you don't know everything."

A handful of the reapers murmured their agreement to each other, with one brave—or stupid—man giving a wholehearted, "Yeah!" The bulk of the reapers simply stood there stoically, but a few looked uncertain.

Dean shook his head and took a step back, distancing himself from Abaddon and the other reapers. "This is not what I signed up for. Replacing a leader who no longer cared was one thing, but you killed Bjorn's soul, Banshee's soul. I'm out," he said before disappearing. A heartbeat later, a woman did as well. Death took note, but wasn't sure what he'd do with those two. They'd chosen correctly in the end, but he had no idea what crimes they'd committed before today.

"You did more than kill Banshee's soul. You murdered Bjorn, murdered Chris, and even killed Blanche," Death said, hating this whole thing. So many reapers had turned against him, and he didn't truly understand why. No, he may not have been the most attentive for the last millennium, but he certainly didn't treat the reapers like his servants. They were his children, in a very real sense. No, they couldn't ever replace the child Ara had never birthed, but he'd created them, cared for them, and now this group had decided to kill him. He didn't really have a choice. Reapers could do a great deal of damage if they were left unchecked. Either they could cause a great deal of chaos within Cindatha, or they could create havoc on Earth. Killing indiscriminately, shoving souls into bodies they didn't belong in, or—with Abaddon in control—kill souls until only their chosen remained.

"Blanche looks just fine to me," Abaddon said, sneering at her. "And like I told her, it was her own fault she's involved."

"Fucking bastard," Blanche said in a low, dark tone. "I trusted you. *He* trusted you. Hell, you're betraying your own twin brother." She looked away from him, her gaze scanning the other reapers. "If he'd betray the man he shared a womb with, what do you think he's going to do to you idiots?" she asked them.

Abaddon snarled and manifested a scythe. It wasn't a weapon Death had seen before, but the similarity to his own scythe made him realize exactly why Abaddon was doing this. Part of it was the insanity he'd seen before, but the bulk of it? Envy. Pure and simple. He'd lost his godhood and become second to a man with ultimate power over death. Which also explained why Grim had been included by the betrayal. Though Death had been equally as fond of both brothers, Grim was generally better liked than his brother.

This was going to be bloody, and he wasn't sure it would be as simple as striking them down. With the relics in their possession, they were at least somewhat hidden from his power. He had no doubt he could penetrate it, but without being familiar with these relics in particular, it wouldn't be instantaneous. Which meant at least some of these reapers were going to be dealt with the hard way.

Though Death had realized that a fight was inevitable, he still felt a pang of sorrow when Abaddon leapt at them, swinging his scythe. Grim, who hadn't moved or made a noise since they arrived, drew his sword and intercepted his brother, sword blocking scythe. "Don't do this, Lugalirra," he whispered. "Don't make me do this."

"You're fucking pathetic, worshiping Death like a god, doing everything he asked. You used to be a god yourself, now you're just a lapdog," Abaddon growled, putting all his weight, his strength, into his scythe. And as skilled, as strong as Grim was, Death could see he really didn't want to hurt his brother. Which meant if those two fought, Abaddon would win. Death wouldn't allow that.

He lashed out with his power, hitting every reaper—but for Grim—as hard as he could, forcing his magic to ignore the power of the relics. Though it wasn't as effective as he'd hoped, he saw at least ten reapers drop as their life was sapped away in an instant. But while it helped their odds, it didn't keep Grim safe.

Two steps were all it took to reach the brothers, and Death kicked out, his booted foot landing in Abaddon's gut, shoving him away from Grim. That sent the remaining reapers into action. They rushed forward, not one at a time like in movies, but as a swarm. Death risked a glance at Blanche, momentarily fearing for her, but he didn't have time to dwell. She was a strong, powerful woman and had already killed a reaper. He had to trust she could handle herself.

Blanche's hands tightened on her borrowed weapons. When she'd insisted on coming, she'd expected to find Abaddon and maybe one or two others. She hadn't expected odds this bad. Three to twenty? Death may be immortal in the truest sense of the word, and Grim might be a former god with thousands of years of experience with his weapons, but she was a two hundred-year-old necromancer who once was a human. She was so far out of her depth it wasn't funny, but she didn't really fear death at the moment. As long as her soul survived, Death would bring her back, and she'd make damn sure it survived.

So she fought beside her lover and best friend, aware they worked hard to keep her between them. It probably wouldn't keep her safe, but right now she appreciated their protective natures.

The reapers fought with a variety of weapons, from daggers like Grim had brought, to huge broadswords. One even had a fucking bow, which Blanche discovered when an arrow slid across her shoulder, sending fire shooting through her system. She hissed and glanced at the blood seeping through the tear in her shirt, but didn't stop. Out of the corner of her eye, she saw Grim was getting drawn further away from her. No, she realized, she was getting pushed back. Half the reapers had fallen to Grim and Death's attacks, but not enough. Not nearly enough.

One of the reapers armed with a sword came for her, and though Blanche fought hard, a particularly powerful swing knocked a knife from her hand. She darted in, ducking beneath the reaper's arm, and thrust the blade into his gut, angling it upward as she attempted to end him the same way she'd tried to deal with Banshee. Though he screamed, he jerked back before she could hit anything vital. A woman, tall and strong as an Amazon, took his place, her short sword slashing at Blanche. She leaned back, far enough to prevent herself from being killed, but not enough to keep the tip of the weapon from slicing a shallow diagonal line almost from her hip to her shoulder.

The move threw her off balance and she stumbled back, tripping over the body of one of the downed reapers. She fell hard on her ass, her other knife clattering to the stone floor. The woman looked smug and murderous as she pressed her advantage. Unarmed, Blanche lifted her hand, intending to light the woman on fire, but as soon as her hand was in front of her, a weapon appeared. It took her only the space of one rapid heartbeat to recognize it.

Death's scythe.

Apparently having a touch of Death's power came with more benefits than just being able to pop around his castle, and right now, she was grateful as hell for that. The weapon held more power than it had when she'd handed it to Death months ago, and she intended to use every drop of it. Swinging, she caught the woman across the stomach, and though she didn't have the reach to cut deep, the woman shrieked like the edge had been dipped in acid.

Using her free hand, she quickly shoved to her feet, feeling absolutely invincible. There was no way a reaper could kill her while she held Death's scythe. In the back of her mind, she realized that was probably flawed thinking, but it didn't prevent her from diving into the battle with everything she had. The scythe wasn't a weapon she'd ever used before, but it felt instinctual as she slashed and swung it toward the traitors. It wasn't effortless. These people had skill and training after all, but she was helping Grim and Death trim the numbers down. One by one the reapers fell, the shadowy souls that remained disappearing only moments after their bodies dropped. Death's doing, she assumed, aside from the one she hit with the scythe. That one had been sucked into the blade instantly.

The numbers were soon down to just a few, though Blanche didn't have time to breathe. They hadn't yet won, so all three kept fighting. Just as soon as she saw Death kill what she thought was the last reaper, she felt an arm band around her chest and something sharp press against her throat, hard enough to draw blood. She tensed, hissing at the sting, but didn't dare move. If she had any other weapon she might fight back, but the scythe was bulky and too long for that. She'd be more likely to lose the weapon or hurt herself in the process. Her magic was equally as useless, as whoever was holding her would probably jerk and slit her throat. Again.

Grim's sword lowered as he looked around for more enemies, and Death did the same. They saw her almost at the same time. "Lugalir-ra...don't do this, not again," Grim begged, taking a step toward them.

"Stop," Abaddon ordered, pressing the knife more firmly against Blanche's throat. She did her best to hold her breath, to not even twitch. It wouldn't take much for him to do to her what she'd managed to do to Banshee, and she really didn't want to die twice in a week, though she was sure it'd be a record. "You can just leave, actually. It's him I want to talk to."

"I'm listening," Death said, waves of power flowing out of him. His eyes had gone completely white, something she'd never seen happen before, but she could only guess what it meant. Absolute killing fury.

"No, not until he leaves. I don't want any...distractions."

Death glanced at Grim, caught his eyes, then nodded. Grim gave a last look to his brother, his expression a mix of regret and anger, before he disappeared.

"He's gone. Talk."

Abaddon chuckled, and Blanche's eyes closed as she heard the crazy in the sound. She may still be holding Death's scythe, but she doubted this was going to go well. As soon as she thought that, the scythe disappeared. She hoped it wasn't a sign. "You know what I want, Death. You either give me your power, or I'll kill her. And this time I'll make damn sure her fucking soul goes too," he snarled, his arm tightening around her as the blade slid just a little. Just enough to deepen the wound.

"It doesn't work like that, Abaddon," Death began, but Abaddon jerked Blanche more tightly against him and she made a low sound as the edge of the knife dragged over her skin.

"Don't patronize me," Abaddon snapped. "I was a god. I know how powers work. You can transfer them to another person. You do that, now, or your precious wife is dead. Again."

Grim had left, but he hadn't gone far. This had been his temple—his and his brother's—so he knew it intimately. There wasn't an inch of it that he wasn't familiar with, so he simply teleported to another area and quickly made his way back on foot. He had no idea who his brother was anymore, but there were a few traits he knew for a fact had been genuine. One of them was Abaddon's inability to back down once he'd committed to something, and he was clearly committed to this plan for whatever reason. And with Blanche at risk, Death likely wasn't thinking clearly. Hell, he wasn't thinking clearly. His twin brother had gone mad and threatened their friends. Which meant Grim had to stop him. Now.

He took the hallway that would lead him behind where Abaddon had been standing, and he hoped Abaddon hadn't turned or this attempt could be over before it began. Fortunately, when he peeked around the doorway, he saw Abaddon's back, and he was still holding Blanche.

Closing his eyes, he took several deep breaths. This could only end one way, he knew that. He also knew extremely well exactly how death worked, even for reapers and gods. His sword would do no good, not with Blanche being held in front of Abaddon. Yes, Death could bring her back, but not if Abaddon managed to get her soul first. So he gripped his knife tightly in his hand, not noticing that there was a fine trembling in it.

Using his powers to move silently, he crept around the wall while Abaddon raged at Death, blaming him for every problem Abaddon had. Death's eyes flicked to him briefly before they returned to Abaddon.

"Fine, if this is what it will take for you to release Blanche, I'll give you my powers," Death said, and Grim felt a hint of relief. Yes, keep Abaddon busy. Keep his attention on Death so Grim could get closer. He might love his brother and desperately not want to do this, but Blanche was innocent in this, and Abaddon had gone too far. This would *save* his brother.

"Good," Abaddon said in a darkly pleased voice. Except the knife didn't ease against Blanche's throat. It was a risk he'd have to take, though, because he wasn't sure Abaddon planned to release her even if he got what he wanted.

Whispering an apology in his head, Grim lifted the blade, and shoved it deep into Abaddon's back, expertly finding the heart with a single strike. Knowing that alone wouldn't be enough, he twisted it as his brother screamed in absolute agony. His body jerked in reaction to the killing blow, and exactly what Grim had been afraid of occurred. The knife he held pressed into Blanche's neck, clearly hitting the artery within that kept her alive.

Grim grabbed Abaddon's arm, pulling the blade away from Blanche even if it was too late to save her from this death. Keeping his own weapon buried in his brother's back, he drew Abaddon away from the necromancer as she covered her throat with her hand and fell to her knees.

"I'm sorry," he whispered as he and Abaddon went down as well, Abaddon landing in a heap in Grim's lap. Tears threatened at his eyes but refused to fall as he withdrew the knife and wrapped his arms around his twin.

"Traitor," Abaddon whispered, a thin line of blood trickling from the corner of his mouth.

"No, I was only setting things right," Grim said, voice thick with emotion. "Why did you do it? What made your life so bad that you'd resort to this?"

Abaddon may be moments from death, but he sealed his lips, stubbornly refusing to give Grim the answers he desperately needed.

Looking up, he saw Death scoop Blanche up, ending up in much the same position as Grim and Abaddon. He expected to see fury or feel Death's power as he tried to save Blanche, but they were absent. Oh, he certainly didn't look happy, but there was no frenzy. He didn't understand it.

"You'll be okay," Death murmured to her, brushing her hair back before he wiped a thumb over her throat, smearing the blood.

"She will?" Grim asked, voice cracking.

"How?" Blanche asked at the same time, her voice strained. Abaddon had likely nicked something vital for speaking.

Death looked uncomfortable for perhaps the first time in Grim's presence. "I...may have done something other than simply bring you back to life," he admitted.

Blanche wiped at her throat and even from a few feet away Grim could see that her throat was knitting closed. What should have been a killing blow was healing, and he wasn't sure why. "What?" she asked.

Before Death could answer, Abaddon gasped and jerked. Three sets of eyes moved to him and the tears Grim had been holding back fell.

"You...betrayed...me," Abaddon whispered before his eyes went blank and his last breath eased out of his lungs.

Unable to keep it inside, Grim threw his head back and screamed wordlessly. The sound tore at his throat as he clung tightly to his brother's body. What had happened to the boy he'd grown up with? The man he'd been so close to. Once upon a time, Abaddon hadn't just been his brother or even just his twin, he'd been Grim's best friend. And somewhere, that connection had broken. Somewhere, Abaddon had lost all reason and morals.

And Grim had never noticed. What did that say about him?

"Sorry, Grim," came the quiet words after his lungs had run out of air to sustain the scream. Lowering his gaze, he saw Blanche, still looking pale from the rapid blood loss, still too weak to move, with warmth and sincerity in her eyes. How was she trying to comfort him when she'd nearly died? When Abaddon had literally killed her only days before?

"As am I," Death said, stroking Blanche's hair. "He was a dear friend to me as well. Once."

Grim could only nod as no more sound wanted to pass his abused throat. Instead, he glanced pointedly at Blanche's injuries, hoping that the explanation for them might distract him from what he'd done, if only for a few seconds. Death fortunately got the hint.

"When I knew we were coming here, I was sure Abaddon wasn't alone, and I just couldn't risk that you'd die and your soul would be extinguished as well," Death told Blanche, and Grim noticed he was very carefully not meeting either of their gazes. "I am truly immortal, did you know that?" He didn't wait for them to answer, but continued. "Not immortal like the gods or reapers. They're simply unaging and hard to kill. I literally cannot be killed. How could I, when I am death itself?" he asked with a wry smile. "When I realized that, and after a few thousand years had passed, I grew to resent that fact. It's why I no longer speak to the Anunnaki, because they did this to me. Did it and either wouldn't or couldn't reverse it. So I swore I would never do this to another. Death and reincarnation are necessary for the sanity of the soul, so why would I deprive anyone else of them?" He finally met Blanche's eyes. "But I couldn't risk it, Blanche. I just couldn't."

"It's okay," she told him with a small smile, tilting her head to rest against his chest.

Holy shit. Blanche was undying, too? Death really did love her, to ensure they were tied together for all of eternity. That was good. Death deserved someone, but Grim couldn't be happy for them right now. Not when he'd just killed his brother. Not when he wasn't sure where Abaddon's soul had gone. Unlike Abaddon, Grim had never had the ability to snuff out a soul, so it had to be somewhere. "Where is he?" he rasped.

"Safe and intact," Death assured him.

That was all he needed to know for now. "Thank you."

"Take all the time you need, Grim. You know where to find us when you're ready."

"We're here for you," Blanche added.

He only nodded again and disappeared, going to the place that had once been his home. There, he would deal with Abaddon's body. Later, he could worry about his soul.

When he was gone, Blanche looked up to Death. "What did you do with their souls?"

"I have a room back in the castle. It's where I keep everything that's too dangerous to be in anyone else's hands. It's also where I keep the souls of those who cannot be freed for whatever reason. They're all there."

"Including Abaddon's?"

Death nodded and shifted her in his lap, needing his arms fully around her. Just because he'd known she couldn't die didn't mean it had been any easier to see Abaddon do something that should have killed her. "Including Abaddon's," he agreed. "Some will stay there until their slates can be wiped clean and they can be reborn. I was going to kill them all," he admitted, looking to where Grim had held his brother's body. "But I don't know that Grim would be able to recover from that."

"No, he wouldn't," she agreed, and his arms tightened as he knew she was thinking of Mira and how she'd blamed herself for that death. How much worse would it have been if her hand had been the one to actually do the deed?

"Are you ready to go home?" he asked, some of the tightness in his chest easing as he thought it being her home as well. He never had to be without her again.

"Gods yes. I need a shower."

Since he had her blood on him, he agreed and took them back to the castle, straight to his room. Before they got undressed, he cupped her face, the one that had become so very precious to him. "I love you, Blanche. You. Not Ara, not the woman who used to be my wife, but Blanche, the stubborn witch who gave me my first headache in centuries."

Though their day had been beyond difficult, she smiled and pressed her face into his palm. "I love you, too Death. Or do you prefer Zirin?"

He grinned. "Either's fine, but maybe save Zirin for when it's just us. I kind of like that only you know my true name."

"Trying to say I'm special?"

"Absolutely." And he made her clothes disappear before pulling her into the shower. And if he took his time cleaning every speck of blood off her, no one could blame him. Nor could they blame him when he laid her down in the bed afterward and spent several hours making love to her.

But in the back of his mind, he couldn't help but to feel for the man who was somewhere by himself, mourning his brother's death.

CHAPTER 33

By afternoon the next day, Grim still hadn't returned. Blanche wasn't really surprised, especially not with how she'd been after Mira had died. And she could see that Death felt his own guilt over Grim's current state, so she decided she was going to kill two birds with one stone. Distract him and relieve her family's minds, because she had no doubt they'd found her body by now and were thinking the worst.

Death had been busy all day dealing with the fallout of the rogue reapers, but she went looking for him now. She found him in the throne room, just as a small group of reapers disappeared. He sat on his throne, looking weary, and she crossed to him. "We're going out."

"Out?"

"Yep. You need a break from all this, and I need to let my family know I'm not dead. So we're going to go visit my family."

"We?" he repeated.

"Yep, we. Partly because I can't teleport outside of Cindatha—" or she didn't think she could— "and partly because, if I'm going to stay here with you, I want them to meet you."

"I really can't. There are still reapers showing up, wanting to know what's going on, and I'm searching for reapers who have more of those coins."

He had returned to the temple that morning to ensure he gathered all the relics, but there was one missing. It could have been destroyed at some point, but he wasn't going to take chances.

"Bullshit. You can take an hour. Remember what I said about taking breaks? Besides, I still can't get there on my own." He was wavering, she could see it, and she pressed. "Please. I don't want them mourning me when I'm not dead."

He sighed and rose, kissing her forehead. "Don't give me those eyes. We'll go."

She smiled and hugged him. "Thank you."

He took them straight to her bedroom. Before she went looking for her family, she looked at the spot where she'd fallen and died. No blood, no body, so they'd definitely found her. Grimacing, she took a moment to grab a few things she didn't want to do without in Cindatha and shoved them in her pockets. Including the small bottle of mithridate she'd gotten from Suni. Since she was immortal, she probably wouldn't need it, but it didn't hurt to keep it on hand. She considered her clothes for a moment, but it brought back a question she'd had earlier. "Was it you or Grim who brought my clothes and stuff to the castle?"

Death looked mildly uncomfortable, but shrugged. "It was Grim."

She grinned and kissed him. "It's okay. I didn't like you much back then, either," she teased.

Taking his hand, she pulled him out of her room and went in search of her family. No one was in any of the bedrooms, so they went downstairs, his hand remaining in hers, and came across the first person at the base of the stairs.

Mira's eyes widened, and she stumbled before her eyes started to roll back in her head. Blanche started for her, but Death was quicker, catching her before she could fall. He eased her to the floor as Blanche rushed over. Fortunately, Mira hadn't actually lost consciousness, though it took her a moment to manage to formulate any coherent words.

"You're dead," she breathed.

Blanche grinned and shook her head, pulling Mira to a sitting position. "Was, but I got better," she said, jerking a thumb in Death's direction as he straightened.

Mira looked to Death, back to Blanche, then to Death. "You resurrected her?"

"I did," he agreed.

"And you're bringing her back to us?" she asked, and Blanche grinned at the skepticism in her voice.

"Temporarily," Blanche answered, now tugging Mira to her feet so she could hug her sister. "I'm staying in Cindatha, but as one of the few living people."

"You're staying?" Mira shrieked.

The commotion brought the rest of her family trickling in. Her brother was first, and he let out a shout for their parents before he pushed past Death, picked her up in a bear hug, and swung her around. Before she knew it, two more sets of arms had wrapped around her and she knew her parents had shown up. Breathing was kind of difficult, but she couldn't begrudge them the opportunity to hold her after they'd found her body like they had. Not to mention they'd only had her back a few days before Abaddon had killed her.

Her mom was the first to realize they weren't alone, and her arms went slack as she drew back, but she refused to let go. "Who are you?" she asked, and Blanche could hear the nerves. No doubt she could feel the death magic rolling off him.

"Death," was his only answer, and Blanche rolled her eyes as her dad's arms tightened painfully around her.

"Yes, he's Death, but he isn't here to kill anyone," she assured her family, slipping free of their hold and stepping over to him. He was the stiff, cold, powerful man she'd first met, but she didn't hesitate to link her fingers with his. "He brought me back."

"You brought my baby back?" Marguerite asked. "You brought both my babies back?"

"Technically Blanche brought her sister back, but yes," Death answered coolly.

That was all it took. Blanche had to stifle a laugh when her mom hugged Death. He stiffened and gave her a 'what the hell?' look, and she shrugged. Her family might be wary of Death, but they were the Arcane family least likely to be put off by his presence, especially under the circumstances. Still, she took pity on him after a minute, pulling her mom away from him.

"Look, I know you guys had to have found my body. I just wanted to let you know I didn't stay dead. I couldn't put you through that, especially not after Mira was dead for a few weeks. But...I'm not staying, either," she told them, knowing they'd prefer the blunt approach. They weren't a beat-around-the-bush family.

It didn't surprise her when they erupted with denials and questions. She let them roll over her for a minute, knowing they needed to get it out, then she cocked her head and arched a brow, waiting for them to fall silent. Another minute passed before they got control of themselves.

"What do you mean you aren't staying?" her dad demanded, watching Death like he was considering his odds of making it out alive if he decked the man. He would, of course, but only because she knew Death wouldn't do that to her. Besides, even if he did, she could just bring her dad back again.

"I mean...I love him and I plan on staying in Cindatha. But," she said, raising her voice to carry over the new round of protests, "I'll visit. It's no different than if I'd decided to move in with someone on the other side of the planet."

"And she has her phone," Death offered. His tone was still uptight, but she smiled at him. Her phone was the first thing she'd grabbed, and it felt good to have its weight in her back pocket. "She can call you whenever she likes."

Her dad crossed his arms over his chest, his gaze still fixed on Death. "And are you planning on marrying our Blanche?"

Death sighed. "It would be redundant. We married centuries ago."

"You *what?*" Mira shrieked. "You bitch! What the hell have you been keeping from us?"

"No, it's not like that." Blanche shot Death a glare. "That doesn't count. You married Ara, not me."

"Our souls wed," he protested.

"Not the same! And maybe I want a wedding now," she said, folding her arms over her chest. "I don't remember the last one."

"Your memory might come back," he countered.

"Remember what I said about not mistaking me for her?" she asked in a warning tone.

He tried to fight off a smile, but she noticed. "Do you want a wedding?"

"One fit for a necromancer who is marrying Death, but yes."

"Then we'll have a wedding."

She smiled brightly at him. "Good." She focused on her stunned family again and nodded. "Yes, I married him, but it was in a past life, so we are *not* married now. It's a long story, but when I died back then, my soul sort of went AWOL until I was born as Blanche."

"Are you telling me you're marrying *Death* not once, but twice?" Aidan asked, his voice surprisingly calm.

"Basically? I mean, he wasn't Death the first time, but yeah."

He chuckled and shook his head. "I always knew you were more of a necromancer than any others I knew."

Death cleared his throat. "That would be my fault."

"Wouldn't say your fault," Blanche said, remembering what he'd said back in the castle before they'd faced off with Abaddon. "Back in that life, it seems like he accidentally transferred some power to me," she explained, leaving out the part where he'd inadvertently killed her. He might have done it to Ara rather than Blanche, but her family would still have some negative opinions about it.

"You bitch," Mira said again. "No wonder you've been able to do some of the things you've done."

Blanche shrugged. "I didn't have any idea until, oh, yesterday."

Her mom just looked proud. Stunned, but proud. "I don't care if you're the most powerful necromancer in the world or an ordinary witch. I'm just glad you're happy." She paused and narrowed her eyes at Death. "You are happy, right?"

Blanche grinned. "I am, yeah." She wouldn't go into the whole thing with Abaddon. It was over—except for Grim—and it felt like reaper secrets. This might be her family, but she also couldn't betray the man who'd somehow just become her fiancee. Again. "I've got a man I love and who loves me, the underworld to explore, and even have a cat now."

"A cat?" Aidan asked skeptically.

Death chuckled as Blanche said, "Well, technically, yeah. I mean, he's the soul of a saber-tooth tiger, but still a cat."

"Only you," her brother said, shaking his head.

"When are you leaving?" her dad asked.

"In a minute."

He shook his head. "No, no. That won't do. You'll stay for dinner."

"But—"

"You'll stay for dinner," he repeated in a tone she knew meant he'd made up his mind.

She looked up at Death and shrugged. He just sighed. This was far from his comfort zone, she knew that. Other than the reapers, he didn't seem to interact with most people. Okay, so he was apparently friends with Hades, and there was her, but that seemed to be it. The fact that he was willing to endure a family dinner only made her love him more.

Her dad went all out in the kitchen, making a meal fit for Thanksgiving or Christmas. She wasn't surprised, either. He loved to cook, but she knew he went overboard when his emotions were high. Having two daughters die and brought back to life in the space of a month would put anyone on edge.

When they sat down to eat, her family didn't ignore Death, but the conversations directed at him were either awkward or the pointed questions families asked of potential romantic partners. To his credit, Death didn't let it bother him, at least not visibly. She did her best to help take some of the pressure off him, but knew she'd still owe him later. Ordinary men had a hard enough time dealing with this kind of interrogation, and for a man as powerful as Death to endure it said a lot for how he felt about her.

It was hours later when her family finally allowed them to leave. There was quite a bit of hugging and more than a few tears before Death took them back to the castle. And there, she proceeded to make up every minute of awkwardness to him as their bodies twined together in the bed until late in the night.

CHAPTER 34

The last several days had been busy for both Death and Blanche. He was dealing with the fallout of Abaddon's actions, including wiping the souls of the reapers who had been involved, then sending their souls back to Earth to be reincarnated. All except for Abaddon's soul. He was waiting for Grim, as he had a feeling Grim would want to say goodbye to his brother. Blanche had mostly been answering questions for the reapers who had shown up in the throne room, freeing Death to do the things only he could do. Which was a relief, as previously he'd counted on the twins to deal with that, and Grim was still MIA.

Then there was clearing the rest of the reapers of wrongdoing. He had found the last coin in Dean's possession, and after discussing the situation with Blanche, had decided not to kill him, but that didn't mean he wouldn't keep a close eye on the man. Second-chances weren't exactly something he was known for, but having Blanche in his life had softened him a little. Generally only when she gave him that look, but it was still softer than he'd been since he was human.

When he wasn't dealing with that—or getting Blanche out of her clothes at every possible opportunity—he spent a good bit of time helping her. Since they'd discovered she had at least some of his powers, they both wanted to ensure she knew how to control them. They knew firsthand how dangerous those powers could be without control. It was easier for her because she'd had necromancy powers almost since birth, but not all magic was equally as simple to control. She'd already resurrected someone, so he had no worries there, but while she'd managed to capture Mira's soul and send her own to Cindatha, there was more to soul magic than that. It sounded similar in some respects to what she did with ghosts, but that was like saying finger painting was the same as creating the Mona Lisa. Fortunately, there were quite a few souls of people who had been absolutely vile in life that he was okay with her practicing on. All they needed to do was hit Tartarus, Hell, and the other parts of Cindatha reserved for the worst of the worst.

And when she needed a break from that, he took her around Cindatha, showing her not just the spots like the waterfall and sapphire cave, but the different parts 'ruled' by other gods. Once, he even introduced her to Hades. He wasn't sure it was a good idea though, as she was awed by the man. Oh, he knew it wasn't romantic or anything, but it hit his pride. In the pecking order of power, Death outranked Hades by quite a bit, and she hadn't acted like this with him. Except, he reminded himself, she'd fallen in love with him, which surely topped a bit of awe. Besides, she'd grown up a necromancer, learning about the gods and goddesses of death and the underworld. And Hades was deeply in love with Persephone, so there wasn't anything for Death to worry about in any case.

Tonight, she'd dragged him into the theater, demanding that he relax. And though he'd protested that sex with her was extremely relaxing, she'd only laughed and told him movie first, sex later. Which was why he was currently sitting in the dark, his arm around Blanche's shoulder, Sa sprawled out on the floor in front of them, while a movie played. To be honest, he had no idea what the movie was, as he'd spent most of his time watching her. While movies were fine, he'd really only put the theater in for Grim and Abaddon, and Blanche was a great deal more interesting than any story.

Grim appeared between them and the screen and Blanche sat up, fumbling for the remote to pause the movie.

He looked terrible. It had been less than a week, and though it shouldn't have been possible, Grim looked like he'd lost weight. He'd certainly lost color. Though his skin was naturally bronzed like the rest of the Sumerian gods, he was now as pale as Blanche's banshee brother.

"Grim, come sit," Blanche said, jumping up and grabbing his hand. He didn't protest when she pulled him over to the couch and pushed him down so he was between her and Death. "I won't ask if you're okay, because I know better, but how are you holding up?"

"I killed my brother. I'm not," Grim said, his voice as bland and empty as Death had ever heard it.

Blanche hugged him and sighed. "He didn't give you a choice," she assured him. "He'd killed people, and I think he would have killed you to achieve his goals."

"I know," he said, tilting his head against hers, but didn't return the hug. "I just don't understand how he changed so much. Or was he always like this and I just missed it? How could I miss my twin fucking brother becoming a murderous, power hungry asshole?"

"Sometimes the people closest to us can fool us the best," Death said, remembering how, all those years ago, it had been his best friend who'd killed him. And back then, it had been envy as well. Not for power, but for his wife.

"He's right," Blanche agreed. "And yeah, you might have lost a brother, and no, we can't undo that, but there's always something to be gained." She smiled faintly and squeezed lightly. "Hey, if the grumpy as fuck Death can find someone, there's always the chance for you to do the same."

"Yeah, maybe," he said, though it didn't sound like he believed it.

"I saved his soul," Death said quietly. "If you want a few minutes, that can be arranged, then I intend to wipe him and allow him to be reincarnated."

"Thanks."

Sa decided to get in on the conversation, by leaping onto the couch and dropping down heavily across all three of their laps. They let out soft grunts and oofs at the impact of the hundreds of pounds of feline, who then promptly started to purr.

"I think that means you're stuck with us until he decides to move," Death said, shaking his head, though he ran his hand over the cat's fur.

Grim honestly wasn't unhappy about that. He'd spent the last few days alone and his mood had only deteriorated. He did know that he hadn't had a choice, but it didn't make the fact that he'd been the one to end Abaddon's life any easier. And despite Death's offer, he wasn't sure he wanted to talk to Abaddon. His soul was still the same as it had been the moment of his death, which meant Grim likely wouldn't get any answers. But there was always a possibility, which meant he needed to at least consider taking Death up on that.

Secretly, he studied Blanche's face for several minutes, then did the same with Death. No, he couldn't undo what Abaddon had done, or how his life had ended, but he could always try to make up for it. He'd start with these two. First, he'd be a better friend than Abaddon had ever been. Second, he'd throw himself into his work. He might not be Death, but he was a reaper with some powers of an underworld god. And now...now he had nothing more to live for really, other than the three beings in the room with him.

And if he was lucky, he'd prove to himself that he was more than just an ex-god, reaper, and brother of a traitor.

After Blanche was asleep, Death eased out of bed. There was still one question about everything that had happened that was nagging at his mind. He understood Abaddon's actions, even if he didn't like them. He also understood how Blanche had taken some of his powers when she'd died the first time. What he didn't understand was where her soul had been in all the thousands of years between then and her birth as Blanche. Which meant he needed to go to the only people in the universe who might know something. And that meant going to a place he hadn't been since he'd realized he could never achieve the peace of death and reincarnation literally every other being got. Even gods had that option.

Drawing in a breath, he took himself from his castle to a place that had existed before any form of sentient life had walked the Earth. It didn't exist on Earth or Cindatha, but sat in its own little realm. Nothing existed there but an island in the middle of a crystal blue sea, with a stone palace sitting in the center. It was a beautiful paradise, and despite his understanding of why the Anunnaki had done what they'd done, he still hated it.

"Ananke? Chronos?" he called as he walked up the steps and into the palace. He didn't call for Tiamat, knowing it wouldn't do any good.

They appeared only a moment later and even he had to tense against the power they radiated.

Ananke was a beautiful woman, tall, blonde, and curvy. Her hair curled to her hips, framing golden skin, and had eyes that were all colors, though they gave the impression of both being a single color and multi-colored at the same time. Even he had never figured them out. Her wings were visible, and though at first glance the feathers looked white, he knew they were like her eyes in that they held every color, like white opals.

Chronos wasn't any better as far as definite appearances went. He was a few inches taller than his mate and had wings that were the opposite of hers; black with a rainbow sheen to them. But where the part of Ananke that changed were her eyes, with Chronos, it was his age. One glance had him looking like an old man, where the next he looked no older than eighteen. Staring too long had always given Death a headache, which was why in the past Chronos had generally taken care to solidify his age. The fact that he didn't now said something, Death just wasn't sure what.

But as two of the three original creators, and the ultimate powers over Fate and Time respectively, they were certainly entitled to be a little different from anyone else.

Ananke smiled at him, looking genuinely pleased to see him. "You came," she breathed, walking toward him, but though he understood why they'd taken his death from him, even had started to forgive them, he wasn't ready for any hugging and took a step back. Her face fell.

"What brings you to our palace? You haven't come here since you came to yell at us for giving you endless life," Chronos said, sliding an arm around his partner's waist.

Death was quiet for a moment, trying to figure out exactly what he wanted to say, and how. He was surprised to realize he didn't want to fight with them. "I still don't like that you took my choice away from me. I chose to become Death, but you didn't tell me you'd also make it I could never experience the one thing I was master over. But I get it," he said when Ananke opened her mouth to try to explain. Again. "And that's not why I'm here."

"Why are you here, then, dear child?" she asked. That was why he'd come to think of her as a mother, and Chronos as a father. Beyond being the creators of literally everything in the universe, including the Earth and Cindatha, they had created the first life on Earth. And they'd always treated him like a son. They could be fierce and deadly, even cold when needed, but they'd never acted that way with him. Once, he'd loved them dearly, and they'd loved him. Which was why he'd come now.

"Right after I died, right after I became Death, I went back to my wife, Ara. Except I didn't know how to control my powers and I killed her. Until just recently, I thought I'd killed her soul as well, erased her entirely from existence. There was no trace of her until her soul appeared in a woman named Blanche. Do you know anything about that?"

They exchanged a look before turning back to him and nodding. "We do," Ananke said cautiously.

"We saw what you had done, and originally..." Chronos sighed. "You did kill her soul as well as her body, and we saw how much it destroyed you."

"And though you know I don't interfere with what is meant to be, I couldn't let you suffer like that," Ananke said, picking up the story. "We don't have any control over death, though. Those powers belong to you, not us. Even we had no way of bringing her soul back from the void."

"So I went back, just a little, and we protected her enough to capture her soul," Chronos said.

"But since giving you her soul then would interfere with fate, would change what was meant to be, we couldn't simply make things right, not then."

"Instead, we kept her soul safe here. We didn't want to risk it being reborn into a life where she'd suffer or her soul would be killed again. Or where you would never meet and the endless cycle of reincarnation would continue. We waited, until Ananke found the right time, the right family. When her mother became pregnant, we placed her soul into the new life, because we knew your path would cross with hers."

Death was silent as he processed that. Even when he'd raged at them, swore he hated them and what they'd turned him into, they'd kept the most precious thing to him safe. More, they'd made sure he'd find her again.

"Are you angry with us?" Ananke asked as she took a step toward him. One of her hands twitched, like she wanted to try to hug him again, but she resisted the urge.

.He shook his head. "No, I don't think so," he admitted. "Do I like that you allowed me to think I'd destroyed her soul for so long? Of course not. But I know fate is as much a part of you as death is part of me. And you saved her for me. You actually went against your own natures to do that for me. No, I'm not mad. I can't be. I have her back. She's not the same person, but neither am I. And she loves me, exactly as I am now."

Ananke smiled. "Of course she does. You two were always meant for each other, in any life. Even if you hadn't become Death and you had both lived lives as human or Arcane, you would have found each other again and again."

"And we know how much we took from you when you took up the mantle of Death. We know how hard it is for you at times. This was the least we could do for you," Chronos said. "We have always wanted what's best for you, even when you refused to speak to us. And the best we could do was ensure there would be someone for you who would stand by your side. To support you when the weight of your duties pushed you down. To make you smile when the dead made you despair. To hold you when it all followed you into the land of dreams."

"And you loved her so much when you were human, and she you. I could see how inevitable the two of you were, and how right. Who else would we put in your path but her?" Ananke added.

Death wasn't given to extreme emotion beyond anger. Blanche drew softer feelings from him, of course, but he hadn't felt anything beyond anger for far too long. Now he felt love and gratitude burning in his chest for these two people. People he'd thought had simply used him and put him into his own personal hell.

"Thank you," he said, his voice not quite steady. And now he gave Ananke what she had attempted to get when he first arrived. He hugged the woman who was both friend and mother, while Chronos stood beside them, smiling at them both.

It had taken lifetimes upon lifetimes for their plan to come to fruition, but now he could spend the rest of eternity with the woman he loved. A woman who was more than just his lover, but his equal. His perfect match. There was just one thing missing. One thing that he'd almost had before it had been stolen from him. And the one thing that he wasn't sure he'd ever be able to get back. Because while he was impossibly old and had learned so much over the centuries, he didn't know it all.

Drawing back from Ananke, he looked between them. "If you know all that happened when I was first killed, were there when I killed Ara, then did you know that she was pregnant? Not far along, but pregnant, nonetheless."

The smile on Ananke's face dimmed and the way she looked like she mourned with him made him soften toward her even more. "We do, yes. Just as we know that the soul of your child was reborn, and has lived multiple lives."

Death nodded. He'd worked to ensure that soul was always given a good life, but had never interfered beyond that. It had never met its parents, never known him as a father, so it had felt wrong to try to keep it trapped in Cindatha with him. Especially since he hadn't had his wife. "It was," he agreed. "But...I'm dead. I truly died all those years ago. Does that mean that children—actual children, not those created like the reapers—are something I can never give Blanche?"

Both the Anunnaki smiled and Chronos shook his head. "You died, but you're not dead."

Death frowned. "I don't understand."

"You were the first to die," Ananke explained, "so things weren't as...set in stone, as they say. You know how the first of anything—the prototype, I think they call it—is never quite right?"

"Yes..."

"That went for you as well. You are something different. Not dead, not alive, not even undead. You are simply you. As unique to the world as Chronos and I are." Her smile dimmed. "As Tiamat is."

"Are you ever going to tell me what happened to her?" he asked, thinking of the third and final member of the Anunnaki, the one who embodied pure chaos. They had all been needed to create the universe, but he hadn't heard of or seen her in too many thousands of years.

"Not now, no," Ananke said. "Besides, weren't you wondering if you were alive enough to have a child with Blanche?"

"I was, yes," he agreed, and her words had hope balling in his chest.

"The answer is...I believe so. It feels true, but you are, as I said, unique."

"Can't you see?" Death asked Chronos, wanting more than just a possible answer.

"Time is a funny thing, you know that," Chronos answered. "Every decision, large or small, can change the entire course of history. But, like Ananke said, I do believe it's possible." He grinned. "Besides, don't you intend to spend as much of your time trying as you can, now that you have her back?"

He did, but just scowled at them. Besides, while he had always regretted that he never got to meet his child, to raise it with Ara, he did have the reapers. They were as much his as they were those they'd been born to. There just wasn't any guarantee Blanche would feel the same, and he wanted to give her everything she wanted. And he'd always mourned that he hadn't been able to be a true father. Now, if Blanche agreed, they could experience parenthood together.

"You know things will work out as they should," Ananke promised him, reaching for his hand and giving it a squeeze. "And you have enough to focus on now. But we are here if you need us. We always have been."

Maybe they had, but he was only just now willing to accept that. With a faint smile, he said his goodbyes and returned to the castle, to find Blanche still asleep in their bed. He stripped and climbed back in with her, drawing her back against his chest as he buried his nose in her hair. They may or may not have another child, but at this exact moment, it didn't matter. He had stopped the reaper rebellion and had Blanche. Everything else would simply be a bonus.

And honestly, all he really needed was her. Someone beside him, to make the hard days lighter, and the good days brighter. Someone to tell him when he was wrong, and support him when the right thing to do was difficult.

He smiled against her hair and, for the first time since he'd died and become Death, he slept and dreamed like the man he'd once been.

Eternity didn't look so bad, not anymore.

ABOUT AUTHOR

Meg M. Robinson is a fantasy author who lives in north Georgia with her husband, teenager, and a small menagerie of animals.

She's obsessed with crows, Halloween, and, of course, books. When she's not focused on either reading or writing a book, she enjoys playing video games, archery, and baking.

www.megmrobinson.com

Please consider leaving a review for this book. Reviews are extremely important for authors, but especially indie authors like me! Believe me, we appreciate it!

www.ingramcontent.com/pod-product-compliance
Lightning Source LLC
Chambersburg PA
CBHW032117310726
48972CB00001B/259